LISA JACKSON

ALMOST DEAD

7000436873 2X

First published in Great Britain in 2007 by Hodder & Stoughton
An Hachette UK company

1

This Mulholland paperback edition first published in paperback in 2017

A CIP catalogue record for this title is available from the British Library

Paperback ISBN 978 1 473 66107 3
eBook ISBN 978 1 848 94552 4

Printed and bound by CPI Group (UK) Ltd, Croydon, CR0 4YY

Hodder & Stoughton policy is to use papers that are natural, renewable
and recyclable products and made from wood grown in sustainable forests.
The logging and manufacturing processes are expected to conform to the
environmental regulations of the country of origin.

Hodder & Stoughton Ltd
Carmelite House
50 Victoria Embankment
London EC4Y 0DZ

www.hodder.co.uk

To sister Nan—You were right.
One bite at a time. . . .

Acknowledgments

I can't thank everyone enough who helped with this book. I have to start with my sister, Nancy Bush, whose encouragement kept me going, and then my editor, John Scognamiglio, who first came up with the idea of "Cissy's Story" as a sequel to *If She Only Knew.* He was the one who came up with many of the ideas which, I think, make this book unique. Thanks, Nan and John.

Of course, there are a raft of other people who contributed. My agent, Robin Rue, is at the top of the list as she is forever encouraging as well as fun as all get out, and also the staff at Kensington for their patience, creativity and support.

On the home front, I have my ace helpers, Matthew Crose, Michael Crose, and Niki Wilkins, as well as Marilyn Katcher and Kathy Okano, Roz Noonan, and Alexis Harrington, who all played a part in getting this book on the shelves (or in keeping me sane!).

Prologue

Bayside Hospital
San Francisco, California
Room 316
Friday, February 13
NOW

They think I'm going to die.

I hear it in their whispered words.

They think I can't hear them, but I can, and I'm listening to every single syllable they utter.

"No!" I want to scream. "I'm alive. I'm not giving up. I will fight back."

But I can't speak.

Can't utter one damned word.

My voice is stilled, just as my eyes won't open. Try as I might, I can't lift the lids.

All I know is that I'm lying in a hospital bed, and I know that I'm barely alive. I hear the whispers, the comments, the soft-soled shoes on the floor. Everyone thinks I'm in a coma, unable to hear them, to respond, but I know what's going on. I just can't move, can't communicate. Somehow, I have to let them know. My condition is bad, they claim. I understand the terms ruptured spleen, broken pelvis, concussion, brain trauma, but, damn it, I can hear them! I feel the stretch of skin at the back of my hand where the IV pulls; smell the scents of perfume, medicine, and resignation. The stethoscope is ice cold, the blood pressure cuff too tight, and I try like hell to show some sign that I'm aware, that I can feel. I try to move, just lift a finger or let out a long moan, but I can't.

It scares me to death.

I'm hooked up to machines that monitor my heartbeat and breathing and God only knows what else. Not that it does any good. All the high-tech machines that are tracking body functions aren't providing the hospital staff with any hope or clue that I know what's going on.

I'm trapped in my body, and it's a living hell.

Once again I strain . . . concentrating to raise the index finger of my right hand, to point at whoever next enters the room. Up, I think, raise the tip up off the bedsheets. The effort is painful . . . so hard.

Isn't anyone watching the damned monitor? I must *be registering an elevated pulse, an accelerated heart rate, some damn thing!*

But no.

All that effort. Wasted.

Worse yet, I've heard the gossip; some of the nurses think I would be better off dead . . . but they don't know the truth.

I hear footsteps. Heavier than the usual. And the vague scent of lingering cigar smoke. The doctor! He's been in before.

"Let's take a look, shall we?" he says to whomever it is who's accompanied him, probably the nurse with the cold hands and cheery, irritating voice.

"She's still not responsive." Sure enough, the chipper one. "I haven't seen any positive change in her vitals. In fact . . . well, see for yourself."

What does she mean? And why does her voice sound so resigned? Where's the fake, peppy inspiration in her tone?

"Hmmm," the doctor says in his baritone voice. Then his hands are on me. Gently touching and poking, lifting my eyelid and shining a harsh beam directly into my lens. It's blind-

ing, and surely my body will show some response. A blink or flinch or . . .

"Looks like you're right," he says, turning off the light and backing away from the bed. "She's declining rapidly."

No! That's wrong! I'm here. I'm alive. I'm going to get better!

I can't believe what I'm hearing, and should be hyperventilating, should be going into cardiac arrest at the very words. Can't you see that I'm stressing? Don't the damned monitors show that I'm alive and aware and that I want to live? Oh God, how I want to live!

"The family's been asking," the nurse prods. "About how long she has."

My family? They've already put me in the grave? That can't be right! I don't believe it. I'm still alive, for God's sake. How did I come to this? But I know. All too vividly I can remember every moment of my life and the events leading up to this very second.

"Doctor?" the nurse whispers.

"Tell them twenty-four hours," he says solemnly. "Maybe less."

Chapter 1

Four Weeks Earlier

Click!

The soft noise was enough to wake Eugenia Cahill. From her favorite chair in the sitting room on the second floor of her manor, she blinked her eyes open. Surprised that she'd dozed off, she called out for her granddaughter. "Cissy?" Adjusting her glasses, she glanced at the antique clock mounted over the mantle as gas flames quietly hissed against the blackened ceramic logs. "Cissy, is that you?"

Of course it was. Cissy had called earlier and told her that she'd be by for her usual weekly visit. She was to bring the baby with her . . . but the call had been hours ago. Cissy had promised to be by at seven, and now . . . well, the grandfather clock in the foyer was just pealing off the hour of eight in soft, assuring tones. "Coco," Eugenia said, eyeing the basket where her little white scruff of a dog was snoozing, not so much as lifting her head. The poor thing was getting old too, already losing teeth and suffering from arthritis. "Old age is a bitch," Eugenia said and smiled at her own little joke.

Why hadn't Cissy climbed the stairs to this, the living area, where Eugenia spent most of her days? "I'm up here," she said loudly, and when there was no response, she felt the first tiny niggle of fear, which she quickly dismissed. An old woman's worries, nothing more. Yet she heard no footsteps rushing up the stairs, no rumble of the old elevator as it ground its way upward from the garage. Pushing herself from her Queen Anne recliner, she grabbed her cane and felt a little dizzy. That was unlike her. Then she walked stiffly to the window, where, through the watery glass, she could view the street and the city below. Even with a bank of fog slowly drifting across the city, the vista was breathtaking from most of the windows of this old home—a house that had been built on the highest slopes of Mt. Sutro in San Francisco at the turn of the century, well, the turn of the *last* century. The old brick, mortar, and shake Craftsman-style manor rose four full stories above a garage tucked into the hillside and backed up to the grounds of the medical school. From this room on the second story, Eugenia was able to see the bay on a clear day and had spent more than her share of hours watching sailboats cut across the green-gray waters.

But sometimes this old house in Parnassus Heights seemed so empty. An ancient fortress with its electronic gates and overgrown gardens of rhododendrons and ferns. The estate backed up to the vast grounds of the university's medical center yet still sometimes felt isolated from the rest of the world.

Oh, it wasn't as if she were truly alone. She had servants, of course, but the family had, it seemed, abandoned her.

For God's sake, Eugenia, buck up. You are not some sorry

old woman. You choose to live here, as a Cahill, as you always have.

Had she imagined the click of a lock downstairs? Dreamed it, perhaps? These days, though she was loath to admit it, her dreams often permeated her waking consciousness, and she had a deep, unmentioned fear that she might be in the early stages of dementia. Dear Lord, she hoped not! There had been no trace of Alzheimer's disease in all of her lineage; her own mother had died at ninety-six, still "sharp as a tack" before falling victim to a massive stroke. But tonight she did feel a little foggier than usual. Unclear.

Eugenia's gaze wandered to the street outside the electronic gates, to the area where the unmarked police car had spent the better part of twenty-four hours. Now the Chevy was missing from its parking spot just out of range of the streetlight's bluish glow.

How odd.

Why leave so soon after practically accusing her of helping her daughter-in-law escape from prison? And after all the fuss! Those rude detectives showing up at her doorstep and insisting that she was harboring a criminal or some such rot. *Humph.* They'd camped out, watching the house, and, she suspected, discreetly followed her as Lars drove her to her hairdresser, bridge game, and the Cahill House, where she offered her time helping administer to unmarried pregnant teens and twenty-somethings who needed sanctuary.

Of course the police had discovered nothing.

Because she was totally innocent. Still, she'd been irritated.

Staring into the night, Eugenia was suddenly cold. She saw her own reflection, a ghostly image of a tiny woman backlit by the soft illumination of antique lamps, and she was surprised how old she looked. Her eyes appeared owlish, magnified behind her glasses, the ones that had aided her since the cataract surgery a few years back. Her once vital red hair was now a neatly coiffed style closer to apricot than strawberry blond. She seemed to have shrunk two inches and now appeared barely five feet tall, if that. Her face, though remarkably unlined, had begun to sag, and she hated it. Hated this growing old. Hated being dismissed as past her prime. She'd considered having her eyes "done" or her face "tightened," had even thought about Botox, but really, why?

Vanity?

After all she'd been through, it seemed trivial.

And so she was over eighty. Big deal. She knew she was no longer young, her arthritic knees could attest to that, but she wasn't yet ready for any kind of assisted living or retirement community. Not yet.

Creeeeaaaak!

The sound of a door opening?

Her heartbeat quickened.

This last noise was *not* a figment of her imagination. "Cissy?" she called again and glanced over at Coco, who barely lifted her groggy little head at the noise, offering up no warning bark. "Dear, is that you?"

Who else?

Sunday and Monday nights she was usually alone: her "companion," Deborah, generally leaving the city to stay with her sister; the day maid gone by five; and Elsa, the cook, having two days off. Lars finished every night by six, unless she requested his services, and she usually didn't mind being alone, enjoyed the peace and quiet. But tonight . . .

Using her cane, she trundled into the hallway that separated the living quarters from her bedroom. "Cissy?" she called down the stairs. She felt like a ninny. Was she getting paranoid in her advancing years?

But a cold finger of doubt slid down her spine, convincing her otherwise, and though the furnace was humming, she felt a chill icy as the deep waters of the bay settle into her bones. She reached the railing, held onto the smooth rosewood banister and peered down to the first floor. In the dimmed evening lights she saw the polished tile floor of the foyer, the Louis XVI inlaid table and the ficus trees and jade plants positioned near the beveled glass by the front door.

Just as they always were.

But no Cissy.

Odd, Eugenia thought again, rubbing her arms. Odder yet that her dog was so passive. Coco, though old and arthritic, still had excellent hearing and was usually energetic enough to growl and bark her adorable head off at the least little sound. But tonight she just lay listlessly in her bed near Eugenia's knitting bag, her eyes open but dull. Almost as if she'd been drugged. . . .

Oh, for heaven's sake! She was getting away with herself, letting her fertile imagination run wild. She gave herself a swift mental kick. That's what she got for indulging in an Alfred Hitchcock movie marathon for the past five nights.

So where the hell was Cissy?

She reached into the pocket of her heavy sweater for her cell phone. Nothing there. The damned thing was missing, probably left on the table near her knitting needles.

Turning back toward the sitting room, she heard the gentle scrape of a footstep, leather upon wood.

Close by.

The scent of a perfume she'd nearly forgotten wafted to her nostrils and made the hairs on the back of her neck lift.

Her heart nearly stopped as she looked over her shoulder. There was movement in the shadows of the unlit hallway near her bedroom. "Cissy?" she said again, but her voice was the barest of whispers, and fear caused her pulse to pound. "Is that you, dear? This isn't funny—"

Her words died in her throat.

A woman, half-hidden in the shadows, emerged triumphantly.

Eugenia froze.

Suspended in time.

"You!" she cried. Panic crept up her spine, and the woman before her smiled, a grin as cold and evil as Satan's heart.

Eugenia tried to run, to flee, but before she could take a step, the younger woman pounced, strong hands clutching and squeezing, athletic arms pulling her off her feet.

"No!" Eugenia cried. "No!" She lifted her cane, but the damned walking stick fell from her hands and clattered uselessly down the stairs. Now, finally, Coco began to bark wildly.

"Don't do this!" Eugenia cried.

But it was too late.

In a heartbeat, she was hoisted over the railing, pushed into the open space where the crystal chandelier hung. Screaming, flailing pathetically, hearing her dog snarling, Eugenia hurtled downward.

The Louis XVI table and tile floor of the foyer rushed up at her.

Sheer terror caused her heart to seize as she hit the floor with a dull, sickening thud. *Crack!* Pain exploded in her head. For half a second she stared upward at her assailant. The woman stood victorious on the landing, holding Coco, stroking the dog's furry coat.

"Payback's a bitch, isn't it?" the woman gloated.

Then there was only darkness. . . .

*   *   *

"Shhh! Beej, you're okay, got it? You are *okay!*" Cissy Cahill leaned over the railing of the playpen and hoisted her eighteen-month-old son onto her hip. His face was red from crying; tears streaked down his chubby cheeks, and his nose was running something fierce. "Oh, baby, look at you." Cissy's heart instantly melted, and she kissed the top of his blond head while reaching for a tissue and dabbing at his nose. "It's gonna be all right. I promise," she said as she found his little jacket and the hat he hated with a passion. She somehow managed to dress him, grab the diaper bag, and head out the door of the old Victorian home she'd lived in for nearly two years. He'd been cranky all afternoon, probably teething, and when the pizza-delivery kid had showed up, for some reason Beej had ratcheted into full tantrum mode. She had no real idea why he was upset. Teething? Too cold because the friggin' furnace had gone out? Too hot because his mother had piled on extra clothes? Whatever the reason, Cissy was convinced it wasn't serious, and the baby would just have to deal with it. She was running late, and her grandmother would be angry.

"The price we all pay for being Cahills," she confided to her son as she locked the door behind her and walked to the driveway, where her car, a silver Acura sedan, was parked, the pizza already cooling in a box on the floor of the passenger seat. In no better mood than he'd been in all day, B.J. wailed and clawed at his hat as she strapped him into the child's seat in the back and climbed behind the steering wheel. It was dark out, a soft rain beginning to fall, the lights of the city a little blurry. She glanced across the street to the spot where the unmarked police car had been parked ever since she'd heard the news that her mother had escaped from prison, but, surprisingly, it was missing.

Gone too was the news van that had camped out for hours on the street, a reporter coming to her door three times and asking for an interview. As if she would ever talk to the press! Cissy had prayed they'd go away, and tonight she'd gotten her wish.

Good.

She was sick of being treated like *she* was some kind of criminal when she'd done nothing wrong. Nothing! It wasn't her fault that her mother just happened to be a narcissistic, murderous bitch—which were some of the nicer adjectives Cissy could ascribe to Marla. As far as Cissy was concerned, the farther her egocentric nutcase of a mother stayed away from her and B.J., the better.

Don't think that way . . . get rid of the negative thoughts . . . count slowly to ten. . . . Cissy's shrink's voice slipped through her brain, but she ignored it. She wasn't in a forgiving mood tonight, and she was just grateful that the police weren't following her to the Cahill estate, where her grandmother had resided ever since marrying into the family nearly fifty years earlier. Cissy's life was in enough turmoil as it was; she didn't need to deal with the cops. In her opinion, she'd already suffered enough melodrama and pain to last her a lifetime or two—compliments of Marla Amhurst Cahill, sick-o extraordinaire and her mother.

"Yeah, Beej, that's your nana," she said, weaving her way through the neighborhood streets rimming Alamo Square. "Nana Psycho." She glanced into the rearview mirror and caught a glimpse of her son, his wailing having stopped, his big eyes devoid of tears. For the moment, he'd stopped fighting the hat.

Relieved that the tantrum was over, she winked at him. "See, you just wanted a date out with Mom in a classy car, right?"

The light ahead turned amber, and she stepped on the brakes. There had been a time when she had run anything remotely yellow, but now, with Beej, she'd suddenly become a model driver and nearly overprotective mother. Who woulda thunk it?

Her rumbling stomach and the clock on the dash reminded her that she was late. *Great.* No doubt she was in for another lecture. Like she hadn't had enough. She was a grown woman, for God's sake.

Once again she looked into the rearview mirror. This time she scanned the traffic behind her, searching for signs of a cop car. Not that she could pick one out. But considering that ever since her mother had escaped, the police had planted themselves near her door, it was odd that they weren't following her now. Though the detectives had been nothing but nice, she knew, behind the concerned words and patient smiles, they were suspicious.

As *if* her mother would contact her.

As *if* she would harbor a woman she hated.

"No friggin' way," she whispered. Every muscle in her body tensed. As a kid, she'd grown up with Marla's cool, aloof attitude toward her. She'd accepted it, accepted the fact that her whole family was a set of cold weirdos. To survive, she'd simply rebelled in any and every way she could think of.

But now, as a mother herself, Cissy couldn't imagine not feeling close and bonded to a child. From the first time she'd laid eyes on her son, she'd been a new person. Life had changed in that sterling instant. Throughout her pregnancy she'd talked to the baby, rubbed her tummy, even named him Juan because of her cravings for tacos or anything Mexican at all hours of the day or night, but it hadn't compared to holding him and hearing him cry at the hospital. Yep, they were a team. Inseparable.

So where was her mother?

How the hell had she gotten out?

Weren't prisons supposed to be escape proof?

What will you do if she does show up at your door?

"Don't even go there," she told herself. She didn't need any more tension in her life. Wasn't it bad enough that she was in the first stages of a divorce and that her son was quickly approaching the terrible twos and had been crabby all week? It didn't help that the furnace had decided to go kaflooey now too. All in all, the last seven days had been hell.

The light changed, and Cissy drove along the panhandle until she reached Stanyan, then headed steadily uphill. Her cell phone rang just as she was taking a steep switchback of a street that climbed Mt. Sutro. Pulling the phone from the side pocket of her purse, she checked the caller ID. She could plug the phone into the slot on her dash and talk hands free, but seeing the number on the LCD caused her to frown.

"Not tonight," she said aloud. She wasn't going to deal with Jack—lying, cheating bastard that he was. Oh yeah, and he was still her husband. Well, not for long. Dropping the phone into its pocket, she concentrated on the narrow road that climbed ever upward past elegant old homes built a hundred years earlier and surrounded by manicured gardens. Near her grandmother's home, she pressed on the electronic gate opener and slowed as the old iron gates groaned open. She pulled into a spot in front of the garage, hit the button again and, once the gates were locked behind her, tried to figure out how she was going to haul B.J., the pizza box, diaper bag, and purse into the garage and upstairs without dropping the baby or ending up with melted cheese and marinara sauce everywhere.

"You win, Beej. You get to go first," she said, tossing her purse into the oversized diaper bag. Slinging the bag over her shoulder, she walked around the car, ignoring the tantalizing scent of garlic and pepperoni as she unbuckled her son. "You can stay with your great-

grannie while I run back down here," she told the boy.
She hoisted him onto the same hip she used to nudge
her car door closed. Rubbing her nose into his ear, she
heard him giggle. "Come on."

Sometimes it was a real headache to visit Eugenia
when the staff had the night off. It would be so much
easier for Cissy to spend time at the old mansion when
someone else was here to help with the baby. Then there
wouldn't be the problem of dinner, or the guilt that if she
didn't show up the old woman would be disappointed.

Carrying B.J., who was making loud smacking noises
with his lips just to hear himself, she walked along a
brick path through tall rhododendrons and ferns that
still dripped from the rain that had stopped over an hour
earlier. This old house, where she had grown up, held a
lot of memories. Maybe too many. Some good and a lot
that weren't, but the brick, mortar, and shake walls,
peekaboo dormers and sharp gables had endured two
earthquakes and generation after generation of Cahills.
For well over a hundred years it had stood on the slopes
of Mt. Sutro, offering up commanding views of the city
and the bay. Cissy didn't know if she loved the old house
or hated it.

Oh, get over yourself, she thought, inserting her key
into the old lock.

"Helloooo," she called as the door opened. "Sorry
I'm late, but . . . Oh God!" She bit back a scream and
turned away, hiding her son from the sight of her
grandmother lying on the marble floor, blood pooling
beneath her head. "Oh God, oh God, oh God!" she
whispered. She dropped her keys and the diaper bag,
then, still holding B.J. close, fished in her purse for her
phone. She was trembling all over, her fingers scrabbling for her cell. "It's okay, it's okay, it's okay," she said
over and over as she found the phone and punched
out 9-1-1.

Beej, picking up on her stress, began to howl. Bracing herself, Cissy placed him on the bench on the porch. "Sit here for just a second, honey," she instructed.

"No!" he screamed and began scrambling down as she hurried inside.

"Gran!" Bending down on one knee, Cissy reached to her grandmother's neck, her fingers searching for a pulse, the phone pressed to her ear. She felt nothing beneath her fingertips, no sign of a heart pumping. "Oh, Gran, please be okay." Her stomach cramped, and she thought she might be sick.

"Nine-one-one, police dispatch."

"Help! I need help!" Cissy yelled. "It's my grandmother!"

"Ma'am, please state your name and the nature of your emergency."

"There's been an . . . an . . . accident. A horrible accident. My grandmother fell down the stairs! She's hurt. Bad. There's blood everywhere. Oh God, I think she might be dead! Send someone quick. Oh God! Oh God, I can't find a pulse!"

"What is your address?"

"Send someone now!"

"I need the address and the name of the victim."

"It's . . . it's . . ." Cissy rattled off the address as she tried again to find a pulse, to hear even the shallowest drawing of breath. "My grandmother's Eugenia Cahill. Oh, please send someone. . . . Hurry!" She glanced over her shoulder, out the door, and didn't see her son sitting on the bench. "B.J.!" she yelled, panicking.

"Ma'am. What is your name?"

"Cissy Holt . . . er, Cissy Cahill Holt. I was coming over here to dinner, and oh, sweet Jesus, I found Gran, and now my son . . . Please just hurry!"

"A patrol car has been dispatched. If you could stay with the victim—"

"I have to find my son!" She hung up and yelled, "Beej!" But there was no answering response from a tiny voice. "B.J.! Where are you?" Frantic, Cissy jogged outside to the dark night where the rain was starting to fall again. There was nothing to do for her grandmother. Eugenia was dead. Cissy knew it. But her child . . . Oh God, where was he? He couldn't have gotten far. She'd let him out of her sight for only a split second. "B.J.!" Panic gripped her to her very soul as she searched the night-darkened grounds. She tried to sound calm when inside she was out of her mind with worry. "B.J.? Honey? Where are you?" She tried to keep the tremor out of her voice, the sheer terror. "Beej?" Dear God, where could he have gone so quickly? The gate was locked . . . right? It had slammed shut behind the car.

Or had it?

"No," Cissy whispered, running down the walk. New panic seized her. "B.J.! Bryan Jack! Where are you?"

In the distance, sirens screamed. "Hurry, damn it," Cissy said, her heart pounding, her mind black with fear. *Don't panic. He's here, you know he's here. He's just as scared as you are. Calm down. Forget that you just saw your grandmother dead, forget that you might have prevented the accident if you had been here on time, forget that your mother, the psycho-bitch, has escaped from prison, and just FIND B.J.!*

Chapter 2

She couldn't believe she'd actually gotten away with it!

Adrenaline sizzled through her blood.

When the old woman had finally looked at her, she'd almost lost it, but somehow she'd found an inner strength to go through with her plan.

Now, as the windshield wipers slapped away the rain, her heart drummed a million miles a minute. Triumphant, it was all she could do to ease off the accelerator of her Taurus. She couldn't afford a speeding ticket, or any kind of interest from the police. Not now.

Calm down. You can savor this later. . . .

Her gloved fingers curled over the steering wheel, but she couldn't quite put aside, not even for an instant, the thrill of the kill and that moment, right before she'd pushed the old woman over the railing, that precise, magnificent moment of recognition when Eugenia had made eye contact with her.

In that smallest of heartbeats, Eugenia Haversmith Cahill had realized that she was about to meet her maker, that she was facing her own demise. Even so, the old bitch probably hadn't expected it to happen so quickly. She probably thought that there would be a way to talk, bully, or buy her way out of it.

Too bad.

Grinning to herself, she turned on the defroster, forcing warm air to blast on the interior of the glass and evaporate the condensation as she gazed through the windshield at the glowing taillights of the sporty little BMW zipping along in front of her. In and out of traffic he wove, his engine whining. *Go for it, you idiot,* she thought. *You get the ticket.*

She remembered the old woman's horror as she'd been pitched over the railing. Oh, Eugenia had fought and screamed, but she hadn't been able to save herself. Her small body had slammed into the hard marble floor, the crunch of bones a sickening, satisfying thud.

Now she flipped on the radio and hummed along to an old song by Sheryl Crow. Staying within the speed limit, she headed over the bridge spanning the night-darkened waters of the bay, following a steady stream of taillights into Oakland.

Still feeling a bit paranoid, she checked her rearview mirror more than once, making certain she wasn't being followed.

She couldn't get caught. Not yet. Not when there was so much to do, so much to accomplish. Squinting against the headlights reflecting in her mirror, she saw nothing out of the ordinary, no red and blue strobe lights announcing a police cruiser pursuing her.

For God's sake, no one's tailing you! No one knows what you did.

Relax!

You got away with it! And the cops . . . they're morons.

Remember that.

Once on the east side of the bay, she headed north toward Berkeley and calmed a little. She quit holding the steering wheel in a death grip and wasn't quite as jangled, nor as afraid, nor as high. She exhaled a calming breath as she drove through the suburbs toward Wildcat Canyon, where the dense population gave way to little bungalows and quiet, treelined streets. One more time, just before turning down the road to her little rental house, she rechecked her mirrors. To be safe, she made a couple of quick right turns, watching behind her. Then, satisfied that she was safe from pursuit, she doubled back into an alley behind the two-bedroom cottage she'd leased under a fake name. She remembered handing the leasing agent her fake ID, biting her lip with anxiety, sure that when it was checked the agent would discover the Oregon driver's license was a fraud. Instead, with a few quick clicks on a computer keyboard to double-check the credit report and job history of Elyse Hammersly, recently of Gresham, Oregon, and acceptance of a cashier's check, she, as Elyse, had been handed the keys. Wonderful! Now she liked to think of herself as Elyse. Why, she *was* Elyse. Why not? It was perfect!

Chuckling to herself, she pulled into the drive. The bungalow had the basic floor plan of post–World War II, with two small bedrooms, single bath, a living area, walk-through dining room, tiny kitchen, and stairs that led to the most important feature of the house: a basement. With special amenities.

The basement was where this house, nearly identical to every other one on the block, got interesting. And perfect for what she needed.

Now, however, she had to face her new guest.

Marla Amhurst Cahill.

Or, as she liked to think of the woman she'd helped spring: Marla the Missing, or Marla the Escapee. Not that she would ever admit as much to her prickly new roommate.

The weeks before the actual breakout had been nerve-wracking, and they'd communicated through several different parties. Never once had she visited Marla in prison. Never had she called. The people who had relayed messages had known nothing of their plot, nor had they known her name. Elyse felt her anonymity was secure. Just for good luck, though, she crossed her fingers and braced herself for the confrontation she knew was brewing.

Though they'd planned this prison break for over two years, and it had gone off without a hitch, Marla, as ever, wasn't satisfied.

Sometimes Elyse wondered if it was worth it.

Of course it is! Millions are at stake! Remember that!

Slinging the strap of her purse over her shoulder, she climbed out of the car and locked it. Nervous as a cat, she glanced this way and that, peering at the corners of the garage, the garbage can, and the long, sweeping porch, half expecting an ambush of FBI agents with badges flashing and guns pointed at her heart.

Don't freak out! You made it.

She dashed up the overgrown cement walk to the back porch, where a now-leafless clematis wound skeletally and ropelike over the eaves. She fiddled with her keys until she found the one she needed and slipped it into the deadbolt.

Click.

Key ring jingling with her case of nerves, she found a separate key for the second lock and had to twist and jiggle it a bit before the ancient deadbolt slid back with a scrape of metal on metal. Using her shoulder, she pushed the sticky door open to be greeted by the smells of must and dead air. She reminded herself to get some of those air-fresheners, as the cottage had been unoccupied for eight months. Maybe there was a way to convince Marla to get off her ass and break out the Lysol and a mop. It wasn't as if she hadn't done just that kind of work in the big house, but Marla was still paranoid, afraid someone might see her.

"I'm never going back," she'd confided in Elyse. "Not ever. They'll have to kill me."

And Elyse believed her.

She locked the door behind her, pulled a white sack out of her purse, and dropped the leather bag on the landing. Up half a flight of stairs was the kitchen, where the leaky faucet dripped and an old-fashioned wall clock ticked off the seconds of its life. But she wasn't interested in what lay upstairs. Instead she double-checked to make certain both locks were latched, then followed the creaking stairs downward into a musty basement that seemed forever damp. The ceilings were low enough that a tall man would have to duck beneath some of the beams, and she'd found more than one nest of spiders hiding in the dark corners of the joists for the floor above.

Her skin crawled despite the fact that the place was perfect for their purposes.

Walking past a rusted washer and dryer, she approached what appeared to be the far wall of the dank room. However, it was not as it seemed. During the course of the last half century, one of the bungalow's owners had made a false wall in one corner of the basement, creating a space for a hidden wine cellar. All of which was odd, as the basement was too damp to create the right atmosphere for anything worth drinking.

But then, she wasn't using the space to hide her special bottles of Pinot Gris or Chardonnay or Merlot.

The fake wall with its dusty shelves and hidden door was a perfect hiding spot, if not for cases of wine, then at least for an escapee from a minimum-security prison.

Careful not to make too much noise, just in case Marla was sleeping, she softly rapped on the back of the shelf. Marla was probably exhausted from the tension of planning and executing the escape.

Elyse waited a second, then pulled on a hidden lever. With a click, the latch unhooked, and she was able to push one section of the shelving into the small room.

She whispered, "Hey, I'm here," as she let herself into the windowless room currently lit only by the flickering bluish light of the television and a small bedside lamp. The compact area was stark: walls devoid of pictures; the only furniture a chair, bed, night table, and dresser to support the television.

Marla barely looked up to greet her.

Oh God, she was in a bad mood.

Great.

The euphoria of the escape had obviously seeped away. "Are you really watching this?" Elyse demanded, recognizing a popular reality show on the screen of the muted television.

Silently, Marla gave her a look that said it all. Somehow, in prison, Marla had gotten hooked on all kinds of weird TV. "I like it. It's escapism," she said and offered a hint of a smile, the old cagey Marla surfacing for a second.

"Okay, whatever. But I thought you'd like to get out of here."

"And go where?"

"Upstairs."

"Someone might see me," she said in a tone that suggested Elyse was an imbecile.

"You can keep the blinds shut, but at least, at least it wouldn't be like . . ."

"A cell?" Marla said, scarcely moving her lips.

"Yeah. Like a cell. Tomorrow, I'll bring cleaning supplies and we'll fix it up. It's already furnished."

Marla snorted in disgust, her eyes wandering back to a group of people locked inside a windowless house together. Well, at least Marla could relate.

"Look, I brought you something to eat." Elyse held out the white paper sack. "A hamburger I picked up before I went to the house. Sorry it's a little cold, but I didn't want to stop afterward."

"The house?" Marla's interest was suddenly sharp, though she didn't seem the least bit interested in the food.

"Yeah, *the* house. On Mt. Sutro." She stepped closer to the chair and leaned down, whispering in Marla's ear. "I killed Eugenia tonight. Just like we planned. Oh God . . . it was . . . perfect. She recognized me, too, the old bitch."

"You killed Eugenia? First?" Marla ignored the bag on her lap and glared at Elyse. "That *wasn't* the way we planned it."

"Hey! Opportunity knocked, okay? And I got rid of her. I don't see what difference it makes when they die or how they die, just as long as they die!"

"You little—"

"Don't," Elyse warned. "I risked my damned neck for you, so the least you could do is be interested or say 'thank you' or 'good job,' but do not, do you hear me, do not belittle me. I won't stand for it."

"Testy, aren't we?" Marla muttered.

"Yes, *we* are. Both of us!"

Marla composed herself. "All right," she said slowly. "I didn't mean to snap. I'm just so damned tired of being cooped up."

"That'll change soon."

"Not soon enough."

Elyse scraped her hair away from her face in frustration. That was the problem with Marla, she was so damned moody. "Listen, I'm sorry. I should have told you, but I had to work fast when I learned that Eugenia would be home alone. Crap, it's not easy, you know."

"It's not easy for me either. I'm the one who's been in prison, and now . . . now this."

"You knew you'd have to keep a low profile for a while."

Marla frowned, but didn't argue, thank God. "I think I just need some time to adjust."

"Yeah, well, me too. Go on, eat and watch . . ." she glanced at the television. "Whatever it is."

"*House Arrest.*"

"Perfect."

Marla laughed then at the irony of it all.

"I'll be back. Tomorrow or the next day, whenever I can be free, and I'll bring things we can use as your disguise. Then you can chance getting out again. How's that?"

"Better," Marla agreed as the show on the television broke for a commercial for some kind of light beer. "Next time you come, make sure the food's at least tepid."

"Right."

As Elyse left she wondered why she even bothered with the bitch.

For the money, remember? The Cahill fortune? Just put up with her for a little while longer. She's your ticket to wealth.

But you're right: she's a first-class bitch.

Live with it.

Heart in her throat, Cissy hunted for her eighteen-month-old son. *Please let him be okay. Please!*

"Beej! Honey? Where are you?" Fear pounding through her brain, a dozen horrid scenarios flashing behind her eyes, Cissy jogged the grounds of her grandmother's house. Her gaze scraped the undergrowth, searching in the darkness. Her heart pounded a horrifying tattoo as the rain began to fall in earnest.

What if she couldn't find him?

What if he somehow slipped through the bars of the gate?

He was so small . . . so innocent.

Oh God, please let him be safe!

"B.J.?"

Where were the damned cops? They could help!

For the last two days they'd been hanging out and . . . thank God! She saw the first set of flashing lights, flaring red and blue on the hill below. The sirens screamed ever nearer, just as she spied her little boy cowering under an azalea. "Oh, B.J." She splashed across the cold puddles in the yard and scooped him into her arms, hugging him tightly. He was dirty. And clinging. And crying. His hat was tilted drunkenly on one ear, tied around his neck like a noose. She untied it and pulled it off. He was safe. Safe. She drank in that special B.J. scent of his and swallowed the lump in her throat.

"Me scay-o-ed," he said, shivering in her arms.

"Me too, baby." She kissed his now-wet crown and held him close. Tears burned the back of her eyes at the thought of losing him. "But you're okay now. Mommy's here. Everything will be all right!" She walked to the gatepost, pressed in a code on the electronic keypad, and, as the gates swung open, the first cop car—an old Cadillac with a light mounted on the dash—roared up the hill, stopping at an odd angle on the street, blocking the drive. The second car, a marked cruiser, found a spot on the crowded street. A fire truck and EMT vehicle were right behind, working their way up the snake-like narrow road.

"The cavalry," Cissy said to her son, though she had a bad feeling about the boatlike first vehicle. It brought back memories she didn't want to recall, recollections of another bad time in her life ten years earlier, the horrific events that had landed her mother in prison.

When the first cop rolled out of the driver's side of the Caddy, her heart sank. He didn't have to flash his badge or utter his name. She knew him because Detective Anthony Paterno had been in charge of the investigation that sent her mother to prison. His hound-dog face sported a few more lines, and his thick hair was more shot with gray, but otherwise he, like his car, had changed little.

"You're Cissy," he said.

"Yeah. This is my son, B.J., er, Bryan Jack. Come on. This way." She glanced past Paterno to the paramedics. "Maybe there's a chance Gran can be revived," she said, hope blooming in her heart, though she was pretty certain it was too late. Holding B.J. as if she thought she might lose him again, she half-ran up the brick walk to the front door. Paterno and his partner, a tall, mannish-looking woman with simple glasses and a short haircut, were on her heels, the paramedics and firefighters a step behind.

"Stay here," Paterno said, motioning to a bench on the porch while his partner, who introduced herself as Janet Quinn, stepped through the open doorway. "Jesus, what happened?"

"I don't know. I wasn't here when she fell. . . . Oh God." Swallowing hard, Cissy cradled B.J. close to her body while rocking back and forth.

"Mama sad," B.J. said, and she nodded.

"Very."

"Mama cry?"

"Oh, maybe." She smiled through her tears and kissed his head. Shielding her son from the open doorway, she didn't try to look inside to the foyer. She'd seen enough.

Two EMTs, hauling equipment, rushed past her.

"Careful. This could be a crime scene," Paterno said as they entered.

"We got it, Detective," the female EMT said. "Back off. Let us work. Oh hell . . . she's already gone."

All of Cissy's hope died.

"Nothing left to do but bag and tag her," the second EMT said so emotionlessly Cissy caught her breath. This was her grandmother, for God's sake! Not just some unknown, unclaimed, unloved body! The woman they were talking about was Eugenia Cahill, a short, sharp, sassy woman who had run corporations, played competitive bridge, and sat on the boards of . . . Oh God, what did it matter what boards she'd sat on? She was gone.

"No sign of forced entry," Quinn said. "We're checking to see if robbery was a motive."

Still on the porch, Cissy turned away from the drama inside. The whole scene was surreal, and Cissy, holding her son, watching rain drizzling down from the night sky, realized for the first time that she'd never see her grandmother alive again. She blinked back a fresh spate of tears. Theirs hadn't been a loving relationship, in fact they'd had more than their share of knock-down, drag-out fights when she'd been a teenager living here, but she'd loved Eugenia, and, aside from an uncle and aunt now in Oregon, and another uncle in an institution, Eugenia was the only family she had left. Certainly her closest relative, besides James, her half-brother.

Except for Marla. Remember her? Your mother? The damned escaped convict. You have to count her.

And what about Jack?

She didn't want to think about her louse of a husband right now. Daring another look inside, she saw one of the EMTs shake his head. Cissy swallowed hard. She'd known from the second she'd seen Eugenia that the old woman was dead, but it hit so much harder when her suspicions were confirmed.

Paterno walked back outside. "Your grandmother—"

"I know." She was shaking inside, but managed to keep some sort of calm. Her mind was racing in a zillion directions, but she tried to focus on the detective with his sober face and dark eyes. "But why . . . I mean, you're

with homicide, I thought. Why did you come so soon?"
Before he could answer, she understood. "Oh, I get it.
This has to do with my mother, doesn't it?"

"We'd like to find her."

She shivered when she thought about Marla Amhurst
Cahill as a free woman. Though Cissy didn't want to
jump to conclusions, it seemed damned coincidental
that her grandmother had fallen down the stairs within
a few days of Marla's escape.

Her mother, if nothing else, was clever. Sly. But it would
have been just plain stupid to return here. The police had
been staked out on the street near the gates. . . . Or had
they? Her grandmother had complained about them
yesterday, but where were they tonight?

A cold feeling settled in the pit of her stomach.

"So, what took you so long to get here? I figured that
someone was staking out the house. Gran had said a
couple of detectives were parked on the street."

"There was a car," he admitted. "But the officers got
called away."

"Called away?"

"A reported shooting just down the street."

"At the same time that my grandmother fell down
the stairs?" she asked, disbelieving. A coincidence? Her
grandmother dies soon after Marla escapes, and while
it's all happening, the officers assigned to watch the house
are suddenly jerked away? "Did they catch the shooter?"

Paterno's long face didn't give up a clue. "Not yet."

"You mean, it just happened?"

"About an hour ago."

"An hour." Her heart knocked as the coincidences
kept stacking up. "Gran hasn't been dead long. She was
. . . was," Cissy's voice cracked. "She was still warm when
I searched for a pulse. . . ."

"How did you get in?"

"I have my own key," Cissy explained dully. It was difficult to process.

Paterno looked at B.J. "Why don't you wait in the car? Where it's dry and warm. We might have a few more questions and in the meantime the house is going to be considered a crime scene."

"She fell down the stairs. Where's the crime?" But Cissy already understood what he was suggesting, and the thought, that her mother might somehow be involved, turned her stomach. This couldn't be happening. And yet here she was, standing on rubber legs, feeling almost as if she were having an out-of-body experience.

"Was anyone else home with her?" Paterno asked, ushering her from the front porch.

Feeling the rain run down her neck, Cissy made her way back to the car. "No . . . I mean, I don't think so." As they reached the Acura, B.J. whimpered in her arms, and she whispered into his little ear, "It's okay, honey. Ssshhh."

Paterno opened the driver's side door, and the pent-up aroma of tomatoes, oregano, and garlic greeted her. She slid the seat back, then, with her child on her lap, sat behind the wheel while Paterno climbed into the passenger side of the car, one foot crushing the lid of the pizza box.

Too late he shifted his shoe. "Sorry."

"Doesn't matter." Right now, nothing much did. She felt numb inside. Aside from her baby, she didn't really care about anything.

Fortunately, B.J. was thrilled with his position and was "driving" the car, both his little hands on the steering wheel.

Sitting with his feet straddling the dented pizza box, Paterno retrieved a pen and small notebook from his coat pocket. "You were bringing dinner to your grand-mother?"

She nodded. "I usually visit her on Sundays, because she's alone. I always come with something to eat, some-thing fun, I think, fix it for her, then we watch some television show, you know, *Jeopardy* or *Wheel of Fortune* with Coco and—" She stopped short, her head snap-ping up. "Where's the dog?"

"What?"

"Gran's usually alone except for Coco. Her little white mutt of some kind that she absolutely adores. I didn't see the dog in the house, and that's really weird. Grandma takes that dog *every*where. They're practically inseparable." She scanned the grounds as if the dog had somehow slipped through the door.

"We'll find it," Paterno said, but made a note in his little pad. He touched her on the arm. "You were say-ing . . . You watch television. . . ."

"Tonight we were going to have pizza because I was running late. . . ." Cissy looked down at the crushed white box and couldn't believe that less than half an hour ago she'd been worried about explaining why she didn't have time to cook something her grandmother liked better than takeout from Dino's. Now she was stuck in a car with a cop she didn't trust, her grand-mother dead. She cleared her throat, tried to think straight. "Anyway, it's usually just the three of us. Me, Grandma, and Beej. Deborah, the woman who is basi-cally her companion and, um, you know, isn't really a 'caregiver.'" Cissy made air quotes with her fingers. "Gran would never put up with that, but she's got the companion. Deborah has Sundays and Mondays off, and the day maid, Paloma, leaves around five, I think. Elsa, the cook, she only works, oh geez, Monday through Friday unless Gran was having company . . . and . . . and, oh, Lars, the chauffeur, works until, I don't know . . .

Five? Six? Something like that, unless Grandma needs him, and then they work something out." She was trying to keep it all straight, though she knew she was rambling. "So then we watch some inane show and . . . and . . . oh damn." She started crying again, then, disgusted with herself, angrily scraped the tears away.

"Mommy?" B.J. asked, twisting his head backward to look at her.

She managed a smile. "Mommy's okay." An out-and-out lie. "Can we go now?" she asked the detective just as a vehicle for the crime-scene team rolled to a stop and added another roadblock to the driveway. Worse yet, she saw through the open gates that some of the neighbors had stepped onto the street, clustering together under the spreading branches of a large oak tree. Cissy groaned, then groaned again as a news van roared up the hillside and double-parked a few houses down. "This just gets better and better."

"I can drive you home. Unfortunately it'll be a little while. It would help if you could give me a list of the people who work here. Names and addresses."

"I don't have them on me, but Gran did. I've got a couple phone numbers on my cell. For Deborah and Lars. I don't have the rest, but I do have some of her friends at home on my computer."

"I'll need what you've got."

She found her phone in her purse, scrolled down her contact list, then rattled off the phone numbers that she had. "Deborah Kropft, here it is." She told him the number. "And Lars Swanson; I know I have his because sometimes he drives Beej and me." Again she gave him a number. "Paloma's last name is Perez, and I . . . I think she lives in Oakland. Her husband is Estevan. There's another maid, Rosa, who has worked for Gran on and off for years. Her last name is Santiago. I'm not sure where she lives, but Gran has records in the library,

I think. By the phone. A card file, not on a computer. . . .
She rarely used her PC. . . ." Oh Lord, she was rambling
again.

"We'll check. Thanks."

"Can we leave now?"

"Not just yet, but soon. Promise," he said solemnly.
"I'll be back in a few minutes, then we can wrap this up,
and if I have more questions, I'll call or stop by, or, if it's
easier, you can come to the station."

"I really don't have anything more to say, and I really
need to get my son home."

"I know. I'll make it quick." Paterno stepped outside
and turned his attention to someone who had appeared from the crime-scene-unit's vehicle. Together
they walked briskly back up the brick walk that now was
cluttered with cops and emergency workers. No way was
she going to take a ride from the detective. They could
just find a way to unblock the damned driveway. For
now, though, it looked like she was stuck. Which really
sucked. "Okay, buddy," she said to B.J. "Nothin' else I
can do. Looks like it's you and me. How about we eat in
the car?"

"I drive."

"Mmm. Later."

He started to wail as she shifted him from her lap,
but she ignored the coming tantrum, strapped him into
the passenger seat, grabbed some extra napkins from
the glove box, and opened the pizza box.

She pulled out a small piece and handed it to him.
His cries quickly subsided. Yesterday, she would have
worried about her leather seats. Tonight, she realized it
wasn't a big deal. Any slopped-over tomato sauce or
strings of mozzarella cheese could be wiped up. Her
grandmother would never be able to complain about
stains ever again.

As B.J. pulled off a piece of pepperoni, examining it

closely before stuffing it into his mouth, Cissy stared out the rain-splattered windshield and up at the old house. Its shingle and brick walls rose four stories above the basement garage, which was flanked by rhododendrons, azaleas, and ferns, all currently collecting rain and shivering in the wind. The windows on the first two floors glowed—warm patches of light that belied the horror inside. She lifted her gaze upward to the third floor and the dormer of her old room, the place where she'd spent most of her miserable teenage years.

At that time she'd hated living in the city, had preferred the ranch. All that had changed, of course.

Maybe Cissy should have moved back here as her grandmother had suggested when she'd kicked Jack out of the house, but she hadn't wanted to give up her independence. And besides, this huge, rambling house didn't hold all that great of memories for her.

Now Gran was dead.

Her throat tightened painfully. Her whole life seemed to be falling apart. Her mother was an escapee, her grandmother dead, her husband . . . Oh, she didn't even want to go there. She glanced at her child, happily chewing on a piece of pepperoni as she broke off a bit of cheesy crust. She offered it to B.J., and he took it eagerly, crushing it in his tiny fist.

So lost in thought was she that she didn't see a shadow pass by the car, didn't realize someone was staring through the window of the driver's door until there was a quick rap of knuckles on the glass. She jumped, turned quickly, nearly sending the rest of the pizza into the steering wheel only to find Jack Holt peering inside.

"Geez!" she said, her heart knocking, then, under her breath, added, "Well, B.J., look who arrived." She couldn't believe it. "Daddy's here."

Chapter 3

The last thing Cissy needed right now, the very last, was to deal with her soon-to-be ex. Reluctantly, she rolled down the window. Along with a gust of rain-washed air, she caught a hint of his aftershave and a whole lot of unwanted memories. As upset as she was, she still noticed the hint of beard shadow covering his strong jaw and the laserlike intensity of his blue eyes.

"You okay?" he asked.

Stupid question. "Do I look okay?" She was shaking her head and trying not to cry. "No, I'm not. I'm not okay at all." She wouldn't break down, would *not* in front of him. "It's Gran. She's . . . she's . . . Jack, she's dead." Her voice cracked over the last word, and she mentally kicked herself.

"Ciss," he said quietly, and it got to her so much she had to look away.

"Dad-dee!" B.J.'s little arms shot straight up as if he could will his father to reach through the window and grab him. Marinara sauce streaked his face, the console, and the seat.

"How are ya, big guy?" Jack asked as B.J. waved his

arms frantically in the air. "Here . . ." He walked quickly around the car, opened the passenger door, and, ignoring the grease and marinara sauce covering his son, unbuckled the seat belt and slid into the passenger seat. "You're a mess," he said, holding the boy, and Beej, the traitor, laughed and showed off all thirteen of his teeth.

"Dad-dee!" B.J. said again, his face shining with delight.

Cissy's headache thundered.

"I'm sorry about Eugenia." Jack touched her on the shoulder, and she tensed.

He seemed sincere, but then he'd always been able to play the part of the attentive boyfriend, romantic fiancé, or loving husband if he wanted to.

She wasn't buying his act. She knew him too well and how pathetically easily he charmed her. Even now, when she was grieving and guilt-riddled, she felt that ridiculous male-female connection that had always been a part of their relationship. Damn him with his open-collared shirt, thick, mussed hair, and dimples that creased when he smiled. The trouble was Jack Holt was too damned good-looking for his own good. For *her* own good. She should have known better than to ever get involved with him. From the first time she'd set eyes upon him at that benefit party for Cahill House, a home for unwed mothers established by her family years before, she'd been intrigued. And doomed. She'd sensed he'd been the only man with a touch of irreverence in the whole damned ballroom, the only person, other than herself, who had found the stuffy affair boring.

Even after Jack's father introduced them, Cissy had avoided Jack. She was just putting in her time at the affair. However, he soon figured out that she too wasn't "into" it and kept trying to strike up a conversation with her. At first cool, she'd eventually had to laugh at his wry, self-deprecating humor. She'd even ended up flirting with him, and, of course, he'd responded. They'd escaped that damned party to start what should have been a short fling and ended up in Las Vegas a few months later with a quickie marriage and promises of love ever after.

What a joke!

A mistake of immense proportions.

Except for B.J.

Their son was the only part of their ill-fated marriage that was worth the heartache. As lousy a husband as Jack was, he did seem to adore his kid. The feeling was obviously mutual, and the one thing she hated about the separation and impending divorce was that B.J. wouldn't grow up under the same roof as his father.

"What happened?" Jack asked, his brows slammed together, his blondish hair artificially darkened with rain.

"I don't know," she admitted. "I think Gran fell down the stairs. She could have tripped or had a stroke, I guess. The thing is, she *always* took the elevator. I never saw her on the stairs. She didn't even consider it. So how . . . ?" Sighing, she leaned back against the seat and fought an overpowering sense of guilt. "I was late. Our furnace was acting up all day, and I couldn't get a repairman out cuz it's the weekend. Then B.J., contrary to how he's acting now, was fussy as all get-out. Nothing made him happy. Nothing . . . well, except obviously you, now."

Jack flashed her a grin.

"So I waited for the pizza-delivery guy to come, then drove over an hour or so later than usual, and . . . and . . ." In her mind's eye she saw her grandmother's tiny, broken body sprawled upon the tile floor, the pooled blood beneath her short hair. Cissy's stomach churned. "And by the time I got here, I found her on the floor of the foyer. I knew she was dead, but I called 9-1-1 and . . ." She clenched her teeth. "I think that if I'd gotten here earlier, when I was supposed to . . . maybe things would have happened differently. Maybe she'd still be alive."

"Don't go there, Ciss. It's not your fault. You know that."

She nodded shortly, fighting emotion.

"I'm sorry," he said again, and this time when he touched the back of her neck, she didn't shrink away.

She would like, for just a few minutes, to not reopen her eyes, to push the pain aside and let someone, even Jack, comfort her. Just until she could pull herself together.

"Can I get you out of here?"

"Blocked in." Blinking rapidly and running a finger under her eyes, she shot a look through the foggy back window. The crime-scene van, Paterno's car, a fire truck, and several police cars, their lights still strobing the night, were parked behind her, clogging the driveway and the street. More people had crowded around the gates—two neighbors whom she recognized, a jogger, and someone walking his dog—all congregating under the spreading bare branches of the ancient oak tree across the street. All their faces appeared ghostly in the watery blue illumination of the flickering streetlight that her grandmother had always complained about.

"My car's out front," Jack said. He smiled faintly at her in the darkness. "We can escape."

Like Marla, she thought but didn't say it.

"I think Paterno wants to talk to me again."

"The homicide dick? The one who put your mom away?"

"One and the same."

Jack's eyes narrowed as the windows of the car continued to fog. "But I thought he left town. What the hell is he doing here? What's he got to do with this?"

"I don't know." The headache Cissy had been fight-

ing all day intensified, pounding at the base of her skull
again. Lately, Jack had that effect on her.

"But homicide? As in murder? Jesus, what is this?"
His jaw turned hard as stone.

"I said 'I don't know.'" She lifted a shoulder, realized
he was still touching her, and looked pointedly at his
hand.

Jack got the hint and pulled it back to wrap around
B.J., who was still happily munching on his squeezed
piece of pizza. Plopped as he was on his father's lap, the
kid was happy, really happy, for the first time all day.
Great. Cissy didn't want to think about the future and
what that might spell.

"I'll get you out of here."

"I can take care of myself."

He shot her a glance that begged to differ, and she
realized she looked a mess, mascara running from her
eyes, hair matted from the rain, grief probably etched
all over her face.

"This'll only take a second." He started to get out of
the car.

"Wait a minute," she said, but resisted the urge to
grab his arm. "How'd you get here so quickly?"

"I was looking for you. I called several times, but you
didn't answer. I knew you came here on Sunday nights,
so I thought I'd surprise you." For the first time since
he'd shown up, there was a bite to his words, something
more than just casual conversation.

"What was so all-fired important that you would interrupt my dinner with Gran?"

"Not interrupt," he corrected. "Join."

"Join?" She gave him a cool look.

His jaw clenched a little harder, and his intense eyes
seemed to drill a hole right through her. "Because I was
served today."

Her stomach lurched. Of course. "The divorce papers."

"Yeah. The divorce papers," he said with more than a bit of acrimony. He shoved his damp hair out of his eyes, and a muscle began to work in the side of his jaw, just like it always did when he was angry.

She winced. "And you thought discussing it in front of Eugenia would be a good idea?"

"I don't think anything about it is a good idea," he said and reached for the handle of the door again. "I'll talk to Paterno and see if I can get you out of here."

"Jack, don't do anything stupid."

"Too late," he muttered and got out of the car, slamming the door behind him and jogging up the path to the front door. She watched him through the windshield. He shouldn't get involved. She shouldn't have let him, and she should *not* be noticing the way his khakis hugged his butt as he ran. Damn it all, she'd *always* found him attractive, even now, when her grandmother was lying dead in the foyer. Sniffing loudly, she confided in her son, "Your mom's a basket case." She reached over and touched his nose. "Don't tell anyone, okay? It's our little secret."

"Secret." He nodded, then looked through the window. "Where Dad-dee go?"

"On an errand; he'll be right back."

"Right back."

"Um-hmm." She caught a glimpse of her reflection in the rearview mirror and cringed. The woman staring back at her was a mess. Layered, streaked hair flattened by the rain, the whites of her eyes bloodshot, her nose red, and, along with the streaking mascara, her makeup a mess, lip gloss long gone, skin splotchy from crying, and a damned zit or two. Crap. She looked like hell.

And Gran's dead.

A lump filled her throat.

She just wanted to go home. And not with either Paterno, and his damned questions and suspicious eyes, or Jack, who had a way of worming himself deep into her heart. "Help me," she muttered, leaning back against the seat and trying not to be irritated that Jack, true to his nature, had decided he had the right to talk to the police as if he were still a member of her family. Couldn't he just go away? She'd already suffered one shock tonight and was still dealing with the thought that her grandmother was dead.

Dead!

Her eyes burned again.

So what was Jack doing here, acting as if he were some kind of knight in shining armor, showing up as if he cared one little whit about their family? What a joke! She would love nothing more than to believe for one little second that he actually loved her and that she could draw from his strength. That, of course, was an idle and supremely ridiculous thought.

Jack Holt was a lot of things, a tower of strength not being one. She didn't dare make the mistake of trying to lean on him again. Cissy sniffed loudly then caught B.J. staring at her, his little face puckering. She forced back her tears. "Hey, little man, gonna eat that?" she asked, opening his fingers and retrieving the squashed piece of pizza. He shook his head, and she scraped the remains of cheese and marinara sauce from his plump fingers. "I don't know about you, but I'd like to get outta here."

"Go home!" Beej said as she wiped sauce from his cheeks, leaving a reddish stain around his mouth.

"You bet, big guy. As soon as we can." She turned on the engine, forcing a little heat into the car. "As soon as we can."

* * *

"The husband. At two o'clock," Quinn warned, barely moving her lips. She and Paterno were in the foyer of the massive old house, both squatting next to Eugenia's body. But Quinn had looked up and out the open front door.

Paterno also recognized Jack Holt, editor and owner of *City Wise*, a slick rag about San Francisco, bearing down on him.

Just what they needed. "What's he doing here?"

"Who knows? The wife probably called him."

"I'll cut him off at the pass." Straightening, his bad knee popping a bit, Paterno ambled to the door to block the entrance to the house. "Sorry, potential crime scene."

"I get it. I'm Jack Holt, Cissy Cahill's husband."

"Detective Paterno." They'd never met before, but Paterno had seen Holt's picture often enough, either smiling from the glossy pages of his magazine or in the local newspaper, his raffish image caught at whatever charity event was in the papers.

Jack Holt, somewhere around thirty-five, was definitely high profile, part of the see-and-be-seen crowd. Whether in a tuxedo or casual golfing clothes, the guy was just too slick for Paterno's taste. Now, though, he was just a worried family member running through the rain, determination and sadness etched into the sharp-bladed planes of his face.

Holt swept in a sharp breath. Looking past Paterno, he obviously caught a glimpse of the dead woman. Momentarily, his expression jolted with pain.

"What can I do for you?" Paterno asked.

Holt forced his gaze back to the detective. "I want to take my wife and kid home. My car's on the street. Not blocked in like hers. I can bring her back here later, maybe tomorrow, to pick up the Acura when you're finished."

Fair enough. "Shouldn't be a problem, but I still may want to ask her some questions."

Holt's lips flattened. "I don't know what more you want from her. Cissy brought our son for one of their weekly dinners with her grandmother." Peering around Paterno to the crumpled body on the floor, Holt winced a bit, and Paterno wondered if maybe there was more to the man than he'd first thought. "Cissy was running late and found Eugenia at the bottom of the stairs. Then she called 9-1-1. End of story."

Paterno didn't like the younger man's tone. Felt his patience slipping. "I'm just asking questions. Trying to get to the bottom of this. I'm sure your wife understands that we want to find out what happened to Mrs. Cahill. And to do that, I'll probably be talking with both you and your wife again." He stepped onto the porch. "So why don't you tell me where you were tonight? You got here pretty damned quick."

Because I was on my way over here already. To see Cissy . . . Every muscle in Holt's body tensed. "Wait a minute," he said, eyes narrowing as the wheels turned in his mind. The temperature on the porch seemed to fall another five degrees as rain gurgled in the eaves and trickled through the downspouts. "Eugenia fell. Tripped and lost her balance and ended up at the bottom of the stairs." He glanced inside again, apparently mentally calculating the distance between the old lady's body and the foot of the stairs. "You're not thinking any foul play was involved?" But as he posed the question, he gave Paterno a penetrating look.

"We're just figuring that out now."

"You're with homicide," Holt pointed out flatly.

"We haven't ruled out any possibilities yet. As I said, we're working on it." Paterno wasn't giving up anything for the time being. At first glance it looked like the old woman tripped and fell, tumbled down the curved steps and broke her neck, but, these days, who knew? Eugenia Cahill was a wealthy woman. The Cahills had weathered a number of financial ups and downs, but it was no secret their fortunes were solid and currently on a steep rise. But the family had suffered their share of nutcases too. Marla Amhurst Cahill a case in point. It seemed like too much of a coincidence for Eugenia to wind up at the bottom of the staircase less than seventy-two hours from the time Marla, her murderous daughter-in-law, had escaped from prison.

Paterno scowled. The thought that Eugenia's daughter-in-law had escaped really gnawed at his gut. He'd worked his ass off to put Marla away years before, and now recently, because of overcrowding and her stellar behavior as a model prisoner, she'd been transferred to a lower-security facility.

What a mistake! He wouldn't be surprised if some of the Cahill fortune had been used to grease the skids on that little maneuver. Within two years of the transfer, Marla had found a way to break loose of that country club disguised as a lock-up facility. It hadn't come as much of a surprise to Paterno, but it pissed him off. In all his years in law enforcement, Paterno would be hard-pressed to come up with a more calculating, murderous bitch than Marla Cahill. The way he saw it, she should have been locked away doing hard time for the rest of her life.

And now she was out.

And her mother-in-law, keeper of the family fortune, had just suffered a quick, untimely death.

Coincidence?

No friggin' way.

Paterno just didn't take much stock in coincidence.

Especially not where Cahills were concerned.

But right now he didn't want to deal with Jack Holt, or anyone else. Not until he'd gathered a little more evidence. Besides, Holt was a member of the press, and at the moment Paterno wanted reporters far away from his crime scene. "Go ahead and take your wife home," he agreed. "If I need anything else, I'll call. And here—" He reached into his wallet, grabbed one of his business cards, and handed it to Holt. "If she needs to get in touch with me, she can reach me at any of these numbers, including my cell."

"Okay." Holt's face was still grim. "If this is a murder, we want to know. Immediately."

"You will."

Holt turned and jogged through the falling rain, his shoes slapping on the wet bricks. He skirted a camellia bush, his shoulder swiping a near-dead bloom, a few red petals dropping onto the ground.

Watching him leave, Paterno couldn't help wondering if Holt had married Cissy Cahill for love or money. That was the trouble with having millions stashed away in stocks, real estate, or the bank vault—someone was always after a piece of it. You could never be certain if they cared for you because they truly found you fascinating and really loved you, or if they were attracted to you because of the number of zeroes on your bank statement.

Greed, before, had cost a few people close to the Cahills their lives.

He made a mental note to check out Holt. Phone records, he told himself, might help. Credit-card receipts and bank balances. *If* the old lady had been murdered. He glanced through the open doorway, spying the broken body of the little dead woman, appearing, in many ways, like a nestling that had fallen from its nest. In life, Eugenia Cahill had been a force to be reckoned with. Sharp as a tack and definitely the matriarch, she'd run this family with tiny iron fists and an incredible will.

Had she suffered an unlucky fall?

Or was it murder?

With Marla Cahill on the loose, he was betting on the latter.

Cissy spied Jack running toward the car and rolled down her window. "What's happening? Can we leave?"

"The police are still investigating. They're not sure what went on with your grandmother, and they're being careful, just in case this isn't an accident."

"Not an accident?" she repeated, her worst fears slicing through her.

"Nothing's decided," he said, standing in the rain, the shoulders of his shirt drenched, his hair dripping, his face a mask of concern.

Cissy gazed at him. *Murder?* "No way . . . no one would want to kill Gran," she protested, though, deep inside, hadn't she considered that Eugenia hadn't just fallen? Her mother's escape. The cops' surveillance. Homicide detectives in the house. They all added up to the simple fact that someone was likely behind her grandmother's death. She felt herself shaking inside, unspoken denials forming on her lips.

"Paterno gave me the green light to take you home."

Cissy didn't want to leave with Jack, but she had to get out of here, away from the creepy old house with its dead body in the foyer and secrets locked away in all the other rooms. Now lights were glowing in the windows of all four stories, as if a giant party was in full swing, when, instead, police, photographers, criminalists, and God only knew who else were crawling through the rooms where she'd spent so much of her life.

"Come on, I'm drowning out here. Let's go."

A van marked as belonging to the coroner's office rolled to the end of the drive and parked between the other vehicles scattered haphazardly on the rain-slickened streets. A reporter, wielding her microphone like a weapon, flew out of a news vehicle and hurried up to the driver of the van as soon as he stepped a foot on the pavement.

Cissy watched in horror as someone she assumed was the assistant ME gave a quick little interview.

"Practice your 'no comments,'" Jack advised, and she remembered that he too had once been with a newspaper, chasing down the latest story not only in Los Angeles, when he was first out of college, but in the Bay Area as well. Now he'd already opened the passenger door and was unbuckling his son. "Come on, big guy, let's go home."

Beej, the traitor, flung his hands up and down and grinned like a goof for his father, who it seemed just happened to be his most favorite person in the world.

Although she wasn't crazy about spending any more time with Jack, she didn't have much of a choice. And, believe it or not, Jack's company was a lot less stressful than the detective's. She hauled her purse, diaper bag, and disreputable pizza box with her. Together they wended their way through the emergency vehicles and police barricade. As soon as they stepped onto the street, they were immediately assaulted by the same determined female reporter that had chased down the assistant medical examiner.

"Miss Cahill!" Cissy heard her name, but ignored the newswoman. "Can you tell us what's going on? Who died? Was it murder?" The woman hardly paused for a breath, and Cissy pressed on, right behind Jack and B.J., refusing to look into the blinding light held by one of the television station's crew, or the camera she knew was following her every move. "Does your mother, Marla Cahill, have anything to do with this?"

Cissy bristled and had to bite her tongue, all the

while waiting impatiently as Jack unlocked the door of his Jeep.

"Have you heard from Marla Cahill since her escape?"

The locks of the Jeep clicked. Cissy opened the passenger door, nearly knocking over the cameraman.

"Back off!" Jack shouted across the top of his vehicle. "No comment!"

Cissy slammed the door with the camera still rolling and with shaking fingers managed to snap her seat belt into place. She'd ridden in this very seat hundreds of times, and yet it felt awkward to be sitting here, staring straight ahead, trying not to meet the eyes of neighbors and the curious who had gathered. It was all so weird. Not just because of the bizarre media circus: police vehicles scattered about, walkie talkies crackling. And not just because her grandmother now lay dead in the big, old house. Her relationship with Jack was weird too.

She sighed. Now that she and he were separated, there was a little bit of "this is yours" and "this is mine" going on. While before it had been natural to share everything, and she'd never felt the least bit uncomfortable about driving his car, using his laptop, "borrowing" his toothbrush, or wearing one of his shirts as pajamas, now the rules had changed. Their way of interacting with their child, the division of their property, the days of the week when they could expect to see B.J., all this was now written in lawyer doublespeak and tied up with suspicion.

Jack strapped Beej into his car seat, then slammed the back door, jogged around his vehicle, and climbed behind the steering wheel. "The press," he said with mock severity as he jammed his keys into the ignition. "All a bunch of vultures." He offered her a self-deprecating smile, as they both knew he'd been a stringer for a local paper, then a full-blown reporter before coming up with the idea and backing for *City Wise,* his latest venture and the very magazine where Cissy now contributed.

She understood all too well about stories, spins, and angles, but she didn't like it when the focus narrowed onto her and her family.

Jack cranked on the Jeep's wheel and disengaged the parking brake as he pulled away from the curb. The SUV shot down the steep hill with its narrow, winding street, and Cissy, unaware that she was holding her breath, let out a sigh. "Thank God," she whispered.

"Yeah, it's good to be out of there."

That was an understatement. Rubbing her temple, she sneaked a glance in his direction. Jaw rock hard, hands so tight on the wheel his knuckles bleached through, he didn't seem to notice that she was studying his profile as the headlights from oncoming cars splashed bluish light into the Jeep's interior, giving her short, almost strobe-light images of his honed features. Deep-set eyes, high cheekbones, rugged jaw, and thick hair that streaked blond in the summer. All he needed was a Stetson and boots and he could be Hollywood's image of a modern-day cowboy. There was just something about him that whispered "rebel" and "independent" and "irreverent," all the qualities in a man that attracted her . . . and now repelled her as a wife. Had he changed? Or had she?

Of course she'd been a fool to fall so fast and hard for him. He wasn't the marrying type. She'd known it. All the warning signs had been there, right in her face, and she'd ignored every last one of them. She'd sensed he was a confirmed bachelor, a man who had wanted to play the field, a workaholic who spent countless hours on the job, ensuring the success and growing popularity of his local magazine. He'd worked with the Internet, rather than against it, when it had threatened circulation, and he'd been ahead of the game every step of the way.

He'd been described as a "rogue" publisher, ruthless and cutthroat with the competition, smarter than most.

And she'd loved every bit of it.

Until he'd stepped over the line.

Now, behind the wheel, he guided the Jeep downhill toward the financial district. As they merged onto Stanyan, she caught a familiar whiff of his aftershave and mentally kicked herself for remembering all too vividly how that scent, and the man, had turned her on. Even on the night when she'd first met him.

Cissy—in college and wondering what the hell she was going to do with her life—had gone to the benefit for Cahill House at her grandmother's insistence. She'd intended to make a quick appearance at the stuffy old hotel on Nob Hill just to satisfy Eugenia's need for "family solidarity," then ditch out. Even though she thought Cahill House a worthwhile cause, Cissy saw no reason to rub elbows with the stuffed shirts on the board or make small talk with staid members of the several foundations who had helped fund the house.

Talk about boring!

What she hadn't expected when she'd stepped into the grand ballroom with its cut-glass chandeliers, patterned carpet, and incredible view of the bay was Jack Holt with his tie already unbuttoned, his shirtsleeves rolled up, his hair messy from shoving his hands through it one too many times, and the scent of that clean aftershave. A drink in his hand, a cocksure smile on his lips, a square jaw, and a glimmer of irreverence in eyes that were a startling blue, he'd had the nerve to wink at her as she passed—as if the two of them shared a secret.

A player, she'd thought and written him off.

She'd run into him a couple of times more throughout the course of the evening, and each time there was something she found interesting, but it wasn't until she was introduced to him by his father, Jonathan Holt, who knew her grandmother, that he'd gotten to her.

Maybe if she hadn't been on the rebound from a rocky relationship with Noah Chandler, a soon-to-be lawyer she'd met at USC, she might not have fallen for Jack's charms, but the truth of the matter was that she'd been looking for something or someone different. Someone edgier and fun. Maybe someone older.

It had hurt when she learned that Noah was seeing another law student, a smart, beautiful LA girl whom Cissy had met and sensed had more than a friendly interest in him. She'd known the girl had set her sights on him, though Noah, always playing the part of the innocent, had denied it and had even gone so far as to accuse her of being paranoid.

It's hell always being right, Cissy thought with an inner snort.

A few days after graduation, she and Noah made a final break. A few days after that, Cissy was back in San Francisco and met Jack, all smiles and dimples and sexy eyes. He'd danced with her, drank with her, and, under his breath, made jokes about all the "stiffs" at the party. Ultimately, he charmed the socks—and her siren red dress—off her.

And it hadn't ended that night. What started out as a hot one-night stand erupted into an incredible, heady affair ending with a wedding in one of those little chapels in Las Vegas being witnessed by complete strangers. The impulsive elopement had resulted in an incredible son and a marriage that seemed destined to fail from the get-go.

Cissy shut down the memory. What was the point? She stared out the windshield, watching the wipers slap away the thick raindrops as some old rock song drifted through the speakers. The lights of the city stretched out before

them in a dazzling display, and beyond the grid of illumination, the inky waters of the bay stretched to the opposite shore, where more lights sparkled like jewels.

The beauty of the view was lost on her tonight.

She felt hollow inside. Numb. She'd never known
life without her kid-gloved but iron-fisted grandmother,
couldn't imagine what it would be like now that Eugenia was dead. It could be easier in some ways, but it would
certainly be less defined. Eugenia Cahill was nothing if
not an autocrat, her rules unbending.

"You okay?" Jack finally asked.

"No."

"I am sorry, Ciss."

"I know." She blinked against a new rush of tears.
She could accept his callousness, even his fury, but not
his kindness, not when they had no chance of reconcil-
iation, which they hadn't. "I just can't help thinking that
if I hadn't been late, if I'd been there, she wouldn't
have fallen."

"You think she fell."

"Of course she did," she said, denying her darkest
fears once again.

"Then why the homicide dick?" Jack's fingers drummed against the steering wheel nervously as he turned
through Haight-Ashbury and past Buena Vista Park. He
hit the brakes for a jaywalker, then, once the guy had
crossed, said, "Paterno and his partner don't just show
up at every crime scene."

"It's because of my mother," Cissy said darkly. "Ever
since she escaped, the police have been all over the
place. As if Marla would come running to me, or to
Gran! That's just plain stupid. She's smart enough to
know that the police would be waiting for her."

"So you haven't heard from her?"

Jack thought Marla had contacted her? She pinned
him with an incredulous glare. "Are you nuts?"

"It's normal that she would want to see you. She might even want to see James."

"She doesn't know where he is," Cissy said, thinking of her brother, who was nearly eleven now, hidden away in Oregon with her aunt and uncle. "My guess is that she's going to run as far away as possible. Maybe Mexico. Canada."

"She'll need papers. ID."

Cissy sent him a don't-be-so-naive look. "She broke out of prison. I think she can figure out how to avoid the police and get forged documents. If she didn't know how to before she was arrested, I bet she does now. Surely some of her 'friends' on the inside know people on the outside who can get any kind of ID she'll need."

"She couldn't get documents without help or money."

"Well, she's getting none from me," Cissy stated positively. "And I think the police figure she had an accomplice working with her."

"Who?"

"That's the million-dollar question," she said. It was one she'd been asking herself ever since learning Marla had broken out. "I can't imagine who would *want* to help her."

"Not everyone hated her."

That much was true, she thought as they eased around a final corner before reaching her street. Her mother had always attracted flocks of people. Not only beautiful, but rich as well. But to help her escape? Not exactly the actions of someone she shopped or played tennis with.

Jack nosed his Jeep into the drive in front of the garage, and she felt a bit of relief at just being home. Had it been less than three hours since she'd unknowingly driven to her grandmother's house? In that short time span her life had changed irrevocably. Now she slid out of the SUV and gathered her things while Jack carried Beej into the house and deposited him into his high chair.

It all seemed so natural.

The tiny nuclear family.

But it wasn't. She couldn't allow herself to be seduced into thinking things between her husband and herself had slipped back into the trust they'd vowed when they married. Even though it seemed perfectly normal for him to be standing in the kitchen, she had to remind herself that things had changed. Forever. A little bit of her heart tore, but she ignored it.

Before her husband could get too comfortable, Cissy said, "I think I can handle it from here. Thanks."

His lips tightened at the corners. "Don't do it, Ciss," he warned.

"Do what?"

"Play the part of the bitchy ex-wife. You know, all prickly and able to handle life on her own no matter what kind of trauma she's just been through."

"But I can. Handle everything."

"Even your grandmother's murder?"

"Don't be such a bastard."

He inclined his head, taking the heat. "I just want to face reality."

She slid a glance at their son, and her voice softened. "Let's not discuss this now, okay? Little ears hear a lot, Jack. Maybe you should just go home."

"This is my home."

"No more. And I'm tired. It's been a helluva week." She slid another piece of pizza onto the tray of Beej's high chair, then poured some milk into a sippy cup. "Careful with this," she told her son, and he, so much like his father, grinned mischievously before taking the handle and swinging the cup to and fro, spraying milk on the wall, floor, tray, and Cissy.

Perfect.

"I was afraid of that. You just lost your 'get out of jail free' card, bud."

She retrieved the cup, and he started winding up to wail before she distracted him with his favorite toy. A little rubber car with no moving parts. It did nothing except look remarkably like Jack's Jeep.

"Dad-dee car!" he said gleefully, his attention diverted as Cissy dabbed at her sweater with a dishrag before swabbing the counter. She glanced up at Jack and saw him smothering a smile. "Don't say it," she warned, pointing at him and dropping the rag by mistake. "Crap." She bent to pick it up and nearly cracked heads with Jack, who had also dived for the soaked towel. "I've got it!" Retrieving the dishrag, she mopped up the sprayed milk, then walked onto what had once been a porch and was now the sunroom. Opening a cupboard door, she dropped the rag into a laundry chute that channeled to the basement.

By the time she'd returned to the kitchen, Jack had retrieved two bottles of beer from the fridge. "Something I forgot when I moved out," he said, then popped the tops. He handed her a bottle, tapped the neck of his to hers, and said, "To better days."

A part of her wanted to argue and throw him out, though another part told herself to let it go for the night. She didn't need another fight. She figured there were enough battles on the horizon. Reluctantly she offered him a conciliatory smile.

"Amen," she whispered. "To better days."

She lifted the bottle to her lips, but paused as a horrid thought hit her.

What if this was the best day?

What if from here on in, things just got worse? She took a long swallow as her son pounded his little car on the tray of his high chair.

Now, there was a happy thought.

Chapter 4

Paterno felt a case of heartburn coming on.

He reached into his pocket and found a near-empty packet of Tums. Popping a couple of the chalky tablets, he took a sweeping glance at the Cahill estate, thinking this was the price he paid for returning to the city. A few years back, he'd taken a leave of absence and spent some time working in Santa Lucia, thinking the quiet life might appeal to him. Instead, though, he'd caught one helluva case involving a firefighting family, and after that he'd slowly become bored with the slower pace of small-town life. He'd done his share of touring wineries, golfing, or fly-fishing, but the quiet life hadn't taken. Truth to tell, he'd missed the hustle and bustle of the city: the steep hills, rich history, and varied elements and ethnicity of San Francisco. He loved the smell of the wharf, the Irish bars, the noise and color of Chinatown, all of it. He still got a thrill driving over the Golden Gate, and hell if he didn't ride a damned cable car now and again. He just liked the feel of the city, the smell of it. So despite this new Cahill mess and the long hours he put in with the department, he was glad to be back.

"Hey! Detective! Over here!" From within the house, Tallulah Jefferson gestured for him to come back inside. She was eyeing the marble tiles of the floor while the ME was examining the body, taking internal temperature, checking for contusions and lividity. A petite black woman, Jefferson was nothing if not an enthusiastic criminalist. She was able to divorce herself from the person within the body in a way that Paterno had never seen. She wore no makeup, and she always sported some kind of headband to scrape her springy curls away from her face. Now her usually smooth forehead was wrinkled in thought as she huddled with Janet Quinn at the base of the stairs while an officer dusted the railing for prints and a photographer snapped off pictures.

"What have you got?" Paterno asked, approaching her.

"No accident, that's what I've got." Jefferson nodded, as if agreeing with herself, then looked up at the landing and squinted. Paterno guessed that in her mind's eye she was watching a slow-motion movie of what she thought were the last seconds of Eugenia Cahill's life. "The way I see it, she fell from the landing, not down the stairs." Jefferson pointed to the sweeping wooden steps covered with an expensive runner. "I can't find any signs of anything hitting the wall, no blood, no unusual scrapes on the risers or railing where either her body or her cane would have hit and bounced as she tumbled down. Nothing on the runner, no tears to the carpet or smears of blood, at least none that I can see." Jefferson scratched a spot near her headband. "And see where she landed . . . over here." The criminalist walked back to the victim's body, where the ME was getting it ready for the body bag.

A thick red stain spread upon the floor, Eugenia's blood in a pool directly under a huge chandelier suspended from the floor above. Dripping crystal and illuminated by hundreds of small lights, the chandelier seemed garish and overwhelming considering the tiny victim directly beneath it. "She's a good six feet from the bottom step. No way would any kind of momentum send her over here, even if she skidded over the tile. This rug"—Jefferson pointed to a small circular carpet at the base of the stairs—"would have been disturbed, but see: not even one piece of fringe is out of place. No blood streaking the floor. No scuffs from her shoes. And I don't think the body was moved. It looks like she landed right where she ended up."

"She was pushed?"

Jefferson glanced up at the landing. "She was not quite five feet tall, and presumably a little stooped. Walked with a cane. The rail would have hit her about here." She leveled a hand on her own body, to a spot just under her breasts. "Even if she tripped, or fell, or had a heart attack or stroke or whatever, how did she get *over* the railing? I could see her stumbling on the landing and falling *against* the rail, and if it was really weak and she hit it with some kind of force, maybe the old railing would have splintered. *Maybe* then she could've fallen through, but I really don't think so. Doesn't matter. I checked. That railing's oak and damned solid. No weak connections, no broken balusters. Besides, I think the body's in the wrong spot. If she fell or were dangled, she'd land over here." Jefferson walked to below the landing, closer to the wall. "We won't know until we take more measurements, but I'm guessing she either did a swan dive from the railing, leaping outward, or, more likely, she was helped over."

"Homicide."

"It's preliminary, but yeah, right now, that's what I'm saying. I didn't see any sign of a struggle on the landing, but I'll look again."

So who would kill her? Paterno wondered, his gaze moving from the foyer to the sitting room, then toward hallways that he knew from previous visits led to the kitchen, dining area, and elevator. If he remembered correctly, this floor was strictly for entertaining; the second was the real living quarters, and included Eugenia's room; the third was bedrooms; and the fourth had once belonged to live-in servants. Beneath it all was the garage. The house was worth millions, and he wondered who would end up with it now that Eugenia was dead. He walked to the sitting room off the foyer, glanced around. "Anyone see a dog?"

"What? A dog?" Jefferson asked.

"A little white dog. It was the victim's. According to her granddaughter, Eugenia never went anywhere without the damned thing." He remembered the little white mutt, a terrier mix of some kind. The dog had been a pain in the ass the last time he'd visited here, and he figured it hadn't improved with age. What was amazing was that the scrappy thing was still alive.

Or had been.

Jefferson walked up the stairs to the landing. "No dog, white or otherwise."

"Let me know if you come across it."

Jefferson flashed him a smile, showing off slightly flared teeth against her mocha-colored complexion. "Does it bite?"

"Probably," Paterno said. "It's a Cahill."

She snorted, already back at the railing above and studying the balusters positioned directly over the body. Meanwhile, the techs had spread out, dusting for prints, collecting debris, and continually snapping pictures in their painstaking search for evidence.

Quinn joined Paterno. "I'll start with the phone records, the computer, and her date book. They're all up in the library."

"She's got a computer?" Paterno asked.

Quinn nodded.

"The granddaughter said she didn't like them."

"I'll check it out."

"See if you can find any legal records," he added. "Insurance policies and a will." Frowning, he stared at the interior of this immense house with its original art and expensive, if worn, furnishings. "A place like this might have a wall safe."

"Already checking," Quinn assured him as she headed up the stairs to the library.

Paterno glanced down at the victim again, a last look before she would be zipped into a body bag and placed on a stretcher. His gut clenched as he stared at the dead woman's tiny body, dressed in its expensive pants, suit jacket, blouse, and scarf. As if she'd planned to play bridge or have tea with her friends. Her hair was messed and bloody now, but he guessed it had been recently done—smooth apricot curls were still teased and sprayed into position.

Damn it all.

He had a bad feeling about this.

Real bad.

At least the beer was cold, Cissy thought, though considering the outside temperature, she and Jack should have been sipping hot chocolate laced with whiskey or Bailey's, the kind of drinks they'd loved on the few trips they'd taken, skiing at Tahoe and Heavenly Valley. Back in the days when everything had felt magical. She recalled coming into the lodge exhilarated from the ski runs, snow melting in Jack's hair, his face red with cold. Clunking in ski boots, they had ordered drinks, then sat outside to stare at the clear, incredibly blue waters of the lake, and later, after soaking in a hot tub outside, they'd spent hours in their room making love.

A lifetime ago.

Cissy took a swallow from her bottle and pushed those particular thoughts back into the locked closet where they belonged. No sense getting maudlin or nostalgic. So she had loved Jack with all of her heart; so it didn't work out. No big deal. It happened all the time.

But you never thought it would happen to you, did you?

Cissy had believed that when she married, it would be for life, to a man who loved her unconditionally. She craved love like an addict—an emotional need any two-bit shrink would say lay in the debris of her broken childhood. And they would be right. Cissy had never experienced that kind of love, not from her grandmother, and certainly not from her egomaniacal mother or narcissistic father. She'd thought with Jack and B.J.—her own little nuclear family—that life would be different.

Oh, how wrong she'd been.

Now, sitting at the table they'd bought at a second-hand store and refinished together, their first of countless "projects," she and Jack shared what they could salvage of the pizza and tried not to let the silence grow too uncomfortable.

She leaned back in "her" chair—the one positioned next to the French doors leading to the backyard. Cissy wouldn't allow herself to think about their search for this house and how excited they'd been when they found it. It had been run-down, in need of "TLC," the real estate ad had said, a "fixer-upper," a "handyman's dream." This hundred-year-old Victorian had been all those things and more, but they'd both fallen in love with it the minute they stepped over its rotting threshold. They'd bought it, hired a contractor, and spent the next year working every night and weekend, ripping up thin, filthy thirty-year-old carpeting then stripping the hardwood floors and refinishing them to a lustrous sheen. They'd replaced or regrouted tile and peeled off layers of the ugliest wallpaper she'd ever seen. They'd worked to exhaustion, loving every minute of it.

And Cissy was certain she had conceived B.J. the very first night they'd moved in. Probably while testing out the durability of the living room floor. Now her eyes strayed to that room and the shining patina of the oak floorboards. Just around the corner was the fireplace, and there, on a sleeping bag that they'd used for camping, they'd created their first and only child. She'd thought she'd love Jack Holt forever.

Pushing that uncomfortable thought aside, she took another swallow of beer, then righted Beej's sippy cup before he sprinkled milk all over himself, the high chair, and the surrounding walls and floor. Her son wrinkled his nose and showed off his new teeth. "Get down?"

"In a sec, honey."

"I know this isn't a good time," Jack said, "but I want you to rethink the divorce."

"Rethink," Cissy repeated. Like she hadn't thought and thought and thought about it already.

"We need to give it another shot, Ciss. Hell, we've hardly been married long enough to have a rough patch, much less survive one."

She studied this man she'd married. Was he a raving lunatic? "You had an affair, Jack. With Larissa. End of story."

"I did not—"

"Sure you did," she cut him off. "We've been through this before, so let's not do it again. You brought me home, and now you can go. You don't live here anymore."

"Not my choice, Ciss."

"Doesn't matter. It's best."

"I miss you."

"Should have thought of that when you were sleeping around."

"For the millionth time, I wasn't. You know it too. You're just looking for an excuse."

"Fortunately for me, you gave me a damned good one." She stood, unstrapped B.J., and plucked him out of the high chair. Wiping a spot of milk from his cheek, she balanced him on her hip, then set him on the floor. As he loped to his toy box in the living room, Cissy squared off with her husband. "I caught you coming out of Larissa's house, Jack. Please don't insult me with the old 'but nothing happened' story. Just leave, Jack. This is pointless." Beej wandered back into the room, a beat-up stuffed frog hanging from one hand, and Cissy said, "Say good-bye to Daddy, honey."

"You just won't listen. You're as pigheaded as ever."

"Pig-headed," Beej repeated on a giggle as Jack lifted him. He patted his father hard on the shoulder and chortled, "Dad-dee! Dad-dee!" so many times that Cissy thought she might puke. Pigheaded? She would have liked to argue the point, but Jack and Beej were doing their male-bonding thing, laughing and playing with each other, so she decided to keep out of it for the moment. As lousy a husband as Jack had become, she couldn't take away the fact that he loved his child. By no means was he a great father, and considering his up-bringing that could be explained, but he did love Beej. He did try.

She grudgingly gave Jack points for that, especially when she thought about her own childhood. For Beej's sake she would try to pull herself out of the anger and pain caused by his betrayal and do the best she could to ensure that father and son had a decent relationship. It wasn't B.J.'s fault that she and Jack couldn't get along.

He hadn't chosen his father.

She had.

"Look who I found." Janet Quinn, who had been searching the library on the second floor, walked down the stairs carrying a shivering little white dog. Paterno looked up from the floor, where he'd been studying the tiles where the body had hit. There was still blood everywhere, but the shell of what had been Eugenia Cahill had finally been hauled away.

"Where was it?"

"Cowering in a cupboard beneath a shelf containing first editions of Sherlock Holmes."

"In good company," Paterno observed.

"And scared to death. Literally shaking. I wonder who put her there. Eugenia? Or the killer? We are thinking homicide, aren't we?"

"Looks that way. Jefferson's pretty certain."

"Who would want to kill a little old lady?"

Paterno flashed on Marla Cahill. "Maybe her daughter-in-law?"

"Pretty bold to come here right after an escape."

"Have you forgotten Marla Cahill? Brazen doesn't begin to cover it." He'd seen a lot of conniving, cold-hearted people in his time, but, as far as women went, Eugenia's daughter-in-law took the prize.

"She's not stupid."

"Not at all."

"And she would have had to have known that we were watching the place."

"Well, *someone* called 9-1-1 before the granddaughter showed up here. I'm willing to bet whoever put in the call that pulled our guys off was involved. If we find out who that is, we might start making some headway."

Quinn nodded. "The caller was a male. I checked."

"Paid to do it. From a pay phone." Paterno already had that much figured out from talking to the emergency dispatch operator. Squatting next to the bloodstains, he twisted his neck to view the landing as he had half a dozen times, replaying what he imagined had happened. It wouldn't have taken Atlas to toss the little woman over the railing, but then again, Eugenia would have fought back. Unless she'd been drugged or had a stroke or heart attack. He'd know more once all the tox screens and blood work came back from the lab and the autopsy was complete. "I'll start calling the staff," he said to Janet Quinn. "You order phone records."

"Planned on it," Janet said. She stroked the dog's head, and it whimpered. "Do you know her name? The dog's, I mean."

"Coco, the granddaughter said." But he remembered the damned dog from the last time he'd been here years ago. Then, though, the dog had been younger and not traumatized. In fact, it had been feisty and yappy and a real pain in the butt. Now he almost felt sorry for the white mutt. "I'll drop it off at her house. She was asking about it."

"*Her*," Janet said. "Coco's a female."

"Why do you think the dog was locked up? Did it get in the way?"

"Maybe she was locked in there by accident. Sometimes my cat will curl up in a closet or in a room where I've closed the door, and I won't find him for hours."

"This is a dog. And I remember it . . . *her*. She wasn't exactly timid or quiet." He glanced into the little black button eyes.

"I'll put her in your car, and you can take her to Cissy Holt's place. I saw a carrier in the bedroom."

"We're not done processing in there," Jefferson said as she measured a piece of cracked, bloody tile directly under the balcony. "Just give us a second before you start taking things out."

"I think I should stay," Jack said, just as Cissy was thinking he should be leaving.

Damn him, Jack could be so muleheaded. Still, she

thought she'd heard him wrong. "Don't use this as an excuse."

He handed B.J. to her. "If you want, I'll camp out on the couch."

"Don't you get the concept of 'separated'?" Cissy demanded in frustration. "Didn't you hear what I was just saying? And, wait a minute." She paused for effect as Beej squirmed in her arms. "Didn't you say you got served today?"

"Don't fight me," Jack said softly, dangerously. "I'd just feel better about it," he said, so close to her she could smell the clean scent of his aftershave, see the striations of darker blue in his irises. In her arms, her traitor of a son had the nerve to rain one of his incredible baby smiles on both of them. As if all were right in the world, as if his loving great-grandmother were alive and his parents were living some fairy tale.

"No," she whispered, though her heart was tearing.

Jack leaned even closer, his breath warm against her ear. "Your psycho mother is on the run, Ciss. Remember her? How relentless and cruel she can be? God knows where she'll turn up or what she'll do. And your grandmother died tonight, possibly the result of someone helping her along to the hereafter."

"You don't know that."

"I do know that things have taken a turn for the weirder, and I don't like it. I'm staying." To prove his point, he walked into the living room, sidestepped an array of B.J.'s toys, and flopped himself down on the leather couch they'd picked out together less than two years earlier.

Her stupid heart squeezed, but she ignored it, just held onto her son a little more tightly. "Jack, you *can't* stay here."

"What're you going to do? Call the police?"

"They're probably already camped outside again,

waiting for Marla." God, he was stubborn. "I don't want you here."

"It's only for a night."

"No, Jack. Not one night, not one hour." She shifted Beej from one hip to the other.

"Damn it, Cissy."

"I know. I'm pigheaded. So are you, actually. We should have been perfect for each other." She was steamed now, all the rage she'd felt after witnessing Jack step out of Larissa's apartment boiling up again.

She remembered the scene in vivid technicolor. Jack had still been tucking his shirt into his pants, his tie was missing, his hair wet and a mess, as if he'd just towel-dried it after a shower. Larissa was in the doorway in a bathrobe and, it seemed, nothing much else. Cissy's heart had dropped to her knees as she'd sat in her car, half a block up the street, sunglasses covering her eyes.

Though they hadn't kissed, Jack had flashed a smile at Larissa as he'd left and sketched her a wave before tripping down the stairs to his Jeep, parked right in the parking lot of the apartment building. Larissa, watching him go, had stepped barefoot onto the outside balcony, leaned over the top railing, and blown him a kiss as he'd fired up his Jeep. Her just-washed hair had caught in the sunlight, her cleavage playing peek-a-boo with the lapels of her robe, a breast slipping free before she laughingly clutched the lapels together again.

All for Jack's benefit.

Even now, just thinking about it, Cissy felt wounded and mad all over again. Her jaw tensed.

As if reading her thoughts, Jack stopped arguing. He reached forward and ruffled Beej's blond curls. Tiredly, he asked, "You sure that's the way you want it?"

She inched her chin up a fraction. "Absolutely."

"Then . . . if you're sure you and Beej will be okay here alone . . ."

"We'll be fine," she assured him as if she meant it, as if it didn't hurt her to face him, as if she weren't already grieving for her grandmother, as if she weren't really worried about her mother's escape from prison. "If I get lucky, I might even end up with two detectives staked outside."

He frowned and looked about to argue, then changed his mind. "Okay, well, then I guess I'll go." He collected his son in a bear hug then set him down. "Good-bye, big guy," he said to Beej, his tender tone squeezing Cissy's heart.

Steeling herself, she walked to the front door and held it open. Jack's lips twisted. He glanced up at Cissy, and the look he sent her stopped the air in her lungs. Dark. Hot. Angry. And sexy as hell. The temperature in the house seemed to inch up a few degrees. But then that's the way it had always been between them, every emotion intense.

"You win, Ciss. Sorry about Gran." As he passed, he swiped a chaste kiss across her cheek, and she nearly changed her mind. Her pulse jumped, and she felt heat come to her cheeks. *Don't do it, Cissy. Don't let him get to you. You'll only regret it.*

She didn't so much as look at him. Let him think her a heartless bitch; it didn't much matter anymore.

As Jack walked outside and a gust of moist air swept in, she heard the furnace wheeze and rumble, trying to come on again, before going silent once more.

In her arms, B.J. twisted and wriggled. "Dad-dee!" he cried suddenly, as if finally understanding that his favorite person on the planet was leaving. "Dad-dee!"

Yeah, Cissy thought, kicking the door shut and feeling miserable inside—all in all it had been one helluva day.

Chapter 5

Jack mentally kicked himself up one side and down the other as he walked to his Jeep. He'd blown it with Cissy, no doubt about it, and she was making life hell for him. He decided he deserved it. Not that he'd slept with Larissa. But he'd come damned close. Too close. "Stupid," he muttered, unlocking the Jeep and sliding behind the wheel. He backed out of the driveway and started heading toward his apartment, but he didn't like the feeling that he was abandoning her.

Driving around the block, Jack found an empty space on the street, just so she wouldn't have a fit about his car being in the drive. Then, using the seat-adjustment lever, he pushed the seat of his Jeep back as far as it would go. He figured if the cops could stake the place out, so could he. He always kept a sleeping bag in the back, and he had a couple of bottles of water in the console, so he was good for hours.

He had an apartment, of course, one he'd rented just this month when Cissy had given him the boot, but he hated it. Cold. Lifeless. Sterile. Even with rental furniture, a fake plant, and a plasma TV that stretched across one wall, the place wasn't home. It was ironic, really, because he'd always considered himself a bachelor for life. Then he'd met Cissy, and everything had changed. His whole damned attitude on the institution. He'd seen enough bad marriages in his lifetime, witnessed firsthand the battlefield wedded "bliss" could be from his parents, then watched as several of his more idealistic friends had taken the plunge into matrimonial waters, only to have nearly drowned.

Still, his relationship with Cissy, as fast and hot as it had been, had changed his mind about settling down. When he'd married her, he'd gladly given up the bachelor basics of recliner, remote control, microwave, and minifridge. And he hadn't missed them.

But he was a realist.

Cissy was still mad.

Really mad.

It would take a lot of smooth talking, crow swallowing, redundant apologizing, and dozens of good deeds before she'd ever trust him again. He wasn't even sure it was possible. The truth from Larissa's pouty and lying lips wouldn't hurt either, but so far, Larissa refused to tell Cissy what really happened. There was a part of her that reveled in his predicament, as she insisted that if Cissy were a truly trusting wife, she would never doubt Jack. Larissa wasn't even going to acknowledge or honor the argument. Cissy had been her friend too, as they all worked together at the magazine, and Larissa proclaimed loud and long that it was up to Cissy to trust them both.

Which was bullshit, and they all knew it. Hurt feelings didn't work that way, didn't answer to what should be in a perfect world.

Now, even if Larissa did come around, it was already too late. Cissy had made up her mind, and she'd seen Larissa's silence as testament to the fact that Larissa and Jack had slept together. Even if Larissa were to come clean—which was a big if—Cissy wouldn't believe her and would, no doubt, come to the conclusion that Jack had put Larissa up to it.

So they were at an impasse.

Damn, what a mess.

Your own fault, Holt. You blew it.

Now he stared out at the street where rain was washing down the hillside, past the rooftops of the Victorian houses to the city below. Thousands of lights winked in the night, warm windows glowing in the high-rise apartment buildings, hotels, and office buildings of the financial district.

Back at their house, a light went on in the baby's room, and Jack visualized Cissy going through the evening routine of bathing the baby, dressing him in pj's, then sitting in the big overstuffed chair to read him a story before laying him in his crib. Gazing up at the window, Jack felt a loneliness he'd never experienced in his life. He cracked open a bottle of water, wished it were a beer, then noticed another car pull into a spot in front of the house.

Great.

He had company.

The cops were back.

He remembered seeing the classic Caddy parked at Eugenia's house. Paterno's old car. He watched as Paterno climbed out of the driver's side then opened the car's rear door. The detective retrieved a plastic carrier of some kind from the backseat, then headed for the house.

A pet crate?

Jack heard another approaching engine. As Paterno started for the door, a news van turned the corner and pulled up on the far side of the street, its nose blocking Cissy's driveway.

Great.

Jack screwed the cap back on his water bottle and left it on the passenger seat.

An Asian woman in an orange parka with the station's letters—KTAM—emblazoned over a pocket practically flew out of the van and popped open a fat umbrella. The reporter, glossy layered hair gleaming, zeroed in on Paterno and headed his way, cutting across the grass as if she hoped to reach him before he got to the front porch.

This didn't look good.

Jack reached for the Jeep's door handle.

"Detective," the reporter called as she closed the distance. "Detective Paterno! Could I have a word with you?" A cameraman was following close behind, his mammoth camera propped on his shoulder as he ran after her. "We've met before. I'm Lani Saito with KTAM."

Paterno turned just as Jack slid out of his rig.

"Can you tell me about Marla Cahill's escape?"

Paterno stopped short as she blocked his way. Tersely, he answered, "I'm sure the prison authorities and state police have issued a statement."

She wasn't budging. "But you were the detective who arrested her, and now, just a few hours ago, her mother-in-law died from a fall. Was foul play involved in Eugenia Cahill's death?"

"We don't know."

As he was behind the detective, Jack couldn't see Paterno's reaction, but there was no mistaking the irritation in his voice. "We're still investigating." He turned toward the house, and inside the pet carrier a dog started yapping.

"Detective, what's in the carrier?" But the howling that came out of the plastic crate answered the question. "You're delivering a dog?"

"It was missing." He turned back toward the house.

"Whose dog?"

Paterno didn't honor the question with so much as a turn of his head, but Lani, spying Jack, switched her attention to him. He suspected she knew who he was; he'd done a lot of promoting when he was getting the magazine off the ground and showed up at a lot of civic and charitable functions.

"Jack Holt?" she said, and he noticed the sharpened interest in her dark eyes. The wheels were turning in her mind. He didn't wait for her to put two and two together. Jogging around her, he caught up with Paterno at the front door. "Don't ring the bell," he said as Paterno was just lifting his hand. Now Coco was having a fit, barking crazily, baying and whining in her little-dog voice. "Cissy just put the baby to bed. Let's not wake him. Here." He slid his key into the lock, and the door swung open. "I'll get her," he said, ushering the cop inside and pulling the door shut.

"Jack?" Cissy called from the top of the stairs. "I thought you understood—"

"We've got company, Ciss," he said as Paterno set the crate on the floor.

"What? Who?" He heard her soft, familiar footsteps on the stairs as he opened the cage's mesh door.

With an excited yip, a scrap of scruffy white fur bolted from inside the carrier and barked excitedly at Cissy's feet as she reached the main floor. "Oh." She had already pulled her hair into a ponytail, and the sleeves of her T-shirt had been pushed up her forearms, slightly wet, evidence of B.J.'s quick bath. She looked from Jack to the detective as she bent down to pick up the frantic, ecstatic dog, who was yipping and jumping up at her.

"I probably should have called," Paterno said. "We found her"—he pointed at Coco—"locked in a cupboard in the library."

"What?" she repeated.

"Would your grandmother ever put the dog in the—"

"Cupboard? No! Never!" Holding the wriggling terrier, Cissy was rewarded with a pink tongue that licked her all over her face. She couldn't help but smile. "Yeah, yeah, I'm glad to see you too," she said dryly to the dog, then actually chuckled at Coco's enthusiasm. Looking at Paterno, she said, "My grandmother adored Coco, and I'm not kidding you, she would have died before she would have locked . . ." She blinked and shook her head. "Sorry. It's . . . still processing. . . . The thing is, Gran would have never locked Coco in anything, including that," she said, hitching her chin toward the crate. "I mean, this dog, from the time she was a puppy, sat on Gran's lap while she watched television or knitted or read. My grandmother was meticulous to a fault. She absolutely detested dirt of any kind, but she didn't care a whit about the dog hair when it came from this one." Cissy rubbed Coco behind her ears, and the dog grunted happily, beady black eyes still glaring distrustfully at Jack and Paterno. "Thanks for bringing her by." She shot a look at her husband as if to say, *So what are you doing here?*

Paterno reached into his pocket and pulled out a little spiral-bound notepad. "Since I'm here already, would you mind if I ask you a few more questions? Some clarification on a few things."

Cissy wanted to tell him to wait till morning. It was on the tip of her tongue, but what good would it do, really? Put off the inevitable for one more night? She inclined her head and asked, "When I pick up my car tomorrow, can I go inside Gran's house?"

"I think it'll be okay."

"Then go ahead with your questions," Cissy said as she carried the dog into the living room. "I don't know what more I can tell you," she said and motioned to the couch from which Jack so recently had been evicted. "Please, sit down."

"Thanks. What I need from you are the names of your grandmother's friends and associates, their phone numbers, or addresses, if you have them. I have the ones that were on your cell phone. I was also hoping you could tell me a little bit about your grandmother, her routine." He dropped onto the couch while Jack walked to the fireplace and lit the gas jets, gold flames instantly flaring over ceramic logs.

"Deborah, Gran's companion, could tell you better than I can about what she did every day. Give me just a minute to take care of the dog, and I'll be right back." To Coco, she said, "I'll bet you're thirsty and maybe hungry too, huh?" She and the dog disappeared into the kitchen, and a few seconds later the sounds of banging cupboard doors and water running were accompanied by a series of sharp, staccato yips. Soon, Cissy, barefoot, returned, while the dog, presumably, was digging into whatever it was she found to feed it.

Jack watched as his wife retrieved her laptop from an upper shelf of the built-in bookcase near the fireplace, a "baby-proof" spot well out of the reach of B.J.'s curious fingers, then clicked it on. "It'll be just a minute," she said as she sat on a side chair while Jack braced himself against the mantel. As the computer began its clicking and humming to life, Cissy pushed her wet sleeves down to her wrists and answered the questions she could about Eugenia, telling the detective as much about her grandmother's days as she knew.

"She's on the board of Cahill House, which is what would once have been called a 'home for unwed mothers.' In fact, I think that's exactly what it was called once. Now everything's more straightforward, isn't strangled by all the secrecy and shame, thank God. Cahill House is now a place for pregnant teens or twenty-somethings who don't have support from their families. They can stay there, go to school, and get counseling while they're awaiting the birth of their child." She managed a smile. "It's one of the truly philanthropic things my family's done. And Cahill House has always been one of Gran's pet projects, along with being on the board at the hospital."

"Which hospital?" Paterno asked.

"Bayside."

Paterno made notes while Cissy added, "Gran plays mahjong and bridge with different women every week. Mahjong on Wednesdays, I think, and bridge on Thursdays . . . or maybe it's the other way around. I can't remember. She gets her hair done without fail by Helene on Friday mornings and has for years. Helene has a shop somewhere around Haight-Ashbury. Lars would know the address." The computer made a series of clicks as it came to life just as Coco trotted back to the living room and made a beeline for Cissy. "Oops," she said, then placed the laptop on a side table while the dog settled onto her lap.

"Okay, here we go." As Paterno wrote in a notepad, Cissy, without any inflection, rattled off names and phone numbers, many of which Jack was hearing for the first time. Afterward, she added, "Of course, there's Cahill International, the family business. It was in bad shape a few years back, but I think it's doing well again. I don't really pay that much attention, but Gran still sits on the board. I mean sat on it. God, it's hard to believe she's gone."

"You were close?"

"I wouldn't say that, exactly." Cissy shook her head. "I wasn't that crazy about her, growing up, and she thought I was just okay. Believe me, she was *all* about a male heir for the family. It was ridiculous, so antiquated, but because of it, I only tolerated her when I was a kid. As a teenager I would have rather been anywhere else, and we lived with her. It was the worst!" She looked away for an instant, her features tightening with emotion. "But over the years we got closer, and then B.J. came along and Gran went nuts. Another boy, I suppose." Her lips twisted wryly, and Jack hated the pain he saw in her eyes. "You know, I sometimes wonder how she would have reacted if he'd been a girl." She looked up at Paterno. "Probably not the same. How is that for unfair?"

Paterno lifted a shoulder. "From what I see, not many families are perfect."

She snorted, glanced through the window to the dark night beyond. Absently she rubbed her arms, as if a sudden chill had swept over her.

"Where are the rest of the family now?" Paterno asked.

"Around here it's just me," she said a little defensively, the way she always did when anyone pried too deeply about her family. She was prickly where they were concerned, and Jack didn't blame her. "There's my aunt and uncle, who are raising my brother in Oregon. You remember them."

Paterno nodded. "You got a number?"

Absently petting the dog, she rattled off the phone number from memory. "Of course, there's my mother too." She looked through the window to the dark night beyond, almost as if she expected Marla's visage to appear in the rain-drizzled glass.

Paterno quit scribbling long enough to click the top of his pen as he thought. "Don't you have some cousins, or half cousins?"

"My father's cousins." Her jaw hardened at the mention of the man who had sired her. Though Alex Cahill had been dead for years, Cissy had never forgiven him for neglecting her while he'd been alive. "Gran always called them the black sheep." Cissy scratched the little dog behind her ears. "Monty, er, Montgomery, is still in prison, but his sister, Cherise, is around. I think her last name is still Favier. It's hard to keep up. She's been married a few times."

The policeman nodded, as if he actually knew who she was talking about. Jack didn't. Sometimes it seemed the longer he knew Cissy, the less he knew about her.

"They never got along with the rest of the family. I think they thought my grandfather did something under-handed and cut their grandfather out of the family fortune. Monty and Cherise never got over it."

"Did your grandfather? Cut them out?"

She lifted a shoulder, and Jack realized she was try-ing to hold on to her patience. He saw the tension in her body, the slight narrowing of her eyes. She didn't like Paterno and didn't like his questions. "I don't know. Gran would remember. . . ." Her voice trailed off, and she cleared her throat. "Look, I really don't know what more I can tell you."

Paterno nodded and acted like he'd heard it all be-fore, but it was news to Jack. The detective asked a few more questions, asking Cissy to check and see if any val-uables were missing when she returned to Eugenia's, then finally left. Jack walked him to the door and noticed that the KTAM van wasn't blocking the driveway any longer.

Good news, at least for now. But it wouldn't last long. Sooner or later, Lani Saito, or someone else who smelled a story, would be back.

He closed the door behind Paterno and watched as the policeman walked to his Caddy. Once satisfied that the detective wasn't coming back, Jack returned to the living room, where the fire hissed in the grate and Cissy sat in the chair, petting the dog, still staring out the win-dow. "So," he said, picking up a framed picture of B.J. on his first birthday, one candle burning on a cake placed on the tray of his high chair. His eyes seemed twice their size as he stared at the cake in awe and amazement.

"So what?" she asked, not even looking at him.

He replaced the five-by-seven on the table. "Are you going to throw me out again?"

"Am I going to have to?"

"You don't *have* to."

She hesitated, as if there were just the tiniest chink in her armor. She slid her gaze to one side, and he had the good sense not to walk close to her, try to touch her, offer unwanted consolation and sympathy. "You keep pushing me."

"No, Ciss, you're the one pushing. You're pushing me away."

"And you know why," she declared, throwing her arms up in defeat. "I am so tired of fighting. You can stay, Jack, on the couch—on one condition. No . . . make that two . . . on second thought, *three* conditions!"

Before he could argue, she held up a finger. "First, you leave early in the morning. You do not pass 'go,' you do not 'get out of jail free,' you do not expect to move in, and you just get the hell out before I get up."

"Okay."

A second finger shot skyward. "You walk the dog tonight."

"The dog hates me."

"Tough!" The third finger joined the others. "Before you leave, you find a way to fix the damned furnace."

"You're not calling a repairman?"

"It's Sunday. The thermometer in here says the temperature is hovering below sixty-two, and the thermostat is set to seventy."

"I'll look at it."

"Okay." Cissy gazed at him uncertainly, as if unsure whether she'd won or lost. "Then, good. Good night, Jack."

"Good night," he said, but she was already striding out of the living room, across the foyer, then hurrying up the stairs, her bare feet nearly noiseless on the hardwood steps. Above, as she walked, the floor creaked. He heard a door open and shut, then watched a pillow and a sleeping bag come hurtling down the stairs. The sleeping bag bounced against the door of the closet in the foyer; the pillow skidded across the floor and stopped when it hit the back of the couch.

"Thanks," he called up the dark staircase toward the landing.

"Don't mention it." A second later he heard the distinctive creak of the master bedroom door as it opened, then shut with a soft thud and a click of the lock. Obviously Cissy was taking no chances that he'd try to sweet-talk his way into their king-sized bed.

He wasn't that deluded.

He picked up the sleeping bag, unrolled it, and tossed it over the slick leather cushions of the damned couch. Throwing the pillow toward one end, he surveyed his work. Not that great, but at least it beat the car, he thought as he walked into the kitchen, found the last beer in the refrigerator, and uncapped the bottle. After taking a long, not-that-satisfying pull, he carried a growling and suspicious-looking Coco outside, deposited her on the turf just off the patio, and waited in the cold drizzle for the damned dog to sniff every damned bush before she finally got down to her damned business.

"This isn't exactly what I had in mind," he confided to Coco as he carried her inside and found a dishtowel to wipe her tiny wet paws. For all his efforts, he was rewarded with a warning growl. He thought for a minute that the feisty bit of fluff might actually bite him. "Don't even think about it," he advised, and when he set the dog onto the floor, she scrambled to get away from him, nearly skidding as she headed for the stairs and ran up them as if she were a dog half her age and was fleeing for her life.

"Good riddance," Jack muttered.

With one look up the darkened stairs, he returned to the living room, flopped onto the couch, and picked up the remote. He thought of the irony of his earlier assessment of the single life. Even married and in his own house, it wasn't much different.

He clicked on the local news, and there, filling up the flat screen, was the last picture his wife had of her mother: Marla Amhurst Cahill's mug shot.

You're a fool!

Cissy peeled off her clothes, let them drop to the bedroom floor, then stepped into pajamas that had gotten at least one size too big for her over the last month. Her appetite had been off; the stress over the separation from Jack had cost her ten pounds she could ill-afford to lose.

And now he was downstairs.

Great!

Stupid, stupid, stupid. Tonight on the couch. Tomorrow up here in the bedroom? And then what? Are you going to forgive him just like that? Set yourself up for more heartache? Put yourself and B.J. on an emotional roller coaster for the rest of your lives? You can't do it, Cissy. No matter how much you want to. Jack Holt is a player, plain and simple. He might not ever intend to hurt you, but if you let him, he'll break your heart over and over again.

She couldn't let him.

It was that simple.

She walked into the small master bath that she and Jack had carved out of an existing attic space, brushed her teeth and stared at a face she barely recognized. Her eyes, whiskey gold, as Jack had referred to them, were rimmed in running mascara, the whites shot with red veins from all of the crying she'd done since finding her grandmother on the floor of the foyer. Her nose was pink, a couple of damned zits daring to erupt on her chin, and her cheekbones more defined than ever. She scrubbed off all remnants of her makeup, dug in the drawer for acne cream she was way too old to be using, then gave up the search when she heard Coco scratching at the door.

"Hang on for a sec," she called, then walked through the bedroom.

She opened the door, half-expecting Jack to be on the other side, his shoulder propped against the door-jamb, an irrepressible grin tugging at his lips, devilment in his eyes.

But the dog was alone.

Insanely she felt a little bit of disappointment.

"Come here," she whispered to the dog, "let's go check on Beej."

She heard the soft noise from the television in the living room filtering up the stairs and noticed the illumination of a flickering screen playing against the wall of the staircase. Sighing, she found it ridiculously comforting knowing that she wasn't alone tonight. That Jack was downstairs. In their house.

Oh man, Cissy, you ARE a basket case!

She pushed open the door that she always left just slightly ajar. Inside B.J.'s room, her son was sleeping in his crib, and her heart swelled at the sight of him in the one-piece pajamas that covered him head to toe in soft, powder blue cotton. His blond curls had dried from the bath, and his lips were parted as he slept on his back. A mobile of airplanes through the ages, biplanes to Lear jets, hung suspended from a ceiling where she and Jack had painted clouds.

"Don't let his angelic demeanor fool you," Cissy whispered into Coco's ear as she stared at her son. "He's been a holy terror all week." With her free hand, she adjusted Beej's blankets and watched his small chest rise and fall.

Satisfied that he was sleeping soundly, she slipped back into the hallway and then nearly screamed when she saw a dark figure near the stairs. Her hand flew to her heart the nanosecond before she recognized Jack. "Holy God, Jack, what're you doing up here! We had a deal."

"I was just going to do what you've been doing. Check on my son."

"He's fine!"

But Jack brushed by her and poked his head into the nursery anyway. She followed and peeked through the open door. Her heart squeezed as she saw Jack smile and place his big hand on B.J.'s tummy.

Her heart squeezed.

Don't let him get to you, do not!

"You're right," Jack said, easing into the hallway again and brushing up against a picture she had yet to take down, an eight-by-ten of their wedding in the stupid little Las Vegas chapel. She was in a short white dress, he in a tux, and no one they knew had been there to witness the event.

Jack saw her quick glance and looked at the picture, righting it. "You don't like Detective Paterno much, do you?"

"He's not exactly been a champion of my family, but let's discuss this some other time."

She thought he might grab her right then and there, close as they were. But the little dog in her arms growled, causing Jack to curb whatever impulse he might have had. "That dog hates me," he said, faintly amused.

"Maybe she has a reason."

"Cheap shot, Ciss," he said, but his amusement didn't

fall away. "You know, I'm getting damned tired of being your whipping boy."

"You're the one who lobbied hard and fast to get back into the house."

"My house," he reminded her. "At least half of it. But listen, I'm not going to argue with you tonight. I know you've been through enough today. So for now, good night, Ciss." He walked the few feet to the stairs and descended, leaving her in the hallway. She glanced at the wedding picture, yanked it from its hook and, once inside the bedroom, tossed it into the trash with enough force that the glass splintered and the frame broke.

Telling herself she didn't care two cents about the damned picture, she set the dog on the floor, but the terrier was having none of it. With surprising agility, Coco launched herself onto the bed and settled on Cissy's pillow. "Oh, no. Not a prayer." Cissy pushed the tiny beast onto Jack's side, where Coco circled about a million times before settling into the spot formerly occupied by the man downstairs.

How pathetic was that? She and this little dog on a bed that suddenly seemed an acre across.

She slid between the sheets and picked up a book, then, after reading the same paragraph three times without remembering a word, tossed the paperback onto the nightstand and clicked off the light. Coco was already snoring contentedly, but Cissy stared up at the dark ceiling.

The police really thought her grandmother had been murdered.

During the very week her mother had escaped from prison.

She shuddered, drew the covers up around her neck, and glanced out the window, where the streetlight illuminated a spot on the sidewalk. No police car was outside, but the rain beat steadily, slashing downward, and for a second, just half a heartbeat, she thought she saw someone standing outside that watery pool of light, a dark, smudgy apparition that could have been a person in a dark coat, or a figment of her imagination.

A frisson of fear skated down Cissy's spine, and her heart nearly stopped.

You're imagining things.

But she slid out of the bed and, in the darkness, walked to the side of the window, obscured by the curtains, peering out into the damp night. Lights from neighboring houses should have made her feel more secure. Jack being downstairs should have made her feel safe.

Her fingers wound in the sheer curtains as she squinted into the night.

There's no one there. Look . . . there's nothing.

But she swallowed against a suddenly dry throat and resisted the urge to call out to Jack.

She thought about Marla as she stared at the spot where she felt she'd seen someone lurking.

Where was she?

Here?

Chapter 6

The couch wasn't made for sleeping.

It was fine for sitting on.

Great for watching television.

Perfect for making out.

But sleeping all night, no way.

Jack woke with a crick in his neck and a bad taste in his mouth. He didn't dare go upstairs and wake his wife, so he walked into the small bath off the foyer and cleaned his teeth with some of the soap from the dispenser and his finger.

He thought about making a pot of coffee and carrying it up to Cissy, maybe even finding a fake flower and placing it between his teeth in an effort to make her smile, but thought better of it. Part of their deal was that he would leave before she awoke. Cissy was not a "morning person" and was still too pissed at him to even think about forgiving him. He walked into the kitchen, ground some beans for coffee, found the filters, and poured in a carafe of water. With a press of a button, java was on its way.

Just as the first fragrant drips were working their way

into the pot, his cell phone jangled. He flipped it open and spied his sister's name and number. Not a good sign. He almost didn't answer, but knew that wouldn't stop her. Jannelle—tall, blond, and five years older than Jack—had been a print model before opening her own school for girls who were on the fast track to the runway. She was tunnel-visioned to the nth degree and relentless when she wanted something. If she was calling at six in the morning, it wasn't just to say hello. She had to be on some damned mission.

"Hi, Jannelle," he said in a whisper so as not to wake his wife, child, or the yappy dog.

"What's this about Cissy's grandmother being murdered?" Jannelle demanded.

That was Jannelle, never one to sugarcoat anything. "Good morning to you too."

"You know about this, right? It's all over the news! Jesus, Jack, did someone really kill Eugenia Cahill?" She sounded nervous, anxious. He heard her breathe in hard, then the distinctive sounds of her lighting a cigarette, though she'd quit smoking a good six months earlier.

"That appears to be the current line of thinking," he said, leaning one hip against the corner of the cabinets in the kitchen. The coffee was really doing its thing, percolating and sputtering and hissing and filling the small kitchen with a warm, rich scent.

"Was it Marla? Did she knock off her mother-in-law?"

"I don't know."

"How did it happen?"

"I don't really know, Jannelle. Enough with the interrogation." He heard his voice rise with impatience and made an effort to bring it back down. "It's early. Slow down. For all I know, Eugenia *could* have fallen down the stairs. It doesn't look that way, but who knows?"

"I've already had a reporter call *here*. Can you believe

it? I think the jerk knew you were Cissy's husband, couldn't find you in the book, and was calling anyone named Holt with a 'J' for the first initial. Jesus, I'm going to have to change that. You know, Dad probably got a call too. And J.J. Brace yourself. They're bound to be as pissed as I am about it. Probably worse."

"I'm braced." Jack wedged the phone between his shoulder and ear. He was already rooting around in a cupboard for a cup, came up with a mug from his days at UCLA, and pulled the pot out of the coffee machine before it was ready.

"So this guy didn't call you?"

"Not yet. But our house . . . Cissy's place is unlisted. I don't have a phone at the apartment. Just use the cell."

"They'll track you down."

Of that much, he was certain. He poured himself a cup while some of the black brew drizzled from the reservoir and through the filter onto the hot plate, where it sizzled. Quickly, he returned the carafe to the coffee machine and listened as Jannelle barraged him with more questions. Rapid-fire, she demanded:

"When did it happen?

"How?

"Who would have done this?"

A bit of conscience hit her, and she asked, "Jesus, how is Cissy? You've talked to her, right? You . . . Oh God, that's why you're whispering! You're with her, aren't you? Oh, Jack, no!" He heard her take another long drag. "Didn't I tell you to divorce the bitch and be done with it?"

Jack wasn't in the mood. "What is it you want, Jannelle?" he asked coldly.

"Answers."

"Why?"

"Because I want to know what to say if the damned media calls again."

"Whatever happened to your stance that 'no publicity is bad publicity'?"

"Maybe that was a little broad. I'm rethinking it," she said from her condo in Sausalito.

"Try 'No comment.' Look, I've got to run, I'll talk to you later." Before she could say another word, he hung up and took another long gulp from his coffee. What was it with Jannelle? Naturally bossy, she was forever sticking her nose into his business.

But then, his whole family had a tendency to get under his skin. All opinionated; no one could ever keep his or her mouth shut. And they'd all chimed in on his separation from Cissy. Jannelle, divorced twice herself, had never liked Cissy and was rooting for the split to be finalized. When he'd given Jannelle the news, she'd arched a perfectly plucked eyebrow, crossed her incredibly long legs, leaned back in her chair in the Italian restaurant on Pier 39, and smiled. Outside, a colony of sea lions lazed on the docks in the cool wintry sun. Inside, Jannelle ordered two glasses of champagne and said, "Let's toast to your new freedom. I've always said you should divorce the bitch."

Jack had walked out, leaving her with the two flutes of expensive champagne and the bill. He'd wandered aimlessly along the waterfront, smelling the brine of the sea and wending his way through tourists willing to brave the sunny, if windy, day.

Things had gone differently with his father. Jonathan Holt had been saddened when he'd heard of the potential demise of Jack's marriage. He'd met Jack in an Irish bar not far from Jack's office in the financial district. "I hope you find a way to bury the hatchet and patch things up," he'd said, sipping a Guinness and glancing at the long mirror that stretched behind the bar. They had been standing, each with a foot on the brass rail, an array of colorful bottles and clean glasses stacked on glass shelves in front of the mirror. "There's a child involved, you know. *My* grandson."

"I know that, Dad. B.J. isn't just your grandkid, he's my son." The old man always had a way of turning the center of the conversation to himself. And Jonathan Holt was no expert on marriage. Though he and Jack's mother had endured nearly forty years of being together, throughout the duration of the union, Jonathan—handsome, fit, and charming—had found it difficult to stay faithful to his wife. In the end, Jill Holt had become weary of turning the other cheek, looking the other way, and pretending not to hear the whispers, while younger women openly flirted with her husband. She didn't divorce him, just moved into a bedroom on the far side of their house, as far from her husband as possible without actually taking the step of "separation." In Jack's estimation, Jonathan Holt was the last one to be giving advice on the sanctity of marriage vows.

Jack hadn't had to face his older brother, Jon, who went by the moniker Jonathan Junior and sometimes was referred to as J.J. Once a major surfer and now "doing time" as he called it as a philosophy professor at a small college in Santa Rosa, Jon often dated coeds and had always been a believer in the old hippy axiom of "doing your own thing." When Jack had delivered the news of his separation from Cissy to his older brother over the phone, J.J. had barely reacted. "Hey, man, it's your life. Mom and Dad made a mess of theirs hanging together for so long. If we learned anything from them, it's you should get out of a bad marriage while you can. I did. It's no big deal."

No big deal. J.J.'s words still haunted Jack, ringing in his ears as he stood by the French doors and looked outside to the predawn morning. He noticed his watery reflection in the glass, seeming ghostlike. J.J. had been wrong. This, the breakup of his marriage, was the biggest deal of his whole damned life. And his marriage wasn't "bad"; it just needed some work. Maybe *he* needed some work. He was the one who'd messed up.

Closing his eyes for a second, Jack could almost hear his mother's voice, as if she were in the room standing next to him instead of dead and buried, having succumbed to liver cancer two months before B.J. was born. Of course, if Jill Holt had been alive, she would have wrung out the old "'til death do us part" line, not that it mattered much.

The divorce had been Cissy's idea.

He heard the sound of little dog paws and then footsteps on the stairs. In the wavy reflection, he spied his wife walking into the room. She was carrying a tousle-headed B.J. in her arms.

"'Morning," Jack greeted her.

"I thought one of the terms of our deal was that you'd be gone in the morning."

"Still haven't worked on the furnace."

To his surprise, she didn't argue. Still in pajamas and bare feet, her sun-streaked hair a mess, no makeup visible while hauling a groggy and seemingly grumpy child into the kitchen, she was still beautiful.

"Hey, big guy," Jack said as Cissy handed her son off to him. "How're ya?"

Beej, usually ecstatic to see him, turned his face away and grumbled, "No!"

"What's this all about?" Jack asked him with a frown.

"No, Dad-dee!" B.J. was emphatic.

Cissy glanced over her shoulder on the way to the coffeepot. "Welcome to my world. This has been his disposition most of the week. I think he's teething again. He hasn't got a fever or anything. Just a bad mood." She poured herself a cup and rested her hips against the counter as she blew across the top of the steaming cup. "You made this?"

"Yeah?"

"The single life must be agreeing with you already. Look what you're learning."

"I'll let you in on a little secret. I *knew* how to make coffee before I met you."

"Never made a pot while you were living with me."

"You're the earlier riser."

She hid a smile behind the rim of her cup. "And how was that couch?"

"Slept like a baby."

"Up every three hours crying?" she asked as Beej, a limp rag, his head tucked in the crook of Jack's neck, looked up at his father and scowled.

"No, Dad-*dee*!"

Cissy shook her head as she started making Beej some oatmeal.

"Maybe he just needs breakfast," Jack suggested, trying to jolly his son out of his grumpy mood by lifting him high overhead and swinging him, but B.J. wasn't having any of it and began wailing as if in pain.

"I see Daddy's missing the magic touch too," Cissy said as she turned her attention to B.J. "We'll have breakfast, then go upstairs and have a real bath, as last night you ended up with only a lick and a promise, and we'll change and . . ." Her voice had lifted an octave as she spoke to her son, smiling at him and wrinkling her nose, but he turned away from her as well.

"Apparently Mom's got an equally magic touch," Jack observed.

"At least this morning," she said, adding, "Coco needs to go out, and the furnace is still blowing cold air."

"I'm on it." He drained his cup, then opened the door to the backyard. The sun hadn't yet risen, but at least the rain had stopped, leaving the air thick and damp. "Come on," he said to the little white dog.

Coco stood as if planted on the hardwood floor under the table. "Come on, Coco, let's do your thing."

The stubborn animal wouldn't budge.

"Oh, for crying out loud!" Cissy said, unable to keep a tinge of amusement out of her voice. "Come on, Coco." Carrying the toddler, Cissy walked outside, and the stupid little dog happily followed. Over her shoulder, Cissy called to Jack, "You could have picked her up, you know."

"And risk being bit?" he asked, following her.

"Wimp!" she said but laughed as Coco started sniffing the wet grass.

The house phone rang. Still holding Beej, Cissy headed back inside to answer it. "Hello . . . Yes, this is she. . . . No, I haven't heard from her," she said, her voice edged with irritation. I don't expect to. . . . What? Look, I have no idea, okay, none! That's all I have to say on the matter. Don't call back!" Cissy slammed the phone down so hard that outside Coco jumped and looked up from her close examination of a clump of crabgrass.

Jack could hear Cissy grumbling under her breath as she walked into the living room. It sounded as if someone had asked her about Marla. He grimaced, imagining what might come next, how many reporters and snoops and gossips would keep bothering her. Wishing he could stave off the flood and help, he let the dog back inside.

Well, there was one thing he could do.

The furnace, a giant rumbling monolith, was in the basement, down steep, switchbacking steps through a door just off the kitchen. Jack found a flashlight in a junk drawer in the kitchen, then headed downstairs and past the laundry area to the ancient heater. It looked like a giant octopus with huge tentacles rising to the ceiling and the rooms above. Its replacement had been next on the to-do list, but, of course, that was before all hell had broken loose and his marriage had crumbled. No, that was wrong. It hadn't completely died, he reminded himself, though Cissy acted as if the marriage were on its last gasps and there was no hope of resuscitation.

Jack wasn't about to give up.

He spent half an hour with the damned furnace, figured out that it wasn't cycling on and that the element was probably kaput. The ducts were fine, might need to be cleaned, but it was the furnace itself that needed replacing. Not a surprise.

He found a towel in the dirty-clothes basket positioned near the washer. Wiping his hands, he climbed the stairs and reentered the living room, where Cissy, having already folded the sleeping bag, was sitting on a corner of the couch, Beej on her lap playing with a toy bunny.

"It's shot," he said.

"Your professional opinion?"

"Yep."

Cissy sighed. "I'll call some places this morning. Get a few bids."

Jack noticed the time on the clock in the living room. No matter what he did, he'd be late for work, and he couldn't bag out. He had a meeting at ten with reps from a major hotel downtown. The hotel reps wanted a feature, and since the unique hotel was a major advertiser, Jack was ready to discuss it. He would have loved to run upstairs and shower, but that was impossible. Cissy had thrown every last stitch of his clothes on the driveway the morning after he'd spent the night at Larissa's. There wasn't so much as a sports jacket in his side of the closet any longer.

There were no two ways about it, he'd have to stop by his apartment to shower and change before driving to the office. "Gotta run," he said reluctantly. "Do you want me to take you up to your grandmother's house to pick up the car?"

"Oh." She glanced at the clock mounted over the mantel. "No, I'll call a cab once Tanya gets here." Her lips tightened just a bit when she mentioned the nanny's name, the nanny Jack had found for their son, a woman of twenty-eight whom, for some reason, Cissy didn't quite trust despite Tanya's stellar list of recommendations.

"Are you sure? I'm not crazy about you going back there alone." He was giving her an out, even though he didn't have much time.

"I'll be fine. Go on. You'll be late."

He hesitated.

"Jack, go. You were supposed to be out of here before I got up, remember?"

No use arguing. Especially when she was right. "Okay, I'll talk to you later, but if you change your mind and want some moral support, I'll come back and take you."

"*Moral* support?" she said meaningfully.

"Give it a rest, will ya? I'm trying to help out."

She started to come back with a hot retort, but instead she backed down and nodded. "Okay. You're right. We both know where we stand."

"Good." He could barely believe it. She'd been so adamant, so prickly. As he passed by the couch, he ruffled B.J.'s hair and pressed a quick kiss to Cissy's crown, surprising her.

"That's not winning you any points, Holt," she said, but she climbed to her feet and, still carrying Beej, walked him to the door.

"I'll be back after work."

"No, wait, you don't have to—"

She didn't finish her thought, and he took that as a

good sign. As he jogged to the car, he felt her gaze on his back. When he reached the Jeep, he looked over his shoulder and saw Cissy standing on the porch in her bare feet holding the baby. Next door, Sara Delano, their neighbor, dressed to the nines, was picking up her soggy newspaper from the bushes near her front porch.

"Jack!" Sara said, waving and offering him a smile that was too wide for so early in the morning.

He waved as he hit the button on his remote lock. "Hey, Sara!" As he climbed into the Jeep, he saw that Sara, in long skirt, boots, sweater, scarf, and jacket, was picking her way across the adjoining lawns to the porch where Cissy stood. Good. He hated to leave Cissy alone even though she'd made damned sure he knew that she liked it that way.

Not that he really believed it. He glanced over his shoulder as he eased from his parking space and caught a picture of Cissy, ponytail blowing over her shoulder in the breeze as she clutched their kid. She was staring after his Jeep, her angry facade slipping, her expression pensive.

He grinned to himself.

Damn, if she didn't look like she missed him already.

Cissy watched Jack pull away. From the corner of her eye she'd witnessed the quick exchange between Sara and him, then observed Sara's eyes follow Jack's movements.

So what?

They were all friends.

Sara and Jack had been close, no big deal.

It was nothing. Meant *nothing!*

And yet a ridiculous spurt of suspicion stole through her. She couldn't help but wonder if Jack and Sara had ever had a fling.

Like Larissa.

Don't be stupid, she instantly chastised herself. *Sara's your friend.*

But it happened all the time, didn't it? The wife was always the last to know. How many times had Sara commented on how "hot" Jack was? How many times had he tried to set her up with one of his friends, always saying that Sara was a catch? Before finding him with Larissa, Cissy would never have thought for a second that there was anything between her husband and their neighbor, but now . . .

Cissy gave herself a mental shake. So the looks Jack and Sara had exchanged once in a while seemed more than just friendly. Who cared?

She would not—absolutely would *not*—become one of those suspicious women she detested. What was wrong with her? If she couldn't trust Jack, she certainly could trust Sara.

You're over the edge because of last night and Eugenia's death. That's it. And because Marla is on the loose. She shivered at that thought and held her son closer as she thought about someone watching the house the night before. Had that been her imagination?

"Hey," Sara called, holding a dripping newspaper away from her rust-colored jacket as she crossed the damp grass that separated their two houses. A redhead with porcelain skin and big eyes that flashed a deep forest green, Sara had been a model in high school and now was a high-powered realtor. She'd been married and divorced twice and now swore that she would remain single at least until she was thirty-five, which was still two years away. "I heard about your grandmother," she said, tossing her hair out of her eyes as the newspaper dripped from one hand. "What a bummer. I'm so sorry."

"So am I," Cissy admitted as a gust pushed a few wet

leaves across the grass and she turned her back to the wind. "It's a shock."

"Hang in there." Sara came to the porch and trained her gaze on B.J. "Hey, there," she cooed. Sara, who didn't have any of her own kids, winked at Beej. The boy pulled his shy act, burrowing his face into his mom's neck. "See that, it's the effect I have on all men."

Cissy doubted it. In fact, she knew better.

"God, Beej looks more like his dad every day."

That much was true. Which wasn't so horrible, Cissy supposed. Jack definitely was good-looking, which sometimes could be more of a curse than a blessing.

Sara squinted up at the sky, as if searching through the clouds for the sun. "Will it ever warm up?"

"It's winter," Cissy reminded her.

"I know. What I wouldn't do for hot sand, warm water, and a cool margarita brought to me by a pool boy named Ramon."

Cissy actually smiled. "Amen."

"You know, Cissy, you could use a break. All that business about your mom? And now your grandmother? On top of the divorce?" Sara shook her head, and sassy, razor-cut red waves bounced around her face as she touched B.J.'s nose with a manicured finger. "Good thing she's got you, though, huh, Beej? You're the bright spot."

He stared at her but clung to his mother.

Sara glanced over her shoulder, spying Jack's Jeep negotiate a last corner and disappear from sight. "Sooo," she said, gaze returning to Cissy. "Jack's back?"

"Oh, no. He just stayed over last night. He gave me a ride back from my grandmother's place. My car was blocked in by all the emergency vehicles."

"Oh God, you were there?" Sara pulled a face. "That's right. You always see her on Sunday. Don't tell me you were the one to find her." When Cissy's jaw tightened and she nodded, Sara's white skin paled even more. "How awful. Are you okay?" She rolled her expressive eyes. "Sorry. Dumb question. How could you be?"

"I'll be fine," she said and meant it. She had to be for Beej.

Sara's mind was already going a mile a minute. "So. Wait a minute." Her gaze swept the driveway. "What about your car? Is it still there?"

"Yeah."

"Do you need a ride to pick it up or something?" She checked her watch as the wind caught in the fringe of her scarf. "I could take you over there."

"Really? Don't you have to go to work?"

"Working from home today."

Cissy's gaze skated down her friend's outfit: maxiskirt, unbuttoned to the knee; expensive boots; big-necked sweater and suede jacket. And the scarf.

"You're working at home dressed like that?"

Sara laughed. "Well, I do have appointments this afternoon, and once I shower, I just get dressed for the day. But I'm going to hang around here for a while. It's one of the advantages of selling real estate and having a home office with Internet access. So if you want to pick the Acura up this morning, I'm available."

"How about as soon as Tanya gets here? Around nine?"

"Perfect." Sara flashed a grin that had probably sealed more than her share of deals. "Call me." Gingerly, she picked her way back to her house. Cissy watched her, then looked down the street to where she thought she'd seen the figure standing in the dark. Curious, she packed Beej across the street and walked to the position where she'd thought the person had been lurking. The neighbor's grass was a little mashed, and there was a cigarette butt in the gutter, but that didn't mean anything . . . or did it? She stood in the spot and stared up at her house. From this very position she could see into the dormer of the master bedroom. With only a partial turn of her head, she had a full-blown view of Beej's room.

Another gust of wind blew down the street, rattling the branches of the trees and chasing a chill as cold as death up her spine. Rain began to fall from the sky in a thick, icy mist.

It's nothing, Cissy. You were imagining things.

But she held her son a little tighter as she dashed back across the street and entered the house to hear the phone blasting. A little breathless, she managed to scoop up the receiver before the phone went to voice mail.

"Hello?"

"Tell me it's not true," a woman's thick voice said on the other end of the line. "Tell me Eugenia's alive." There was a loud sniff.

"Deborah?" Cissy guessed, thinking of her grandmother's companion.

"I just got a call from the police, and then I saw on the morning news that she had an accident. Oh Lord, I should never have left her."

"It's not your fault," Cissy assured her.

"What am I going to do?" Deborah asked, and Cissy spent another twenty minutes consoling her. Deborah flat-out asked about the terms of her employment now, and Cissy really didn't know what to say. Eugenia was gone, and there was no need for her. As gently as possible, Cissy pointed out the obvious, saying that she would be paid through the end of the month.

After she hung up, she decided to call Lars, the chauffeur; Elsa, the cook; the maids; and the groundskeeper. They deserved to hear what had happened from her, and she wanted to assure them that she appreciated their loyalty. In that moment she determined they could stay on staff and be paid for another two months, and that they would be given excellent recommendations if it was decided that they were no longer needed at the house.

As soon as the thought crossed her mind, she caught herself up. Was it even up to her to make these decisions?

She decided that, yes, it was. Someone needed to talk to the Cahill employees. Someone needed to keep some semblance of order.

Thanks, Gran, she thought, feeling a mixture of pain and frustration. Cissy wasn't that crazy about Lars, and though Elsa and Rosa were both sweeties, Paloma was hard to read. Still, she needed to deal with each of them.

Her shower would have to wait.

Chapter 7

"So what do we know about what happened to Eugenia Cahill?" Paterno asked the next morning as Janet
Quinn, ever efficient, dropped a cup of black coffee
onto the corner of his desk while she sipped from a similar cup that held all kinds of goop. Milk, sugar, caramel,
foam, everything *but* coffee.

"Not much," she said. "There was no sign of forced
entry on any of the doors or windows, though one window, near the back stairs leading to the basement, was
open just a fraction, probably to air out the old staircase, but we couldn't find prints beneath it, and it's
pretty high, five feet off the ground. There was a step-
ladder in an outbuilding, but it looks like it hasn't been
moved in months, cobwebs all over it. The electronic
locks on the garage and main gate were working."

"Someone could have known the code. All the servants have to have a way to get inside. Same with friends
and workmen. I'll check. What else?"

"Phone records have been requested. Autopsy's scheduled in a couple of days, and the lab will be working on
her tox screens, to see what's in her blood." She took a

sip and then had to lick a little foam from her lip. If another woman had taken the same action, it would have been sexy. With Quinn, it barely registered in the male side of his brain. "Nothing seems to be missing. She had jewelry in a box in her bathroom, looks like the real thing—diamonds, rubies, you name it—and we found the safe, had it opened. More jewelry, a little cash, and I did come across a couple of insurance policies and her will."

Paterno looked up, interested, as a phone in the department started ringing and a fax machine began sputtering out pages just around the corner.

"A little money thrown at charities here and there and to loyal members of her staff, but the inheritance falls to three: Cissy Cahill Holt, her brother, and uncle."

"Who are still in Oregon. Never left. I checked. So far, I think the last person to see Eugenia alive was Deborah Kropft, who usually has Sundays off but stopped by to take Eugenia to church services. She walked Mrs. Cahill into the house, offered to fix her something to eat, but Eugenia had said she was fine. Deborah claims she left her very much alive in the living room." Paterno leaned back in his chair and sipped some of the hot coffee.

"You think she's lying?"

Paterno shrugged. "I think we should interview her in person."

Quinn was nodding. "I don't like changes in any routine. Why did she call Deborah?"

"They both go to the same Methodist church, and Eugenia usually rides with her friend, a widow, Marcia Mantello, but Marcia was ill. I'm checking it out." He took another swallow of his coffee. Despite what he said, he didn't like the change in Eugenia's routine either. "So what about the insurance policies?"

"Originally the beneficiaries were split between the

same three—Cissy, her brother, her uncle—but eighteen months ago, about the time Cissy had the baby, Eugenia changed the beneficiaries. Only Cissy and her child are listed. Cissy for a million, her child for two."

"Millions? The old lady had that much life insurance?" Paterno asked, whistling through his teeth.

"Yeah, it looks like she took the policies out about ten years ago."

"Oh." Paterno picked up a yellowed file on Marla Cahill, flipped it open, and found his notes. "Let's see . . . Yeah, now I get it. There was a time when Cahill International was in financial trouble. I didn't think the old lady knew about it, but it could be that she's smarter than we all gave her credit for. She might have figured that if she kicked off, everything the family owned would be gone." He scowled, studying his own chicken scratchings. "That's probably it. She was the matriarch of the family, felt responsible."

"And then, when the company turned around and Cissy gave her this new great-grandson, she changed the policies."

"I wonder if Mrs. Holt knows?" Paterno said.

"Doesn't matter. The estate is worth so much that *if* she were greedy and needed money, she'd inherit a fortune *without* the insurance benefits."

Paterno drummed his fingers on the cluttered desk. He didn't figure Cissy for a killer. He'd already talked to a couple of members of the staff. Deborah Kropft and Elsa Johanssen, who both had solid alibis, told the same story of familial devotion, of Cissy Holt visiting her grandmother like clockwork on Sundays. He glanced at the list of names Cissy had given him and frowned. He hadn't been able to get through to the chauffeur or either of the maids.

And there was still the matter of Marla Cahill, he thought, spying her mug shot in the folder. A cold-hearted bitch if there ever was one, but beautiful and bewitching as well, a woman who had a history of twisting men around her little finger. There had been sightings reported, to the state police, to the FBI, and to the station. None of the "leads" had led authorities to anyone resembling Marla Amhurst Cahill.

He scratched at his chin while another detective dragged a reluctant suspect or witness toward an interrogation room. The man was protesting all over the place.

Paterno barely noticed as he studied Marla's file.

Where the hell was she?

Who was her accomplice?

The state police were looking into that angle of the investigation, and, in truth, Marla's whereabouts weren't a part of his caseload. Yeah, he was the cop who had nailed her, but now she was someone else's problem.

Except that her mother-in-law was killed within days of Marla's escape.

Paterno took another swallow of the coffee, felt a case of heartburn coming on. He opened the second drawer in his desk, where he found a bottle of antacids, and popped a few, washing them down with the coffee.

"Did you drop off the dog?" Janet asked.

"I was glad to get rid of that yappin' thing."

"She's sweet."

"My ass."

Quinn was an animal lover. All animals. Period. If it had two legs or four; hard shell, fur, or feathers; beak, wings, scales, or webbed feet, she loved it. She'd even gone so far as to give up meat, becoming a vegan, which, when they were on the road together, was a royal pain.

"I bet Cissy was glad to see her." Quinn's eyes lit up behind her glasses. She'd probably wanted to adopt the damned thing and add it to her already swarming brood of five cats.

Paterno snorted derisively.

"Oh yeah," Quinn said, finishing her drink. "You're so tough."

"That's just the kind of guy I am," he said as his cell phone rang and Quinn took her leave. He made some notes to himself as he heard the frustration in the voice on the other end of the line. Oscar Benowitz worked with the California State Patrol. A good friend, lousy poker player, and ace golfer, Oscar and he traded information between the two agencies, especially when cases overlapped.

"I saw you called," Oscar said. "I figured it was about Marla Cahill. Well, the truth of the matter is we got squat. Unbelievable. It's like the woman literally vanished into thin air."

"Someone on the outside helped her."

"That we got figured," he snapped, then added: "We're checking all the phone calls and visitors who came by to say 'hi.' Her cell mate claims she didn't know a thing, which is what we're hearing from all the inmates. We're still looking, working with the prison, but so far we've got nothing."

Paterno glanced over at the open file on his desk to Marla Cahill's mug shot. Her damned eyes seemed to stare back at him, taunting, as if she were thinking, *You'll never get me.*

"Anyone talking inside the first place she was locked away in? The real prison?"

"She hasn't been there in a while."

"My guess is she's been planning this for years."

Oscar seemed to want to argue, but said simply, "I'll keep you posted."

Paterno hung up and finished his coffee. He wasn't surprised that Marla Cahill hadn't left any clues. He suspected she'd planned this a long, long time ago, and the truth of the matter was, from Marla friggin' Cahill, he expected no less.

* * *

"A dog?" Tanya said, stepping backward at the sight of Coco. She was a short, frail-seeming woman whose looks were deceptive as she spent hours rowing on the bay or running to keep in shape. "You got a dog when you know I'm allergic to all animals, including dogs!"

"She was my grandmother's, and she'll be staying with us."

"Permanently?" Tanya asked, her brown eyes round and wide beneath shaggy bangs. "I'm serious about the allergies."

"I don't know how long she'll be here," Cissy said tightly, fighting back her annoyance. "She's an old dog. She'll just sleep in her basket. . . . Look, if she bothers you, put her in the crate, with a pillow or blanket or towel. That—detective—just brought her over here without any of her things. But I'll pick them up and bring them back."

"You're seriously thinking of leaving me and Beej with it?" Tanya said, recoiling as if Coco were a ferocious wolf, snarling in the darkness, blood dripping from her snout. As if sensing Tanya's abhorrence, Coco growled and yapped.

"Give me a break, will ya, Tanya?" Cissy snapped. "My grandmother died last night. I found her body. She might have been murdered, so deal with the dog, okay?"

Tanya's eyes widened. "Oh, wow, I'm sorry. I didn't know. . . . That's too bad, but really, I'm allergic." To prove the point, and too much on cue for Cissy to fully believe her, the girl sneezed.

"I'll take care of it," Cissy said through clenched teeth. She marched across the room, found a towel in the upper hallway, a small dish in the kitchen, filled the bowl with water, and stuffed the towel, dish, and Coco into the carrier. "If she drives you nuts with her whining and scratching, just take B.J. for a walk in his stroller."

"It's supposed to rain." Tanya glanced through the patio windows. Cissy wanted to scream. Tanya was trustworthy enough, but the girl would rather whine about something than do it, which was weird because, as far as Cissy could see, Tanya could do about anything she wanted. She was artistic and smart and, at times, clever. Cissy believed that Tanya would never do B.J. any harm, nor neglect him, and if spurred, as in a crisis, would ultimately do the right thing, but Tanya was *forever* grumbling, and it was a total pain. Nothing was ever right, and that less-than-sunny disposition bothered the hell out of Cissy. She didn't want her kid being partially raised by a downer. As soon as she dealt with Gran's funeral and found a replacement, Tanya would be history.

"Perhaps the dog could go outside," the girl ventured, as if it was a new, incredible thought.

"You just said it was going to rain."

"The garage?"

"Believe me, this animal has never spent one minute in a garage. You'll be okay. I'll be back in about three hours at the latest, it all depends." She didn't wait for any more complaints, just told Tanya that Beej had already had breakfast and been bathed, then, using her cell, called Sara.

She was out the door before Tanya could muster up another complaint and crossed the yard quickly. Sara was backing out of her driveway. She stopped, and Cissy climbed into the new Lexus, buckled up, and started pointing the way to her grandmother's house.

"Oh, I know where it is," Sara said. "On Mt. Sutro, backs up to the college's medical school, right?"

"You've been by?"

"Half a dozen times since I met you." Her eyes were on the road as she wove through traffic that was still thick from the morning rush hour. "It's a great place. I would love to see it. Never been inside, you know, but it has to have a fantastic view."

"It does," Cissy said carefully. She knew where Sara was going with this.

Sara flipped on her blinker as they reached Golden Gate Park, and Cissy gazed out the window. Bikers, joggers, and people walking their dogs were already on the paths cutting through the trees and grass. Normal people who didn't have to worry about psychotic escapee mothers and dead grandmothers. They rode up the hill to the house, and Cissy glanced at Sara, who was practically salivating as she parked on the street. The gate was left open, thankfully, as Cissy's remote was in the car. "Mind if I take a peek?" Sara asked, and Cissy decided it really didn't matter.

"Sure, why not. But remember, the police were here. They searched the place for evidence, dusted for prints. I don't know what it's going to look like."

She and Sara walked up the brick path, Sara eyeing the exterior, obviously calculating the home and property's worth.

Cissy unlocked the front door, steeled herself, then pushed it open.

"Oh God!" Sara gasped, spying the bloodstains on the foyer floor, the black powder covering everything, and the cold, certain feeling of death that seemed to settle throughout the old house's bones. "Oh, I didn't know. . . ." Sara, to her credit, swallowed hard. "I'm sorry, Cissy."

"It's all right."

Sara's eyes were drawn to the marble tile floor and the dark stains. "This house . . . this house is worth a fortune . . . if, um, if you ever want to sell. . . ."

"Sell the family home," Cissy responded flatly. She couldn't think about it.

"I figure you'll inherit, right? You might want to un-
load the property, what with the bad memories and all.
I'm telling you, it's worth millions. Exactly how much,
I'm not certain yet. But I'll walk around, and when I get
back to my computer, I'll pull up some comparables.
However, I'm sure they'll be few and far between. This
place is almost one of a kind." She was on a roll now,
looking beyond the black dust and blood, eyeing the
woodwork, the floors, the wainscoting, as she traipsed
from room to room. Her mental abacus going into
overdrive, Sara mounted the stairs to the next story.

Cissy let her go. Selling the house was the furthest
thing from her mind. She strolled slowly through the
cold, empty rooms and felt as if the estate had somehow
lost its heart with her grandmother's death. It just felt
different.

She could hear Sara walking upward to the third
story, so Cissy climbed to the second. She paused on the
landing, envisioning her grandmother, who had probably been in the library, walking across this strip of hardwood toward the elevator and stopping about . . . here.
Cissy positioned herself over the spot and wondered
what had happened. Gran had to have gone over the
railing right here, but who would push her? How would
the killer get into the house? And why? For God's sake,
who would hate Eugenia enough to want to kill her?
She'd made her share of enemies over the course of her
seventy-plus years, but for someone to come in and
murder her?

Could it be Marla? Could it?

Cissy shook her head. If she had arrived in time,
could she have saved her grandmother's life? Or would
she and B.J. have been attacked as well? Killed?

She swallowed hard, then walked into the living area,
where she and Beej had hung out with the older woman.
Cissy felt a new sadness when she noticed the knitting

bags now turned over at the foot of her grandmother's favorite wing-backed chair, the remote control for the television aimed at her twenty-year-old TV. In her room, she saw her outfits, sorted by color, shoes and handbags in cubbies, at the ready near the appropriate jackets, slacks, and skirts.

"Oh, Gran," Cissy said, her heart breaking all over again.

Before she could become too grief-stricken, she gathered up Coco's multiple dog beds, leashes, bowls, grooming kits, and blankets, then carried them out to the car. She also found two bags of dog food and a tiny little sweater, which, she was certain, she would never put on the dog.

On her way back inside the house, she nearly collided with Sara, who was smiling. "This is a wonderful, wonderful property," she enthused. "Really, Cissy, if you want to sell, I have clients who have been looking for nearly three years for a house as unique and 'San Francisco' as this one. It would be perfect for them. Perfect."

"It's not mine to sell, Sara."

"Then who's the legal owner?"

"Maybe my uncle or brother. . . . I don't know." She tried to hide her irritation. "Gran just died. Let's not even speculate."

"You're right, of course." Sara pulled a face. "I tend to get ahead of myself sometimes. I don't mean to be insensitive." She actually appeared sympathetic. "I've got to go. You okay?"

"Sure. Thanks for the ride."

Sara hugged her without pressing a business card into her palm; about as sincere as she could get. She then marched back to her Lexus, climbed inside, yanked out her cell phone, and was already talking a blue streak as she backed out of the driveway.

The minute the sleek car was out of range, Cissy reached into her own car and pushed the remote button to close the gates. With a grind and whir, the old iron behemoth swung into position. "Fortress secure," she told herself, but paused before heading into the house again. If someone had killed Eugenia, how did they get in? The front door had been locked, the gate closed when she arrived. True, there was a code everyone employed at the estate knew, the code that electronically released the locks and swung open the gate. Punch the same numbers on the way out, and the gate would close. The same was true of the garage. Her grandmother changed the codes every two or three months, just to keep the house more secure, but someone must have learned them. How else had they gotten in?

As she was looking at the gates, they clicked and began to open, groaning with the effort. She whipped around. Her heart nearly stopped.

Paloma was walking toward her, pocketing her remote control for the gates. Cissy released a shaky breath and tried to smile at the newcomer. Tall, almost regal looking, with shiny black hair clipped away from her face, sporting a long, spy-type trench coat, she walked up the street smartly in high-heeled boots. She seemed unconcerned, on her way to work as normal, earbuds plugged into her ears from the iPod hidden in her pocket. She was humming, her voice right on key, but when she caught a glimpse of Cissy through the opening gate, her face immediately crumpled, the humming stopped, and she yanked the earbuds from her ears. Her demeanor changed in an instant. "Miss Cissy, I'm so sorry," she said, one hand splaying over her heart. "Even though a policeman called me, and you called me, too, I . . . I still can't believe it!" She wasn't crying but was shaking her head sadly.

"I can't either."

"And the authorities, they think it could be murder?"

Cissy saw Eugenia's neighbors, Dr. and Mrs. Yang, in their town car as it backed onto the street. Their grand house was a little lower on the hillside, on the other side of the street. She'd met them before; he was a retired dentist, his wife was a quiet woman who had regularly beaten Gran at mahjong.

"I should speak to them," she said to Paloma. "Just give me a minute."

She crossed the street, and as she approached the Lincoln, Mrs. Yang rolled down her window. "Cissy," she said softly. "This is so awful. Are you okay?" Concern etched a face that had few natural wrinkles. Her hair was short, its black now shot with silver, her glasses small and dark-rimmed.

"I'm fine," Cissy lied. Then, while Dr. Yang let the car idle, she gave them a quick report, promising to let them know when the services were. Mrs. Yang sympathetically patted her hand, which was resting on the open window.

By the time Cissy recrossed the street, Paloma was finishing a cigarette. As Cissy approached, she tossed the remains of her filter tip onto the driveway, crushed it with the toe of her leather boot, then picked up the butt.

Cissy said, "Let's go inside before I have to talk to any more of the neighbors."

They went through the garage.

Paloma discarded the cigarette into a trash can as they waited for the elevator. Then they rode up in silence while the old car ground its way to the main floor before stopping with a bit of a bump.

Bracing herself, Cissy stepped into the house again.

Once again, the place felt empty.

Lifeless.

Almost tomblike.

Then there was the foyer.

Paloma's hand jumped to her mouth. She swallowed hard and paled, her gaze moving from the landing to the stairs and then once again settling on the dark near-purple stain on the floor. "This is horrible."

Cissy couldn't agree more, and when Rosa arrived five minutes later, the plump little woman began sobbing and making the sign of the cross over her chest and speaking rapid-fire Spanish to Paloma. Cissy caught some of the phrases, though she didn't need an interpreter to realize that Rosa was upset and grieving.

"*Dios!* Oh *Dios!*" she sobbed into several tissues, her face red, her dark eyes watery and full of misery. She shook her head over and over, as if in her vehement denial she could change what had happened. Then, just when she had nearly controlled herself, she glanced at the stain on the floor and wailed even louder.

Paloma, calmer, spoke softly to her and hugged her, but the woman was inconsolable.

"Coco? Where is my little Coco?" Rosa asked around a hiccup.

"I've got her."

"Thank God. I thought . . . Oh, never mind what I thought," she said in her thick accent. "What're we going to do?"

"We're going to clean up the mess," Cissy said with renewed determination. They could all grieve, all feel a little bit of guilt somehow for living when Gran was dead, just as she did, but life had to go on. "Can you handle it?"

"*Sí* . . . no . . . yes, yes, I can," Rosa said, nodding her head emphatically. "Miss Eugenia, she would not like this mess." Despite the tears streaking her face, Rosa's nostrils flared as she spied the offensive dirt tracked across the floor: the blood, of course, and all the black dust. "It's a pigsty in here!" Again she sputtered out Spanish, but this time she was more angry than sad. "Look at this!" she said, spying a potted plant that had been accidentally toppled. "And this!" The rug at the bottom of the stairs had been tracked upon. "My God!"

Armed with new purpose, Rosa began the therapeutic task of putting the house back together. Paloma too went about cleaning up. Cissy braced herself to deal with Lars, Elsa, and Deborah as each one arrived. Each was grim, but each found a way to assist, Deborah showing up to offer a hand despite the fact that Cissy had basically given her her walking papers.

Cissy was grateful to all of them. She helped where she could as Elsa set about straightening the kitchen, throwing out food that wouldn't be eaten, cleaning and polishing all the small appliances, counters, and utensils. Lars headed to the cars and the garage, and Deborah tackled Eugenia's calendar and engagements, canceling appointments and explaining a little about what had happened, referring Eugenia's closest friends to Cissy. She said she would e-mail Cissy all of the important phone numbers and names of contacts such as accountants, lawyers, and, of course, the prepaid funeral arrangements that Eugenia, years ago, had compiled. She promised to help Cissy with the arrangements and also to start on the obituary.

As they went about their business, Cissy, satisfied that the house and some of the affairs were being overseen, was finally able to leave.

She'd just pulled out of the drive and was heading down the steep, fog-shrouded road when her cell phone jangled. Driving with one hand, she fished it out of her purse and slid it open. "Hello?"

"Cissy, hi. It's Nick."

"Nick." Her uncle's voice was like something from a distant past.

"We heard about Mother," he said, then launched into a spate of "we're worried about you, we'll be there for the funeral, if there's anything you need, please call . . ." All the same crap she'd heard for ten years. Nick, her father's brother, was okay; she kind of liked him, but she wasn't sure about his wife, the bad girl gone good, or some such nonsense. Cissy had tried living with them in their podunk, nowhere town on the Oregon coast and had jettisoned herself out of there ASAP! Talk about boring! She'd hightailed it back home, then lived with Gran for the last few months before high school graduation. After that it was southern California and USC all the way. Uncle Nick, his wife, and even her small brother were fine, just not what she considered her immediate family.

Like Jack? her mind taunted. *He's your immediate family, isn't he?* Or he was supposed to be.

It was a little sad, she thought, maneuvering down the hill, still listening to Nick. She wasn't even that close to her brother, who seemed to be thriving with all of that backwoods stuff. Uncle Nick flew down every other week or so, as he still had his hand in the company business, but most times he'd shown up Cissy was able to duck out of their "family" dinners. She just couldn't make herself join in the happy family stuff. Not with her mother's crimes hovering over everything like a bad smell, even if she had been locked away in prison.

Which she wasn't now.

"So we just thought you might need us. We know you've got Jack and B.J., but thought, oh hell, you know."

"I'm fine, Nick," Cissy assured him, just as she had when he'd called about Marla a few days earlier. But she felt tears touch the back of her eyes. She hadn't told him about the impending divorce, didn't want him or his wife involved, didn't need to hear their opinions one way or the other. "I'm grown up now. I guess I should be saying 'I'm sorry' to you. Gran was your mother."

He hesitated just a beat, which said volumes about his relationship with Gran. "That she was."

"Look, I'm sure the attorneys and all will be calling you, and I'm driving and have another call coming in."

"Okay, Cissy. Take care."

Her throat tightened just a fraction. "You too, and say hi to James for me." She clicked off, feeling slightly guilty. She'd lied about another call coming in, but she did *not* want or need Uncle Nick and his wife putting their noses into her business.

The phone rang again, and this time she looked. Her friend Tracy. From high school. Oh great . . . the word about Gran and her mother had hit the street. She didn't pick up. Wasn't ready to face the onslaught. Tracy would be just the first.

Before driving home, she stopped by Joltz, the local coffee shop and deli where she sometimes set up her laptop for a few hours of uninterrupted work, parking in a spot that still had a little time on the meter.

Joltz offered tables, couches, and free wireless, and there were days when Cissy had been surrounded by the warm scent of roasting coffee, the gentle buzz of conversation, and the sputter of the espresso machines. She didn't mind the occasional burst of laughter or the whine of the coffee grinder. Sometimes the little table she always used as a work area was a respite from the office, where she shared a cubicle with three other freelance writers, or home, where she was always distracted, knowing her baby was nearby. Here, in relative anonymity, she had found it surprisingly easy to work, drink coffee, or even choose lunch from the array of sandwiches and salads in the deli case.

"The usual?" one of the baristas asked. "No-fat double-mocha with whipped cream?"

"I owe it to myself," Cissy said and reminded herself to climb on the elliptical machine tucked into the extra bedroom when she got home.

"You got it."

The workers behind the counter didn't wear name tags, but Cissy was in here often enough to recognize Diedre, with her quick smile and sharp wit. She was slender, blond, and friendly, whereas the woman who worked with her, Rachelle, was a little quieter, not quite as outgoing, and was always rotating the colors of her hair. Today's hue of choice was a rich mahogany shimmering with deep purple highlights. Modest by Rachelle's standards. Both baristas were attractive and witty enough to keep the regulars coming back.

Rachelle saw her in line and said, "I heard about your grandmother." She shook her head. "I'm sorry."

"What?" Diedre asked as she took Cissy's credit card. "Oh . . . wait." She glanced back at Rachelle. "It was on the news, wasn't it? The old woman in the mansion. Found dead."

By me, Cissy thought. "Yeah," she said, slightly uncomfortable as there were two other people in line, staring at the offerings in the bakery case while waiting to order.

"And all that business about your mother," Rachelle added. "That's gotta be tough."

Cissy didn't know how to respond. Yes, these women knew a little bit about her; she'd gladly offered up a few details, as she'd been virtually alone with them in the early afternoons when business was slow. Obviously, she should have kept her mouth shut. She knew she was blanching but managed to force a thin smile. "You have no idea."

"What?" Diedre said again, and Cissy groaned inside.

Rachelle caught Cissy's mortification. "Sorry," she mouthed, whispered something to Diedre, then turned her attention to the next woman, a jogger with beads of sweat still sliding down her face. Fortunately the woman, panting from her exercise, hadn't heard the exchange. Only Selma, a regular positioned in her favorite reading chair near the corner window, seemed to be paying attention. She took a long swallow from her cup, then buried her nose in her paperback again.

Diedre brought Cissy the mocha as Rachelle hit the grinder. A hard whir roared through the room. In a soft tone, Diedre said, "Look, I'm really sorry. I didn't know about your mother, and believe me, I understand. My family"—she rolled her eyes—"they're the worst."

Not even close, Cissy thought as she signed the receipt and tucked it, as well as the card, back into her wallet. Deciding not to stay, Cissy headed outside. She pushed the heavy door open with her shoulder and stepped into the late-morning chill, nearly running into a man in a long, dark coat, a frustrated expression etched into his narrow, pissed-off face. He stepped around her, his briefcase hitting her on the thigh. She reacted, the lid came off her drink, and hot chocolate, coffee, and whipped cream sloshed all over her jacket.

"Hey!" she called, but he never turned around, just walked as if wherever he was going was more important than stopping long enough for a quick "Excuse me."

"Damn it all," she grumbled to herself. After picking up the now-dirty lid, she walked into the shop again.

"What a jerk," Rachelle said. "I saw what happened." She had already plucked a stack of napkins from behind the counter and handed them to Cissy.

"It's okay. I just need a new lid."

Rachelle offered, "I can refill the mocha." The line waiting for service was already stacking up, Diedre taking orders.

"I'm fine," Cissy told her as she wiped her hands and refitted her drink with a lid. Once again, she took a sip of the hot mocha and, more carefully this time, stepped onto the street.

After that, the walk to the car was uneventful, but as Cissy reached the Acura, she noticed the parking meter had expired. After everything else she'd gone through, a stupid parking ticket might just send her over the edge.

Fortunately, she'd lucked out. The meter reader hadn't been by, but, as she pulled out of the tight spot, she nearly hit the car in front of her, missing it by inches.

She drew in a couple of slow breaths, taking her time, searching for her own equilibrium. "Count your blessings," she told herself, whispering one of Gran's favorite sayings. She'd gotten no ticket. There was no fender bender.

But it was still morning.

God only knew what the rest of the day would bring.

Lost in thought, she drove down the hill. She stopped for a red light at a crosswalk near the park. As her engine idled, a brightly colored bus belched clouds of exhaust her way, the smelly smoke mingling with the bits of fog still trailing through the city.

Cissy waited, foot on the brake, fingers tapping the wheel.

Several pedestrians crossed in front of her. An old man walked his impossibly tiny dog, a young couple held hands, lost in their own world, a teenager on a skateboard with a stocking cap pulled down to frame his face rolled past, skating around a businessman in a long, dark coat.

Cissy snapped to attention.

She focused on the man in black.

Sure enough, it was the same creep who'd nearly knocked her down. As she contemplated blasting him with her horn, he turned to look straight at her. She froze. Had she seen him somewhere before, not just on the sidewalk in front of the coffee shop? He never stopped walking to the bus stop, but he stared at her long and hard with eyes that seemed to have no soul. And then, before he stepped onto the curb where the bus was waiting, he smiled. A cold, toothy grin that quietly promised they would meet again. Though no word was spoken, Cissy understood the silent message.

The bump on the sidewalk at Joltz had been no accident.

This appearance in front of her car had been planned.

She thought of the figure she'd seen just the night before staring at her bedroom window. At B.J.'s window.

Her heart jackhammered.

Her blood froze in her veins.

What the hell was this all about?

She needed to pull over and accost the man, right here, in broad daylight, with witnesses.

And what?

Accuse him of hitting her with his briefcase on purpose?

Of walking in a crosswalk and grinning evilly?

She, the daughter of Marla Cahill?

Impotently, she watched him disappear behind the idling bus, then heard the honk of an angry horn. The light had turned green, and the guy in the Range Rover behind her was in a hurry. "Get a life," she muttered, stepping on the gas, but as she drove through the intersection, she kept one eye on her rearview mirror, where fog was clouding her view and the bus bullied its way into traffic.

The man in the black coat with the frighteningly cold grin was gone. Like a scary-looking marionette yanked quickly off the stage by unseen hands, he'd vanished.

Chapter 8

Marla was sitting on the bed, propped up by pillows, a book on the night table, the television turned on, but muted, a rerun of some reality cop show casting shadows in the poorly lit room.

And she wasn't pleased.

Big, big surprise.

Nor had she gotten off her sorry ass and cleaned the upstairs, claiming that she might be "seen" by some nosy neighbor peeking through the blinds or windows.

What a crock!

Elyse had known dealing with Marla would be difficult, of course she'd known it! The woman was notorious for being self-serving and wanting to be treated like the princess she'd thought she'd been born to be. But she'd never been lazy before. And all during the planning of the escape, she'd done her part. Eagerly. Anxiously. Cleverly.

Now all her sly aggression had flown out the shuttered windows, replaced by idle ennui and sharp remarks. "I thought you'd be back earlier," she accused.

"I'm bored sick. And don't start in with that garbage about me going upstairs and cleaning toilets or sweeping floors. I've had enough of that."

Elyse bit her tongue. She didn't know how much more of the woman's complaining she could take. "After work I stopped by a couple of stores and bought you some things to wear, as a disguise."

"You really think I'd risk that?"

"Not right now, but soon, yeah." Elyse had carried two shopping bags down the rickety steps and behind the false wall to Marla's room. "Take a look." She felt a little zing of triumph as she pulled out the clothes, body padding and wig that would transform "Marla the Beautiful" into "Marla the Frump": old-lady shoes, support hose, and an ugly brown housedress that was voluminous enough to hide the fat suit she would wear beneath. The wig she'd found was short and neat, somewhere between platinum blond and gray.

Marla gazed at the items, repulsed. "You're kidding, right?"

Ignoring Marla's sarcasm, Elyse placed each item of clothing next to the other. "No, I'm not kidding. They're perfect! I found them all at the thrift store."

"I bet. You know, maybe I'll just stay in."

"You can't hide forever."

"I'm not hiding!" she snapped. "I'm just being careful. Can't you get that? I'm not going to wear any of those!" She sneered at the floral print in brown and gray. "God, it looks like you tried to find the ugliest clothes in the universe and succeeded!"

"I just tried to find you things that would make you blend in."

"Oh, right, like this is the pinnacle of haute couture in San Francisco this year! Everyone's wearing ugly prints and shoes that look like they came out of the sixties." She threw a look of scorn at the plain, flat loafers. "You're out of your mind."

"You're not going to be walking through the business district or having lunch at the Four Seasons," Elyse replied with forced patience. "You'll just be in the car, and we don't want anyone on the street who has seen your picture on TV to recognize you. I thought you'd want to get out."

Marla turned quiet.

Again.

She had the whole passive-aggressive act down to a science, and Elyse knew what this was all about. She'd altered the plan enough that Marla was still pouting. Punishing her. Giving her the silent treatment.

Elyse reached into her bag again, this time coming up with a sandwich from the deli just down the street from where she really lived. "You might like this: turkey, lite mayo, even some cranberries. Kinda like Thanksgiving." She took the wrapped sandwich out of the bag and left it on the night table along with a can of diet soda, a pickle and a small bag of chips.

"You know I like beef," Marla reminded her in that same cool soft voice that irritated the hell out of Elyse. The quieter Marla got, the stronger her words seemed to be. Oh, she was so sly, a master at the psychological game-playing.

"I just thought, after the hamburger, you might want something different." But maybe not. Marla's mini-fridge was stocked with salads and soups in cups that only required heating in the microwave. There were apples on top of the refrigerator and instant oatmeal along with the coffeemaker and special French roast blend that Marla had insisted upon, some kind of obscure coffee she'd had ten years earlier. Elyse had worked hard to find that stuff and had Marla even uttered one word of thanks? Of course not!

"Just try on the clothes and we'll go out in a week or so, once they're convinced that you're in Oregon or Washington. I've got a guy who agreed to drop off your prison clothes at a rest stop on I-5, somewhere around Roseburg. The cops will think you're heading north or making a run for the Canadian border. Either way, the heat will be off San Francisco."

For once, Marla looked relieved. "Good," she said, and actually showed some interest in the sandwich. "I don't try to be a bitch."

It just comes naturally, Elyse thought, but clenched her teeth and didn't let the words pass through her lips. "And I'll look for something else for you to wear."

"Do I have to be fat?"

Here we go with the demands.

"It will help. No one will expect you to have gained weight. It's just a disguise."

"I've never been heavy in my life."

"Exactly." *Time to experience new lows in self-esteem.*

Marla gave up a long-suffering sigh, but didn't argue.

"Look, we can start with your hair. Let me trim it a little," and to her surprise, Marla didn't argue. "Here, you can watch." She found the hand mirror that Marla always kept near her and handed it to the vain woman, forcing it into her tense fingers.

"I don't know . . ."

"Marla, please."

"Not too much," Marla warned.

"Just a trim . . . We can talk about color later." She found a pair of scissors and began snipping carefully at Marla's long, mahogany-colored tresses. She was careful with her scissors, clipping around the edges of Marla's hair and sneaking a few locks into her pocket. Fortunately, Marla was too busy gazing at herself to notice.

Only when Elyse pulled harder, as if her finger had gotten caught in a few hairs, pulling them out by the roots, did Marla look up sharply, her gaze finding Elyse's in the mirror. "Ouch!" she shrieked. "What're you trying to do? Scalp me?"

"Sorry. Mistake," Elyse lied.

"Well, for Christ's sake, be careful!" Marla hissed in a low, angry whisper as she shot Elyse a baleful look full of mistrust.

"I said I was sorry, okay?" Elyse pretended to be wounded. "I'm just trying to help. See how nice this is going to look when I'm finished?"

"Fine." She eyed her reflection critically, and Elyse held her breath. "So, tell me again about Eugenia," she finally said, calmer now, nearly smiling, in fact. It was almost as if the pampering had mollified her.

God, the woman had an ego! And a temper.

Elyse felt a little niggle of trepidation. Marla could be so deadly. Elyse had witnessed Marla's volatile mood swings with her own eyes. She reminded herself to watch her back. On the day that they'd made good on Marla's escape, she'd been elated. There had been an almost manic jubilation on Marla's part; her eyes had been as green and deep as the waters of San Francisco Bay, her smile absolutely infectious. No wonder men had fallen all over themselves to be with her. She was pushing fifty, but you'd never know it. She'd kept in shape in prison and even with minimal makeup she was beautiful. She'd let her hair blow free on the day of the escape, rolling down the window of the car that they'd picked up at a rest stop, drinking in the fresh, damp air despite the cold and fog that had socked in the entire Bay Area.

But now, of course, some of that euphoria had worn off. The gleam of triumph that had been so evident when Marla had slipped away from the prison in a delivery van had disappeared. She was paranoid. Hiding behind double locks in a dark basement, the jubilation having dissipated to become something akin to depression . . . silent, moody, dark depression. Sometimes Elyse had to work hard to scare up a smile, or even a word, from the woman.

Not for the first time Elyse wondered if the risk of springing Marla had been a mistake.

Well, there was no going back.

It was all part of the plan, all for the money.

Remember the money.

They had planned that she'd hide out here, and the escape had been years in the making. Years! Elyse couldn't blow it now. Wouldn't.

Marla had promised to bide her time, change her appearance, then leave once some of the fervor of the hunt had died down. But now Elyse sensed she wanted to speed things up, that she was getting impatient.

"I can't stand it here," Marla complained.

"I know, I know, but now we don't have a choice. Remember, we talked this over."

"But I didn't know it would be so dark, so . . . alone."

"I told you that you can go upstairs. Just keep the curtains drawn. You should move around more, get your blood pumping."

"As if I could!" Marla said with a sneer. "Don't you get it? Someone might see me. I may as well be back in prison!"

"No way," Elyse argued. She couldn't have Marla thinking that! Not after all the risks she'd taken.

Marla seemed somewhat mollified. "Fine. You were telling me about how you killed the dried-up old prune."

"Your mother-in-law," Elyse reminded her gently.

"Eugenia." Marla made a moue of distaste at the memories of her mother-in-law. "So go on, tell me, did she recognize you?"

"Oh, yeah. It was great," Elyse admitted, rubbing in her victory a bit, still feeling the thrill running through her veins. "She didn't even see it coming." Smiling down at Marla, Elyse said, "I wish you could have been there to see it, the way she flew over the railing, sailing and screaming and landing on the floor with such an incredible *crack*. It was so loud, it was like *I* could feel it in my body. Then it was silent, and she was staring up at me vacantly. I don't even know if she was dead yet, but I picked up that stupid little dog so that the last image she had was of me stroking it."

"Did you kill it too?"

"The dog?" Elyse recoiled as if she'd just encountered a horrid smell. "Of course not. I left it there, locked in a cupboard so it wouldn't follow me, but the police or someone would find it."

"I hate that dog," Marla said.

"You hate everything."

"I *liked* being a Cahill," she said with sudden longing. "It was even better than being an Amhurst, let me tell you."

"If you say so." Elyse checked her watch. "Look, I can't stay. I've got to keep up appearances, you know. But I'll be back soon, when it's safe."

"It'll never be safe," Marla said.

"You don't know that."

"Sure I do." She was nasty again. Angry. Pouting.

More trouble than she's worth. . . . But that wasn't true. Marla was worth a bundle . . . a damned fortune. If they played their cards right. And Elyse intended to. Along with a stacked deck, she had an ace up her sleeve. One Marla wasn't privy to.

"Good-bye, Marla," she said, but the other woman wouldn't so much as look at her. In the blink of an eye, Marla had gone back into her morose pouting. God, her act was already getting old.

Too bad.

Elyse knew what she had to do.

She pushed the fake wall back into place and wound

her way through the dank basement, then up the old stairs. She had to return to their original plan. It was the only way to keep Marla satisfied.

Well, so be it, she thought, locking the house with her key and hurrying to the Taurus.

Marla wanted her brother Rory dead.

So Elyse would take care of it.

The retard was history.

Cissy's concentration was shot. She couldn't outline the article she'd planned to write—the same article that had sat on her computer for weeks was still a bunch of jumbled notes. Four weeks earlier she'd interviewed a new, young candidate for mayor, but it was the same week Cissy had found out about Larissa and kicked Jack out. Not long after that, when she'd tried to pull her notes together, her psycho mother had escaped from prison. Now her grandmother had fallen to her death— or been murdered—and she was dealing with grief and guilt. Maybe the article wasn't meant to be written.

Cissy sighed. Between the house phone and her cell, she must've fielded over twenty phone calls: all short, one-sided conversations about her grandmother. Family members, including her father's cousin Cherise, whom she could not stand, had phoned. People who knew her grandmother from her civic work, or friends of Eugenia who had played cards or taken trips with her, even some woman from Sacramento who claimed to have roomed with Gran at Vassar had called. Cissy's e-mail in-box was filled with inquiries and expressions of sympathy. Heather, a friend from her sorority at USC; Gwen, her personal trainer; and Tracy, who had ridden horses with her when they were in grade and high school—all of them had e-mailed or sent text messages to her phone. Of course, there was the press too:

reporters fishing for some information about Gran's death, and, if they got the chance, they asked about Marla as well. As promised, Deborah had e-mailed her the names of the Cahill attorneys and accountant, so Cissy was dealing with legal matters and tax issues as well. It was getting so overwhelming, she'd started screening her calls, avoiding those she didn't want to take and just leaving them in her voice-mail box to access later. Ditto for the e-mail.

It was a flippin' nightmare.

And things were only getting worse as the afternoon wore on. Cissy was working in her office, a little niche by the exercise room, while Tanya was supposed to be taking B.J. for a stroll before it got dark. The sun, setting low, was peeking from behind a veil of clouds, out for the first time all day. For the next forty-five minutes, if they were lucky, there would be some light. Since Tanya hadn't gotten around to taking Beej out yet, Cissy decided it was time she and her son hit the streets. She clicked off the computer, nudged aside Coco, who had been sleeping at her feet, and stretched out of her chair. Snapping a rubber band around her ponytail, she then changed into jogging pants, finding her favorite running shoes in the back of her closet. After snagging a hooded sweatshirt for herself, she headed to B.J.'s room and grabbed his little down coat and stocking cap, another piece of headwear he detested.

"Tanya, I'll take Beej out, I need the exercise," she said as she hurried downstairs.

The front door opened as she reached the bottom step, and a gust of cold air and her estranged husband swept inside. Cissy instantly put on the brakes and tried not to notice that it seemed right for him to walk into the house after a day of work. Just like he had every weekday throughout their ill-fated marriage. She ignored any sense of nostalgia as he glanced up at her.

"Did you forget you don't live here anymore?" She shot Tanya a don't-interrupt-me look when she saw an explanation or protest of some kind forming on the nanny's lips.

"What?" he asked, in the cocksure way of his that irritated the hell out of her as he slid his arms out of the sleeves of his overcoat. "No martini waiting for me? No wife in a cute little French maid outfit?"

"Oh, excuse me. Let me run upstairs and change," she said with an edge.

He laughed, and Cissy, who'd tried for sarcasm, found herself melting a bit. Damn the man.

Coco, slower than she once was, hopped awkwardly downstairs. Realizing there was an interloper in the house, she began to bark wildly at Jack in her high-pitched yip, growling and snarling at him as if he were a murderous intruder. Tanya, uncertain which way to jump, said quickly, "I'll go get B.J.," then hurried off to the living room.

Too late. Beej, who had been playing with a toy that made animal noises upon pressing a button, had already realized his father was home. He'd just hit the cow button, and the room echoed with a loud "Mmm-mooooo" as he, squealing in delight, let out the predictable "Dad-dee home!" Like a rocket, he was on his little feet and scrambling to greet his father with uplifted arms.

"Hey, big guy! Glad to see you're over your bad mood." Jack hooked his coat over the curled iron arm of the hall tree, then grabbed his eager son and lifted him into the air. An eruption of giggles and "More! More! I want more!" came flying out along with wiggling legs and arms.

The dog was in a froth.

"Coco, hush!" Cissy snapped.

The terrier didn't listen. As Cissy stepped into the

foyer, the little beast hid behind her legs and kept up the racket.

"Miserable little rat-dog," Tanya muttered under her breath as she gathered up her things. "I guess B.J.'s in good hands already, so I'd better go." She found her raincoat and umbrella at the hall tree and with one eye on the furious little white terrier said reluctantly, "I'll be back tomorrow."

"See you then," Cissy said, though she was already mentally replacing Tanya with someone who was nonallergic and animal-friendly.

Jack and B.J. had moved into the living room and were playing with the animal-sounds toy together. A cacophony of braying, growling, roaring, bleating, and peeping was erupting, one noise after the other, as if Noah had just dumped the contents of his ark in their living room. "Hey, how about this one," Jack said, seated cross-legged on the floor with his son on his lap. He pressed a button and a loud "woof, woof, woof" echoed through the rooms.

"Doggy!" Beej said. "Like Coco!"

"Just like Coco," Jack agreed, though the recorded dog bark sounded more like an eighty-pound German Shepherd than a tiny terrier mix.

It was utter chaos, and Cissy, filled with conflicting emotions, detached herself a bit. Through the window, and in the gathering dusk, she watched Tanya climb into her battered Subaru, light a cigarette, then take off, red taillights disappearing around a corner farther down the street.

Yeah, she was overdue for a new guardian for her child.

A lion's roar reverberated through the house. "Does that thing have a volume control?" she asked.

"We like it loud."

Cissy walked to a side chair and dropped into it. B.J. was delighted to be with his father. Of course. Was he more "into" Jack since he'd moved out? Had her son already missed his father? Guilt gnawed a big hole in her heart. She hated being the bad guy, and if she looked at it from her eighteen-month-old's eyes, she was. She'd kicked Dad-dee out.

"So," she said when the roar had died down for a second, "you came back here for a reason?"

As an elephant trumpeted, Jack said, "I wanted to see that you and B.J. were okay."

"We are." She clasped her hands between her knees and noticed that it was already getting dark. Too late for the stroller. "But even if you were coming here after work, you're early. It's not even five."

"Well, I do have an ulterior motive."

"This should be good."

"Actually, it is." He looked up at her, his expression serious. "I didn't think you'd want to face my family alone."

"What do you mean?"

"They want to stop by and offer their support. All of them. Dad, J.J., and Jannelle."

"You're kidding!" She couldn't imagine facing any members of the Five Jays, as they referred to themselves, based on their same first initials. "No way. I don't want any company."

"I told them that, but you know how Dad is when he gets an idea in his head."

"Then stand up to him, Jack. Man up! I do *not* want to deal with any member of your family, much less all of . . . oh damn!" She saw headlights flash against the living room window. "Too late," she said as a snake hissed from Beej's favorite toy. She shot her husband a look that said it all, the this-is-your-mistake-so-now-fix-it glare, as she carried Coco into the dining area and placed her into her kennel. "This won't be for long," she promised the dog, mentally crossing her fingers.

Holding B.J., Jack opened the door before his father could hit the doorbell. As Jack had said, both Jannelle, looking pissed off, and J.J.—Jon Junior, his I'm-cool-to-be-here expression neatly in place—were with Jonathan. They were all good looking, some Scandinavian ancestor having handed out tall bodies, blond hair, high cheekbones, and varying shades of blue eyes.

"Oh, honey," Jack's father greeted Cissy, arms outstretched. He crushed her to him.

"I'm okay," Cissy said, barely able to breathe.

Jonathan's face was remarkably unlined for someone near sixty, and he still had lots of hair, an ash blond color just beginning to gray. He was fit, tanned, and could pass for fifteen years younger than he was, which of course he loved. Cissy guessed that only the ages of his children prevented him from stretching the truth about the years.

"I'm so sorry for your loss," he said, releasing her, his eyebrows pulled together, sadness evident in those Nordic eyes.

"It's a bummer," J.J. said.

Jannelle rolled her eyes at her brother's phraseology. "Dad thought we should come by and, you know, offer support, bond as a family, all that . . . sensitive bullshit." She plopped into a side chair and crossed her long legs.

"Don't go there," Jack warned.

"Jannie, come on." Their father was obviously irritated. To Cissy, he said, "What Jannelle said is essentially right, without the editorial comments. I know this is tough . . . so here we are."

"One big happy family," Jannelle chimed in. "Hey, when *is* that divorce final?"

"Enough!" The lines around Jonathan's mouth showed white in irritation.

"I *knew* this was a mistake," J.J. muttered, shoving a hand through hair that was long enough to curl over the collar of his leather jacket. He always dressed in what Cissy thought of as casual cool—trendy, but never too upscale. She really didn't know him, didn't much want to; another Holt male to avoid. Then she caught a glimpse of Jannelle rolling her eyes again. So, okay, she needed to avoid all Holts, regardless of gender.

"There's Grandpa's boy!" Jonathan motioned for Jack to step a little closer so he could get closer to his grandson. "How're you, Bryan Jack?" he asked, but when he attempted to pry Beej from Jack's arms, their son, independent kid that he was, said loud and clear, "No, Poppa!"

"Ugh," Jannelle muttered under her breath.

J.J., looking uncomfortable, sat on the ottoman and stared at the nonexistent fire.

Yeah, this was a great idea, Cissy thought wearily. But she was stuck with it. "So, does anyone want anything? Coffee? A beer?" She glanced at Jack for help.

"Actually, we thought we'd take you out to dinner. Something simple. How about a place that deals with kids?"

"Are you talking McDonald's?" Jannelle asked, horrified. "Really, Dad, I'll pass." She looked pointedly at the watch glittering around her wrist.

Though she wanted to tell them all to just get out and leave her alone, Cissy bit back the urge, saying instead, "You know, that's really nice, but I thought Beej and I, we'd just kind of camp out here tonight." She forced a smile at Jonathan, who had been so instrumental in her hooking up with Jack in the first place. "Thanks."

"Good enough for me." Jannelle shot to her feet.

"Me too." J.J. wasn't one for gooey family togetherness.

The older man was disappointed. "Come on now, we're all here anyway."

"It's okay, Dad." Jack walked to the window. "Jannelle, that's your Mercedes. So, you drove?"

"Now look who's the detective."

"Jesus, Jannelle, stuff it," J.J. said, irked.

"Why don't you and J.J. take off? If Dad wants to stay, I'll drive him home in a while."

"Great idea!" Jannelle slung the strap of her bag over her shoulder, then made fast tracks, her high heels clicking over the hardwood as if she were afraid someone would change his mind. J.J., who so recently wanted to shut her up, was only one step behind, zipping his jacket and muttering phrases like "Hang in there. Things'll get better. At least she didn't suffer." The usual platitudes that Cissy already found tiresome. Jannelle said only, "Let me know about the funeral," and was out the door. A few seconds later a powerful engine sparked to life, and the Mercedes reversed, then tore down the street.

"I'm sorry," Jonathan said, and B.J., as if sensing his grandfather's sadness, finally allowed the older man to extract him from his father's arms.

"Hi, Poppa," he said and patted the older man on his shoulder.

"Well, hi, yourself. So, the old man's okay, huh?"

Cissy saw Jack's father's tenderness where B.J. was concerned and felt her heart warm a bit. She tried to forgive him the ancient history of cheating on his wife, though she couldn't help thinking, as she walked into the dining area, if Jonathan had remained faithful, maybe Jack wouldn't have crossed that same line.

Jack's inability to stay faithful is Jack's problem. Not his father's. Not yours.

She let the little dog out of her kennel, and after a few sharp barks, Coco gave up the fight and hopped onto the chair Jannelle had so recently vacated.

"Why don't you stay here with Cissy and Beej, and I'll go get takeout," Jack suggested. "There's a great Thai place five minutes away." He glanced at his wife. "Okay with you?"

"Why not?" Cissy capitulated. "You know me. I just roll with the punches."

Jack snorted as he walked to the hall tree and snatched up his coat. "That's you, Little Miss Mellow."

Walking unnoticed into the assisted-living area of the care facility proved relatively easy. Elyse posed as a woman working with a local church group, and, wearing the same kind of disguise at which Marla had sneered, she'd visited the place enough during the past few weeks. There was a security code, of course, but it was simple enough to watch another visitor punch it in, then do the same thing herself. The front desk was usually manned by a woman who had duties that extended little beyond sitting in the same chair hour after hour. After five, the staff really thinned out as the office workers went home, and the phone system was switched to an answering service which networked with the adjacent brick building where the nursing-home patients required round-the-clock care and the staff was more vigilant.

The security cameras were no issue, and Elyse toddled slowly down the hall, saying "Hello" and "God bless you" to the few residents she met. She could feel her adrenaline spurt through her veins in anticipation.

This was it.

Her final visit to the retard.

Rory Amhurst. Marla's brother. A healthy child who as a toddler had been in a horrible car accident, run over by his own mother. The result had been permanent brain damage.

Surely Marla, who had been in the car with Rory

when her mother had dashed back into the house, leaving the car idling for just those few moments, hadn't known what would happen. Rory, a toddler, had screamed, and older Marla had unlatched him from his seat restraint, let him outside, and closed the car door. When their mother, Victoria, returned, she didn't notice the boy wasn't in the backseat. She jammed the car in reverse and hit the gas, running over her own child as he crouched behind the car, presumably to look at an ant or some other insect on the pavement. Marla, a child herself, couldn't have had any idea of the consequences of her actions that day. Right? Certainly she wasn't born evil. That was a fiction, wasn't it? Born evil?

Or was she?

Not that it mattered.

Now Marla wanted Rory dead.

And Elyse was her messenger.

Rory's room was at the end of the hallway. As Elyse entered, she found him sitting up, staring at the television where a rerun of *South Park* was playing.

"Hi, Rory," she said sweetly. "You remember me, don't you? Mrs. Smith?"

He nodded, grinning, his eyes vacant, his head still a little misshapen. It was too bad, Elyse thought as she pulled the batch of brownies she'd made from her oversized purse with gloved hands. "Do you mind if I turn up the television? My hearing, you know." She upped the volume to hide any sounds he might make, then grabbed a can of soda from her purse and, while he was watching television, added enough Valium to drop a racehorse.

She handed him the can. He smiled gratefully and drank it down.

Elyse felt a twinge of conscience as he swallowed. He really was an innocent and, as far as Elyse knew, had never hurt anyone.

But Marla had been insistent.

"That basket case has got to go, you understand me!" she'd said vehemently. "Do you know how much money it costs to keep him in that overpriced institution? All his physical therapy and speech therapy and God only knows what else. It's a wasted life. Wasted. It'll be a mercy killing. Who would want to live that way?"

"But he seems happy," Elyse had argued, and Marla had pinned her with those furious green eyes.

"Because he doesn't know any better."

"Then what does it hurt?"

"Are you going to do this, or do I have to?" Marla had snapped. "I will, you know. Without a second thought. He won't feel much pain. . . . Just give him the shellfish: disguise it in a brownie."

"Shellfish?"

"He's violently allergic. He'll go into anaphylactic shock, but the Valium should knock him out. Just cover the whole thing in lots of chocolate frosting. He'll eat it, trust me."

Elyse had been skeptical as she'd baked the batch, then tasted one. The shellfish taste was masked well enough. The brownies tasted "off," but not necessarily bad, and when slathered in goopy chocolate frosting were pretty decent.

"Here ya go, Rory," Elyse said, looking over her shoulder, hoping none of the aides accidentally wandered in. Rory had a remote-alert device, a call button he wore around his neck that, if pressed, would notify the staff that he needed help. She couldn't take a chance that he would use it. "Here, let's put that on the dresser. You wouldn't want to mess it up with all that chocolate."

He looked up at her with trusting eyes and bit into the brownie. Would it work? There should be enough crab oil and ground shrimp to start a seizure and cause his throat to swell. *If* he ingested it. But that didn't seem to be a problem. He ate one brownie and was reaching for another when it hit. He started convulsing, and Elyse hurriedly took his call button and put it in the bathroom. Then she carefully wrapped up the rest of the brownies and returned them to her purse. Fear and adrenaline zinged through her bloodstream. Her mind spun crazily as she realized how close she was to being found out, to being caught in the act of murder, to losing everything she'd worked so hard to achieve.

Rory, gulping and gasping, eyes rolling upward, exposing only whites, slid to the floor, his seizure wild. Elyse pushed his wheelchair and rolling table away from him so that his flailing arms and legs wouldn't strike the metal, banging and creating a racket louder than the strangled noises coming from his mouth. Again she adjusted the volume of the television upward. She stepped into the hall, closing the door behind her. Strolling slowly, she had to fight the urge to run like crazy. Instead she smiled casually at passing residents as she headed toward the double doors at reception. The corridor was so damn long! It seemed to have lengthened to the size of a football field while she was in Rory's little studio.

She passed by other rooms where elderly wheelchair-bound residents sat like automatons in front of televisions. A nurse spied her and smiled, and Elyse, behind her thick glasses and tinted contact lenses, smiled back and nodded. The fat suit was uncomfortable, the makeup making her sweat even more than her own sense of panic. It was all she could do to keep from looking over her shoulder. Crossing her fingers, she hoped the stupid floor nurse wasn't going to Rory's room.

At the main desk, an aide was arguing with a woman in a wheelchair who was refusing to return to her room. Elyse slipped by. The aide glanced up briefly, catching her eye before Elyse could toddle through the double doors to the vestibule. She punched in the code to open the exterior doors.

Nothing happened.

What?

She tried again, her heart racing, and this time, thankfully, a green light and buzzer told her she had fifteen
seconds to shove open the door.

Now to make good her escape.

Pulse pounding in her eardrums, she headed for her
car. Slowly. Painstakingly. As if fear weren't propelling
her to run.

Just outside the door Elyse clicked the remote to unlock the car, but she heard the sounds of panic forming
inside the building.

Running feet. Shouts.

They'd discovered Rory.

Too soon!

This was way too soon!

Fingers shaking, she ran to the car, pulling her purse
to her chest. In her haste, she dropped the key ring, and
it fell between the front seats.

Oh God.

It was too tight to get her hand through the crack.

Damn!

The keys were there—she just couldn't reach them.

She was trapped!

She couldn't go back inside. She had to flee. Now. As
soon as they revived Rory or called an ambulance . . . it
would be over. *Think, Elyse, think.* Heart pounding frantically, insides quivering, she tried to edge her hand down
through the tight crevice again and ended up scraping
her knuckles and breaking a nail. Somewhere in the
distance a siren wailed. Blood bloomed on the back of
her fingers, and her skin burned from the scrape.

She leaned over, the fat suit rubbing against the
steering wheel as she forced the passenger seat back
and scrabbled for the damned keys. Still, she couldn't
reach them.

Shit!

Desperate, she looked around for something, *anything*, to retrieve the key ring and spied a hanger on which the dress that she'd picked up at the thrift store had hung. Sweating like a pig, she snagged the hanger, crammed it between the seats, and, breathing rapidly, flipped her wrist, shooting the keys onto the floor mat of the passenger seat.

Thank God!

Quick as lightning, she snatched the ring up, jammed the key into the ignition, turned the switch. The engine fired, and she wasted no time throwing the car into reverse and backing up, then shoving the Taurus into drive.

Calm down. Don't do anything stupid. Don't burn rubber or drive too fast. Keep cool.

Fingers wet on the wheel, Elyse drove out through the main gates. She had to pull to one side as a screaming ambulance flew by. Oh God, they must've seen her. Someone would know. The nurse would put two and two together and call the police and . . .

Stop it! Just drive! Away. Out of the city. South toward San Mateo. Put some distance between you and the institution. Then, drive to a park-and-ride and trade out license plates. Find a Taurus with similar plates and make the switch. Then you can go home.

Calming a little, she glanced in her rearview. No one was following, no police cars with lights flashing, sirens *woo-woo-wooing*. No one passing even looked her way.

Slowly her heartbeat lessened its frantic tempo as she joined traffic on the Pacific Coast Highway.

She was safe.

If Rory wasn't dead already, he was as good as.

Marla would be pleased.

Maybe.

Chapter 9

"It's Rory Amhurst," Janet Quinn was saying from the other end of the connection, "Marla's brother. DOA at Bayside."

"What?" Paterno had been sitting in his recliner, beer in one hand, slab of takeout pizza in the other, when his cell had gone off. His eyes had been trained on his new flat-screen television, but his concentration on the basketball game stopped short with Quinn's announcement. "You're talking about the mentally disabled guy, right?"

"One and the same. Looks like someone left him with a lethal dose of chocolate. We won't know for certain until all the lab tests come in, but the staff doesn't know where the chocolate around his mouth came from. Probably a visitor, an older woman, one Mrs. Mary Smith. A nurse saw her in the hallway a few minutes before Rory was discovered."

"Marla in disguise?"

"Highly possible. You wanna meet me at Bayside and we'll go to the assisted-care center together? There's already a unit there, and they've cordoned off Rory Amhurst's room."

"I'm on my way." Paterno left his pizza, beer, and remote on the table, then found his service weapon, coat, and keys. His notepad and recorder were already in the pockets of his overcoat.

Would Marla kill a man who was mentally disabled?

She'd certainly been involved in killings before.

Corpse number two this week, compliments of Marla Amhurst Cahill.

He locked the door to his condo, the one-bedroom unit he'd bought after his wife died, then took the stairs two flights down to the garage. He didn't much like the place, but he was rarely here, so he figured it didn't matter much. His and his wife's marriage had been rocky, her unhappiness stemming from the hours he'd spent at work, and they'd separated time and again, but, damn, he still missed her.

He shouldered open the door to the garage that was located underground. His Caddy was wedged into a tight spot between a Ford Focus and a Toyota, and he could barely get the door open, but he slid inside, turned on the ignition, and carefully backed out of his assigned spot. The Cadillac was just too big for newer parking spaces, but he couldn't sell it, even though getting parts for it was growing tougher every year.

He drove slowly up a narrow ramp that wound up to the street. Waiting for the electronic garage door to open slowly, its warning system beeping loudly to make pedestrians aware that he was coming through, he thought about Marla. Obviously she was still in the area. Otherwise the body count of people she knew wouldn't be going up.

And someone had to be helping her. Hiding her out. But who? He'd checked everyone she'd known on the outside and talked with her cell mates in that country club of a prison. No one purported to know anything.

But someone did. Either someone was lying, or he'd missed a person close to her, close enough to harbor her and help her commit murder, someone with his or her own agenda. Someone who would benefit by Marla's freedom and the resulting deaths.

Who?

The gate swung open, and Paterno eased the big car's nose outside. Then, carefully, he rolled across the sidewalk, waited for the light a block down the street to change, and wended into the ever-heavy traffic of this section of the city.

It took him nearly half an hour to reach Bayside, and he had a helluva time finding a parking space, but eventually he was walking through the hallway and into the ER, where he caught up with Quinn and the emergency-room doctor, who explained about anaphylactic shock. Again he heard how it would take some time for the blood work to come back, and, as he looked down at the peaceful face of Rory Amhurst, the dead green eyes, still-thick brown hair, heavy beard shadow, and skull that wasn't quite evenly shaped, Paterno felt rage. Deep-seated and hot. Marla was behind this, he knew it, and her brother would still be alive today if she hadn't escaped. The system had failed Rory. Big time.

"Send everything you get on this guy to us," he instructed the ER doc, who looked as if he wasn't yet thirty. "Then we'll want a full autopsy."

"I already called the ME's office," Quinn said.

"Good. Let's go to the care facility. I'll drive."

Fifteen minutes later they arrived at Harborside Assisted Living Center, which wasn't near any harbor, but, Paterno supposed, you might get a glimpse of the bay from the roof, if you looked down a street, through a series of buildings. But then again, maybe not.

Rory Amhurst's room was small, roped off by crime-scene tape, and Paterno had to weave through residents with wheelchairs, scooters, or walkers as he made his way down the hallway.

"This has never happened before, not at Harborside," the director of the facility, Anne Baldwin, insisted as she walked with him. Paterno tried to ignore the smell of the institution—cleaning solvent, urine, and the remnants of some meat that had been served for dinner. Mixed in with the depressing odors was the feeling of overall malaise and sadness, despite the cheery, yellow-painted walls and the smiles of the staff.

Anne was thin and direct. Her blond hair was frizzy, her glasses as skinny as she was, and she wore a prim pink sweater and pressed black slacks. "I just can't imagine who would want to hurt Rory. He was such a sweet man, a favorite with the caretakers and staff."

Paterno held his tongue about Marla. "I heard he had a visitor last night."

"Mary Smith, yes. She's from a local church and visits fairly often."

"When did the visits start?" he asked, since Marla had been on the loose less than a week.

"A month, maybe six weeks ago."

That stopped him short, and he looked directly at her. "You're sure?"

She nodded so fast, he thought her glasses might fall off. "It was in December, the holiday season . . . sometime between Thanksgiving and Christmas." Her forehead puckered above the bridge of her long, straight nose. "I remember she commented on the decorations the first time I met her. Said she liked our light display."

So Mary Smith was *not* Marla Cahill, as Marla had still been locked up at that time. "Can you describe her for us?"

"Oh, yes. She was, oh, five six or seven, I think, heavy, in her late fifties, probably. She wore big glasses, the kind that turn dark with the sun."

"Hair color?"

"Dishwater blond, going gray. Cut short."

"Does the facility here have any cameras?"

She shook her head. "No. We don't believe in invading the residents' privacy."

"But in the parking lot, right? Or the grounds?"

She was shaking her head some more. "Really, Detective, you have to believe me, we just don't have any need of them. There is no crime here—" She heard herself and sighed. "Well, I guess that's all changed now, hasn't it?"

"Maybe someone had a cell phone, the kind that takes pictures? Or a camera?" Quinn asked.

Anne let out a short, amused laugh. "The residents aren't exactly high-tech, and the staff, I don't think so. But I'll ask, send a memo."

"Would you mind talking to a police artist?"

"Not at all. If it will help, of course!"

They'd reached Rory's room, and one look inside was enough to silence Paterno for long moments. A single dresser with a television on top, a twin bed, wheelchair, night table, and movable bed table were the extent of Rory Amhurst's furnishings. There wasn't even a personal picture on the wall, almost as if the man had no family or friends.

So much for being an Amhurst.

Crime techs were already dusting for prints, collecting evidence, and taking pictures of the place, but Paterno was willing to bet dollars to doughnuts that they'd come up with diddly-squat. "I'd like to see his records."

"You know that's a breach of patient rights."

"I'll get a warrant."

Anne nodded. "And when you do, I'll hand everything over. As much as I want to help you, Detective Paterno, I have to go by the book on this. It's a matter of liability."

He'd expected no better. "We'll need to notify next of kin."

"That might be difficult," she admitted. "Marla Cahill is listed as his closest relative."

I got away with it!
As she drove into the city, Elyse couldn't believe her good luck. She glanced at the other drivers, all caught up in their own private worlds, their own little problems, never once knowing that she was beside them—or that the frumpy woman in the nondescript car was a murderess, a genius, damned near infallible.

Elyse was so convinced she needn't worry that she hadn't bothered switching license plates after all. It would just be her luck that some anal jerk would be hanging around, watching, wondering what she was doing. The kind that would report the anomaly and send the police screaming her way. No, this time it was safer to keep things status quo.

But, oh God, what a high!

Yanking off the itchy wig, she rolled down the windows, inhaling salty-fresh air mingled with exhaust as she ripped down the freeway.

A part of her, that stubborn egotistical part, considered driving back to tell Marla and crow about her feat, but Elyse decided to wait. Marla was such a downer, and Elyse wanted to celebrate. She'd driven around the south side of the bay and stopped at a minimart where she changed her clothes quickly and tore off the padding around her neck, spitting out the stuffing in her mouth. Now, after wiping off the wig glue, she stripped out of the rest of her hated Mary Smith disguise.

Once again she was Elyse, her alter ego. She gassed up the car and made certain again that she wasn't being followed as she drove the last few miles to her townhouse, pulling into her garage. Relieved, she plotted out the next steps. She planned to leave pieces of her fat suit in dumpsters all over other parts of the city. She would roll up the wig and glasses, put them in a sack, and toss the bag into a garbage bin behind a restaurant in Oakland. She'd leave the dress and shoes anonymously at a thrift-shop collection site in San Jose. Eventually there would be nothing to link her to the nefarious and murderous Mrs. Smith. She'd even hoist her fake set of rings into the bay for good luck.

Adios, Mary!

Grinning to herself, Elyse hurried upstairs to her bathroom, needing to wash the remnants away. She stepped into the shower and felt the hot needles of water ease the tension from her muscles as it washed the thick makeup from her face. She was thankful that she'd never have to return to Harborside Assisted Living ever again. The place was so depressing. How did the retard stand it?

Besides, she had others who would meet a similar fate as had Rory; others she was more interested in seeing suffer. First and foremost was Cissy, that miserable, spoiled brat. What a loser! Elyse couldn't wait to confront the bitch and make her understand just how useless and stupid she was.

But tonight she wanted to celebrate, so she would avoid crossing the bay. Seeing Marla would only make her miserable. Tonight, she was going to have a little fun, and she wouldn't tell Marla about it, not ever. Elyse would meet the man she intended to marry and spend the rest of the night with him. Hot sex after a chilling killing. Oooh, she liked the sound of that.

Licking her lips, she thought about the evening ahead and was already fantasizing. Should she reveal to him what she'd done? Or wait?

She thought it best to keep her secret to herself. He

might not understand, and she didn't want to risk losing him. But it would be hard not to brag about it. She wanted to boast and shout it to the world.

See how smart I am?
How clever?
I'm the one who sprang Marla Cahill.
I'm the one who killed her mother-in-law.
I'm the one who took care of the retard.
And I'm the one who bloody well will reap the rewards.
No matter what Marla thinks.

Detective Paterno stood on the porch outside her front door.

Cissy couldn't believe her bad luck as she caught a glimpse of him through the window. *What now?* she thought, bracing herself for another barrage of pointed, privacy-invading questions. The guy just never gave up. His face was long and drawn and reminded her of a bloodhound, but his personality was more like a pit bull with a bone.

Lucky me, she thought.

It was as if she couldn't get away from the man.

She waited for him to ring the doorbell, and Coco went nuts. Of course the dog had to bark madly, as if Cissy didn't already know that someone was on the other side of the door panels.

"Coco, hush!" Cissy commanded, and for once the little white scruff stopped yapping, cowering behind Cissy's ankles and peering around her legs as Cissy opened the door to find that Paterno wasn't alone. The mannish-looking woman detective, Janet Quinn, was with him, and Cissy could tell from their expressions they were not the bearers of good news.

Would it never end? Last night she'd been subjected to Jack's less-than-warm-and-fuzzy family, the night before Gran had been killed, and now . . . Oh God, what if something had happened to Jack?

Her knees threatened to buckle, and her heart lost a beat as she recognized the detectives' grim expressions for what they were.

"What?" she said, her voice hoarse.

"Can we come in?" Paterno asked. His tone was almost kind.

"I-uh-yes, of course." She backed up on rubbery legs, then somehow guided them into the living room. B.J. was asleep upstairs, thank God, but Jack . . . Where the hell was Jack? Now that he'd invaded her life again, she'd come to expect him. "What is it?"

"There's been another death."

Cissy inhaled sharply. She couldn't believe it. *Not Jack. Please, God, not Jack!* "Who?" she whispered.

"Please, sit down," Paterno said, and she dropped into a chair, letting the force of gravity pull her into the deep, soft cushions.

"Rory Amhurst was killed earlier tonight."

Cissy blinked. "Rory . . . ? Killed?"

"Murdered."

She felt cold inside. Numb. "My uncle in the care center." She was shaking her head. This was crazy. "There must be some mistake. No one would want to harm him. He's . . . well, he's not all there."

But both the detectives were nodding. "I know," Quinn said. "I'm sorry for your loss."

"But this is wrong. No—" She couldn't believe it. First Gran, now Rory?

"Do you have someone who can stay with you?"

"What?"

"You probably shouldn't be alone."

"No, I'll be fine." It was an automatic response, knee jerk, a lie, and everyone in the room knew it.

"Do you remember the last time you saw your uncle?"

"Uh . . . no . . . well, yeah, maybe around Christmas. I took B.J. to visit him. We brought him some Christmas cookies. I don't really know him, not well. All my life he's been at one home or another." The numbness was wearing off now, and her mind was starting to piece things together. "You think this has something to do with Marla's escape," she guessed and read a silent acknowledgment in Paterno's eyes. "You think she's behind his death? That's what you're saying."

"We don't really know what happened. Yet."

"Just like you think she killed Gran?"

"It's possible."

Cissy shoved the hair from her eyes and tried to think straight. "You're insinuating that she broke out of prison and now is on some kind of killing spree, annihilating members of her, of *my*, family?"

"We don't know what her involvement is at this point."

"But you think it's something."

Janet Quinn said, "Marla Amhurst Cahill is the link between Eugenia Cahill and Rory Amhurst. She's related to both of them. As are you."

Cissy felt a chill deep in her soul.

"As is your son," Paterno added, and she felt colder still. Fear and despair clawed at her. Her baby. Oh God, no one would ever want to hurt her baby. Surely not.

"Just a second," she said, her throat catching. Before anyone could say another word, she ran upstairs, taking them two at a time, hearing Coco on her heels. On the second floor, she tore down the hallway to Beej's room, pushing open the door that was already ajar. Heart thumping with fear, she hurried to the crib and found him fast asleep, his eyes closed, his tiny lips open as he breathed.

"Oh, Beej," she whispered. Her heart felt bruised. He was safe, and she would make certain he would always be safe no matter what it took. Her eyes burned, and Cissy fought back tears. Then she checked both of the windows in his room to see that they were latched and double-locked.

She couldn't think about losing B.J., about his life being in jeopardy. Feeling unsteady, she splashed cold water over her face in the bathroom before returning downstairs. "I'm sorry," she said to the two detectives as she returned to the living room where they sat unmoving, waiting. "You scared me so much I had to make sure Beej was all right."

"We understand." Did they? She doubted it, but she just listened while they explained they weren't certain of the details of her uncle's death, but it looked like he'd been poisoned. They would know more once the tox screens and other lab work and autopsy were performed.

Cissy felt her insides quiver.

Of course they were doing the same with her grandmother's remains, but they promised to release the bodies as soon as possible because they knew she had to make funeral arrangements. They asked her to stop by the station to look over a computer-generated sketch of the assailant, as several people at Harborside had seen her.

"Her?" Cissy repeated.

"Yes, a woman. In her sixties, maybe even seventies."

"That doesn't make any sense."

"She could have been disguised; in fact, we suspect she was," Paterno said.

"Does she have a name?"

"Mary Smith. Claims she was from a local church, and, of course, the church in question has four Mary

Smiths, and one Mary Smythe, in their congregation. We're checking them all out, but figure the name is an alias."

"You think it's Marla," Cissy stated flatly.

Quinn shook her head. "This Mary Smith has been visiting Rory since before your mother escaped. So, no, it wasn't Marla."

Paterno said, "Unless she started impersonating the real Mary Smith."

"But why?" Cissy said. "My uncle could hurt no one."

"We're working on that too." Paterno stood. "Is there anyone who can stay with you?"

"Believe me, I'm fine."

"Your husband's not home?"

"No," she said, and smiled. "Not yet." Why go into it? She'd consider telling them the true state of her relationship with Jack when she went to the station, looking at the picture of the suspect, whoever Mary Smith was.

After escorting the detectives to the door, Cissy closed and locked it behind her, throwing the deadbolt and punching in the lock on the knob. She thought of the figure she'd seen outside her house and the guy who'd bumped into her outside the coffee shop. Were they related to all this or not? Little goose bumps raised on the back of her arms, and she hurried upstairs again, walking directly to B.J.'s room. He was inside, of course. Just like earlier. He hadn't been snatched away in the last thirty minutes.

Nonetheless, she adjusted his blanket around him and sent up a silent prayer for his safety. Downstairs, Coco growled, and for the first time since the dog had come to live with her, Cissy decided it might not be such a bad thing to have a furry little house alarm always on guard.

"Sleep tight," she said and couldn't help but wish

Jack were with them. It would be comforting, knowing he was here to protect them.

Even if he was a lying, cheating son of a bitch.

Bayside Hospital
San Francisco, California
Room 316
Friday, February 13
NOW

Oh God, I'm going to die. The hospital staff doesn't know I'm alive. This is so wrong. So damned wrong.

I'm so frustrated! With all my might I try and fail to move any part of my body—an eyelid, an eyebrow, a finger, my lips—but my muscles are frozen, useless. As hard as I try, I can't do anything!

Please, God, let them understand that I'm awake, I can hear them. Don't let them kill me. . . . Please . . . It's a miracle they've kept me on life support, I know that. But now they're talking about discontinuing it. At any second they could pull the plug and not give me the time to prove to them that I'm awake, I'm alive, and I have so much to tell!

How can I make them understand? If only I'd had a real mother, one who embraced me, one who was not so cold, always unavailable. Everything, it seems, was more important than her daughter. Her parties. Her "women's retreats." Her charity work. Everything! She acted like she wanted me, but it was just that—an act. The truth of the matter is, I was an inconvenience, something to be kept in a drawer until she needed me, like one of her precious pieces of jewelry.

And so I'm alone.

Again.

As always.

The nurses have given up hope, and the doctor is convinced I'll never wake up. Here he comes now. With his low voice, bright light that he shines in my eyes, cold stethoscope that he puts on my chest. Can't my damned body please react so that he can understand? If only I could hold my breath. Or freak out enough to elevate my heart rate or anything!

"Condition unchanged," he says.

*No way! My condition has changed. Listen to me, you old fool—I'M ALIVE. **ALIVE!***

If only I could scream or even whisper!

Surely they can't make the mistake of thinking I won't completely wake up. Yes, I've dozed; yes, I've had only a few moments of lucidity; and yes, I can't seem to communicate with anyone, but please, please give me a chance. It's not *hopeless.*

"I don't know how much longer we can keep her like this," the doctor says. "I've consulted all the specialists in the area. No one has any hope."

But they're wrong! Can't you see that?

Oh, sweet Jesus, if I just had more time!

If only I had one more opportunity to tell Jack that I forgive him, that I love him, that I was wrong . . . so wrong. I remember what happened . . . every little detail . . .

Chapter 10

A funeral should never be a media circus.

There should be a rule about that somewhere.

But Eugenia Haversmith Cahill's funeral ceremony and internment were nothing less than a three-ring circus for the press, Cissy thought angrily as she stood at her grandmother's grave. A stiff breeze blew in from the ocean, causing the ribbons on the standing floral sprays to snap and the roof of the small tent near the grave site to flutter, but the weather hadn't deterred the police or reporters from showing up.

Bastards! Cissy thought.

Grief-riddled, she watched as her grandmother's casket was lowered into the earth. She made a mental note that when she died, she wanted the ceremony to be quick and simple, as Rory's had been. Just a few family members, the preacher saying a couple of short verses, a prayer, a hymn, and that was it. Rory Amhurst had been interred without a lot of fuss.

But this was different.

The century-old church where Eugenia had been a member for fifty years had been filled to capacity, voices of bereaved members lifted in song and prayer. A long-winded pastor had read from the Bible, prayed, reflected on Eugenia's celebrated life, and her sudden, violent death when "God had called her home." Cissy had felt tears gather in the corners of her eyes during the ceremony and wished she were alone. Completely alone. Not standing in a sea of friends, relatives, neighbors, and strangers under the soaring ceiling of the very church in which her grandmother and grandfather had been married half a century earlier.

During the church service, Jack had been by her side, which she supposed was comforting, though it seemed such a lie, a fraudulent display of a marriage that was being ripped apart. He was with her now too, standing under a portable awning beneath a cold winter rain as Gran's casket settled into the wet dirt next to the burial plot of her husband, Samuel J. Cahill. Eugenia's name, birth date, and the words *Loving Mother* had already been etched into the marble—only her date of death still needed filling in.

Oh, Gran, Cissy thought miserably, guilty for every bad thought she'd held against her grandmother as a child, teenager, and adult. For all the times she'd wished her grandmother had butted out of her life. For her favoritism, at least early on, of her grandson. For her strict rules and discipline.

As wind chased the rain into the city, Cissy was seated. Jack, again, was on one side of her; her uncle Nick and his wife, along with her estranged brother, on the other. Jack's family and Eugenia's friends were scattered around the grave site, all half-hidden by umbrellas. At a distance were the police and the camera crew from one of the stations in town that had made the drive up to the cemetery overlooking the city and bay. The cops were clearly expecting Marla to show up. Several plainclothes detectives were mixed in with the crowd, and the media waited discreetly at the periphery. They wanted Marla: her mother, the notorious murderess and prison escapee.

Cissy swallowed hard. She couldn't wait for the ceremony to be over. She still had to get through the gathering at her house, where friends and family were invited to stop by and have something to eat or drink. Cissy had decided to host it at her house rather than at the big house on the hill. There was something too macabre about returning to the place where her grandmother had died and throwing a party, albeit a quiet one. She imagined Sara mentally calculating the value of the real estate, or one of her greedy relatives asking about the disposition of Gran's jewelry or furniture. No, it was better to return to her own house, where Tanya was watching Beej and Cissy could take some time, if she needed it, in the solace and solitude of her own bedroom.

The preacher asked them to stand, then led them in a final prayer. Jack grabbed Cissy's hand as images of her grandmother slid through her mind: Gran hosting charity events, Gran knitting while the television blared, Gran teaching her bridge and suffering through impossibly long board games, Gran buying Cissy her first horse, a palomino gelding they kept at the ranch, Gran delighted when Cissy's brother, James, was born.

Now, through her tears, Cissy glanced over at James. The kid was close to going to junior high. He was all arms and legs and geeky hair, still a boy, but already over five feet tall. Trying not to squirm in his seat, James looked uncomfortable and awkward in a dark suit, crisp white shirt, and tie, all probably purchased for the funeral. He slid a glance her way, and she managed to give him a smile. One side of his mouth lifted. Then, as if realizing how grim and serious the situation was, James turned his gaze back to the coffin.

When the last "amen" was whispered, Jack squeezed her hand, then released it. Cissy stepped forward and, in the drizzling rain, tossed a white rose onto her grandmother's coffin, said a silent good-bye, and turned toward the waiting limo. She wasn't going to stick around and watch the dirt being flung over the casket.

Her vision was a blur as she made a beeline for the waiting limo. She smiled or nodded at familiar faces, but she didn't stop to talk. There was time for that at the house. For now, she just wanted to get home, where her son was already waiting. She'd asked Rachelle of Joltz to cater the event, and Tanya was watching Beej, as Cissy had decided eighteen months was too young to attend a funeral. Nor had he been with her for the tiny ceremony for her uncle.

God, what a week. In the backseat of the limo, she kicked off her shoes and didn't argue about Jack joining her. For today she'd decided to call a truce and just try to get through the slated events.

"It was a nice service," Jack said as the driver pulled the black limousine away from the curb.

Cissy gave him a look as she unsnapped her small purse, found a small bottle of Ibuprofen, and popped a couple dry. "No platitudes, okay? I'm going to hear plenty the rest of the day."

He didn't argue, just glanced out the window. Cissy followed his gaze and saw a man seated on a backhoe, ready to fill in the grave with the big, rumbling machine after the guests had dispersed.

It all bothered her. The kind words, sympathetic cards, gorgeous bouquets—but it all boiled down to a dirt mover shoveling wet earth over a fancy coffin. She shuddered a little at the thought and reminded herself that it wasn't Gran's or Rory's body that was the important thing. Surely their souls were in "a better place," as the preacher had intoned.

She certainly hoped so.

Leaning her head back against the seat, she closed her eyes and prayed for strength to get through the next few hours. It had taken the police nearly a week to release the bodies, and then she'd worked with Deborah on the obituaries and funeral arrangements, also squeezing in time to meet with the lawyers, insurance agent, and accountant. The week had flown by in a series of appointments where she'd seen little of her son and more than she'd wanted to of Jack.

He'd made himself available, and she'd let him, almost falling into the trap of thinking they could work things out. Almost. They'd eaten takeout, talked over the funeral arrangements, and discussed everything in the world *but* their impending divorce. He'd watched Beej when she'd had meetings and Tanya wasn't available, had even taken his son out for a walk while she'd finished the damned story on the mayoral candidate. He'd also been there while the new furnace was installed and the old one removed. All the while, he'd helped her screen calls from sympathizers, well-wishers, or the merely curious. Together they'd watched the news, snapping it off whenever Marla's face was flashed on the screen or her name was mentioned.

Cissy hadn't asked the police what, if anything, they'd learned about the murders; she'd just been too busy and exhausted. But every night she double-checked each window and door latch, deadbolt, and safety lock in the house, sometimes three times, before she went to bed.

She wasn't being paranoid, she tried to convince herself. She was just being doubly careful.

Opening her eyes, she shot Jack a glance, and he sent her just the hint of a smile, not that cocksure, irreverent grin she had grown to love and hate, but a gentle curve of the lips that meant he planned to stand by her throughout the afternoon.

Her silly heart *ka-phlumphed* painfully, and she had to fight another burn of unshed tears. Why did she let the man get to her? She looked away, through the fogging windows to the city streets where traffic rolled through puddles on the pavement and the skyscrapers looked as if they could pierce the underbellies of the somber clouds hanging low in the heavens.

She felt cold and disembodied, as if all this hoopla and tragedy were happening to someone else.

But it's not, Cissy. This is your life.

Using her finger, she traced a small heart on the foggy window, then, surprised at herself, quickly erased it as the big car slid to a stop in front of her house.

"Brace yourself," Jack said. "It's showtime."

"That it is," she said and slid out of the limo, allowing Jack to tip the driver as she squared her shoulders and strode into the house she and Jack had purchased only a few years earlier.

Many of the guests who had elected not to visit the grave site were already milling around, and for the first time Cissy second-guessed her decision to make her home the gathering area. The rooms were already crowded, and the people who'd gone to the short service at the cemetery hadn't yet arrived. It was going to be tight in here. Eugenia's house on Mt. Sutro could have handled the mourners easily.

Still, maybe this cramped space, where everyone would be stuffed in elbow-to-elbow, might force people to leave earlier, which would be just fine.

Planting a smile on her face that felt as false as it was, Cissy inched through a sea of "I'm so sorry about your grandmother" and "If there's anything I can do, please call" and "Eugenia, what a force she was. I remember a time . . ."

By the time she'd wended her way from the living room to the dining area, she felt as if she'd just been squeezed through Bloomingdale's department store on the last weekend before Christmas.

Diedre and Rachelle were working in the kitchen, pulling out trays of hors d'oeuvres from the refrigerator, microwave, and oven before sliding them onto silver trays. While Beej was down for a nap, Tanya was hauling the new trays into the dining room and returning with empties while Rosa and Paloma mingled with the guests, offering wine, napkins, or food. Cookies, cakes, and pies were lined up on one counter. The goodies had been brought by the legions of women who heard there was a death in the family and instantly donned aprons and grabbed spatulas to whip up something for guests and company. The array was dazzling, everything from decorated chocolates bought at boutique candy stores to homemade apple pies and rich, towering cakes.

"Don't you know that you'll gain five pounds by just looking at those," a soft voice said to her.

Cissy turned to find Gwen, her personal trainer, shrugging out of a knee-length black cardigan sweater. Gwen had been instrumental in helping Cissy lose the extra weight she'd gained during pregnancy. Her hair was dark, layered, and shaggy; her toned body visible in a clingy black dress; her expression sober. "I haven't seen you in the gym in a while, but you look great. On second thought, maybe you should indulge in a piece of pie. You seem to have lost weight."

"A little. But I'm not hungry. Maybe later."

"So how're you doing?" Gwen's dark eyes were sympathetic.

"I'm surviving."

"It'll get better," Gwen said, then patted her on the shoulder. "Go and talk to your other guests. I'll catch up with you later."

"Thanks."

Gwen gave her a quick I'm-here-for-you hug, then, after grabbing a shrimp canape, she spotted Jack, who was standing near the table of pictures and awards that showcased Gran's life. She headed straight in his direction. While candles flickered at the shrine Cissy and Deborah Kropft had created so hastily this past week, Gwen struck up a conversation with Jack, her expression changing from serious to almost buoyant.

Did Jack even know Gwen? Cissy wondered. Cissy, on her own, had joined the gym where Gwen worked. But, from the way Gwen was talking animatedly to him, it sure seemed like they were acquainted.

Don't go there, Cissy warned herself. *You're divorcing him, remember? What do you care who he knows? Besides, it's Gran's funeral gathering. Pull yourself together.*

Still, she couldn't help being aware of Jack and Gwen as she spoke to several women from Gran's bridge group, all bright-eyed women over seventy who were genuinely sad to have lost a good friend and "ruthless" contract player.

Cissy moved through the crush of people who were either pouring themselves cups of coffee and tea from urns in the dining area or picking up glasses of wine set on a table in the nook. Deborah, who had arrived from the cemetery, had taken charge, making certain that the food and drinks were never lacking, grabbing coats that she handed to Lars as people entered. Windows steamed, glasses clinked, the smell of candles burning and coffee brewing filled the rooms, and the buzz of conversation was like white noise echoing in Cissy's head.

"Is Beej still sleeping?" she asked Tanya as the nanny passed her with an empty tray.

Tanya nodded, wisps of hair falling from the knot at the base of her skull. She looked flustered and a little frantic, and for once Cissy didn't blame her. "I checked on him a little bit ago. He just fell asleep when the first guests arrived. He was tired. He should be down for another hour or so."

"Good. And Coco?"

Tanya's expression changed to irritation. "In her kennel in your office." She had to raise her voice to be heard over the din as more guests were arriving and the noise level escalated. Each time the door opened, the candles flickered, but the cool air was a relief as the temperature in the house was climbing with the combined body heat and newly operational furnace.

Tanya began arranging a platter of tiny puff pastries filled with mushrooms while Diedre placed skewers of oriental chicken around a bowl of peanut sauce on yet another tray. All the while Rachelle stacked bite-sized tea sandwiches on the mirrored shelves of a three-tiered server.

Saying "Hello" and "Nice to see you again" and "Thanks for coming," Cissy found her way to the foot of the stairs, catching a glimpse of Jack as he gathered coats and umbrellas and purses. Carrying two leather jackets and a scarf, he followed her upstairs, adding the coats to the growing pile of outerwear on her bed.

"See anything you like?" he asked. "I bet we could make a fortune on eBay."

"I thought Lars was handling the coats."

"He couldn't keep up. Eugenia had a lot of friends."

"More than I even realized. A better idea would have been to hold this in the church hall," she said, "but it was booked for a wedding reception, and I didn't want to go up to Gran's place." She hadn't been back to the big house where her grandmother had died since the day after her death.

"We'll muddle through," Jack assured her. His gaze found hers, and it was so sincere, so caring, she almost believed him, believed there was a chance for them.

He's a player, Cissy. Just like his father. Identical to his brother. You know that. Don't be fooled again.

"I saw you talking to Gwen."

"Gwen Crandall? The trainer."

"My trainer."

"Yeah, your trainer."

"How do *you* know her?"

He gazed at her hard, as if he couldn't believe they were having this conversation, especially at this point in time. "I met her when I scouted several gyms for an article on exercise clubs in and around the city. Her club was featured. Don't you remember? We were comparing 'all-guys' boxing gyms to those women's circuit training franchises and to hotel athletic facilities and private clubs." He stopped, then said, "I hope you're not asking for the reasons I think you are."

"She's beautiful."

"Uh-huh. I know a number of beautiful women."

"Well . . ." She turned away, feeling slightly foolish. "We won't be married much longer."

"Oh hell!" He suddenly grabbed her. Just yanked her into his arms and kissed her so hard she couldn't breathe. She gasped and tried to push him away.

"Let go of me!"

"You really want me to?"

"Yes!"

She could feel the tears she'd fought all day well in her eyes, and she angrily dashed them away. Jack had the audacity to kiss her cheek and fold her into his arms. "Oh, Cissy," he sighed, his breath ruffling her hair. "Why do you try to be so damned tough? Why won't you let anyone get close, anyone love you?" She let out a little sob and hated herself for it. "Why don't you think you deserve it?"

Her fingers were curled over the lapels of his jacket, as if she were clinging onto him for dear life. Horrified, she released her grip. She looked up at him and shook her head. "You've got it all wrong, Jack. I know I deserve love. And I want it. From a husband who is faithful to me. That's the kind of love I want. The forever kind. I know we got married on the fly, in a rinky-dink ceremony at a chapel that made you wonder if the ceremony was even legal, but I meant those words I said. I meant every word of those vows, and I thought—hoped—you did too."

"I did. I do."

"Well, you have a helluva way of showing it!" she said, pulling away from him. The day was enough of an emotional roller coaster as it was; she didn't need to go through any more heart-wrenching scenes with her estranged husband.

"Cissy."

"No, Jack," she said emphatically. "Not now. Not today."

"Then for God's sake, let's declare a truce. Just for today. You don't accuse me of screwing everything that moves, and I won't try to convince you otherwise. What do you say?"

Cissy drew a breath. "Oh . . . I don't care."

"Oh, you do, Cissy. You care plenty. You just don't want to."

"Don't try to psychoanalyze me."

"Then don't try to find ways to hate me."

"I'm not trying to—"

"You've been building a case against me for over a month, and, just for the record, I did *not* sleep with Larissa. I came damned close, yeah, I admit it. But I didn't, and you know why?" he demanded. "Because I'm in love with you."

After that he strode away, leaving her trembling, fighting tears and wishing that she dared, even for a moment, to believe him.

Why not, Ciss? Why not give him another chance?

Trying to get a grip on herself, she walked to her baby's room, half-expecting Jack to return. But he didn't, and she felt disappointed as well as relieved.

Why won't you let anyone get close, anyone love you?

His words echoed through her brain. Is that what he really thought?

She stepped close to the wooden crib and found her son sleeping peacefully, his eyes closed to show off impossibly long eyelashes resting upon his rosy little cheeks.

Just looking at him, some of her sadness dissipated. She curled her fingers over the top railing and smiled down at her son. Whispering a soft "I love you," she finally walked out of the room, partially closing the door behind her. She was almost at the staircase when she heard something and turned, looking down the long corridor with the doors, all ajar, opening from it.

Her heart stuttered.

Had she imagined the sound?

You're just distraught. Expecting the worst.

She retraced her footsteps to check on Beej, whom she *knew* was fine; she'd been in his room seconds earlier. Of course he was still sleeping, his room as she'd left it.

How odd.

Unconvinced, she walked farther along the corridor and pushed open the door to the guest room. It was empty, the bed untouched. Across the hall was the exercise room and her little office, and inside, as Tanya had said, she found Coco inside the crate, a bowl of water next to her scruffy white body. The little dog thumped her tail and looked up expectantly through the mesh of the kennel's door. "You'll be fine," Cissy said and decided the terrier had been the source of the noise.

She turned into the bathroom and glanced at the mirror over the sink, cringing at the sight of her reflection. Red eyes, streaked mascara, flat and stringy rain-soaked hair. As quickly as possible, she executed a speedy makeup repair. With a wet cloth, she swiped away any trace of running mascara and tilted her head back as she added Visine to her eyes. Once some of the veins had disappeared in the whites of her eyes, she brushed on some waterproof mascara, then ran a tube of pink lip gloss over her lips and dusted her pale cheeks with a thin layer of blush. Finally, she rubbed a dab of hair gel through her bedraggled tresses. The result was somewhere between a 1980's grunge rocker and someone who just woke up from a restless sleep, but it would have to do.

The truth of the matter was everyone expected her to look like hell today. She only had to get through another couple of hours.

In the hallway she nearly ran into Lars carrying up a stack of what she hoped was faux fur coats. She side-stepped him then headed downstairs. Halfway down she spied Jack, grinning, holding a glass of wine and talking with a woman who stood with her back to the staircase. Instantly Cissy's neck muscles tightened. She would recognize that wavy auburn hair anywhere as belonging to Larissa White.

She felt the blood drain from her face as she walked down the remaining steps.

What in the world was Larissa doing here?

"Talk about brass balls," a voice said as Cissy reached the main floor. Turning, she spied her sister-in-law, Jannelle, sipping wine at the foot of the stairs. Jannelle too was observing the interaction between Jack and Larissa. "You might want to piss on your husband, you know, like a dog, to mark your territory."

"Last time I saw you, you made a crack about my pending divorce, so there'll be no territory marking," Cissy reminded her coolly. If anyone could give lessons in being an A-one bitch, it was her sister-in-law.

Jannelle lifted an eyebrow. "Touché. Guess I'd better extract my foot from my mouth and find another glass of wine."

"Do that," Cissy said, irritated. But since this *was* her house, and Jack *was* still her husband, she snagged a glass of wine for herself and walked up to Jack and Larissa, bold as brass.

Larissa took one look at Cissy, and the smile fell from her face. "I'm so sorry," she said while Cissy's guts churned. "You know I worked with your grandmother a lot at Cahill House, and she . . . she was such a great lady."

Cissy nodded.

"I just wanted to pay my respects."

"Really?"

Larissa looked uncertain at Cissy's cool tone. "Well, I'll see you later," she said to both of them, casting a last glance toward Jack.

Cissy took a long gulp of her Chardonnay, her teetotaling grandmother's drink of choice on the rare occasions when Gran actually broke down and had a sip of something alcoholic.

"I didn't know she was coming," Jack said.

"Odd, don't you think?"

"She did know Eugenia."

"That's not what it was about, Jack, and we both know it. Paying her respects." She snorted. "Larissa could have done that at the church. She came here to make a statement."

"About what?"

"You," she said and took another sip. "She's staking her claim."

"That's nonsense," he said, but watched as Larissa hurried upstairs to retrieve her coat.

"Don't think so." Cissy spied Dr. and Mrs. Yang heading her way and took advantage of the chance to break off the conversation that was quickly escalating into an argument.

Not here. Not now. Not in front of all these people.

Any heated discussion with Jack would just have to wait, but she was thankful to see Larissa stuff her arms into the sleeves of a long leather coat, wrap a scarf around her neck and walk to the front door.

Jack didn't seem to notice, not even when she paused to look over her shoulder as she searched for him. Instead, her gaze met Cissy's, and she didn't even bother to smile, wave, or say good-bye, just opened the door and stepped outside.

"Good riddance," Cissy said under her breath, not realizing that Sara had walked up to her.

"I can't believe she had the nerve to show up here. What was that all about?" Sara sipped from her drink and glanced toward the door. "I went through this twice, you know. Both my exes couldn't keep their hands off other women. But then none of those women had the guts to show up at my house." She tossed another look at the closed door. "A good thing too. If any one of them had, I would have killed her."

Chapter 11

"Let me guess, Marla didn't show up at the funeral," Quinn said when Paterno, after long hours at Eugenia Cahill's funeral and grave-site service, returned to the station.

"Doesn't look like it," Paterno grumbled. He'd spent two days doing surveillance at the funerals—yesterday Rory Amhurst's, a small, private affair for the family, and today the larger, grander event held at the Presbyterian church Eugenia had attended, followed by the interment at the cemetery. He'd attended all of the events. Of course, he hadn't really expected that Marla would show her face, but with that woman, who knew? He wasn't going to take the chance that she might appear and that he wouldn't be there to nab her. He scanned each crowd, searching for anyone who resembled her, or the composite sketch of Mary Smith. The artist had interviewed everyone at the Harborside Assisted Living Center and come up with a composite drawing as well as a computer-enhanced picture, but no one who had attended Eugenia's or Rory's services looked like the chubby woman in the print dress. Nor had any other Mary Smith who attended the church shown up.

An alias.

A disguise.

But not Marla.

Paterno walked to his desk and tried not to notice that his feet were cold from standing in the rain. He shook the water from his coat, hung it on the peg near his desk, then grabbed a cup of coffee and tried to connect Marla Cahill's escape to the killings. Who was her accomplice? One of the people he'd seen at the services?

The autopsy report on Eugenia Cahill confirmed that she'd had some Valium in her bloodstream, but she'd also been prescribed the drug.

Valium was also found in Rory Amhurst's veins, but he hadn't had a prescription. Traces of Valium were in the soda can left in his room, a soda can that had no fingerprints other than his own. The ME decided he had died from asphyxiation, the result of anaphylactic shock, a reaction to what he'd ingested. An examination of his stomach contents showed chocolate laced with some kind of seafood.

Paterno's bad stomach acted up just thinking about it. He reached into his drawer for an antacid and frowned. The two murders were different—the old lady pitched to her death, the handicapped man poisoned. But in both cases the killer knew where they would be, was brazen about killing them, had the murder planned. *Why not poison Eugenia?* he thought, picking up his pencil and tapping the eraser on the desk. Because the murderer had to get in and out fast and didn't know if she had any allergies that would kill her. Hence, whoever had iced Rory Amhurst had an intimate knowledge of him. Either a nurse or family member. And someone no one at the facility recognized.

He took a swallow of his coffee.

It had to be someone linked to Marla.

But who?

Who the hell was close enough to want to spring her, then help systematically kill people related to her? He thought of her daughter, but as sharp-tongued as Cissy Holt was, she didn't strike him as a killer.

Who stood to gain from the killings?

Once again Cissy Holt's name loomed front and center.

He couldn't scratch her from the list of potential suspects, but he would be surprised if she were the actual murderer.

But Marla Amhurst Cahill . . . She would be in the money, if she could ever retrieve it. That would prove to be quite a trick, considering she was a fugitive.

No, Cissy would be the more likely candidate. Unless the will and insurance policies weren't the reason Rory and Eugenia had been killed. Maybe there was another motive, one he just hadn't yet uncovered, one so strong it would force someone to help Marla escape and kill the people close to her.

So if Cissy wasn't the killer, and Marla too hadn't actually murdered her brother and mother-in-law, then who?

He spread the autopsy reports on the desk with Marla Cahill's case file. Pictures of Eugenia's broken body, Rory's corpse, and Marla's mug shot stared back at him.

How were they connected?

Eugenia and Rory are connected to each other THROUGH Marla.

So what?

He tapped his fingers and shook his head. He'd scoured Eugenia's date book, looked into the woman who couldn't drive her to church the day of her death,

Marcia Mantello. Marcia's story was legit as far as he could tell. He'd also checked through everyone else listed in Eugenia's book. And he'd gone through the logs at the care facility and interviewed the staff and residents as he had with all of Eugenia's friends and relatives. So far he'd come up with a great big goose egg. Nada.

His stomach was really roiling now, and he hoped the antacid would kick in soon.

Looking out the window to the building across the street, he tried to figure it all out.

He knew he was missing something. He just didn't know what.

Cissy finished another glass of wine and told herself she'd probably consumed enough for the day. She was feeling a little light-headed as it was and still needed to keep it together. At least for a little while longer.

The crowd was thinning, and though Lars tried vainly to get each person's coat as he or she left, people were going up and down the stairs, retrieving their own wraps. She could hear them walking around upstairs. Doors opening and closing. Snooping. Peering into her life. Two women from Cahill House had come down the stairs and declared the baby's room "adorable," as if they had a free pass to take a tour of the upstairs.

Soon it would be over.

Fewer and fewer guests were talking, visiting, noshing, or making noises of sympathy.

Unfortunately some of the people who were still hanging around weren't her favorites. Though most of Eugenia's friends had left, the remaining mourners were either tied more closely to Cissy than to Gran, or were unlikely attendees whose appearance had been a total surprise. Selma, for instance. What the hell was the woman from Joltz doing here? She'd come up, said she was sorry, hung out in the kitchen with Diedre and Rachelle, and was finally getting ready to leave. Cissy didn't even know her last name.

As if feeling Cissy's eyes on her, Selma turned, tucking her scarf around her neck. "'Bye. I'll see you at the coffee shop."

Cissy lifted her hand in acknowledgment. She was glad to see the woman go. Now if some the others would take the hint.

Her second cousin Cherise and her preacher husband, the Reverend Donald Favier, were still in the dining room, picking at the remaining food, the little sandwiches and cookies arranged on silver trays on the table. Cissy had avoided them at all costs. She didn't know them well and decided to keep it that way. From the way Gran had talked, and from what she remembered growing up, Cherise's pro-football player husband turned preacher was a large, handsome man and a master manipulator, the puppeteer who pulled Cherise's strings. Both he and his wife always had one eye on the Cahill money.

According to Gran, Cherise thought, and her husband agreed, that Cherise's father, Fenton, had been screwed out of the family fortune by Cissy's grandfather, and Fenton's brother, Samuel. The alleged shady financial double-cross had all taken place many years earlier, but the bad feelings and envy had seemed to grow over the generations rather than diminish.

Blond, forever-tanned, Cherise was always looking for a gift or handout, a piece of what she thought was rightfully hers. Gran had always refused to loan her even a dime, and there was no love lost between them, yet here Cherise was, paying her last respects and scarfing up another shrimp canape.

Jack's family, probably under the insistence of his father, hadn't left yet either. Jannelle spent most of her time on the back patio, smoking cigarettes and looking miserable. Jack's brother, the usually reticent J.J., was in his element in a group of strangers. He, like his father, was never without female company. Cissy's neighbor Sara had zeroed in on him. Even Jonathan had, after a few drinks, let his facade of formality and respect for the dead disintegrate as he flirted with women half his age.

From the corner of her eye, Cissy had seen him turn the Holt charm on to everyone from her college friend Heather, to Rachelle, to Diedre, and even Paloma. The man had no shame and even less good judgment.

Heather, of course, had eaten it up. She'd beamed up at Jonathan as she'd sipped wine, then had the nerve to tell Cissy that her father-in-law was "adorable for an older guy."

Cissy's high school buddy Tracy had disagreed. "If you ask me, he's just another old lech. Sorry, Cissy, but it's the truth."

Cissy hadn't argued. She'd noticed when Jonathan had tried to flirt with Tracy, she'd said something sharp that Cissy hadn't been able to overhear, then turned her back on him and stalked away, her whole body seeming to tense in revulsion. *Good for you,* Cissy had thought.

. Jack too had witnessed the confrontation. "Jesus, Dad," he'd muttered under his breath so that no one but Cissy could hear, "give it a rest."

"He can't," Cissy had said. "It's in his blood."

"That's a cop-out. It just takes a little self-control."

Now Jack was surveying his father as Diedre, carrying a tray of wineglasses, walked past. She offered Jack's father a glass. He responded by flashing her his most disarming smile and winking.

To Cissy's horror, Jonathan appeared about to touch Diedre's butt.

She'd kill him. Cissy had witnessed Diedre's temper in the coffee shop when a regular customer had gotten too fresh with her. The tongue lashing had been swift and cutting. Cissy had never seen the guy in the shop again.

"Uh-oh." Jack anticipated what was about to happen. "I'd better see if someone can take him home before he embarrasses himself."

And everyone else, Cissy thought. She couldn't face another scene.

Before Jonathan could put his wayward hand on Diedre's rump, she moved deftly away, doing a quick step to the side, as if she were used to dodging unwanted advances. She didn't give him a tongue-lashing like Tracy had, just sent him a sharp are-you-out-of-your-mind glare as she turned away and almost bumped into Jack.

She stopped short, and somehow, by the grace of God, the teetering platter didn't fall. Diedre managed to right the platter. Some wine sloshed over the rims of the glasses, but the damage was slight, as the glasses remained upright.

Jack said a quick apology and then escorted his dad outside, where Jannelle was cradling another cigarette from the wind, huddling with two men Cissy thought had once worked for Cahill Limited, the family's company before it downsized.

Shaking her head, Diedre returned to the kitchen. "Men," she muttered under her breath, then, spying Cissy, said, "I thought you said something about divorcing your husband."

"It's in the works."

Diedre seemed to want to say something, hesitated, then shrugged. "Well, maybe this isn't the time to hand out advice."

"Diedre," Rachelle warned. She was already covering

some of the extra food with plastic wrap and wiping off empty trays with a towel.

"What kind of advice?" Cissy asked.

"You don't want to know," Rachelle said, but Diedre ignored her.

"I was married for a few years. We had a house, and when we got divorced, because the snake was cheating on me, I couldn't afford to keep the place and he bought me out. I ended up with a few thousand dollars, and now he's moved in with the girlfriend and the house has gone up nearly a hundred grand. So I got screwed. Whatever you do, keep the house." Diedre glanced at Rachelle, who, as far as Cissy could tell, was happily married. "Okay, there, I said it."

"I'll keep that in mind," Cissy told her. At least Diedre wasn't telling her what a hunk her husband was.

Cissy rubbed the back of her neck and glanced through the glass doors to the patio, where Jack was still lobbying for someone, presumably Jannelle, to haul his father home. Geez, she was tired. She glanced at the clock and hoped everyone would leave soon. "Cissy?" Cherise's voice was right in her ear.

Inwardly Cissy groaned. She'd taken her eyes off her father's cousin for less than five minutes, and the woman had taken the opportunity to approach her. "Can I talk to you a second?"

No! Cissy thought but pasted a smile on her face. "Sure. What's up?"

As if she didn't know.

"Well, this is a little awkward, it being Auntie Genie's funeral and all."

Auntie Genie? Gran was probably rolling over in her newly turned grave.

Cherise inched away from the kitchen to a quieter spot at the base of the stairs, and reluctantly Cissy followed, only to discover Cherise's big husband waiting near the hall tree. Six five or six, the Reverend Donald in his clerical collar, black shirt, and leather jacket offered a smile that hinted he and God were tight. "I'm so sorry for your, for *our,* loss," he said. "Eugenia was a wonderful woman."

Oh, really? Cissy thought. As far as she knew, Gran had never given Cherise or any of her husbands the time of day. And now, after she was dead, she was wonderful?

"I'll miss her," Cissy said.

"We all will." The Reverend Donald's voice was smooth as ice.

Cherise touched Cissy's arm. "Maybe we could go to lunch somewhere later in the week or," she added quickly, seeing the denial forming on Cissy's lips, "if that doesn't work for you, how about dinner?"

"What is it you want to talk about?" Cissy asked, stepping out of the way as Rosa, carrying a few dirty dishes, aimed for the kitchen.

"The family, of course. There's been such a rift, and I absolutely hate it. I've talked to Nick. He knows how I feel." She motioned toward the dining room, where Uncle Nick and his wife were speaking with a man Cissy had met, but couldn't quite place . . . maybe an insurance agent or a banker who'd worked with Eugenia? Her brother James was scavenging at the table of desserts, and she felt a tug on her heart. She should have been closer to him. Gran would have wanted that. A part of her wanted it as well. Their family was so small, and shrinking by the day, it seemed.

Because of Marla. Somehow, she'd orchestrated Gran's death, and Rory's as well.

Cissy's stomach burned, as it always did lately whenever she thought of the woman who had borne her. Could she be so different from the psycho? Her own mother?

But she couldn't think of her now.

Not today.

Cissy turned back to Cherise with her big, pleading eyes. "So, what do you want to do to mend this, uh, 'rift'?" Cissy asked, trying to keep the sarcasm from her voice and wishing there was some way to get out of the conversation.

"First, we should have a family get-together," Cherise said, glancing at her husband as if for confirmation. That was the problem with Cherise. She wasn't a bad person. Just weak. Always leaning on her husband, looking at him as if he might just be the embodiment of the Second Coming of Christ.

She couldn't remember all the details, but there was something unsavory in Donald Favier's past, something that had less to do with football and more to do with underage girls. Wasn't that right? It didn't matter to Cherise, obviously, as she was gazing adoringly at Reverend Donald, entwining her arm through his.

Donald was nodding. "Afterward we can hold a more formal meeting with family attorneys involved. There are still a few issues that haven't been settled."

"What issues?" Cissy asked cautiously.

"Oh." Cherise lifted her shoulder. "You know, the family trust, that sort of thing. Now that you're in charge."

"I'm in charge?"

"Well, you're the primary beneficiary of Aunt Genie's estate."

"I am?" Cissy asked. "And you know this . . . how?"

Donald smiled and held out his hands, his fingers open, several gold rings catching the light. "Of course we've talked to the attorneys."

"Ahh . . ."

His thousand-watt smile was nearly contagious. "We're family."

Cissy turned her gaze back on Cherise's near-desperate face, a face that was aging despite what Cissy guessed was the latest in plastic surgery. "You know, you were right when you said this was awkward and you thought maybe we shouldn't discuss it now."

"But we have to."

"I don't think so." The more she thought about it, the less she liked it. "And no, I don't think we're going to have lunch or dinner. I'm not comfortable discussing any of it. Not now, and probably not at any other time."

Dumbfounded, Cherise took hold of her arm. "Cissy, please, be reasonable. We both know things aren't right. They haven't been in a long, long while. I thought that you were different and that you would—"

"Would what? Write you a check? For how much? Ten thousand? Fifty? A hundred? Or maybe a million?" Her voice was rising at the audacity of the woman and her supposedly God-fearing husband. "Gran was just buried today, and here you are at the gathering after her funeral and you're already bringing up the will and money and picking at Gran's bones!"

"Oh, Cissy, no—"

"And you know why you're doing it? Because you think you can steamroll right over me, and I'm too young to stand up to you and to you," she said, turning her furious eyes on the reverend. "Well, you were both wrong."

Cherise's hand flew to her mouth, and Heather, who had been walking by, stopped in her tracks. "Is everything okay?" she asked.

"Just peachy," Cissy muttered.

"You're sure?" Heather asked, her smooth brow knitting.

"We're fine," Cherise's husband said tightly, then, "Thanks for asking, Heather."

Cissy's gaze swung between them. "Do you know each other?"

Heather looked like the quintessential "California girl" with her blue eyes, deep tan, and blond hair streaked platinum, not an ounce of fat daring to show on her toned body. She and Cissy had met at USC, and now Heather taught third grade at a private elementary school in the Bay Area.

"Didn't you know?" Heather asked, surprised. "I belong to the Holy Trinity of God Church. It's just a few blocks from my apartment."

"In Sausalito?" Cissy said, putting two and two together. She knew that Heather lived on the other side of the Golden Gate Bridge, but she didn't have any idea that she was one of the Reverend Donald's flock.

"I thought I'd mentioned it."

"I think I would have remembered," Cissy said and told herself it wasn't a big deal. So what? The church had hundreds of parishioners, but Heather? One more odd connection.

"Heather doesn't just belong to the church," Reverend Donald said as he rained one of his charismatic smiles on Cissy's college friend. "She's being modest. She works with the church secretary, helps with the computers, makes sure there are no broken links in the prayer chain."

"Is that right?" Cissy said, trying to think what she did know about Heather since they'd graduated from college. Other than hearing that she'd broken up with her long-time boyfriend, taught school, and liked green apple martinis, it wasn't much. They hadn't kept in close touch. Hadn't Heather been involved in drugs during their four years at USC? Hadn't there been ecstasy and cocaine use? But that had been years ago, and then there was something about Campus Crusade. Come to think of it, Cissy had known that Heather usually wore a gold cross on a chain around her neck, but she'd never been vocal about her religious views.

"Heather's a big help to us." Cherise nodded, her smile a bit less enthusiastic than her husband's.

"So," Heather said brightly, "are we all okay now?"

Before Cissy could respond, she heard a noise she recognized. Over the hum of the surrounding conversation, she heard B.J.'s distant voice. "Mom-mee! Get up! I get up now! Mom-mee!"

Thank God!

"Oh, gotta run," she said without looking anyone directly in the eye. "My little guy's awake." Before Cherise or Reverend Donald or Heather could stop her, she bolted up the stairs. She was *not* going to lunch or dinner with her father's cousin or her husband. Not ever. If Heather wanted to cozy up to them, fine. But as far as Cissy was concerned, if she never saw either Cherise or her husband again, it would be just fine. "Vultures," she muttered softly, then, at the top of the stairs, took a deep breath, cleared her head, and shoved all her negative thoughts aside.

She pushed open the door of B.J.'s room. He was standing in his crib and pounding on the top rail. "Mom-mee!" he said, grinning widely at the sight of her.

"Hey, Beej!" Her bad mood disappeared in an instant. "How's my guy?" Pulling him out of the crib, she hugged him so fiercely, he giggled. "Not a Grumpy Gus today?"

"Not grumpy!"

"Good."

"Dad-dee downstairs?"

"That he is," Cissy said. "So let's get you changed, and we'll go down and see him. But I gotta warn ya, he's not alone. There are tons of people down there, and they're going to fawn all over you."

"Tons of people," he repeated.

"That's right." She carried him to the changing table, and switched out his wet diaper for a dry one. He kicked and scooted, all part of the game, but eventually he was clean and dry, the new diaper in place. Once he was dressed and she'd finger-combed his curls, she carried him downstairs, where, it seemed, even fewer guests were mingling.

Good!

The Reverend Donald and Cherise were nowhere in sight.

Talk about a blessing!

"Is this the infamous B.J.?" Heather asked, grinning, her eyes sparkling. "You know, I haven't seen him since he was a couple of months old." To the child she said, "Come see Auntie Heather."

"Auntie Heather?" Cissy repeated.

"Well, you know, I'm just trying to connect with the little guy. Come here, pumpkin."

Connect with the little guy? Everything Heather said was hitting Cissy wrong today. Was it her? The funeral? Or was Heather being a little weird?

Beej grinned shyly, but allowed himself to be hugged and cuddled by first Heather, then Tracy, who declared him "more handsome than his father."

Even Sara was beguiled. "What a cutie!" she said and touched his button nose with a manicured finger before lifting another glass of wine from a passing tray.

Rosa was already helping clean up, but she took the time to coo over the baby, and Paloma offered a stiff smile to a child she'd seen often enough but had never warmed to.

B.J. put up with the attention and was eventually passed back to Cissy, but when he saw his father, he went nuts. "Dad-dee!" he cried, wriggling in Cissy's arms again and struggling to get down. She set him on his feet, and he took off like a shot, running through people's legs until he reached his father, who swept him into his arms.

"There he is!" Jonathan crowed, standing next to Jack. "I wondered when you were going to wake up."

Cissy saw Jannelle and J.J. exchange glances and realized that not all members of the Holt family were as thrilled with Jack's son as their father was. The look that passed between them was more than just boredom or irritation that their father was too into his grandson. It was darker than that, an acknowledgment between allies that there was an enemy in their midst.

Cissy experienced a chill as cold as all of December, but when Jannelle looked up and spied her sister-in-law staring at her, she just lifted a shoulder. "Never was a kid person," she admitted. "Look, Jack talked to me. I'm going to take 'Poppa' home. He's been hitting the booze pretty hard, even dipped into your stash of whiskey. Apparently he knows where it's kept."

"Maybe I'll have to put it under lock and key."

"Not a bad idea," Jannelle said, then, "Okay, *Poppa*, you've had your fun, time to go home."

"So soon?" Jonathan seemed distressed.

"It's been a long day. Cissy needs to chill out for a while." She linked arms with her father while Jack retrieved his son and J.J., spying Gwen standing alone, grabbed another glass of wine and zeroed in on the trainer. He was obviously looking for another score.

Would the day never end?

Jannelle anticipated what was going on and cut him off at the pass. "Don't even think about it, bro. You and me, we need to get the old man home."

"I'm not an old man," their father protested, and, it was true, he looked no more than ten years older than his oldest son. "And, damn it, I want to be with my grandson."

Jannelle sent J.J. another warning glance.

Or did she?

There was more than a small chance that Cissy was

overthinking it all, letting paranoia creep in, observing nuances that didn't exist.

Telling herself that she was imagining things, she suffered through the next hour as the last of the mourners eventually said their final good-byes, leaving only Rosa, Deborah, Diedre, Rachelle, and Jack to finish cleaning up. Beej was in his element, tearing around the rooms, playing with anything he could find. When, eventually, the house was back to some semblance of order, the sympathy cards and donations had been picked up, the extra food either meted out to friends or stored, the candles extinguished, and all the pieces of furniture returned to their original positions, Cissy set down her wineglass, feeling as if she might collapse. She promised the tearful Deborah, the last person out the door, that she would write her a letter of recommendation. Then, as the door closed behind Eugenia's "companion," she turned the lock. "No more," she whispered, shoving her hair from her eyes. She was so exhausted she couldn't even summon up the heart or energy to suggest that Jack leave.

"Go upstairs, have a bath, go to bed," he said as he and B.J. settled onto the couch. "I'll watch Beej; we'll hang out, and then I'll get him to bed. You just take it easy."

It sounded like heaven. "And then what about you?"

"I'll be around." He gave her a smile, and she felt the ice around her heart thaw a bit.

"That would be great. I owe you." Leaning over, she kissed her son's head and then headed upstairs. She didn't bother with the bath, just washed her face, changed into her favorite pajamas, and tumbled into bed.

She was asleep before her head hit the pillow, and, dead to the world, she never noticed when, hours later, Jack slid into the bed next to her.

Chapter 12

". . . I'm telling you, it was great! *Great!* No one suspected a thing! You would have been so proud of me! I walked through Cissy's house as if I owned the place, and no one gave me a second glance." Elyse was talking fast, exhilarated, still on a high as she explained to Marla what she'd done, how she'd mingled with the enemy and showed up not only at the funeral but at the gathering after the service. Her nerves were still jangled, and she felt breathless, as if she'd spent the last five hours in the company of hungry wolves. And she'd survived! Thrived!

"I should be proud of you?" Marla scoffed. "As if it was hard for you to blend in? Give me a break."

Elyse stared. She'd expected praise.

During her last visit to the bungalow Marla had been pleased to hear that Elyse had killed Rory, just as Marla had requested.

"About time that half-wit got what was coming to him," Marla had said with a little more animation than she'd shown for a week. "This is all working perfectly." She'd actually ignored the damned television for once.

"Do you know how much money it costs every month to keep him at that swank facility?"

Swank? There had been nothing swank or posh or expensive-looking about Harborside Assisted Living, but, of course, the kind of care Rory Amhurst needed hadn't been cheap.

"He was lucky to be alive," Marla had added. "I was there when dear old Mom ran over him. I heard the thump and the crunch of his bones." She'd had the grace to shudder at the memory, but added callously, "But I guess he was an Amhurst. All of us are pretty thick-skulled." She'd actually laughed and Elyse had felt strangely put off, even though, she was certain, she'd heard the same joke before.

"It was a freak accident. The poor kid . . ."

"Was it? An accident?" Marla had repeated enigmatically. "I guess dear old Mom didn't set out to kill him, but you—defending him—when you baked him the brownies that killed him. What did you call him, 'a poor kid'? He was a man; that accident was over thirty-five years ago! And don't be acting all caring and warm and fuzzy. For God's sake, you watched him die, you told me you did, and you *liked* it. That 'poor kid' didn't know up from sideways. He's better off dead."

"I'm not sure that's true."

"Then why the hell did you kill him?"

"For you," Elyse had blurted, stung. "What? Did you forget?"

"Oh, come on."

"For the plan. Our plan."

"You did it for the thrill," Marla had said knowingly. "Because you could. It's an incredible sense of power knowing you can take a life, even a pathetic one. Tell yourself it's for our plan . . . we both know differently. But it was a good job. Now we can move forward."

Elyse had let herself bask in Marla's praise, grudging

as it was. And Marla had been right. She had enjoyed the kill.

But now they were back to their same roles: Elyse trying to placate a testy, surly Marla. For God's sake, the woman acted as if she were a prisoner, when Elyse had risked her neck to spring her. Ungrateful, self-centered bitch!

"You think you're something special, don't you?" Marla suddenly accused, as if reading her thoughts. "Because you killed two people who deserved to die. Oh, don't deny it. I saw it on your face when you burst in here after killing Eugenia, and then Rory. You were on a high like no other. You felt invincible."

Elyse was thunderstruck. Was it possible that Marla understood her better than she'd thought?

"But really," Marla said stiffly, "just how invincible are you? Eugenia was tiny and old, had already taken her dose of Valium, right? She couldn't have weighed a hundred pounds soaking wet, and so you tossed her over the rail. Big deal. And then Rory, just an innocent boy in a man's body, right? Not a mean bone in his body. Crippled enough that he used a wheelchair and you slipped him some doctored brownies. How much intellect or skill does it take to trick a retard?"

"You wanted me to kill them. You *told* me to," Elyse burst out.

"Yes, I did. And it's fine that you feel exhilarated with the kills, but let's just keep it all in perspective, okay? You preyed on the weak and the helpless. Things are going to get harder. A lot harder."

Elyse didn't know what she'd expected but it hadn't been a lecture on the finer points of murder, a discussion of what was morally right or wrong.

Jesus, what did Marla want from her?

"You know, if I could get out of here, everything would be already done."

"These things take time."

"Easy for you to say. You're not stuck in this hellhole. It's a miracle I haven't gone flippin' insane down here!" she said, then continued to whine and feel sorry for herself again. After all Elyse had done for the bitch. All the risks she'd taken. While Princess Marla was fighting boredom. Well, who the hell cared?

The trouble was, it appeared that Marla was getting weirder by the day, more paranoid about being caught. Not once had she gone up the stairs. She usually just sat in her damned chair in front of the boob tube. This was getting bad.

Yes, Marla wanted to hear every last detail of the funeral and the gathering afterward, asking about people Elyse didn't know, but Marla was pouting as well. They had talked about her attending the funeral with Elyse in disguise, but had decided against it. The cops would be looking for her, and no matter how good the makeup, padding, wigs, contacts, and clothing, there had been the chance that someone might have recognized her.

Elyse said now, "I'm certain the police are thinking you're behind Eugenia's and Rory's deaths. Even though I gave your prison wear to the guy who's going to leave it in Oregon, the authorities won't buy that you've left the state unless we stop now."

"We can't," Marla said fervently. For once, she seemed to understand. "Not yet." She seemed upset now, fretting. "You just have to work faster. That's it. Take care of everyone who's in our way. Then send your man to Oregon. No, wait a minute. I'm going crazy here anyway. I'll help."

"How?" Elyse asked, not liking the turn of the conversation.

"I'll leave here . . . go to a local hotel. I can take a taxi from there. Disguise myself, have the taxi put me near BART and I could take a bus or—"

"No!"

"Then I'll drive the car," she said with more animation than she'd shown in a long while. "I *need* to get out of here."

"Not yet," Elyse said, panicking. "You can't leave yet."

"I don't see why not."

"Just show a little patience. Everything's going according to plan."

Marla glared at her.

"First go upstairs. See if you can handle being out of this damned basement. If you can, then we'll see."

"You're like a damned warden!"

"I'm just making sense," Elyse told her. She didn't want to upset Marla, because there was nothing to prevent her from leaving if she so chose. Even if Elyse decided to lock her inside, Marla had keys, and she was a master at escape. No, Marla had to be convinced that she needed to stay inside for a while longer. Till they were both safe and the job was done. "Really, everything's going perfectly."

So don't blow it!

Marla let out a long-suffering sigh. "Fine. We'll do it your way."

That was more like it.

"I can stay hidden for a few more weeks. It's god-awful, but it won't be forever," she said as if she were convincing herself. "I just have to keep telling myself that. This place is worse than prison. At least there I had people I could talk with."

"You mean cons and guards?"

"I saw sunlight."

"I know, I know, I'll take care of it." Secretly Elyse was glad to ratchet up the schedule. The highs of the killings didn't last long, and she was anxious for everything to fall into place.

She picked up some of the garbage Marla let lie

around. . . . Jesus, couldn't she smell the rotting apple cores and bits of sandwiches? Maybe it was because she was trapped down here with it. She also, nonchalantly, cleaned the brush Marla used on her hair.

"Look," she suggested, pocketing the snarl of hair when Marla wasn't looking. "At least walk into the other room of the basement and stretch your legs. Go up and down the stairs and walk around on the other floor. I'll go up there now and make certain the blinds are drawn. No one will see you."

"I do need to get out." Longingly, she eyed her coat draped upon a hook and the boots on the floor below.

"Absolutely. Go upstairs," Elyse agreed, trying another tack to mollify the older woman. "I'd go stir crazy if I just sat down here all day and night."

"But you're not me, are you?" Marla asked, a sense of new-found pride in her voice. "You've never been penned up like an animal." She smiled almost wickedly, her green eyes sparkling in the half-light of the little room. "You don't have the same backbone I do, the same sense of purpose. That's the difference between us."

Not the only one, Elyse thought, but held her tongue. *I've never been caught.*

She left Marla, the weirdo, and took the garbage with her. She would put it in a bin in a park, as she didn't have pickup service. She didn't want to take the chance of someone going through it here.

Sliding behind the wheel of her Taurus, she glanced back at the house. What if Marla did leave? She could take off when Elyse wasn't here and never return. Elyse would never know the difference, and Marla could screw up everything. Damn! Still lost in "what ifs" she jammed the gearshift into reverse, backing out of the driveway quickly.

BAM!

A thud echoed through the car.

"Hey!"

Elyse slammed on the brakes.

Somebody had pounded on the trunk of her car.

In her rearview mirror, she caught a glimpse of a blur.

She gasped, looked again, just in time to see a bicyclist, one hand raised, middle finger extended, fly past in the glow of the street lamps. "Watch where you're going, you lunatic!" he raved, and she paused a few minutes to catch her breath. Her heart was knocking so fast she couldn't think. Sweat bloomed over her body, and she felt her insides tremble. She couldn't afford to hit a bicyclist or pedestrian or dog or *any*thing. She couldn't risk getting caught. *Could not!* She was too close to having everything she wanted.

Cautiously, her heart jackhammering, she eased out of the drive and onto the street.

What if the bicyclist remembered her license plates? What if those same plates had been caught on some security camera at the nursing home, or on the street near the Cahill home on Mt. Sutro? These days, everyone had a cell/camera phone which they carried with them. Tons of crimes were caught on camera. Yes, it was dark, but the blue glow cast from the street lamps was enough illumination to read her license plate.

Don't panic. The biker was flying by too fast to catch the plate's numbers, and so what if he saw you: you're leasing this place, remember, Elyse?

Inside she was quivering, but she set her jaw and regulated her breaths, her tense muscles relaxing a bit as she drove through the near-dark streets without another incident. No one stared at her. No one turned to follow the Taurus with their eyes. No one lifted a cell phone high and zoomed in to take a picture of her car. She wondered if the trunk was dented where the biker had driven his fist. She didn't want any mark on the vehicle, nothing that would allow it to stand out or be identified.

Calm down, you're safe. What you have to do is steal a license plate off another car, not switch it with the ones you've got now, just find another silver Taurus that looks similar, one parked in a Bay Area Transit station, and take the damned plate or two. They don't have to match front to back; no one will ever know, and the driver of the car from which it's stolen will just think his fell off somewhere and get a duplicate. You can do this. You'll be fine.

Her fingers eased over the steering wheel. She clicked on the radio, listening to some smooth jazz. Cracking the window as she approached the bridge, she smelled the scent of the ocean, and she leaned back in the seat as she drove toward town, back to her real life. She thought about calling her boyfriend and making a date, but she knew that they were both tired. And he'd probably play that stupid cat-and-mouse game that seemed to be his favorite, as if he was always on the verge of breaking up with her, calling the whole thing off.

She knew better.

He was in too deep to back out.

"Silly man," she chided as lonely notes from a saxophone drifted from the speakers. She would visit him another day. As much as she wanted to see him, to kiss him, to feel his hands on her, to straddle him and fuck his damned brains out, another time would be better. She needed to think things through, focus on her plan. Not Marla's. Just hers.

She thought of Cissy Cahill Holt, the ultimate target.

God, she couldn't wait to see the look on Cissy's face when she realized she was about to die. Then there would be that other, unique moment of realization and recognition when she understood who "Elyse" really was. A little tingle of adrenaline slipped through her bloodstream again, a rush of anticipation. She licked her lips as the car's tires sang over the bridge, the night-dark waters whipping by.

Yeah, Cissy. Just you wait, Elyse thought as she drove toward San Francisco, where the city lights were winking seductively over the black water. Things were working out so well. She thought about the cell phone she had tucked in her purse and the key, two items she'd managed to pick up when no one was looking at the gathering of the bereft for poor Eugenia Cahill. She smiled to herself as she thought what she would be able to accomplish with Cissy's cell phone and the key that was "hidden" by the staircase leading to the basement, a key probably no one would miss, not even Cissy herself. Elyse had left another key, one that looked identical. As long as no one tried to use it, no one would be the wiser that it was a dummy key, a decoy, just like those fake ducks hunters floated on a lake.

A pure stroke of genius.

But the cell phone was a different story. Cissy would miss it, freak out, and, when she didn't find it, cancel her service. Elyse would have to work fast, use it before Cissy got wise.

But then, she intended to.

As she drove off the bridge and toward the city, the traffic snarling at some of the stop lights, Elyse stared at the taillights of the minivan in front of her and imagined Cissy's frustration when she realized the phone was missing. She wouldn't cancel her service immediately; she would expect the damned thing to turn up, probably lost when someone at the gathering had inadvertently moved it.

How perfect was that?

You're in for the shock of your pathetic, spoiled life, bitch.

Cissy Cahill Holt didn't know the meaning of the word *fear.*

Not yet.

But she was going to learn.

Soon.

And, better yet, so was her mother.

Cissy yawned and rolled over.

And bumped right into something solid and warm and snoring.

Her eyes flew open, and in the early hours of dawn she saw Jack lying beside her.

"What are you doing here?" she said, shaking him awake. "You can't be here, you can't be . . . Oh God . . ." What had she done last night? She didn't remember, and the headache behind her eyes told her that she'd had a lot, maybe too much, to drink.

Jack opened one eye. "'Mornin' beautiful," he said, one side of his mouth lifting into a sexy grin.

"What the hell do you think you're doing sneaking into bed with me when I'm asleep?"

His grin widened. "I thought I might get lucky."

She stared at him as if he truly had gone round the bend. "We're separated, remember?"

"So you keep reminding me."

"We do *not* sleep together."

"I wasn't thinking about sleeping," he admitted, and something deep inside of her responded.

She started to fling the covers off, and he grabbed her wrist, pulling her back, so that her pajama-clad body was touching his, which of course was naked.

"I thought we had a truce," he murmured.

Cissy could feel his warmth where their bodies touched. "It was for yesterday and didn't include the bedroom," she said, trying not to notice how her body yearned for his. It was semidark in the room, the only light coming from a nightlight that gave off a soft white, luminous glow, enough that she could see his features, catch shadowy glimpses of his expressions but not read what he was thinking.

"Cissy," he said in a voice that sounded an octave lower than usual. "I—"

"Don't say it," she said and placed a finger over his lips. She didn't want to hear any apologies or mention of the word *love*. Here, in bed with him, under thick, downy blankets, in a room where they'd made love more often than not, she didn't want to be emotionally ambushed. "Just don't."

He kissed her finger, and she felt a tingle deep inside.

She should have removed her hand, but didn't, and he wrapped his lips around that finger. The warm wetness of his mouth sent a shot of desire to her core. And that desire, deep inside, in the most feminine part of her, grew in intensity. Memories of making love to Jack cut through her mind, quicksilver images of him staring down at her, levered on his elbows, his blue eyes intense, or of him kissing her breasts, his tongue teasing at her nipples, or of the feel of him as he nudged her legs apart, then held himself for a few moments, just touching her, rubbing against her, making her writhe with want before he actually . . . Oh God.

She slowly pulled her finger out of his mouth. "This is not going to happen, Jack." Her voice was raspy, her heart tripping expectantly.

"We need to start over."

"We're past that."

"Are we?"

Damn the man, he had the nerve to slip his arms around her and kiss her.

Hard.

Warm lips found hers, and she closed her eyes. *Stop this, Cissy, stop it now! Before it goes any further. You do not want to make love to Jack, do not!*

But she moaned softly, and Jack's big hands seemed to envelop her, pulling her tight against him, fingers sliding beneath the hem of her pajama top to splay against her back as he slowly moved downward, kissing her neck, her collarbone, the hollow of her throat.

Don't let him . . . Oh God, he's doing it, isn't he?

Her back arched of its own accord as he began working the buttons of her pajamas, opening each with his tongue, a trick that amazed and seduced her. Warm breath, wet tongue, the click of the button against his teeth as each pearly little disc was slowly released.

It would have been easier and faster to just jerk the damned piece of cotton over her head, or for either of them to unbutton the fabric with their eager fingers, but this slow method, where his hot breath seeped through the cotton, the fabric parting, his lips and tongue skimming her breastbone, moving ever lower, was magical and sexy and turned her on to incredible heights. His hands were free, and he used them to hold her tight, one across the small of her back, the other, as he eased himself down, cupping her buttocks and holding her fast as the pajama top parted from the pants. With his teeth, he pulled her bottoms down, exposing her, leaving her partially dressed as his mouth scraped lower, past her abdomen and belly button, his breathing hotter now, faster.

Desire pounded through her veins. Her throat was dry, her hands entwined in his hair as he began to kiss her between her legs, his lips and tongue touching, flicking, toying with her as sweat sheened her body and the wanting deep inside began to throb.

Moaning, she began to move with him. A quick tug on her pajama bottoms took them off, and he gained closer access, his tongue working magic, his hands on her buttocks.

"Oh God," she whispered and was undone. "Jack . . ." Hot need thrummed through her. She wanted more. So much more. Just when she thought she would go mad with the yearning, he came to her, sliding up her body more quickly now, hands at her breasts, lips skimming her nipples.

All denial fled. She didn't care about the ramifications, didn't think about tomorrow, just wanted him. All of him. Now.

He kissed her again, his mouth clamping over hers as his legs pushed hers apart. She arched upward, her fingers digging into the smooth muscles of his back. "Jack," she whispered when he lifted his head to gaze at her.

"I hate to tell you this, Cissy," he said, "but I love you. I *love* you."

As the words left his lips, he thrust into her. Any argument that might have been forming in her mind quickly fell away. Her body met his eagerly. Hungrily. She wanted so much more from him, *so much. . . .* Her thoughts fled, her breath came in short gasps, her blood thundered through her ears as he made love to her. Faster and faster. Harder and harder. Pressure building. She was sweating, gasping. She saw the veins bulging in his forehead. Her entire body centered on the joining of his body to hers.

"Cissy . . ."

A jolt rocked through her. A soft scream erupted from her throat. Spasm after spasm. She clung to him, felt him tense, and then in one instant he let go, pouring himself into her, whispering her name. "Cissy . . . oh . . . damn . . . Cissy."

He collapsed atop her, his body as covered in perspiration as hers, his own heart echoing the frantic beat of hers.

She was gasping, but managed a smile.

"And you thought this was a bad idea," he murmured.

"I still do."

He lifted his head and cocked a skeptical eyebrow. She laughed.

"Okay . . . I think it was a bad idea, but I'm glad it happened."

"Are you?"

Sighing, she wound her arms around his neck. "You are still my husband, for a few more weeks." His grin widened, and she almost gave in to trusting him again. Almost.

"That's not set in stone either," he reminded her, kissing her forehead.

"Let's not ruin this morning talking about the divorce. I'm going to shower, and you go downstairs and make coffee, and about the time we're on our second cup, Beej will wake up and we'll have a perfectly pleasant morning."

"It could be that way every morning," he said softly, then, as if realizing he was overplaying his hand, said, "Okay . . . coffee it is. And I'll take care of the dog."

"Coco!" she cried.

"Relax, B.J. and I took her out of the crate last night, walked her, and played with her. Surprise, surprise, she didn't bite me."

"How could I have forgotten?" She felt horrible.

"You had a lot on your mind. I think she'll forgive you."

"Where is she?"

"Downstairs in her bed, I think."

"I'm a terrible dog owner," she said guiltily.

"You'll get the hang of it. Besides, no harm, no foul."

"Yeah, right."

He rolled off her. The cold air in the room touched her skin, and she wondered why it was she couldn't get enough of him. Why couldn't she just throw him out and be done with it? True, she thought, as she pulled up her pajama bottoms and walked into the bathroom, she'd used the excuse of her grandmother's violent death to let Jack back into her life. Twisting on the faucets, waiting for the water to heat, she admitted to herself that it had seemed petty and selfish to keep the divorce front and center when people were being killed. But by putting the divorce on the back burner, she'd sent out mixed signals to her estranged husband.

Was that what she wanted?

So what's the big deal? her mind taunted as she stepped out of her pajamas and into the shower. *Another week or two? Who cares? You're separated . . . well, kind of.* Allowing the hot needles of water to wash away her anxiety, she picked up a bottle of shampoo, poured a dab in her hand, and worked it through her wet hair. Steam rolled through the room, and she felt her mind clear and her body relax. *You're on no timetable, no schedule; you can do this any time you want.* She'd been outraged, of course, when she'd seen Jack coming out of Larissa's and had told her attorneys she wanted the fastest divorce possible, but her anger had tempered a little over the past few weeks, and Jack, damn him, had been incredibly charming.

But you know that about him.

From the first time you met, he got to you.

All-blue eyes, athletic body, irreverent bad-boy smile, and maverick appeal.

From the moment he turned his attention your way, you were had. Don't be played again, Cissy. Do not!

Damn it all.

She rinsed and lathered, hot spray running down her face and neck.

Rap. Rap. Rap.

He was knocking?

"What?" she called over the glass door and heard the door to the bathroom creak open. This wasn't a good idea.

"Coffee," Jack announced through the steam. "Geez, it's like a cloud bank in here."

She smelled the rich aroma, heard the clink of a cup being set on tile.

"And that's all? You came in just to bring me coffee?" The lather had drained away.

"Well, that's up to you."

"That sounds like a bad line from a B movie, Jack. A real bad one." She clicked open the shower door, reached for her towel, and stepped into the small, foggy room. Jack was there, of course, standing naked as the day he was born. "For the love of God." She wrapped the terry towel quickly around her. "Did you make the coffee that way?"

He glanced down at his nude body, unconcerned. "Gave Coco a thrill."

"You'll scandalize the neighbors."

"I hope so."

She thought he'd pull her into his arms, force her back into the shower and do all kinds of incredible things to her body while the water cascaded over them and the soap made their skin slick and pliable. Instead, his blue eyes sparkling, as if he knew exactly what she was thinking, he eased around her and stepped into the shower. "It's big enough for two," he said pointedly.

She gazed at him, knowing if she wanted him, he was ready. But he wanted her to come to him.

"I'll see you downstairs," she said after a long moment.

"Tease."

"Oh, yeah, right."

She toweled her body and rubbed the water from her hair, then tossed on her robe. Quickly she reached for her brush, but it wasn't in its usual spot in the drawer. What? She searched, but came up empty-handed. Rather than worry about it, she found a wide-toothed comb and ran it through her hair, pulling water out. Then she picked up her cup of coffee and, after peeking into B.J.'s room and finding him sleeping soundly, headed down the hall.

Jack had to go. He *had* to. For her sanity. He couldn't just hang out here, she thought, walking downstairs.

It's the weekend. Let it go for now.

At the base of the steps, she saw Coco, lying in her little bed near the couch in the living room, her scruffy white head propped on the bed's edge. Dark button eyes blinked. At the sight of Cissy, her little tail wagged, and she yawned, stretching, then shot to her feet, trotting over to be picked up.

"I'm sorry," Cissy said as she scratched Coco behind her ears. The little dog grunted in pleasure. "I should have let you out last night."

Thank God for Jack.

Wait. No. Strike that! She didn't like the turn of her thoughts. "Let's see what we've got." Carrying the little white scruff and her cup into the kitchen, she set the dog down, then opened the refrigerator. She found a few scraps of chicken left over from the gathering and, tearing off a couple of small bites, hand-fed them to the dog. She then took Coco outside, where dawn was streaking the sky in shades of magenta and gold. The air was cold and brisk but, for once this winter, there were no clouds scudding across the sky, no fog wisping through the spires of the skyscrapers visible above the trees.

She rubbed her arms and told herself she'd been six kinds of a fool for letting Jack spend the night.

You didn't let him stay; he crawled into bed with you while you were sleeping.

But she could have stopped him from making love to

her. This morning, when she discovered him all warm and hard-bodied beside her, she could have pushed him away. Sleep hadn't clouded her mind. Grief hadn't devastated her willpower. Too much wine the night before hadn't clouded her judgment. Oh, no. She'd wanted to make love to Jack as much as he apparently had wanted to make love to her.

Idiot!

Damned fool woman!

Now they were back to square one.

What was wrong with her? She knew he was bad for her, and yet she was like some of those stupid women always attracted to the wrong kind of guy, the guy with an edge, the bad boy they wanted to tame.

What a load of garbage!

"Hey," she said to the dog. "Let's go inside. It's not exactly red hot out here, and I'll get you some real breakfast." Coco lifted her head. Finished with "her business," as Gran used to call it, she shot across the grass and through the opened French door. Cissy followed, shut the door, then really took a look around. The place needed work, no doubt about it. Though the house was tidied up from the gathering after the funeral, there were recycling and garbage to deal with, the floors needed mopping, and . . . *and what are you going to do about Jack? You can't just bury yourself in menial jobs and avoid the issue.*

"Damn it all," she muttered, taking another bag of garbage and depositing it into the already overstuffed can.

You know you love him. No matter what you say. You've never stopped.

After feeding Coco and refreshing the dog's water bowl, she filled a bucket of water and added some lemon juice, then set to work with the mop.

You have to make him leave. Now. You can't let yourself be lulled into this feeling of security. You know better.

Working like a demon on the floors, washing them vigorously while Coco barked and played, pretending to attack the mop as it slid in front of her, Cissy worked out her aggression and tried not to think about Jack as she heard him moving around upstairs. He was such a big part of her life, and when he finally walked down the stairs carrying a rosy-cheeked and groggy B.J., her heart melted. "Did someone wake up?" she asked, smiling at her son.

"Dad-dee got me."

"He was just beginning to stir," Jack said, and Cissy caught a whiff of his aftershave, the one bottle she'd forgotten to toss out, the bottle that at least twice she'd opened and smelled, secretively drinking in the scent of him in the long days over this past month.

"Don't let him down. The floor's still wet. How about breakfast, hmm?" she asked her son, who was still in his pajamas. "I'm sure your daddy changed you."

"Last night and this morning, yeah," Jack said. "I do know how to take care of him, y'know." He handed Beej to her, and she kissed his curly head.

"You sleep well, baby boy?"

"I not a baby!"

"Always to me."

"No, Mom-mee!"

"Okay, you're my big guy, is that better?"

"Big guy," B.J. said seriously.

"He's got 'no' down pat, doesn't he?" Jack remarked, pouring himself another cup of coffee.

"Absolutely."

"Dog-gie!" B.J. suddenly saw Coco and began wriggling like crazy to be set on the floor. "Dog-gie!"

She set him on his feet, and Beej, in footed pajamas,

took off a little unsteadily after the dog. Coco barked, and the chase was on.

"I thought she was old," Jack said.

"Believe me . . . she'll show her age pretty soon, and she'll start hobbling and probably sleep the rest of the day."

The doorbell rang, and Cissy glanced at Jack.

"Beats me," he said to the unspoken question. Barefoot, he walked through the foyer and yanked open the door. Beej trotted after him.

Jannelle was standing on the front porch. Her eyes traveled up and down her brother's half-dressed body, and her expression said it all: she was not pleased.

"Don't tell me," she said, not bothering to hide her disapproval. "You're getting back together."

It's not what it looks like, Cissy wanted to deny. But Jack said, "Maybe." Then, as he picked up his son, "Want a cup of coffee?"

Jannelle was shaking her head and ignoring her nephew. "No, I just came by because I left my sunglasses here, I think. They must've fallen out of my purse. I didn't put it upstairs; I had it over here. . . ." She walked into the nook and searched in the corner behind a potted plant. "Voila." She glanced at Cissy's state of undress. "You know, I tried to call and let you know I was dropping by, but you didn't answer your cell."

"Oh. I turned it off for yesterday's service."

"The landline works." Jack placed B.J. in his high chair as Cissy found a box of Cheerios, poured some of the cereal into a small plastic bowl, then put the bowl on the tray of the high chair.

"I don't have the house number in my contact list on my cell." Jannelle looked at her brother again, shrugged, then slid her sunglasses onto the bridge of her nose. "I wish you guys would just make up your mind. Either you're married, or you're not."

"We're not divorced yet," Jack said and then, as if to derail her, asked, "How's Dad?" as Cissy searched in the cupboard for Beej's sippy cup. She found it, but noticed that his tiny silver mug, the one that Eugenia had engraved with his name and birth date, wasn't where it usually sat. Strange. She knew she'd seen it just the other day, but she didn't have time to search for it now. Instead, she took the sippy cup from the shelf and poured a little milk into it.

All the while, Cissy ignored her sister-in-law's comments. Jannelle, who took being the older sister to the nth, had always butted in. Her remarks were always pointed, always full of judgment.

Jannelle's brow furrowed as she glanced around the house through her glasses. "Talk about smudged." She yanked off the shades and polished them with the hem of her sweater. "I haven't talked to Dad today, but I imagine he's got one helluva hangover. He's probably still sleeping it off." She slid the glasses on again, and once more swung her head, testing the clarity of the lenses. "By the time J.J. and I poured him into his condo, he was feeling no pain." Her eyebrows shot up over the rims of her designer sunglasses. "I mean *no* pain."

Jack offered, "I'll call him later."

"Do that."

As Coco patrolled the kitchen, B.J. picked up several Cheerios, put one in his mouth, and, grinning, tossed several over the side of the tray.

"No," Cissy admonished.

"No!" He pounded on the tray. "No!"

Beneath the highchair, Coco was ready, sniffing and eating whatever little tidbit fell to the floor.

"How about J.J.? Did he get home okay?" Jack asked.

Jannelle lifted a shoulder. "How should I know? He kept yammering about all the 'hotties' who he'd met here. I thought he might show up again, you know, and

start asking for phone numbers and e-mail addresses."
She made a face. "I don't really think he understood
the gravity of the situation. I dropped him off at Dad's
since his car was there, and I assumed he went home,
but then again, I don't know, and it's really none of my
business." She was already heading for the door. "I'll see
you around. Keep me posted, will ya? Once you decide
whether you're going to stay married or not?"

"You'll be the first to know," Jack said dryly, following
her barefoot to the vestibule. "Well . . . right after Cissy
and me. I think we should get the info first."

"Funny man," she said.

He held the door for her, and once she was over the
threshold, swung it shut. "She didn't even say 'hi' to
Beej," he observed.

"I noticed."

"Maybe she's jealous, you know. Thirty-eight and
never been married."

"Thirty-eight isn't exactly ancient."

"Maybe she feels like she's running out of options. If
she wants kids, she's got to find a guy, get to know him,
decide he's the one, get married, and then plan a kid
that may or may not happen right away. That takes
time."

"She could have a baby next year if she wanted to,
Jack. She doesn't need to do the whole dating-courting-
marriage thing. I just think she doesn't like or want
kids. And that's okay."

"Maybe." Jack forced his hands into the front pockets of his pants as he walked to the French doors and
stared at the yard. "Sometimes I think my family is more
dysfunctional than yours."

She had to laugh. "Is that possible?"

"Let's face it, Cissy, between us, we have our share of
nutcases and lunatics."

"It's possible the Cahills don't have the corner on

neuroses and psychoses, but you Holts can't hold a candle to us." She thought of her psycho mother running from the law, and Cherise and her brother, Monty, another criminal. She slid a glance at her son, who was contemplating shoving a Cheerio up his nose. "Oh, Beej," she said, distracting him before he actually pushed the bit of cereal up his nostril. "You are the cutest, smartest boy I know, but genetically, you've got some major strikes against you."

"Amen," Jack agreed and glanced up at Cissy. She started to say something about him leaving, but he read the message in her eyes.

"I'll get my things."

Her heart tore a little, but she didn't fight it when, dressed in the same clothes he'd worn to the funeral, he hugged his boy, then dropped a kiss on her forehead.

"Dad-dee!" Beej yelled from his high chair. "Dad-dee stay!"

"I'll be back," Jack promised, then closed the door behind him.

"Nooooo!" the boy wailed, beginning to sob. Cissy quickly unstrapped him from the high chair. He kicked and cried and wrestled, then wept as if his little heart would break.

Cissy felt terrible. How could she do this to her child?

How could she do it to herself?

Forgive him, Cissy. Give Jack a second chance.

"And then what?" she wondered aloud, but there was no answer.

Chapter 13

Paterno walked along the waterfront. It was the week-end, Sunday, two days after Eugenia's funeral. He was trying to follow everyone's advice that he should take some time off, if for nothing more than to clear his head. But he couldn't. The case ate at him.

He took a deep breath and watched seagulls swoop over the green water, calling and wheeling, looking for scraps of food left on the docks. The air was brisk, smelling of brine, a cold breeze blowing in from the Pacific Ocean, slapping at his face and billowing his windbreaker. He stopped into a coffee shop, where he grabbed a cup of black coffee and an oatmeal muffin because it sounded like it had a chance of having some nutritional benefits; not that he cared, but his doctor was on his case.

He should go fishing. Or golfing. Or sailing. Or friggin' stay home and try to find a game on TV. But he'd decided on this walk on the piers, and now, dodging other pedestrians, joggers, strollers, and skateboards, he was still thinking about the case.

Always the damned case.

He eyed the sailboats cutting across the murky water, but he was still sifting through the evidence. Phone records for Rory Amhurst's room at the care center and Eugenia Cahill's house gave up no clues. All tire and foot impressions and fingerprints came back as belonging to members of the staff at Harborside, or the Cahill family members and staff at Eugenia's house on Mt. Sutro. There had been no evidence collected that pointed to a specific killer, and as the hours and days passed, Paterno knew the cases were getting colder and colder. He'd gone over the last days of Eugenia Cahill's life, talking to the people who saw her last, tracing the footsteps of her final hours, but no one had seen or heard anything that had offered a lead to the killer.

He walked to the railing of the dock and stared down into the ocean, spying his own watery reflection. He knew in his gut that Marla Cahill was behind this, but he couldn't prove it, nor could a statewide manhunt locate the slippery bitch.

Where had she gone?

Who was harboring her?

Why, in all of the dozens of calls from people who had thought they'd seen her, had not one solid lead evolved?

And Mary Smith—who the hell was she? The name was a phony, of course, as was her affiliation with a church, but why hadn't anyone seen her? The composite sketch made by the police artist, and another one generated by a computer, had been broadcast over the news, and, as in the case of Marla, nothing solid had appeared.

"Son of a bitch," he growled and noticed a seagull hovering nearby, eyeing the remainder of his breakfast. Dropping it into the water, he said, "Knock yourself out." The bird swooped down and gobbled up the soggy piece of muffin, and two other seagulls squawked and tried to steal it away. "I hear it lowers your cholesterol," he said to the birds, then finished the last of his coffee and tossed the empty cup into a trash bin.

So what did he have to go on to find Marla, to solve the murders?

"Very little and not much," he said to no one as he hiked back to his car. He was tense. Agitated. Knew that if they didn't find Marla soon, there would be more deaths. He'd tried to call Cissy Cahill on her cell phone and warn her, but he'd only been able to leave messages. Maybe she was dodging him. He didn't need to be a rocket scientist to see that she didn't trust him.

Not that he blamed her.

It seemed as if he'd been dogging the Cahill family for years, though there had been nearly a decade between the first case and this one. The decade when Marla Cahill had been safely behind bars. Now that peace had ended, and the murderess was on the loose again. She'd been involved either directly or indirectly in the deaths of three people ten years ago, and now she was adding to the total, though once again, he thought, she was most likely behind the scenes. Someone else was doing her dirty work. Just like before.

But who?

He'd been in contact with Benowitz, but the state police weren't having any luck with nabbing Marla Cahill, and the feds were frustrated as well.

Welcome to my world.

He found his keys in his pocket and was about to unlock the doors to his Caddy when he saw the scratch, a long, ugly mar that went down the driver's side. "Shit." He looked around, hoping to spy the culprit who had keyed his car, but he saw no one running, no one watching, no one hiding in the other vehicles parked here. "Son of a bitch." Anger pounded at his temples, and his fists balled impotently. "Son of a goddamn bitch."

He took another look around, zeroed in on a couple of kids walking and laughing and talking on the waterfront, two boys with iPods and baggy shorts, Oakland Raiders jackets and self-important saunters. They looked about fourteen—one Hispanic, the other white—but they didn't so much as glance over their shoulders as they bought tickets to visit Alcatraz.

Whoever had scratched the hell out of his car had gotten away with it, and it pissed the hell out of him.

"Take it easy. Clear your head. Get a little exercise." He mimicked his own advice as he backed out of the parking space. "What a load of crap."

He drove straight to the station, his mood foul. There was work to catch up on. He had more on his plate than the recent murders of Eugenia Cahill and Rory Amhurst. A Jane Doe had been found in the bay yesterday. And there was a pretty cut-and-dried case of domestic violence, the beaten wife still holding her husband's .38 in her shaking hands as he lay dead on the floor, the baseball bat he'd swung at her still in his hand. These were people who had once pledged to love each other for better or worse. Worse had definitely won out. Jesus, the world was a sick place.

He parked in the station's lot and cast another angry look at his car. It would cost him a fortune to have it repainted.

So get yourself one of those hybrids. Retire the old Caddy. Be kind to the environment. Save yourself some gas dollars.

"Humph." Jaw set, he turned away and walked into the station house, which was a little quieter than during the week. He got a lot more work done, plowing steadily through paperwork. There were always a few detectives doing the same, or working weekend cases. Murderers, unfortunately, didn't work nine to five. Even so, Paterno was more at home during the week, when everyone was on duty. The station house was alive then, crackling with an energy that he found stimulating.

Today, he caught up on his paperwork, made a few phone calls, and went over his list of suspects, some of whom, with alibis, had been crossed off.

Cissy Cahill's name was still there, big as life, a woman who had just inherited a fortune, more money than Paterno could save in his lifetime. And yet he didn't believe she was involved . . . it just didn't fit. He couldn't picture the young mother as a murderess, nor did she seem particularly fond of her mother, so she wasn't about to try and please Marla by knocking off her enemies.

Is that what this was about?

Marla Cahill's enemies?

So far the two victims had been her relatives, her brother by blood, her mother-in-law by marriage.

He drummed his fingers on the table and looked at the pictures of the two victims, alive and then dead. He picked up the composite of Mary Smith. "Who the hell are you?" he wondered out loud as he heard footsteps behind him.

"Your partner," Janet Quinn said, thinking he was talking to her. She was carrying a backpack over one shoulder and a water bottle by its neck in her other hand.

"I thought you were taking the weekend off, going to Reno." He dropped the composite onto the clutter of open files, empty cups, and scratched notes.

"Plans fell through," she admitted, and he wondered about her private life. Quinn was one of the most close-mouthed people he knew. He had no idea what she did on her off hours. "You?"

"Don't ask."

"I saw your car." She was shaking her head. "Ouch."

"It's a pisser," he said, angry again.

"Any idea who did it?" She dropped the backpack onto the chair he usually reserved for suspects or witnesses.

"Some brainless, dickless asshole." He snorted and picked up a pen, clicking it in frustration. "Could be someone I sent away, could be random. I'm going to check if there are any security cameras in the area, but I figure my chances of finding the guy are nil."

"So what have you got?" She nodded toward the Cahill file, open on his desk.

"Nothin'. You?"

"Same as you." She rested a hip on the corner of his desk and uncapped her bottle. "I'm still going over the things we found in Eugenia's safe. Stock certificates, cash, jewelry, the will, and a few other personal items."

"Such as?"

"A family history, I guess you'd call it. Or maybe Eugenia's memoirs. She was pretty meticulous. As if she was going to write a book someday." She took a long swallow of her water, then recapped the bottle.

"Anything good?"

"Nothing that means anything. At least not that I can sort out. There are pictures too. Some look about a hundred years old. I'm trying to do a little who's who and figure out all the major players."

"Interesting?"

"Not so far, but I'm not quite through it yet."

"Good luck," he said.

"What about tips? Anyone seen our Mary Smith?"

"Nah. Nor Marla." Marla Cahill's photo had been circulating through the media ever since her escape. Now the police had released the artist's sketch, and all the tips that had come in had turned out to be either mistakes or freakoids who wanted to be a part of the investigation. They were looking for their fifteen minutes of fame any way they could get it. Well, not on his watch.

"Maybe something will turn up."

He leaned back in his chair as she grabbed the strap of her backpack and walked to her desk. As she dropped into her chair, her cell phone spewed out some tune from the eighties. God, he hated those special ringtones. Waste of time and money. He cracked his neck, winced, and picked up the sketch of Mary Smith again.

Who are you?

On Monday morning, Cissy decided to leave the house and finish her article at the coffee shop. She hadn't been back to Joltz since she'd seen the weird man in black, but she told herself that her encounter with the creep was just an anomaly, a product of timing and over-heightened senses.

Things were crazed right now, that was all. As she scraped her hair away from her face and snapped it into an untidy knot at the back of her head, she told herself to buck up and get on with her life.

Sooner or later she'd have to deal with the lawyers and her grandmother's house, but today she was going to work for a couple of hours, jog if the weather permitted, then spend the rest of her day with Beej while going through the cards and flowers and donations to Cahill House that had been sent after Gran's death.

Tanya, still eyeing Coco dubiously, had arrived and promised to take B.J. to the park if the sun dared peek through the clouds. Cissy's resolve to replace the young woman had wavered since Tanya had helped out so much at the funeral.

Looking at the weather, Cissy figured Tanya was off the hook for the park. The sky was gun-metal gray. No rain was falling yet, but with the approaching thick clouds, it was only a matter of time.

Traffic was thick, and Cissy had to circle the neighborhood a couple of times before she found a parking spot two blocks down the hill from Joltz. Hauling her laptop with her, she hiked to the coffee shop, telling herself the exercise was just what she needed to get her blood pumping and her mind clear.

Though she knew she was being stupid, she couldn't help but keep an eye out for the man in black with the creepy smile. Isolated incident or not, the confrontation still bothered her.

"Get over it," she told herself as she ordered a mocha from Rachelle, thanked her and Diedre again for helping out with the post-funeral gathering, then settled into her favorite table in the corner. There was a lull in the activity at the popular shop. Most of the pre-work crowd had already been in, then out, and it would be a few more hours before the lunch crowd gathered. Right now only a few patrons were sitting at the tables or at the counter. Some were reading a paper, some were talking, while others just sipped their hot beverages as they gazed out the window on the cold, gray day.

One woman who always came in and ordered a frozen coffee-and-cream blend was at the counter. She made small talk and placed a dollar in the tip jar while Diedre arranged croissants and scones in the glass case. A man Cissy didn't recognize was seated near the window. His black beret was cocked upon a head that had been shaved bald, and he was working feverishly on a Sudoku puzzle with a tiny pencil usually used for marking golf score-cards.

Not much happening. Nothing out of the ordinary.

No man in a dark trench coat and with a cold grin.

Of course Selma showed up. Either she lived in the area or was following Cissy, because every time Cissy spent any time at the coffee shop and deli, Selma arrived as if on schedule.

She seemed to always be here.

As Cissy surreptitiously watched, Selma, the slim, reddish-haired funeral crasher, ordered her usual latte, then stopped by Cissy's table and asked about Marla. Cissy murmured a noncommittal response, then Selma drifted to her favorite chair, where she sipped her drink and read a paperback thriller. Or peeked over the top at Cissy and the other patrons, almost as if she were gathering data, like some kind of Gen-X spy.

Oh, stop it! Cissy took a big swallow of her mocha, fired up her laptop, then spread her handwritten notes on the small table. Resting the heel of one of her running shoes on the empty chair on the opposite side of the table, she began pulling her story together.

At first it was slow. She was distracted by people coming into the shop. She was afraid she wouldn't be able to concentrate, that all of the stress of the last couple of weeks would jam up her creative juices. But after a few failed attempts, surprisingly, the story that had been gelling for nearly a month in the back of her subconscious began to take shape. She wrote text from her notes, double-checked quotes, and moved paragraphs around. She remembered liking the black woman running for mayor, and as she reread her notes, brought out most of the candidate's ideas.

Her fingers flew over the keyboard, her mocha grew cold, and she smiled to herself at a particularly clever turn of phrase.

"Cissy?"

She nearly jumped, knocking over her drink then grabbing it before it tumbled to the floor. She glanced up to find her neighbor Sara standing by the table.

"Sara." Cissy's voice lacked enthusiasm.

Sara scraped a nearby chair toward the table. "Working?" she asked, then winced. "Sorry. Dumb question. Can you take a break?"

"I've been on a break all month," Cissy said.

"I know, I know. I won't keep you, but I had to track you down. I tried your cell, couldn't get through, and called the house. Tanya told me where you were, and please," she held up a hand, "don't get mad at her; I had to pry the information from her."

Oh, sure.

"Don't you answer your cell phone? Or are you screening me out?"

"No, sorry, it's lost. Got misplaced the day of the funeral, and I can't find it because I turned it off for the service and never turned it back on."

"That's what 'vibrate' is for."

"Yeah, I know. I was just so scattered. Anyway, if I don't find it soon, I'll have to get a new one."

"I'd die without mine."

Cissy didn't doubt it. "So what was it you wanted?" she asked, but knew. In her heart of hearts, Cissy understood that Sara had tracked her down because of Gran's house. She wanted to list it.

"I thought we should talk about your grandmother's house," she said, leaning back in her chair, and for the first time Cissy noticed that rain had begun to pepper the street and drip from the awnings.

"Sara—"

"Look, I'm serious. I have clients flying in from Philadelphia, and they want something with a view, something old, something authentic San Francisco, and something with room for live-in servants and an elevator. Am I describing Eugenia's house or what?" she asked, her eyes sparkling.

"I can't sell it. I don't own it. It's part of Gran's estate, and that might not be settled for a long time. The attorneys are working on it, but really, Sara, there's nothing I can do."

"I've talked with the attorneys," she admitted just as the coffee grinder roared through a pound of fragrant beans.

"You what?" Cissy couldn't believe her ears. "You went behind my back? After I told you that I didn't want to sell it? Wait a sec—how do you even know which legal firm I'm dealing with?"

Sara gave that little girl smile and lifted a shoulder to acknowledge that she'd been naughty. "I saw their names when I looked at the house," she said. "Right there on Eugenia's writing desk."

"So you called them?"

"I just left my name and phone number and the name of the company I work for. I said I'd love to represent the estate in selling the place. Was that so awful?"

Cissy was dumbfounded. "You should have talked to me."

"I did. You showed me the house."

"You *begged* to see it."

"Okay, okay, I confess. I wanted to see it, yes." She leaned closer and grabbed Cissy's arm. "And I love the place. *Love it.* That house is one of the premier properties in the city. And get this, my clients, the ones flying in from Philly? They're not only able to afford the house, well, just about any house in the city for that matter, but he's a doctor, and his new job is at the medical school, which butts right up to your property. Look, I've got the plan." She opened a sleek leather briefcase, pulled out legal documents and pictures of the house, digital images she'd taken the day after Gran had died. Gratefully, there were none of the blood-stained foyer.

"I can't believe you did this. I told you then, and I'm telling you now, I'm not selling," she said firmly. To her embarrassment, several people glanced in her direction. Cissy shrank away from the stares and snapped her computer closed. She wasn't going to have this discussion here.

"Cissy, I'm sorry," Sara said, and she actually looked mortified. "I didn't mean to upset you. I thought you'd be pleased. . . . Oh hell. I really am sorry. Hey," she turned to Rachelle and waved at her. "Another drink, what is it you're having, Cissy? Latte?"

"No."

"Chai tea?"

"Mocha, but I don't need another one."

"Sure you do. Let me do this," Sara barreled on. "Please. I'm going now. Go back to work." She wiggled her fingers at the laptop. "I'll talk to you later. I'm sorry," she said again. "Really." She pushed her chair back and, with a seemingly genuinely rueful expression, slid a few bills from her wallet and handed them to Rachelle. "Keep the change," she said, hiking the collar of her coat around her neck and shouldering open the door. A gust of rain-washed air swept inside, along with two blond teenage girls, who, for some reason, weren't in school. Noses red, they approached the counter and Diedre.

Cissy had lost the mood and her inspiration. The story was about finished. She could put the final touches on it tonight, after B.J. went to sleep, but she was finished for the time being.

"She's a pain," Rachelle said as she handed Cissy the new mocha.

"Amen," Diedre said.

Rachelle picked up a few dishes and swabbed the table where the guy in the beret had been sitting just as a brown-haired girl bustled in. "Sorry I'm late," she said, peeling off her coat to reveal a Joltz apron over her slacks and a long-sleeved T-shirt.

"The cavalry has arrived!" Rachelle teased.

"If I'm the cavalry, do I have to do dishes?" the girl asked.

"What else?"

Cissy left, hiking the two blocks back to her car in the rain. She'd left her umbrella in the backseat of the car, so by the time she'd unlocked the door of her Acura, she was soaked to the skin. Only her laptop in its leather case had thwarted the elements. So much for jogging later or taking B.J. out in his stroller. She glanced at the dark sky and frowned.

Though she hadn't planned it, she drove around the block and headed up the hill, turning on her headlights and wipers. It was late afternoon, and already, because of the cloud cover, the day was dark as dusk, the rain cold as winter.

It had been a week since she'd visited Gran's house, and she thought it was about time to face her demons, maybe look at the place with new eyes . . . as Sara had.

Using her remote, she opened the gate, nosing the Acura into the parking area in front of the garage. Ducking her head against the chilly rain, Cissy ran up the walk to the front porch and let herself inside with her key.

No one was here. As she walked through the gloomy rooms snapping lights on and off, she could tell that Rosa and Paloma were keeping the place up: the floors and woodwork gleamed; the smell of pine and lemon was heavy in the air. Nothing was out of place, but the house seemed old and creaky, a cavernous tomb.

She mounted the stairs to the floor where she'd spent most of her waking hours, checking out the library and the family room, each seeming cold and dark without Gran's vitality and strong personality. Snapping off lights, she climbed up another flight to the bedroom suites on the third floor. Almost feeling as if she were treading on the grave of her parents' marriage, she opened the door to their suite and stepped inside. They'd each had a separate room linked by this shared sitting area complete with a fireplace and a private verandah, like their own private apartment within the massive old house.

Cissy felt a chill that cut deep to her soul.

Looking out the glass doors to the private garden, she realized how dark the day had become. Night was falling fast. She touched the back of her mother's favorite Queen Anne chair and trembled inside.

It seemed like eons ago when they'd all lived here. She felt a pang of nostalgia, of regret, though she didn't know why. Cissy had never thought of her family as loving, far from it. But it was her family. Or had been.

She left her parents' living quarters and made her way around the staircase to her room. As she walked into the cozy space where she'd spent so many hours as a teenager, she felt a stab of loneliness for what now seemed a simpler life.

Before your mother turned into a psycho.

Refusing to dwell on Marla, she turned back to the hallway and started for the guest room.

Crrreeeeaaaak!

The sound swept up the dark staircase.

Cissy froze.

What was that? A door opening? Or something else? What?

No one was here. She'd checked.

Goose bumps raised on her skin.

She waited, counting her heartbeats, then told herself it was nothing. Her mind playing tricks on her. She hadn't heard anything. Still . . . maybe Rosa or Paloma or Lars had returned. They all had keys. For that matter, so did Elsa and Deborah and God only knew who else. Gran had gardeners and repairmen over all the time.

"Hello?" she called down the staircase to the second floor, where she'd left a single light burning in the library. "Anyone there?" Eerily, her own voice seemed to echo slightly, a hollow sound reverberating against the walls. "Hello?"

She waited.

All was quiet.

Your imagination, she told herself sternly.

Starting for the stairs, she heard a footfall, the quiet scrape of leather against hardwood.

Her heart nearly stopped.

Fear shot through her.

Someone was definitely in the house.

"Hey!" she called again, telling herself it had to be someone who worked here. Someone she knew. Someone with a key.

Why? Did you lock the door behind you?

Did you wait until the gate swung shut behind your car?

And why the hell aren't they responding?

Cissy's insides turned to water. "Who's there?" she called. *Please let it be one of the staff. . . .*

Again there was silence.

Deafening, paralyzing silence.

And darkness. . . . Why hadn't she left on most of the lights? The house was so damned gloomy and still.

God Almighty, was she going crazy?

She knew she heard something.

Some*one.*

Swallowing her fear, she stepped back into the bedroom that had once been hers, the room her grandmother had never redecorated. As rain pelted the window, she looked around for a weapon, anything to ward off an attacker.

Who, Cissy? Who would be assaulting you? That's nuts!

Or was it? Someone had killed Rory, hadn't they? Someone had murdered Gran in this very house. Someone who hadn't broken in.

She thought about using the phone. . . . She didn't have her cell, but there was a landline.

And call whom?

The police?

And tell them you heard a noise?

Come on, Cissy.

Or would you call Jack?

Tell him you're really scared, that you got freaked when you heard a noise while snooping around in your grandmother's house?

He'd want to know why you came up here alone in the first place.

For God's sake, deal with it.

Insides shaking, she quietly opened the closet door and found her old riding crop, a weapon she'd never used on the horse, but which might come in handy now. Feeling foolish, she carried the whip with her to the hallway.

Was it darker still?

She reached for a light switch, and the sconces surrounding the staircase offered a soft, warm glow. That was better. Maybe there was no one—

Clunk!

What?

Her heart nearly stopped as she recognized the sound of the elevator as it groaned into gear and started to whine as it rose upward.

Oh Jesus!

She nearly screamed.

She didn't wait for it to reach the third floor, but scrambled for the stairs. Her feet nearly tripped over each other as she flew down, pausing briefly at the second floor landing.

What if the elevator stopped here?

Who said whoever was inside was getting out on the third floor?

Oh God, who was it? The killer?

Cissy, don't freak out. Maybe the elevator's malfunctioning.

LIKE HELL!

The house was so cold, so suddenly cold.

She paused long enough to hear the elevator car clunk to a stop on the second floor, the very level on which she was standing, the area where her grandmother was pushed over the railing to her death. Frozen, the stupid whip squeezed in her fingers, she felt another cold rush of air sweep up the stairs.

The elevator doors whispered open.

Fear clutched her heart.

Her pulse thundered in her ears.

She stared into the elevator.

The car was empty.

No one stepped out.

All she saw in the dim light of an old bulb was her own terrified expression caught in the mirror mounted on the back wall of the ancient car.

Every hair on the back of her neck stood at attention. *Someone* had sent that car upward. It didn't just rise on its own. A finger had pressed the button of the panel, choosing the second floor as its destination . . . almost as if whoever had done it had known she was here.

The car doors closed, and Cissy was left on the landing, her nerves stretched to the breaking point.

Someone was definitely in the house.

Someone who didn't want to be known.

Someone who knew she was here and was hellbent on scaring the wits out of her. Well, it was working.

She swallowed hard, panic shooting through her as she stared at the closed doors of the elevator. If no one was in the elevator, then . . . She looked down the darkened staircase to the floor below.

A scream died on her lips.

In the open doorway, backlit by the barest of afternoon light, was the silhouette of a woman, a shadowy figure of a woman in a long coat with an upturned collar.

Cissy grabbed the handrail.

The woman's features weren't clear, but her hair was a deep red. . . . Oh dear Lord.

Cissy's throat turned to sand.

The riding crop slid from her hands to tumble down the stairs.

"Mom?" she whispered, her heart in her throat, her brain screaming denials. "Mom? Is that you?"

Chapter 14

The door slammed shut.

Cutting off Cissy's view of her mother.

It couldn't be! Marla wouldn't have risked coming here! No way.

So what then, Cissy? Are you imagining things? Pulling up her image when you know she can't be anywhere near?

On rubbery legs she raced down the stairs and out the front door. Rain was pouring from the sky, gurgling in the downspouts, puddling on the ground. Cissy stepped off the porch. "Mom!" she yelled. "Damn it, Mom, where are you?"

But she was talking to the wind.

She saw no one, heard no running footsteps.

It was as if a ghost had appeared, only to fade again.

No!

She knew what she'd seen. Damn it, if she'd only had her cell phone. Following the path to the back of the house, she searched through the gardens and shrubbery, but in the ever-darkening gloom, she saw no one. Not near the trellis, nor the arbor, nor . . . She saw the swing, hanging from its rotting wooden frame, slowly shifting to and fro, the old chains barely rattling.

The wind?

Or a hand that had swiped it as Marla had fled?

"Mom!" she yelled again, but her only answer was the soft rush of traffic down the hill, the sweep of fir branches in the wind, the plop of raindrops.

She turned, eyeing the big house rising four stories above the ground, mullioned windows dark and ominous.

Determinedly, she trudged to the front of the house. No one was here. Lord, had it been her imagination? Had all the talk of her mother's escape finally gotten to her? With the murder of Rory and Gran, had she, Cissy, snapped? She wasn't afraid of her mother. Never would be. Marla wasn't the most loving mother on earth, that much was true, and Cissy had suffered from her share of neglect, but she didn't fear her mother. Never would. Whoever had killed Gran and Rory was not Marla Amhurst Cahill. She wouldn't believe it.

So what the hell had just happened?

With no answer, she locked the front door, pulled on the handle to make sure it latched, then walked along the brick path to her car. All the while she eyed the shadows and stygian umbras; the wet, shivering plants; the dark, sheltered nooks where the exterior corners of the house met.

But she caught no glimpse of a running woman, heard no frantic footsteps or rush of wild breathing.

Marla's image was gone as quickly as it had appeared.

Cissy was alone.

Trembling, she rubbed her arms, finally noticing the rain that was running down her neck. Had she seen her mother?

Or had her stupid, twisted mind hallucinated, creating an image she secretly wanted to see?

"You're a basket case," she said as she climbed into her car. Inside she noticed the scent, the faintest fragrance that she remembered from her childhood, the odor of the perfume that her mother had worn.

"No," she said and fought tears, denied that she might be losing her mind. "You are not going to haunt me, you bitch, do you hear me? I won't let you." Her mother had not been in her car. And the gates to the estate were closed. Locked. Marla hadn't opened them.

Cissy hit the button on the remote lock and shoved the Acura into reverse, waiting as the gate's old gears groaned and clicked. But the gate didn't move. She hit the button again. Heard the same clicks and groan of grinding gears. In the mirror's reflection, she caught sight of the slightest movement of the massive wrought-iron gate, as if it were trying to open but couldn't.

"What the hell?" Disgusted, Cissy climbed out of her car and examined the gate. Deep in the latch, crammed into the release mechanism, was a rusted screwdriver.

A tool that hadn't been there when she arrived, as the gate had swung open easily.

All the blood in Cissy's body turned to ice.

Her mother's image had been no ghostly apparition.

The perfume hadn't been her imagination.

Marla Cahill had returned.

Cherise Favier checked caller ID before answering the phone. When Donald was out of town, as he had been since yesterday's noon sermon, she was a little more cautious about answering either the phone or the door, or even going outside. It wasn't that she was scared, not really, it was just that over the years of their marriage she'd ceased being just Cherise. She and Donald were like two halves of a whole. She was used to being with him, a part of something special, bigger than herself.

She liked being married.

She'd always liked being married, and this time, she wasn't giving up. Third time was the proverbial charm, and she'd move heaven and earth to remain Mrs. Donald Favier forever.

Her life had been in turmoil before she'd found Donald, and she wasn't going to let him slip away. Now she lived in a large house, supplied by the parish, of course. It was even larger than the last one they'd shared, which only proved how much the parishioners loved her husband.

Nonetheless, sometimes she was lonely, and her children, all three at college, rarely called, hardly ever came home for visits.

So she checked caller ID, saw that Cissy was calling, and almost didn't answer, not after that hideous scene at her house after the funeral. Good heavens! Cissy had acted as if Cherise were asking for more than was her due! They all knew that was wrong, all realized that her father, and all of his progeny, had been scammed by that vile grandfather of Cissy's.

She picked up the phone. "Hello?" she said, as if she didn't know who was on the other end of the line.

"Hi, Cherise, it's Cissy," a raspy nasal voice responded, then erupted into a fit of coughing. "Sorry. I guess I strained my voice talking so much or something. Who knows? It's mainly laryngitis." Cissy sounded as if even speaking in a whisper was a real strain.

"Oh. I, uh, hope you feel better," Cherise said. She was slightly mystified. Cissy never called. Never. She wasn't phoning just to make conversation. There had to be a point to this.

"Look, I'm sorry about the other day. I didn't mean to blow up at you like that. I was just overwrought, you know. Freaked out about Gran and all. I want to make it up to you."

Cherise liked the sound of that, but she was suspicious. She'd known Cissy all of her life, and the younger woman wasn't one to capitulate or change her mind. "You do?"

"Yeah . . . well, I don't know. I just thought we should talk, and I promise I won't freak out."

That sounded better. Truer to form. "When?"

"How about tonight? I can get a sitter."

"Oh, well . . . Donald's out of town. I know he wants us all to get together for a family dinner."

"Actually, I thought it should be just you and me anyway. Not Jack or Donald, because they're not really Cahills."

"I don't make any decisions without talking things over with Donald."

"What decisions? I just want to hear what you have to say, but if you're not interested, then I'm sorry to have bothered you."

"No! I mean, of course we should talk. Tonight would be fine," Cherise agreed quickly, her mind spinning ahead of her tongue. She couldn't afford to squander this opportunity. She felt something wasn't right about this, but she couldn't put her finger on what it was. There was a chance that Cissy was up to something. But what? "What time?"

"You name it."

"How about seven?" That way she could call Donald, tell him what was up, and have him let her know the best way to handle Cissy.

"I'll come to your place. If you need to change anything, call me on my cell. I'm going to be out of the house all day."

"Okay, I've got your number," Cherise said, knowing that her phone had saved the number.

"Perfect." Cissy hung up, and Cherise called her back, just to make sure.

"Hello?" Cissy answered, sounding just as raspy.

"Oh, Cissy, I was just checking to see that you know how to get here. Do you have the address?"

"Gran had it, and I've got her Rolodex. She never did trust computers."

That sounded legit. Still, Cherise wished Donald were here rather than in Sacramento with a group planning a mission to Mexico. She should just say 'no' and insist Cissy wait, but as up and down as that girl was, Cherise knew she had to act fast, strike while the iron was hot. "Well, great, I'll see you then." She hung up; then, because she still felt weird about it, she called Cissy's home, where Tanya informed her that Cissy was out for a while.

Everything checked out. So why was she being so paranoid?

Cherise gave herself a talking to. It looked like Cissy's guilt was finally getting to her. Good, Cherise thought with a smile as she lit the candles in the living room, the same as she did every twilight. It just made the house so much cheerier. Next she sent up several prayers—one of thanks and one for Donald's safety. Everything in her life was getting better.

So why did she still feel so nervous?

"You think your mother was here?" Paterno asked. Cissy Holt had called from her grandmother's house and sworn she'd seen her mother. Paterno hadn't wasted a second. He'd driven straight to the mansion on Mt. Sutro, where Cissy, arms wrapped around her torso, had met him in the living room, just a few steps from the foyer where she'd found her grandmother's body.

He'd been to a lot of crime scenes, seen mutilated

corpses, bloodied bodies, witnessed the most bizarre acts of cruelty done to one human being by another. But never had he felt such a sense of malevolence as he did in this house, not a feeling of out-and-out brutality, more a sensation of cold, calculating, psychological horror.

That's what was happening here.

Marla was purposely terrorizing her.

And it pissed him off, even more than the keying of his car had . . . or, well, at least as much. He was still enraged at the dickwad who had scarred his beloved Caddy.

Cissy had told him a bizarre story about arriving here—how she'd thought she was alone, how she'd spied Marla Cahill in the doorway. She'd almost thought she was imagining it but for the smell of perfume in her car and the screwdriver jammed into the lock on the electronic gate.

Paterno, using a flashlight, had looked around. He bagged and tagged the screwdriver, looked for footprints in the earth, but the rain had pretty much taken care of anything solid. He wondered why Marla would risk coming here. Had she thought she could hide out? Why hadn't she spoken to Cissy? And what was the deal with the elevator being sent to the second floor?

Nothing made sense.

He called Quinn, and they decided to ask the crime lab to come and look for clues. Eventually Tallulah Jefferson and Roger Billings, another tech, arrived. They made short work of the place, dusted the front door for prints, searched again for footprints, and collected what little evidence there was, even dusting Cissy's car and vacuuming it in hopes of finding trace evidence.

"So has anything else strange been happening?" Paterno asked.

"Everything seems . . . off," Cissy revealed. It was dark now; the rain had stopped, but water was still running down the hillside and into the grate in the middle of the driveway. "I've misplaced some things."

"Such as?"

She seemed embarrassed. "Nothing valuable. My cell phone, a silver cup that Gran gave B.J. when he was born, and . . . oh, and my hairbrush, but I think they might all be at the house. There were so many people there the day of the funeral, things got moved."

"Your cell?"

"It was turned off. I thought it was in my purse, but maybe it fell out. Everything else was there. I checked. Credit cards, ID, and cash. Right where I left them. Only the phone's missing. I've called, thinking some-one might have found it and would answer, but it goes right to voice mail. And no one's called home to the landline which is listed in the cell's phone book, in case someone found it and wanted to get hold of me. It's a real pain, let me tell you. That's where I store every-one's number."

"You think someone stole it?" he asked again, trying to understand.

She looked away over the iron fence on the lower side of the property to the city, where lights twinkled through a bank of fog. "I don't know what to think," she admitted. "My whole life is upside down right now." Sighing, she checked her watch and said, "Look, I've really got to run. The sitter expected me fifteen min-utes ago."

"Okay. Just let me know if you think of anything else."

"I will," she promised, and for the first time ever, he sensed she trusted him.

Cissy's nerves were jangled, stretched thin, her hands grasping the steering wheel as if she were afraid to let go. She drove down Mt. Sutro and merged into Stanyan, following the taillights of an SUV.

Ever since Gran's death, her life had been careening out of control. People were dying. Things were missing. She felt as if she were being watched by unseen eyes, and now this . . . this sighting of her mother. Did that make any sense?

"No," she said aloud, and as she stopped for a traffic light she thought about the impending divorce and how torn she was about that too. Had Jack had an affair with Larissa? Was he lying through his teeth, or, as he'd protested, had "nothing happened"? Did it matter whether he'd slept with her at all, or was it the fact that he'd ended up spending the night in the redhead's apartment?

Ever since that one disastrous event, she'd suspected nearly every woman she knew of trying to seduce her husband. "That's nuts," she told herself, then glanced in the rearview mirror to see her own pained eyes staring back at her. Frightened eyes. Paranoid eyes. Oh God, was she losing her mind? She felt herself quivering inside and gnashed her back teeth together. *Get a grip, Cissy!*

She eased around the edge of Buena Vista Park and turned onto Haight Street. She'd go home, play with B.J., make dinner, give him a bath. Once he was in bed, she would strip out of her clothes, cast off her cares, and settle into a tub of hot, scented water. She'd turn on the stereo to her favorite CD, light candles, and even sip some wine. Pamper herself. Find herself.

She wouldn't think about her mother, the murders, her estranged husband, her missing things. No, she'd relax and de-stress.

At the house, she clicked her remote and drove into the garage. Hauling her purse and computer into the house, she called "Hello" but heard no excited little footsteps, no small voice calling excitedly "Mom-mee home," no giggling. No frantic barking from Coco. In fact the house was silent as a tomb.

Oh no!

"Hello?" she called again, heartbeat accelerating. Then she spied Tanya on the patio outside in the dark. She was huddled against the wind, her cell phone to her ear, and when she turned at the sound of Cissy's voice, she quickly ended the call, snapping her flip phone shut.

As she stepped inside, she said, "I get lousy reception in the house."

"Where's Beej?"

"Jack came by and picked him up."

"What?"

"I said, Jack came—"

"I know what you said, I just don't understand it," Cissy cut her off. "I thought you understood that Beej isn't to leave—"

"With his own father?" Tanya looked at her as if she'd gone around the bend.

"Did they take the dog too?"

"Yeah, thank God."

"Where?"

"I don't know. He called and said that I didn't need to bother with dinner. Then he picked up Beej and the stupid dog and they took off about ten minutes ago."

"But—"

"I couldn't call you," Tanya pointed out. "And you're late."

"I . . . ran into some unexpected problems."

"Sure." The corners of her mouth pinched. "Look, I know you don't like me. I don't know why. I do a good job, but it's never good enough, is it? It's like you were ready to hate me from the get-go. I figure it has something to do with the fact that Jack hired me, and you're pissed at him. Anyway, it doesn't matter, I'm giving my notice."

"You are?"

"I'm not sticking around so you can fire me. I know you're thinking about it, so let's just get it over with. It's too bad in a way, because I love Beej. Jack's great too, but you and I"—she waved her hand back and forth between Cissy and herself—"we just don't click."

Cissy couldn't think of anything to say.

Tanya was already reaching for her coat, which hung on the hall tree in the foyer. "Call the nanny school; they have girls they need to place." She slipped her arms through the sleeves of her raincoat and flipped the hood over her head. "Be sure to mention that you've got a dog. It's kind of a big deal. And . . . while I'm giving out advice, maybe you should see a shrink. I know you've been through a lot, but I think you should talk it over with someone instead of taking it out on me." With that she walked through the door, slamming it shut behind her.

Cissy stood in the middle of the hallway.

What had just happened?

The nanny had fired *her*?

Shoving her hair from her face, she started upstairs when a horrid thought hit her.

What if Tanya's lying? What if Jack hadn't been by? What if B.J. wasn't with him? It seemed crazy to think that the nanny was hiding something. Why then would she wait for Cissy?

Who says she was waiting? Maybe you caught her before she left. Maybe that's what the furtive phone call on the patio was all about.

No way. She was probably just calling about another job. *Don't make more of it than there is.*

Cissy grabbed the handheld phone and quickly punched out the number of Jack's cell phone. One ring. Two. "Come on, pick up." Three rings. Cissy walked to the front window and stared into the black night. No one was out there, and Tanya was long gone, her car no longer parked across the street. Four rings. "Jack, come on!" she nearly screamed as, with a series of clicks, the connection went to voice mail. Nervously tapping one foot, she waited as the mechanical voice told her to leave a message after the tone. "Jack, it's Cissy. Do you have Beej? I'm home, and I've had a horrible day, and Tanya said that—"

Headlights showed down the street. They moved closer until they reached the driveway, then splashed against the wall as Jack's Jeep wheeled into the driveway. Cissy was out the door in a flash. "Have you got Beej?" she asked as Jack climbed from behind the wheel.

"Didn't Tanya tell you?" He looked around and said, "Oh hell, she took off! I told her—"

"No, no. She told me . . . she was here. It's my fault that I'm freaked out. I had a hellish day!" She was already across the lawn and opening the back door of the Jeep to find her son staring up at her with wide eyes.

"Hi, Mom-mee!" he said, and his legs kicked in excitement.

She unbuckled and unsnapped him and pulled him tight against her. He hugged her neck.

"You miss me?"

"Oh yeah, honey, Mommy missed you big time."

"Big time," he repeated as Jack pulled out two white sacks that smelled of garlic, tomato sauce, and cheese.

"Takeout Italian," he said, "and definitely *not* pizza. So, you had a bad day?"

Cissy's mind replayed the image of Marla in the doorway. "You wouldn't believe," she muttered as they headed across the lawn to the still-open front door.

"Try me."

"Later, when B.J.'s asleep."

"Would wine and scampi primavera help?"

Her stomach rumbled. She didn't know whether she wanted to laugh or cry.

Seeing her, Jack said, "Ciss . . . ?"

"Yes. Wine and scampi primavera." She smiled shakily at him.

"We've also got old-fashioned spaghetti and meatballs and Caesar salad."

"Perfect."

"You look like you're about to fall down."

He reached for her hand, and she let him. Tonight she needed his strength and, though she might regret it later, she decided that they could share dinner and a glass of wine, and draw the shades. She glanced over at Sara's house and swore she saw her neighbor peeking through the blinds. As Jack pulled the door shut behind them, she caught a glimpse of the street lamp across the street and wondered if the person she'd seen there the other night would return.

Or was it all a part of her own wild unpredictable imagination?

She carried Beej into the house, heard Jack throw the lock on the door, and told herself that for a few hours she was going to close her mind to all her fears. Tonight, she was going to drink Chianti with her husband, suck up spaghetti with her son, and maybe, hours later, confide to Jack about what she'd experienced today at her grandmother's house.

"You're telling me that you found hairs around the screwdriver that was jammed into the gate at Eugenia Cahill's house, and that they might be Cissy Holt's?"

"That's right," Tallulah Jefferson told Paterno from her end of the phone in the lab. "We had samples of her hair from the crime scene at the Cahill house. Under the microscope, they match the ones from the screwdriver in color and texture. I can't be certain until I do a DNA test though, and that takes time. There were follicles on both samples, so I'm asking the lab to put a rush on them, but we're still talking weeks."

"So this is just your educated guess?" Paterno said, leaning back in his chair, hearing it creak in protest.

"Very educated. PhD educated," she reminded him, though he could hear the smile in her voice.

"Yeah, yeah, I know," he said. "The department's lucky to have you and all."

"Damned straight. I've got to run, but I thought you'd want to know."

"Damned straight."

She hung up, and he scratched at his chin, hearing the scrape of his fingernails against his five o'clock shadow. What would Cissy Holt's hairs be doing around the screwdriver? Why would she jam the lock, then call the police?

To fake them out?

Because she was cracking up?

He thought she might be on the verge of a breakdown . . . but that might be a ruse on her part. Maybe to sabotage the investigation? Tell the authorities she'd seen her mother, when she really hadn't?

Was she trying to turn the police in the wrong direction?

Was Marla long gone, out of the state, and Cissy the one behind the murders?

His stomach started burning once more, and he thought he should really see the doc again, but right now, he was too damned busy to hang out in a waiting room. He opened the drawer to his desk, sifted through the pencils, paper clips, pens, and rubber bands before he found a bottle of Tums. It was nearly empty. Great. Popping the last two into his mouth with one hand, he tossed the empty bottle into the trash with the other.

So what did Cissy Holt stand to gain by twisting the truth?

More of the family fortune?

Her mother's safety?

A scapegoat for her own crimes?

He glanced at the open files in front of him. Two dead bodies. Rory Amhurst and Eugenia Cahill, connected by one woman, Marla Amhurst Cahill.

Cissy Holt's mother.

He decided it was time to do a little more digging into Cissy's privileged life.

Who knew what he'd find?

Cherise hung up.

Alone in her own home, standing in the middle of the kitchen, she didn't know what to do.

She'd left three messages on Donald's cell phone and one in his hotel room, but he hadn't called back. No doubt he was deep into discussions about the mission the church was planning to create in a small Mexican village. Nonetheless, she wished he would call, prayed that he would. He was such a good, wise husband, and she leaned on him more than she should. They'd had some rocky times in their marriage, but really, what couple hadn't shared the bad with the good? Recently, though, she and her husband were solid. Right?

Don't question him! Learn to trust.

Perhaps that was why God, or the Reverend Donald himself, had decided he shouldn't return her calls. So that she would make her own decisions, be the strong one.

She hated the fact that everyone thought she was weak, that her previous three marriages seemed to indicate that she couldn't handle her life by herself. But that wasn't it. She could. She just didn't want to. She liked being married, loved being part of a couple, needed that feeling of being a half of a solid whole. The few months she was single between her marriages, she'd always felt adrift. At sea. Almost as if she were doomed to drown.

But Reverend Donald had saved her, and they'd married to create this perfect union. Well, near perfect. And so she wanted to talk to him, to tell him that she was certain that she'd actually seen Marla driving a silver car near the Cahill estate, a place Cherise often drove by. She'd been cruising along a road that wound near the university hospital which backed up to the estate and there, clear as day, driving a little erratically, had been Marla. Or she thought it was Marla. She'd caught only a quick glimpse as the approaching silver Taurus had shot down the road, but the woman at the wheel, who was the spitting image of Marla Amhurst Cahill, had looked over as she'd sped past. For a split second their gazes had locked in recognition before the Taurus had rounded a corner and disappeared from view. Cherise had been so startled she'd nearly hit the curb. She hadn't had time to write down the license plate number. She'd managed a quick U-turn, but by the time she'd reached the corner of the winding road, the Taurus was long gone.

So now, she considered calling the police.

First, though, she'd like to talk to her husband, get his advice. If only he'd call back.

She picked up the plant mister she kept on the mantel and sprayed the leaves of the potted philodendron that grew between the window and her piano. If Donald wanted her to be strong, so be it. If the Lord thought she needed to make her own decisions, then so she would.

Aside from her view of Marla, Cherise had other things she would like to discuss with her husband. The truth of the matter was, she just didn't really know how to handle Cissy. The girl was a blasting cap, ready to go off at a second's notice. Cherise would have to tread carefully, flatter her and the boy, remind her that they were all part of an ever-dwindling family.

At that thought, too, Cherise felt edgy. She set the plant sprayer on the mantel, adjusted the sparkling barrettes she used to hold her hair away from her face, and caught sight of her reflection in the mirror hung over the mantel. Oh dear, she was getting old. Wrinkles had begun to line her face, dark spots on her skin had to be hidden with makeup, her teeth needed bleaching again, and gray hairs were threading through her blond tresses at an alarming rate. She was still thin, but things had begun to sag. Uneasy, she walked to the liquor cabinet, where she kept her bottle of gin. She drank rarely but tonight, well, she needed a little liquid courage, so she poured herself a healthy shot into a short glass.

"Oh, please, Donald, call!" she said to the empty house, a three-bedroom Southern California-style home with a red tile roof and gold stucco walls. She tossed a splash of tonic water into her glass of gin, then carried the drink into the kitchen, adding a twist of lime and three ice cubes. Staring outside, she wondered if she'd done the right thing. She even considered calling one of her kids, but decided against it. She'd received only one phone call from them since Christmas, and that had been about money.

Of course.

Ungrateful children.

She suspected that her two oldest had turned their backs on God completely. Her husband, kind man that he was, had advised her, when she'd broached the subject, that "They'll be back in their own time. Let them make their own choices. God will guide them." She wasn't so sure. In fact, she was afraid all their hard-earned money was going for beer and weed, maybe even ecstasy or mushrooms. Dear Lord, she knew what a tainted path drugs led to, and the thought that her babies were experimenting scared her half to death. And made her angry.

"Oh, well," she said and took an experimental sip. Ummmm. Another sip, and the chilled gin slid smoothly down her esophagus.

She walked into the living room again and started plotting what she would say, how she would appeal to Cissy. After all, the girl was little more than a kid, in her mid-twenties. Cherise could handle her. Another long swallow, and she felt the warmth in her bloodstream.

It was almost time.

She closed her eyes.

Willed her muscles to loosen.

Heard the creak of a floorboard.

Her eyes flew open. No one was in the house. And the sound was too heavy to be the cat, right? "Patches?" she called, searching for the calico. "Here, kitty, kitty . . . Oh, for heaven's sake, where are you?"

She rounded the corner and looked into the darkened front vestibule, where the cat often hid under an antique table on which the family Bible was displayed. "You naughty girl . . . oh!" She stopped short. Sheer terror shot through her.

A woman stood in the shadows. A woman with a gun leveled squarely at Cherise's chest.

Cherise dropped her glass. It crashed onto the tile floor, shattering, glass flying, liquid splattering, ice cubes skittering.

"Don't say a word," the woman ordered in a low hiss that caused Cherise's blood to run cold. "Not one word."

Cherise swallowed back her scream.

What could she do? She had mace in her purse, but that wouldn't help. She could run, but there was nowhere to hide. She could—

The woman stepped out of the shadows and for a second Cherise thought she'd gone mad.

"Marla?" she whispered, disbelieving. She nearly peed her pants as she saw her assailant's cruel expression. Other than the quick glimpse earlier, Cherise hadn't seen her cousin's wife in ten years, but this woman . . . oh dear God, she looked so much like Marla. "Please don't. Show some mercy. . . . We're related . . . Please, oh God . . . no!"

"Uh-oh. I guess you didn't hear me," Marla said. Her lips twisted in an ugly grin.

Before Cherise could utter another word, the woman fired point-blank. Cherise fell back, stumbling against a small table.

"Ssss!" The cat, hiding behind a potted plant, hissed loudly, arched her back, and dashed into the kitchen.

Cherise landed on the floor. Her head cracked against the Mexican tiles.

Pain exploded behind her eyes.

A hot, oozing sensation spread through her abdomen.

Her assailant stepped closer, holding the gun on her. "You miserable, money-grubbing bitch. I hope you go to hell."

Marla? Why? No . . . no . . . not Marla . . .

As darkness pulled her under, Cherise watched her killer drop something soft and floating onto the floor in the vestibule before she slipped out the unlocked front door.

Why? she wondered futilely, knowing she couldn't make it to a phone, to anyone in time. She felt the lifeblood seeping out of her.

I'm going to die . . . oh God, Donald, I'm going to die . . . Please know that I love you. . . . I . . . love . . . The blackness dragged her under. A blessing and she gave herself up to it.

Please God, take my soul.

Chapter 15

Elyse's blood sang through her veins.

Killing Cherise had felt so right. And the confusion and sheer terror in her eyes when she'd thought she was facing off with wicked Marla.

Priceless!

Almost as satisfying as watching that pampered bitch Cissy nearly stumble down the stairs when she'd thought she'd seen her mother in the doorway of the house on Mt. Sutro. God, what a rush! It would have been so easy to kill her then, and Elyse had considered it. She'd had the gun with her. But she wanted Cissy to twist in the wind a bit more, feel a little pain, the kind Elyse had lived with for years.

"You'll get yours," she said and thought about the man she loved. . . . Oh, wouldn't it be perfect to make love to him tonight, when the thrill of the kill was still in her bloodstream, the adrenaline rush still pounding through her.

Eyes on the road, she reached into the side pocket of her purse, pulled out her cell, and hit the "2" pre-set button. It rang once, and a male voice answered.

"Hello?"

Holy Christ! This was the wrong phone. She'd used Cissy's damned phone.

She clicked off and cussed herself up one side and down the other. What had she been thinking? Had she been too high, too revved up not to notice the subtle difference in the cell phones?

She had to ditch it now. Fast. Fortunately, she was near the bridge. Stepping on the gas, she drove across the illuminated span and tried hard to keep the needle of her speedometer under the limit. Her heart was pounding, her skin hot, sweat collecting under her hair.

"Son of a bitch," she whispered, and at the south end of the bridge, before driving into the city, she turned into the park and left her car so that she could walk back along the span and, once she was a distance from the shoreline, wipe Cissy's cell phone clean and drop it over the railing and into the water so far below. It would never be found. Quickly, once her mission was accomplished, she walked briskly back to her car and climbed behind the wheel. She had to be more careful. She'd already nearly run over a bicyclist, and then there was the woman walking her damned dog when Elyse had left Cherise's house. Fortunately she was wearing the disguise and it had been dark, but there was always a remote chance either she or her car would be recognized. And then she called the wrong number by dialing Cissy's bloody phone. God, she had to be smarter if this was going to work. She had a few people on the payroll; the guy from whom she'd bought her fake ID had also done a great job of terrorizing Cissy, bumping into her at the coffee shop and then walking in front of her car. But he could talk. Elyse just wasn't too sure how much she could trust him.

And she couldn't afford any more slipups.

Not now.

Not when she was so close to getting everything that was due her.

Though she wasn't as high as she had been a few minutes earlier, she was still keyed up, and so she tried again, this time with the right phone. Her phone.

The phone rang three times before he picked up. "Hello?"

"Hi," she said a little breathily. "What're you doing?"

"Not much," he admitted, and she heard the wariness in his voice.

"Are you alone?"

"No," he said, giving nothing away to whoever was close by.

"I thought we could get together."

"I don't know," he said. "I don't know if we can meet tomorrow."

"I'm talking about tonight."

"I know." He was covering, trying to hide the fact that he was talking to her because of the other person or persons he was with. That was the trouble with cell phones, the double-edged sword of anonymity. Not only could the person you called not know where you were, but you too had no idea where he was when he picked up. He could well be in the city, across the country, or at home in bed . . . with whomever.

She felt a burning in her gut, but disguised it. "I'll be waiting for you."

"I told you this wasn't a done deal."

"You know where I'll be," she said in a low voice. "And you know what I'll be wearing. . . . We'll have ourselves a really good time."

"I just don't know."

"Trust me, you want to see me. To touch me. To kiss me. I'll do things to your body you can't begin to imagine."

He laughed a little then. "Look, I'll be in the office in the morning. I'll call you."

And then the bastard hung up.

"You goddamned cocksucker!" she hissed, knowing full well that he'd show. He couldn't resist her. Oh, sure, there were other women in his life; she knew that. He wasn't the kind of man to be satisfied with only one woman, but hell, she intended to change that. Maybe tonight. She was sick to the back teeth of him admitting that he still loved his wife. What a crock!

"Bastard." He'd better be careful.

Now that the phone was properly ditched, she swung the car around again and headed back to Sausalito, to the place to which she knew he would return. It was there that they laughed and made love, there that they'd plotted out how to spring Marla from prison, there that they'd laid out their plans.

He'd show up.

He couldn't resist. She knew that about him.

She considered meeting him in her Marla garb, but decided against it. Once she was back at the house, she'd ditch the green contacts, red-brown wig, padding in her bra, enhancers in her cheeks, and lifts in her shoes.

She didn't look that much like Marla, but the power of suggestion was a strong and wonderful thing, especially if one was seeing ghostly elevators open or staring down the barrel of a handgun.

She smiled to herself, gave herself a pat on the back. "Good work, Marla," she said and thought of the real Marla Cahill, that pathetic creature in the basement.

She couldn't wait to take off anything that remotely resembled the woman. In only a few minutes, she'd shower and be herself again.

And then she'd wait for the turn of the key and the

familiar sound of his footsteps as he climbed the stairs
to her bedroom. . . .

"The Sausalito police just called," Janet Quinn said,
strapping on her sidearm as she reached Paterno's desk.
It was ten in the morning, and she was serious. "Looks
like we've got another dead relative of Marla Cahill."

"What?" He glanced up from his notes. The homicide unit was bustling this morning, conversation loud,
phones ringing, computers humming, shoes scraping
against the floor as detectives walked from one area to
the next. "Who?"

"Cherise Favier. Shot dead in her own house."

"Jesus!" Paterno said. He hadn't seen that one coming.

"The neighbor she usually goes walking with called
9-1-1 this morning. She was so upset the operator could
barely understand her. Come on, I'll drive and fill you
in." They walked out of the station together and headed
for Quinn's car rather than use a department vehicle.
Paterno forced himself into the passenger side of Quinn's
red Jetta and clicked on his seatbelt as she tore out of
the lot. The traffic was thick, morning rush hour still
creating gridlock in the city, but a few rays of sun fil-
tered through the thick, gray sky.

"This is what we know so far," Quinn said, turning on
her blinker and looking over her shoulder as she wove
her way into the next lane. "Cherise was alone. Her husband was in Sacramento on church business."

"He's got an alibi?" Paterno had never liked the Reverend Donald and thought the preacher was full of hot
air and BS, heavy on the BS.

Quinn's mouth twisted wryly. "You're going to love
this one. Turns out he was with Heather Van Arsdale."

"Cissy Holt's friend?" He remembered seeing her at the funeral. Young and hip. Pretty. Good body.

"One and the same. And it gets more and more interesting. Heather, when she's not an elementary school teacher, volunteers at the church. She's some kind of computer whiz or something. Anyway, she and the reverend, they were a little more than business associates, or preacher and parishioner. They were pretty cozy. Had connecting rooms at the hotel in Sacramento."

"Figures," Paterno said. "I never trusted the guy." He slid Quinn a glance. "You remember, he was in trouble before. Can't seem to keep his zipper up."

"It goes further than that," Quinn said, cutting through traffic toward the Golden Gate Bridge. On the north end of the span lay the community of Sausalito and Marin County. "Heather was a college friend of Cissy Cahill."

"I know. So how does that all work together?"

She shook her head and reached into the console for her sunglasses.

"Optimist," Paterno said as she slipped the shades onto her face and eased toward the incredible rust-colored bridge with its spiraling towers and wide span. There was more traffic flowing into the city than flowing out, but the lanes were still clogged. Paterno barely noticed the view as they spanned the neck of water connecting San Francisco Bay with the Pacific Ocean. Two hundred feet below, green water sparkled in the wintry sunlight, a few sailboats and islands visible, but Paterno was trying to piece together the puzzle that was the Cahill murders. He reached in his pocket, withdrew a pack of Juicy Fruit gum, and offered a stick to Quinn.

She shook her head and kept talking, giving out what little information they had on the case. Already Favier, who'd been called hours earlier, as soon as the first detectives had gone to the house and seen the dead woman, was at the Sausalito Police Station being interviewed. Heather Van Arsdale, who had taken "personal days" from her teaching job, was in a separate interrogation room, but so far their stories matched.

"Why would anyone kill Cherise?" He unwrapped the gum, folded the stick, and shoved it into his mouth.

"Don't know. It doesn't look like robbery was a motive. Cherise had some pretty high-wattage rocks on her fingers and in her jewelry case. Computer, stereo, iPods, televisions—all untouched."

Paterno didn't like it.

"The Sausalito police have been canvassing the area near the church and Favier home. A few neighbors remember hearing a 'pop' last night, around eight, about the time, according to the ME, that Cherise died. One neighbor, Mrs. Bangs, reported that she'd been out walking her dog about that time. While the dog was taking a leak, she saw a woman coming out of the Favier house through the front door. The woman climbed into a silver car and drove away."

"That's it? Just a silver car? No license, make, or model?"

"Silver car. Sedan. Probably. That's it."

"What about a description of the person leaving the crime scene?"

"A woman. Average. Nothing special. Probably white and not fat. Maybe dark hair."

"Some eyewitness."

"She was busy with her dog."

"Great," Paterno groused.

"It's something."

"And gets Favier off the hook."

"Does it?" Quinn asked. "If the blessed reverend wanted out of his marriage without going through a divorce, he could have hired a hit. It would have been perfect timing, as we're all looking for a way to connect the murders. That's why we were called in."

"We'll see," Paterno said, chewing the gum and thinking the jury was still out on that one . . . way out.

"The Sausalito detectives are talking to the witness, offering up a photo lineup of various people, including Marla, to see if she zeroes in on her."

"What are the chances?" Paterno muttered.

"As I said, it's something. We're closer than we were yesterday."

"Yeah, and another person is dead."

Could Marla Cahill, Cherise's cousin by marriage, be involved in this too? The woman seen driving away from the crime scene? Paterno was willing to stake his badge on it.

On the far side of the bridge, Quinn drove through the quaint hillside village. Once known for fishing, it had become trendy with its Victorian cottages perched on slopes offering breathtaking views of the city and bay. Artists and craftsmen and people who wanted to live a quieter lifestyle, yet be minutes from the city, had driven real-estate prices through the roof.

Yeah, the Reverend Donald, reinventing himself after a career-ending tackle had forced him from the NFL, had carved himself out a nice little spot in one of the wealthiest communities in Northern California. A coincidence? Paterno didn't think so.

"So, did you know the Amhursts were from Marin County?" she asked.

Paterno nodded; he remembered that from the last time he'd been on Marla's trail. "She grew up in a fancy house overlooking the bay around here somewhere, I think. Her father, Conrad, lived out his final days in a care facility in Tiburon, just a few miles away."

"And now someone related to Marla dies up here."

"Related by marriage, through Marla's husband."

"It's all a little incestuous if you ask me."

"Won't argue that," Paterno agreed.

Hours later, after viewing the interview tapes of Favier and Van Arsdale, he still found it hard to think that the preacher had iced his wife. He had too much at stake.

And now he was exposed.

If not as a murderer, as an adulterer and a liar.

The media was out en masse, of course, and as Donald Favier left the police station, he made a statement to the media, admitting his sins to God and his flock at Holy Trinity of God. He stood in the winter sunlight, his breath fogging, his hair neatly in place, his mistress nowhere in sight. In jeans and a dress shirt with the sleeves rolled over his forearms, he asked Jesus's and everyone's forgiveness. Gold rings flashing, he clenched his fist and promised, if God would help him on his quest, to find the sorry, misguided soul who had taken precious, loving Cherise's life.

"Can you believe this guy?" Quinn asked as they stood to one side and watched the display.

"Not for a minute." Paterno eyed the reverend, hypocrite that he was. With a determined, square jawline, conviction in his intense eyes and talk of Jesus's forgiveness, he turned the crowd. He vowed to find the killer of his beloved wife, and, though he was but a man, a man with flaws and weaknesses, with Christ's help, he would seek justice.

"Touching, ain't it?" Paterno muttered to Quinn as he watched the charismatic man work the crowd. "Almost makes me want to believe him."

"You think he's our killer?"

Squinting against cool winter sunshine, Paterno shook his head. "Don't know," he said, "but I doubt it. I'm talking about his whole act. The forgiveness, the shame, the vows of becoming a reformed sinner." He watched the reverend nod at the cameras and slide behind the wheel of his Mercedes.

"You don't think people can change?"

"My old man had a saying. A leopard doesn't change his spots. That's all I'm telling you. Nothin' more."

His cell phone rang, and he picked it up. "Paterno."

"It's Underhill," a voice said, and Paterno pictured the detective, a strapping black man of about thirty-five or thirty-six. With short-cropped hair and a take-no-prisoners attitude he'd picked up in the military, Underhill was all business. "A security guard at the medical school up on Mt. Sutro issued a ticket to a silver Taurus, older model, that was parked up on the hill the day Cissy Holt said she saw Marla Cahill. The parking lot backs up to the Cahill mansion, and I thought you might like to know."

Paterno couldn't believe it.

"And there's more. A security camera not only caught the license plate of the vehicle, confirming the ticket, but also might have got a picture of the driver."

"Marla Cahill?"

"Could be. A copy of the tape is being sent here to the station by messenger. I've got one coming for the state police and the feds as well."

"Good. And put out a BOLF for the license plate."

"Already done," Underhill said. "I've got the name and address of the registered owner. One Hector Alvarez. Lives near San Jose. I already contacted the authorities down there. Someone should be knocking on Mr. Alvarez's door as we speak."

"Keep me posted."

"You got it."

Paterno clicked off.

"Good news?" Quinn asked.

"Could be." Paterno tamped down his enthusiasm until he'd actually looked at the tape. "Let's go. We might have our first serious lead in the Eugenia Cahill case."

"Hallelujah and amen."

"I'm not ready to celebrate quite yet." Marla Cahill was still on the loose. A silver car and a videotape didn't ensure her capture. He'd wait before he cracked out the champagne.

"What do you mean, Cherise is dead?" Cissy said, the pit of her stomach suddenly like ice. She'd been wiping the remains of B.J.'s lunch, a combination of macaroni and cheese and vegetables, from his face when Jack had walked in. Coco, momentarily distracted from patrolling the floor for pieces of Beej's lunch that had accidentally or purposely fallen to the floor, started barking, but stopped when Cissy reprimanded the dog with a sharp "Oh, Coco, hush! Give it up, would you?"

Today she was taking care of her son. Tanya had called in sick, but Cissy thought she was probably on a job interview. Not that she cared. Now that she was over the surprise of it all, she was glad the decision had been made and the nanny was leaving.

As for her and Jack, they were basically living together ever since Cissy had told him about her "encounter" with Marla. He'd been camped out on the sofa, and sometimes he slipped into the master bedroom. Neither of them was addressing the issue. Neither wanted to break the fragile truce.

Now Jack's face was pale, his lips compressed. "Cherise was killed, Cissy," he revealed. "Shot."

"What do you mean? How do you know?"

For an answer, Jack clicked on the television, turning to an all-news station, and, sure enough, within five minutes a picture of the front lawn and porch of the Favier house came into view.

Cissy sank into a chair, feeling detached from reality. What was going on?

The reporter was telling a story about an intruder, a gunshot, and a husband who was out of town, apparently with his mistress.

"They're saying Cherise's husband was involved with Heather?" Cissy whispered, disbelieving, as she saw a camera shot of her friend scuttling away from reporters, heading out the back door of the police station while Donald Favier held court on the front steps. She listened in stunned silence. Coco settled onto the couch beside her. B.J., unaware, babbled to himself as he tried to put a series of plastic, rainbow-colored rings onto a spindle.

Cherise was dead.

Murdered.

Like Gran and Rory.

"Who's next?" Cissy asked.

"I'm moving back in for good," Jack stated flatly. "Permanently. As your husband."

Cissy didn't have the strength to argue. She wouldn't have if she did. Whatever was wrong with her and Jack's relationship would have to be set aside. This was a matter of safety.

"This killer seems to be knocking off every member of your extended family. I'm moving back, and we're getting an updated security system that we're going to use."

"Okay . . . you're right. Of course."

"And you have to trust me, Cissy," he insisted. "I'm going to tell you this one last time, and then I don't want to hear about it again. I never slept with Larissa. I never made love to her. That's not to say that it didn't cross my mind that night. I was tempted, because I thought it was over between us, but even so," he said, shoving his face nose-to-nose with hers, "even so, I couldn't go through with it. Because I fell in love with you, Cissy Cahill Holt, the first time I saw you in that hot little red dress; and even now, when you're driving me out of my head with your insecurities, your doubts, and your accusations, I still love you." He said it all without touching her, but that took nothing away from its power.

"I love you too, Jack," Cissy said around a lump in her throat.

"Are you willing to try again? Do you believe me?"

The honesty and pain were so evident on his face. "Yes," she whispered, nodding. "I do."

He wrapped himself around her and kissed her so hard her breath was lost somewhere in her soul. It felt so right to be in his arms again. She held him tightly, her arms wound around his neck.

The phone jangled, and Cissy jumped.

Jack said urgently, "Let's not answer it." He kissed her again.

"With everything that's going on . . . you know we have to," Cissy said, extricating herself.

Muttering under his breath, Jack walked into the kitchen and snatched up the receiver. "Hello?" he answered.

She picked up B.J. and carried him into the dining area. She saw Jack's expression turn from exasperation to something darker. The brackets near the corners of his mouth tightened, and his gaze slid to hers.

Now what?

Holding Beej as if she might lose him, Cissy stared at her husband. She felt as if the temperature in the house had just dropped ten degrees. During the one-sided conversation, Jack nodded but said little. "Yeah," he finished, "we caught it on the news. . . . sure . . . we will . . . you got it . . . Thanks." He hung up and walked back to the living room, where Cissy, numb, was still sitting, clinging to Beej. "That was Paterno," Jack said, frowning. "He was calling to tell us about Cherise and warn us to watch our backs."

"He thinks we're in danger too."

"He thinks anyone remotely related to your mother could be a target."

It wasn't a surprise, but it deepened the chill in Cissy's soul.

Checking his watch, Jack said, "I'll go and pack my things. It'll take a while, but I'll be back. Until then, lock every door and don't let anyone in but me."

"You're really worried?"

"Maybe you should come with me."

"No . . . we're okay. Beej and I'll be fine," she said. "We've got Coco to protect us."

Jack snorted. "Now I know we're in trouble. You're sure you'll be okay without me?"

"Just . . . hurry . . ."

Marla was being a pill.

Again.

Elyse was tumbling down fast from the high of killing Cherise, her good mood having been evaporated by the fact that her lover had stood her up. Well, not completely. He'd called her and explained that he'd have to "take a rain check" and see her "another time."

As if he were planning to break up with her.

Elyse had been furious, ranting and raving. The son of a bitch was playing her, and she knew it. Why couldn't he see that he loved her? *Her!* No one else. Not his damned wife. She'd been near tears, and the horrible thoughts that she usually kept at bay, the taunts that she was never good enough, had rolled through her mind.

You're not good enough for him.

No one's ever loved you.

Why would you think he would fall for you?

He's using you, Elyse, just as everyone in your life has!

Sometime after two AM she'd calmed enough to watch a boring movie in the big, empty bed, finally falling asleep. She'd awakened at the usual time, her head thundering, her spirits quashed.

She'd had a few moments of triumph, however, when she caught bits of the news and realized that Cherise's death was making a splash. Her lover had called too, and apologized, promising to meet her soon; if not tonight, then as soon as he could get away.

Which was far from perfect, she thought, looking around the basement room, trying to cajole Marla out of another bout of depression. God, the woman was impossible! Her lover would come around. She was sure of it. For now, she had to deal with Marla. Elyse had even gone so far as to give the bitch a manicure, painting her nails a deep shade of red that bordered on purple, and when Marla had been cross about the color not being right for her, Elyse had resisted the urge to poke the manicure scissors through Marla's eyes and blind her. "I think you're wrong, it's perfect. Goes with your hair."

"I don't know. . . ." Marla was unconvinced.

"It's just soooo you!" Oh, gag, she hated kissing Marla's ass, but she reminded herself it wasn't forever. She just had to keep the older woman mollified a little while longer.

"Would you do my toes too?"

"Can't you do them yourself?"

Marla sighed, and Elyse acquiesced though she hated the thought of touching anyone's feet. Talk about gross! But she'd do anything—any-damned-thing—to keep Marla from blowing all her plans. So far Marla was hanging in there, keeping out of sight. If painting her nasty toes would keep her satisfied, then so be it.

"I'm glad you took care of Cherise," Marla finally admitted as she sat in her chair and gazed down at her

glossy toenails. The television was on again, this time
turned to a reality show where the contestants vied against
each other in some kind of celebrity fitness competition.

"One step closer," Elyse agreed. "Closer to D-day."

"D-day?" Marla repeated, barely interested as her attention was again caught by the television screen, where
a particularly heavyset man was attempting to carry his
partner across a fake river before the other "couple" could
get to the other side. It was kind of like that game one
played as a kid in a swimming pool, where one smaller person sat on the shoulders of a stronger, bigger person and
tried to knock a like competitor into the water. The two
scrappier, tinier people would go at it tooth and nail while
their bigger partners just tried to stay upright.

Except the competitors on television were battling
for fifty thousand dollars and the opportunity to go "on
to the next level." It was amazing Marla watched such
crap, but maybe it was because her time watching television in prison had been monitored. Who knew? And as
long as it kept her out of trouble, who cared?

"What are you talking about, D-day?" she asked, turning her gaze back to Elyse.

"That time when everything we've worked for comes
to a head," Elyse said evasively. "Look, I've got to run . . .
but I'll be back."

"Soon, I hope," Marla said as a commercial for a new
diet soda blazed on the screen.

"Hang in. It's almost over," Elyse said. "I promise."
She left Marla in her room and walked up the stairs.
The place was beginning to smell musty again, and she
was irritated with Marla for being such a slob. What was
with her? Where was her spunk? She didn't seem to pos-
sess the same fire. It was as if she'd completely lost her
nerve. Luckily, Elyse had balls enough for the both of
them.

"Goddamned princess," she muttered under her breath as she locked the house and found her way to the car. She was starting to get nervous about it and thought it might be time to ditch it completely and get another vehicle or switch out the plates again.

Though her pulse was pounding and she wanted to get as far away from the bitch as possible, she was careful as she drove, not attracting any unwanted attention.

She wondered when her lover would show. Surely he wouldn't stand her up again. She felt a little sliver of worry about it and didn't like the turn of her thoughts.

Patience, she reminded herself, was a virtue.

It just seemed virtues were often vastly overrated.

Bayside Hospital
San Francisco, California
Room 316
Friday, February 13
NOW

I can hear them talking—the doctors, nurses, and others, people I cannot see, as I can't open my damned eyes. How long have I lain here? Five minutes? Five days? For the love of God, can't they, with all their expensive equipment, realize that I'm not as near death as they think? I just need a little more time.

I hear them talking about me, discussing me as if I'm just another case, not a living, breathing woman. Sometimes they argue—oh, please, let the believers hold sway!

It's my life that's in the balance.

One deep voice is holding out for my life, insisting that they give me a little more time to recover, to show some sign that I'm improving.

Jack?

Is Jack my champion? The one with all the faith?

No . . . not Jack, but a doctor, the one who insists that I'll respond soon. His name is Reece; the nurses speak to him with deference, and, when he's not in the room, talk about how "hot" he is, how good looking. This man, this Dr. Reece, could be my savior, my only chance for survival.

Dr. Reece, please, please don't listen to them! Trust in me. In my life.

He's speaking now, but his arguments are fading; the other voices, that of a woman doctor named Dr. Lee and a nurse, are persuading him that I'm a lost cause.

No, oh, please, no . . .

I can do nothing but wait anxiously, praying they will not end my life, but eventually even my one last hope is convinced. Dr. Reece finally listens to reason, to medical charts, to data and computers. He touches my arm, and I try vainly to respond.

Don't do this!

Don't give up on me!

But it's too late.

He agrees with the others: there is no hope. I won't come out of this coma. The specialists think I'll never awaken.

For the millionth time, I strain to move my hand, to flutter my eyelids, to force some kind of wheezing noise through my vocal cords, but nothing happens; there is only stillness and the ever-present atmosphere of resignation.

This is all so wrong!

"There's nothing more we can do," Dr. Lee says.

No! Oh no! Please don't let me die. . . . I can hear you. . . . Don't give up on me.

Call my family. Call Jack. . . . I'm sorry for all the mistakes I made, I'm sorry if I let anyone down, I'm sorry if I hurt anyone, but please, I'm too young to die. If I could change anything I would, but I can't.

Now all I can do is remember. . . .

Chapter 16

Damn it, this house should have been hers!

Elyse stripped off her clothes inside the once-commanding Queen Anne mansion mounted on the cliffs overlooking the bay, a place her mother had pointed out to her, a place that once was almost as regal as the Cahills' mansion. As a child Elyse had gazed up at the ornate, arched Palladian windows, wide porches, and elaborate turrets and dreamed about what was hidden inside, what secrets the house built a century before held.

Now, she knew.

With her inheritance, she would finally be able to rent the place, and soon, if all went according to plan, it would be hers, and she would restore the deteriorating home to its once-regal grandeur.

It was all just a matter of time. And the clock was ticking.

She showered and found her favorite robe. This was the place she belonged, the place she secretly called home, the place no one knew about. The house had long been abandoned and was starting to show signs of neglect, which was a shame. She knew that at one time there were grand parties held here, and if she closed her eyes, she could hear the tinkling of stemware, the laughter, and the soft strains of music filling the hallways and staircases. In her mind's eye she witnessed the dim, romantic glow of chandeliers that had been forever polished and gleaming. The grounds were manicured, the kitchen always gave off warm, mouth-watering odors, servants abounded.

And there would have been love. . . .

Or . . . was she imagining it all? Sometimes she got caught up in her own fantasies . . . or did she?

But she was certain there would have been happiness and hope here, a warmth and security she'd never been allowed to feel.

And it's where she belonged.

Her heart tore a bit for the time that never was, the life she hadn't lived . . . or had she? Sometimes the memories of her past blurred a bit, which was disturbing. She relied on her sharp senses and her keen mind, but the past . . . It was something she didn't like thinking about too much, and it wasn't always crystal clear. Sometimes it was like the dripping glass chandeliers had grown dusty—blurred and indistinct in her mind. As if she were losing it. But she was far too young for anything as disturbing as dementia to be thwarting her. No way.

No, she was just overwrought.

Emotional.

That's what being around Marla could do to people . . . push them to the brink of insanity.

Casting her dark thoughts aside, Elyse lit the fireplace in the bedroom, uncorked a bottle of wine, and waited as the clock in the hallway ticked off the minutes of her life, as the candles she'd set around the bed burned softly, as the gas fire hissed.

She glanced at the clock. For the smallest of moments she worried that he might cancel again.

What if it was really over?

What would she do then?

She felt suddenly tiny and alone. . . . All her life she'd been alone. Oh, sure there had been parents, but had they ever really talked to her, showed any interest? Only around their schedules. For two people who had claimed they'd badly wanted a child, they sure had proven themselves lacking in the parental-concern department.

Elyse hadn't grown up poor, but she'd never had as much wealth as Cissy, nor the attention that Cissy had garnered just by being a Cahill.

Cissy. God, how had she gotten that stupid, little-girl name? She wondered how it had felt growing up in that huge mansion overlooking the city, never overhearing her parents squabble about money when they thought their darling daughter wasn't listening. Cissy had been surrounded by parents and grandparents, a daughter of one of the most prestigious families in the entire Bay Area. At least that's the way Elyse saw it. What little fortune *her* parents had managed to amass during their lifetimes didn't hold a candle to the Cahill-Amhurst estate.

Life wasn't fair, she reminded herself. *You can't expect fate to hand out fortunes. You have to make your own luck. That's what you're doing.*

And now she was waiting for a man she knew didn't really love her, a man who would never care for her the way he did his damned wife.

So who's the fool?

Look what you've done for him.

Think about how many people you betrayed, you killed. For him.

Oh, you tell Marla it's for her, but you know better. You're only kidding yourself, and now you're in this big bed, in a room overlooking the bay, in a house that should have been yours but has been denied you while you wait for a man you don't really trust.

"He'll come," she said aloud, and her voice seemed to ricochet off the walls. "He *will* come. He'd better."

Her shrink had told her not to hold false hope, not to expect more from people than they could give. But why couldn't they give? Why couldn't she have had a real mother's love? Or a husband's? The louse she'd married had never had any time for her, was married to his job, had never understood her. In fact, he acted as if *she* were the one with the problem! As if *she* were crazy. What had he called her? A "psycho whack-job"? She was lucky to be rid of him. Lucky!

But still it bothered her that she couldn't find a man who cared about her, who would love her, fight for her, even die for her.

Soon, all this mess with Marla would be over, and Elyse would have what she wanted. Then she wouldn't have to run over to the bungalow where Marla was hiding out any longer. God, that was getting tough. Sooner or later someone would see her. There had been the incident with the bicyclist, and just the other night she'd stumbled over a cat. The damned thing had shrieked as if she'd stabbed it, and a nosy neighbor had peeked through her blinds, the same old bitch who had looked through the slats before.

Elyse couldn't take any more chances.

It was time to end this thing. Go for the real prize.

So where the hell was he?

Through the open window, she heard the low sound of a foghorn and then the quiet rumble of a smooth engine. She smiled with relief as she recognized it.

He wasn't standing her up.

No way.

He'd come! Her smile broadened as she imagined

what she would do to him to prove how much she loved him, to show how much she cared. Her heart beat a little faster, and she adjusted the lapels of her robe, glancing in the mirror to assure herself that her hair was freshly tumbled, that a sexy glimpse of her cleavage was visible, that her lips were glossy and wet, promising oh-so-sinful delights.

The engine was closer now, louder, and then suddenly died.

She waited. Counting her heartbeats.

Within seconds a key turned in the lock.

Her fingers twisted in the sheets.

He didn't say a word, but the door shut softly behind him. She heard his footfalls on the floor of the foyer a story below. *Darling,* she thought.

Up the stairs he came, his footsteps quickening as he reached the second story.

He tapped lightly on her door and pushed it open. She lay back on the pillows, every sense alive as he stepped into the darkened bedroom where the candles burned.

His grin, always seductive, widened.

God, he was handsome.

"I'm sorry about last night," he said without preamble as he unbuttoned his shirt. She watched every little pearl disc slide through its hole. He was tanned and fit, his abdomen a washboard of muscles, his chest hair thick and springy.

"Don't let it happen again."

"I won't." He said it easily, too easily, not as if it were a vow.

"Come here, you," she said, and he did, tumbling onto the downy mattress, grabbing her and kissing her until she couldn't breathe. His hands were all over her, untying the knot of her robe, pushing the soft velvet over her shoulders almost roughly. As if he couldn't wait. He kissed her breasts, his fingers kneading her back, but she wouldn't let him get away with a quick, fast fuck. That was *not* what was going to happen. He was going to satisfy her long and hard, and she would do the same for him.

"Slow down," she whispered into his ear even as she was melting and wanting inside.

"I can't."

"Sure you can. . . . We've got all night."

He didn't argue and took his time, but long before she was ready, he was inside her, lost in wild abandon. She too was caught up in the frenzy of the lovemaking, begging him for more. "Harder," she cried. "Oh, come on, faster." She wanted so much from him. She was sweating and screaming and scratching as he pushed her to the brink and then over. No teasing, no making her beg only to deny her and then start over again.

Tonight was different. There was a desperation to his lovemaking. So fast. So hard. So furious. Almost as if he thought it would never happen again.

But that wasn't right . . . was it?

As he collapsed on top of her and she stared at the flickering candles, she sensed how wrong things were becoming. He still loved his wife. And he always would. And it was killing her.

"I'm sorry, but I have to leave," he said, catching his breath. "But, hey, that was . . . great."

"Great," she repeated.

"Always." He kissed her forehead, and she felt a disappointment so deep it was a dark abyss in her soul.

"I thought you'd stay."

"Can't. Not tonight." He rolled away and was already hastily donning his clothes, as if he couldn't get away fast enough.

"Why?"

"You know why. Can't risk getting caught. I'm dealing with the cops all the time, and the family, and we just can't take any more chances."

"You're breaking up with me?" she asked, hating the sound of hysteria that had crawled into her voice, raising it to an unbecoming shriek. She had to get a grip on herself.

"Oh, no, no! Are you kidding? This is the best sex I've ever had, but we've got to keep our eyes on the prize."

"And once we get it? The prize? What then?"

"The sky's the limit," he said, zipping up his pants and pulling in his abdomen as he buttoned the top button. "Just you wait." He'd already picked up his shirt and was shoving his hands down the sleeves. She adjusted herself, tried a pouty, disappointed look, but he ignored it as he slid into his shoes in the candlelight.

"Don't leave me, Jack," she whispered, but he pretended he didn't hear her, didn't even have the balls to confront her. Instead he slipped out of the bedroom forty minutes after he'd slipped in.

And then the son of a bitch was gone.

"So get this," Paterno said as Janet Quinn climbed into the passenger seat of his Caddy. "The Sausalito PD found hairs left at the scene of Cherise's murder. Red hairs. Not Cherise's, not anyone in the family's."

"Red?"

With a flick of his wrist, he fired the engine, and the old V-8 roared to life. "And they don't match the hairs found around the screwdriver that was used to jam the gate at the Cahill house the night Cissy claims to have seen Marla."

"Which she probably did, if the hospital parking-lot tape is to be believed." Quinn shook her head and frowned. "Does that make sense?"

"Who knows?" Paterno sighed, still puzzling it out as he nosed the Cadillac into traffic and noticed how narrow the streets were. "Cissy claims her brush went missing along with her kid's cup and her cell phone. Maybe Marla planted the hairs."

"And then shed her own at the Favier house?" Quinn said skeptically.

He cranked on the wheel and headed north. "There were quite a few hairs found near the front door, along with one that wasn't the same. In fact, it was synthetic."

"A wig?"

"Yeah. And the Sausalito PD didn't find any on the premises. The cleaning people were there the day before, so it's not likely it was from another visitor."

"So what're you saying?" she asked. "That the real hairs, or the fake ones, were a plant?"

"That's the problem. I don't know what I'm saying," Paterno admitted, easing his big car around a delivery van double-parked in the street. A new model Jag heading in the opposite direction had to wait for Paterno, and the driver, a white male in his twenties, honked at the Cadillac. As soon as the Caddy's tail was out of his way, he peeled rubber to show off his manliness and impatience.

"Prick," Paterno said, unruffled as he drove toward the Golden Gate Bridge. He was headed back to Sausalito to check out the Favier crime scene again. He'd heard the reports, seen the pictures, and had let the other cops and feds do their collective things, but he wanted to eyeball everything himself, get his own "feel" of what went down.

The sky was clear, the winter sun bright, spangling the water and beating through the windshield with enough power to heat the interior of the car. At another time Paterno would have relished the day, gone down to the docks, maybe done a little fishing. Today he was knotted up, the case getting to him. Again, the connection was obviously Marla Cahill, but there was something more going on as well, and it centered on Marla's accomplice, a ghost with evil intent.

On the off chance that Cherise's murder wasn't related to the other deaths, he'd checked out her ex-husbands, kids, and extended family and friends. No red flags had shot up. Heather Van Arsdale, the reverend's mistress, had the alibi of being with the preacher and also the other attendees at the meeting in Sacramento. There was no indication that she'd put a hit out on her lover's wife. It was a long shot in the best of circumstances.

Paterno had studied maps of the area and pegged the spots with pushpins where the victims had been found, trying to find a pattern, something on the map that would tell him where the killer lived. So far it had all been a waste of time, an exercise in futility. In his gut he knew that Marla Cahill was behind the murders. Where they had died was no indication of where she was holed up. What it told him mainly was that she was systematically, one by one, wiping out the members of her family. She seemed to have plotted her prison break to seek some kind of revenge. Make some kind of statement.

Meanwhile, the police had procured a copy of the phone records to both the Favier home and Cherise's cell. Most of the people who had called the cell were friends, members of the church, all of whom had iron-clad alibis. There was one anomaly. The last person to phone Cherise was Cissy Cahill Holt. She'd called from her cell phone—the phone that had been "missing"—and talked a few minutes. According to the cell phone company, the call had originated near a cell phone tower close to Cissy's home. . . . Had Cissy lied about the stolen phone and placed the call herself? Or had someone phoned Cherise from near Cissy's house, hoping to misdirect the investigation and lay blame at Cissy's feet?

What were the chances of that?

Cissy's phone records also indicated that she'd called her husband right before phoning Cherise but had hung up quickly. There had been no other outgoing calls that night, and the incoming were always short, less than twenty seconds, probably messages. A lot of people would have been calling to express condolences or sympathy, and one call was from the Holt house itself, possibly Cissy calling to try and locate her cell.

Paterno flipped down his visor against the unlikely glare. His instinct was to trust Cissy, especially since Marla's image had shown up on the security camera at the medical school near the Cahill home after Cissy had reported seeing her at Eugenia's. The police had been circulating that tape along with the artist's sketches to the press. Local television stations and the newspapers had eagerly aired the tape from the hospital and discussed it at length. Newspapers had released the sketches of Mary Smith and a still of "Marla" taken from film footage.

Calls to the police station from people who thought they'd seen Marla had flooded in. So far none of the "Marla sightings" had panned out.

And they'd come up empty handed with the vehicle as well. The owner of the silver Taurus caught on the hospital security camera had apparently been nowhere near the hospital, nor had his car been stolen. Hector Alvarez had been home with his wife, the car parked in their driveway at the time the ticket at the medical school was issued. Two neighbors vouched that it hadn't moved. And his back license plate didn't match with his front. Someone had switched them.

And that someone was probably the driver of the car—who was Marla Cahill or someone who resembled her. The plates and Alvarez's car had been searched and printed by the crime unit.

So far, nothing.

But they were getting closer. Paterno's fingers tightened over the wheel. He only hoped they would nab Marla before another one of her relatives went to meet his or her maker.

A surveillance team was in place at Cissy Cahill's house as well. Whoever was killing off Cahill relatives would surely have her on the hit list.

Unless it turned out she was the murderess.

Either way, she would be followed.

He changed lanes at the far end of the long suspension bridge. "You find anything interesting in the old woman's diaries?"

"A few things," Quinn said. "I'm still trying to sort them out." She sat lower in the Caddy's big bucket seat, her eyes trained out the passenger window. "It turns out the Cahill family has more than a few skeletons in its closets."

"Tell me something I don't know."

"You want to hear this?"

"Give me the condensed version."

"Hell with that. You're getting it chapter and verse." She ignored his groan and said, "Here's some ancient history: first of all, Eugenia was engaged before she met Samuel Cahill, but she deep-sixed the first fiancé in favor of the man she married. No big news bulletin, and the guy's long dead, so I doubt he held any grudges. He married a few years later; he and his wife had three daughters. His wife is dead too, and the daughters are all married with kids. Their lives don't touch anything remotely close to Eugenia Cahill, so I think that's a dead end."

Paterno stopped at a red light, waiting as a woman with a cane and bag of groceries made her way across the street. It was easier to let Quinn ramble than express the frustration he felt.

"Then there's Alex, son number one. He had a few affairs during his marriage to Marla."

"Not a one-way street," Paterno observed as the light changed and he headed through the now-familiar streets of Sausalito.

"Fidelity didn't seem to be a part of their marriage. The interesting thing is how Marla first came into contact with the Cahill family: She spent some time at Cahill House—the home for unwed mothers—not as a volunteer, but as a resident."

Paterno felt his eyebrows shoot skyward. "She had a kid that she gave up for adoption?"

"That's what Eugenia's diary suggests. It's probably not a big deal in and of itself, but I did some digging. The records are sealed, of course, but I'd like to find out more about this kid. What happened to him or her? Who was the father? All I get from the notes is that Eugenia didn't approve of Alex's marriage to Marla Amhurst. She was, and I quote, 'socially acceptable but morally reprehensible'."

"That's gotta bite."

"If Marla knew her mother-in-law's feelings."

"Eugenia was pretty starchy. She might have put up a front of acceptance to the rest of the world, but if she didn't like Marla, I'll guarantee Marla knew it."

Quinn nodded. "Stoic to the outside world, a raving bitch with the people she loved."

"So we don't know where the kid is now?"

"Not yet, but I'm looking into it. The records may be sealed, but there are people who were employed at Cahill House during the time of Marla's pregnancy—people who have long since retired. I've got a list, and I'm working my way through it. Someone's got to know about that child."

Paterno drove past the Holy Trinity of God Church, where a message on the reader board was simple: "Go with God, our Sister Cherise," and then the notation of a verse from the Bible.

He frowned as he saw the sign, experiencing the same burning sensation in his stomach that he'd felt when he'd seen the newscasts where the Reverend Donald played the grieving, broken husband who, though he had been a sinner, was taking Cherise's death as a "sign from God" to mend his ways. The news cameras had been trained on both him and the crowd surrounding him, and Paterno had taped all the local channels.

Heather Van Arsdale's face had been missing from the flock, though other newscasts showed reporters hounding her at her apartment, even camped out at the school where she taught, but she'd never honored any requests for an interview. Paterno didn't blame her. She was the "other woman" in a bad play. Somehow the reverend was turning the situation around, once again the spinmaster, creating publicity and an image of a re-pentant adulterer mourning the violent and tragic end to his wife's life. He was blaming himself—and his act was working. Everyone in the church was standing be-hind him, the weakened man who had bowed to temp-tation and was now strong. Like Heather's, Favier's alibi was tight. So far the police hadn't been able to track down any money trail indicating he'd paid off a hit man . . . or woman, if the myopic dog-walking witness could be believed.

Paterno found a parking spot big enough that he could ease his car into it across the street from the Favier house, a nice rambler with a Spanish motif. Sickly looking palm trees offered a bit of shade to the red tile roof. The lawn was neat and trimmed, the house painted with a fresh coat the color of sand. A brick walk led to a matching porch where big pots were filled with trailing plants that promised to bloom in the coming months.

"Look like a crime scene to you?" he asked as they climbed out of the car.

Quinn shook her head. "No, but it sure must've to Cherise Favier."

A headache pounded behind Elyse's eyes, and she had to squint as she reached into the medicine cabinet. She found a bottle of ibuprofen and tossed back double the dosage. Lately the headaches had become more severe, nearly debilitating.

It's just because everything's coming to a head, that's all. You've nearly accomplished everything you want . . . except for Cissy, and that's about to go down.

After taking a swallow of the wine from the near-empty bottle on the nightstand, she stretched her muscles, unwound the tension from the back of her neck. It was time to go to her regular job, to pretend to be a woman she wasn't. The thought irked her.

Just a little longer . . . that's all it's going to be.

The wheels have been set into motion.

She glanced at the big rumpled bed and thought about the man she loved. He was key, of course, to all her plans. He'd been instrumental, had even contacted her from the get-go, but then she'd gone and fallen in love with him.

Once a fool, always a fool.

But only if you let yourself.

Don't let him use you.

Don't let him belittle you.

Don't give too much of yourself to him.

And for God's sake, don't let him have your heart.

He's not worth it. No man is.

Remember: he's expendable.

Everyone is.

Now, get your butt to work. This is the last day you'll ever have to go there and pretend to be someone you're not.

Today is the beginning of the end.

Chapter 17

"You sure you don't want to come with me?" Cissy asked, as she grabbed her keys and purse from the kitchen counter. She was so glad Jack had moved back in. So glad to feel safe and protected. So glad she'd managed to let go of most of her anger and insecurities, because she needed him now. Really needed him.

And she hated the thought of spending two or three hours alone with the lawyers for her grandmother's estate, absorbing legalese and responsibilities. She'd avoided this meeting as long as possible, but there was no more putting it off. She'd twisted her hair into a sophisticated bun, donned her best pair of slacks and a decent sweater, and was ready to go.

But it would be nice if Jack would come with her.

Jack, however, was standing near the French doors, a shoulder propped against the wall, drinking from a beer.

"Talk to your lawyers? The same guys who wanted to stick it to me in the divorce?" Jack shook his head and scooped up Beej, who was nearly wiped out as he careened around a corner while chasing Coco. "Whoa, buddy."

"Doggie!" Beej cried, pointing at the little dog, who at the moment was hiding under the table, her back toward the wall. Beej squirmed to get down and give chase again.

"I'm the babysitter, remember? By the way, you look great."

Cissy felt her cheeks warm. God, she was pathetic, responding to Jack's compliments like a blushing schoolgirl.

"Down, Dad-dee! I want down!" Beej, thwarted, was getting mad.

"In a minute," Jack said, holding fast to the little dynamo.

"We could take Beej with us."

"Oh, he'd be a blast in the lawyers' office. Let's take his sippy cup and binky and have him sit on our laps for an hour or two. Maybe we could bring Coco."

"Point taken."

Jack smiled into Cissy's eyes. "Actually, maybe that's not such a bad idea. Those tight asses down at the law firm need a little shaking up."

"Thanks, but you're right. I'll take a pass."

"Down, Dad-dee!" Beej slapped his fist against Jack's shoulder in frustration.

"Hey, no hitting." Jack was suddenly serious as a heart attack.

Beej, surprised by his favorite person on earth's sharp tone, buried his face in his father's shoulder in embarrassment and mumbled a soft but defiant, "No, Dad-dee."

"Careful, Beej," Cissy warned. "Dad-dee is pretty tough."

Beej turned his face her way and scowled. It was so comical, Cissy nearly laughed. "'Bye, sweetie," she said, kissing him on his head, but Beej turned away.

"No kisses!"

"I'm going to kiss you too," Jack threatened.

"Nooooooo!"

Cissy did laugh then, and Jack succeeded in giving B.J. a loud kiss to the top of his head, which Beej quickly swiped off. Jack and Cissy shared a moment of amusement. Their relationship had improved over the past few days, their life taking on a new togetherness since that final showdown over Larissa. Cissy believed him. She trusted him. She was glad he was home. And now they were moving forward one day at a time.

Unfortunately, while their relationship continued to improve, the circumstances surrounding the deaths in her family kept them under a shadow of suspicion and fear—and the watchful eye of the police. Cherise's murder had been another shock, and Cissy also hadn't gotten over seeing her mother in the doorway of Gran's house. It was just one unpleasant surprise after another, but she was determined not to shut down and cower in her house. She had a life to live, and Jack was with her now. And with the police providing protection, and the ever-alert Coco on the premises, Cissy felt secure enough to strive for some kind of normalcy. Jack had ordered a new security system, and it was scheduled to be installed by the following week.

Nonetheless, she was wary and a bit nervous. Her request for Jack to join her today hadn't been idle.

But she couldn't—wouldn't—let him see that she felt any fear. They were tiptoeing their way back to each other, and she couldn't appear too needy, too eager. Their relationship had to be equal and solid for them to ever reach that same level of trust and commitment.

Cissy gazed out the window. The unmarked police car was parked across the street, courtesy of Detective Paterno. He claimed he was concerned about her welfare, as well as that of her uncle and brother, and that was the reason for the continued protection. The police in Oregon were watching Nick and James while Paterno considered Cissy his responsibility. This was both comforting and annoying. It was weird having two officers stake out her house 24/7.

Cissy cast an eye toward the sky. It was still sunny, but cold. She opened the closet door in the foyer and pulled out her jacket. "Tanya's supposed to come by in a bit and pick up her final check. If you want to get out for a while, you could ask her to watch Beej."

"I thought you didn't trust her."

Cissy made a face. "I don't know. It's not really a matter of trust. We just never quite clicked."

"Because I suggested her upon my dad's recommendation?" Jack asked, daring her to argue the point. "You were prejudiced. Thought maybe they'd had a fling or something?"

"Tanya? No."

One of his eyebrows arched.

"She wasn't his type," Cissy explained, shrugging into her coat. It wasn't that she didn't think Jonathan would hit on any attractive younger woman; he seemed to think it was practically a job requirement. But Cissy felt he wouldn't have recommended Tanya if they were romantically involved. The man was a cheat, but he didn't like untidiness in relationships. At least that was Cissy's take. He wouldn't want the woman he was currently "seeing" working for his son.

And lately Jonathan had seemed more interested in his various business endeavors than women. He was always looking for the big score, a man who would rather chase rainbows than work. The same could be said for Jack's brother. J.J. was a chip off the old block if Cissy had ever seen one, except that he wanted next to nothing to do with Jack's life. Where Jonathan insinuated himself into Jack's affairs, J.J. stayed away. Cissy had met J.J.'s ex-wife, Amanda, long after they'd been divorced and was sorry that hadn't worked out. She'd liked Amanda right away. But Amanda couldn't take the womanizing and the big dreams that never materialized, so she divorced J.J. and struck out on her own. She'd done well since the divorce, much better than when she'd been married.

"What are you thinking about?" Jack asked when Cissy went quiet.

"Your dad . . . and Tanya. Not as a couple. Remember, Tanya fired me, not the other way around. She suggested I check with the nanny school. She also thought I should see a shrink."

Jack snorted derisively.

"I probably should." Cissy smiled. "I mean, look. I let you back in the house."

"That was pure sanity on your part."

"Uh-huh. Anyway, Tanya's check's on the counter." Cissy walked into the kitchen and tapped the white envelope with a finger. "I'll be back in a couple of hours."

"With those guys, don't count on it." Jack took another pull from his beer, set the bottle on the counter, and eased Beej to the ground.

"'Bye." She brushed a kiss over Jack's lips, and he grinned. In one swift motion, he wrapped his arms around her and kissed her long and hard enough to steal the breath from her lungs and make her think longingly of their recent passionate nights in the bedroom.

When he lifted his head, he casually picked up his beer again, as if he hadn't experienced the sensations that were still sizzling through her bloodstream. He took a long swallow, eyeing her with amusement.

"You're a big tease, Jack Holt."

"Stick around and see how much teasing there is."

"Promises, promises . . . I'd love to, but, you know, I have this hot date with three stuffed shirts who want to talk about wills and trusts and limited liability corporations and tax advantages, and gee . . . it just sounds so damned fun, I'll have to take a rain check."

She headed toward the garage and hit the button for the garage door opener. As she climbed into her car and backed down the drive, she saw Sara wheel in next door. Sara climbed out of her car and left the engine running. Spying Cissy as she headed toward her front porch, she sketched a wave, then stopped. A moment later she was heading Cissy's way.

Inwardly groaning, Cissy pasted a smile on her face and rolled down her window.

"Hey, I want to apologize for the other day," Sara said. "I know you're going through hell. Sometimes I just forge ahead and damn the consequences. I'm sorry."

"It's all right."

Today Sara wore espresso-colored slacks and a matching jacket with a V-necked cream sweater and a dull-pink, cream and taupe silk scarf looped artlessly around her neck. "I'm meeting some clients," she said. "Had to run home and pick up some docs. Thank God the sun's out, at least for the moment. Sales are hard enough without a torrential downpour."

"The clients from Philadelphia?"

"No, they've decided to come in a couple of weeks." Sara peered at Cissy more closely. "You changing your mind about the house?"

"It's not mine to change."

"Well, when it is, promise you'll keep me in mind?"

Her persistence was awe-inspiring. "As I recall, you already gave the attorneys your business card," Cissy reminded dryly.

"I'm a bitch on wheels," Sara admitted with an embarrassed laugh. She shot a glance at the unmarked police car with its burly driver. "What's going on there?"

"The police are watching the house just in case Marla shows up."

She snorted. "I'm surprised the press aren't camped out here too. One of 'em came to my door, wanted to know if I'd give an interview. I said sure."

Cissy blinked. "You agreed to an *interview?*"

"I didn't give away your family secrets, if that's what you're worried about. It's not like I know anything, but I thought maybe if they put my name on the news, I'd get some free publicity out of the deal." To Cissy's look of consternation, she said, "I must have been beyond boring, because it never even aired. I spent the whole time telling them how great you and Jack were and how unfortunate it was that you had to deal with all the bad publicity, and then I asked, oh, by the way, did I mention that I sell real estate? They didn't go for it."

Cissy almost laughed. Then Sara asked, "You going somewhere special?" She was looking over Cissy's choice of dress.

"Meeting with those same attorneys over estate issues."

"Ahh." She looked hopeful.

"I'm not selling the house, Sara."

"Maybe not today. Maybe not tomorrow, but never say never." She glanced over at Jack's Jeep, which was parked on the street in front of the house, across from the unmarked car. "Looks like Jack's back. Is he part of the protection, or is it more than that?"

"Maybe a little of both."

She nodded. "Well, he's a great-looking guy, and he loves his kid."

"We're working things out," Cissy said.

"So all that talk about divorce was just—talk? You never intended to go through with it."

"I had every intention of going through with it," Cissy responded heatedly. "But things have changed."

"Can I ask how?"

"All this with my mother . . . losing my grandmother . . .

it's kind of put things in perspective, you know? Makes you ask yourself, What is family? What's important?"

"But you said Jack was having an affair."

"I was wrong."

"Oh." Sara's brows lifted.

Cissy could tell she didn't believe her. Well, fine. She didn't have to. It wasn't up to Cissy to convince Sara that she'd made a mistake. That just because women looked at Jack in "that way" didn't mean he acted on their unspoken invitations. Maybe it was because Sara herself liked Jack's company, became flirtatious and animated when he was around, that she was reacting now as if Cissy were burying her head in the sand.

"I'd better go," Sara said, moving away from Cissy's car. "Tell Jack I'm glad for both of you. And I hope things get resolved with your mother soon too."

Cissy watched Sara hurry back to her house, steamed for reasons she couldn't fully explain. She searched inside herself and realized it was because of the way Sara treated her. As if she never really mattered. Sara had a tendency to negate Cissy's importance without even realizing it. It was as if she'd deemed Jack the prize and Cissy unworthy of his love, or even his interest. As if she expected Jack to wake up one day and recognize he'd made a mistake—that Cissy was too young, too inexperienced, too unsophisticated for the likes of Jack Holt.

And some of Cissy's own insecurities where Jack was concerned had been triggered not only by Sara's attitude, but by others' attitudes as well. Larissa, for instance. She'd supposedly been Cissy's friend, but that had all been a fantasy, she saw now. Larissa had merely put up with Cissy because she was married to Jack, but like Sara, she'd dismissed Cissy as a serious threat for his attentions. Sure, Cissy was married to him. Yes, she'd borne him a son. But Jack was out of her league: older, wiser, and too intelligent to want to seriously be with her "till death do us part." Both women felt that it was only a matter of time until Jack was back on the market; Cissy could tell.

And she'd damned well almost followed through on their expectations!

Now she shook her head in disbelief. Had she been so affected, so unsure of her own worth, that she'd believed as they did?

Jack had told her that she was on a search for unconditional love, a product of her uncaring mother, selfish father, and remote grandmother. Maybe he wasn't that far from the truth. Cissy had certainly let other women feed into her insecurities about his love for her.

Pulling out of her drive and heading into the city, Cissy realized that blaming Jack for cheating had almost become a self-fulfilling prophecy. She was sure he would cheat, she'd *expected* it based on his father's and brother's history, and therefore she'd pushed Jack away so hard that he damned near slept with Larissa. Then she'd compounded her error by kicking Jack out of the house and demanding a divorce!

Cissy pulled up in front of Joltz, feeling as if she were having some kind of epiphany. A parking spot had miraculously appeared, and she slid into it almost by reflex. She had some time before the appointment with the attorneys. Enough anyway to grab a coffee and take advantage of the parking spot, which was almost a must-do in San Francisco whenever one came available.

She felt slightly dazed. Both with the events of the past several weeks and her own self-realization. She wanted the police to catch her mother. She wanted to know how Marla had killed Eugenia or orchestrated her death. She wanted Cherise's murder to be solved.

But she was glad she had Jack back. And she resolved that she would never let anything break them up again.

Never.

Diedre and Rachelle were behind the counter as Cissy walked inside. They were both busy helping customers, so Cissy got in line. Across the room Cissy saw Selma seated at one of the small tables near the window. It figured. There was no escaping her. If Cissy was anywhere near Joltz, Selma was there. Spying Cissy, Selma waved and headed her way. Cissy inwardly groaned. She wasn't ready for Selma to take their "friendship" to the next level.

"Hi," Cissy said, trying to infuse her voice with enthusiasm, failing miserably.

"You're all dressed up," Selma observed. "Where are you going?"

She managed to make the question sound cheery and perky instead of downright nosy, but it grated on Cissy's nerves all the same. "Financial meeting with lawyers."

"No jeans. Dead giveaway that you weren't planning to spend the afternoon writing here." Selma sounded proud of her powers of observation.

Cissy reached the front of the line, and Rachelle shot her a smile. "The usual?"

"Please. And a muffin. Those apple bran ones?"

"You got it."

Cissy moved to one side to wait for her order. Selma moved with her as if they were old pals. She started telling Cissy how she'd always wanted to be a writer but was thinking of becoming a novelist rather than a newspaper and/or magazine writer. Cissy wondered if this, maybe, was what was driving Selma's seemingly deeper interest in her. Did the woman hope she could help her in her writing ventures? Or was it something else?

Rachelle handed Cissy her latte and a plate with her muffin, and Cissy moved to an open spot at the bar surrounding the baristas, hoping Selma would take the hint and return to her own table. But Selma said, "Let me get my coffee," then hurriedly gathered her things and settled onto the stool next to Cissy. Other patrons quickly scooped up Selma's table, and Cissy was stuck with unwanted company. Rachelle caught her eye and looked sympathetic.

When Selma winced and rubbed above her right eye, Cissy tried to ignore her. But after the third time, she felt obliged to ask, "You okay?"

"I've been trying some decaf the last couple of weeks, but weaning off the caffeine gives me a headache. I guess that's what it is. I thought caffeine was making me tense, but this is almost worse. Maybe if my problems went away, it wouldn't matter."

She'd opened the door for Cissy to ask her about those problems, but Cissy was already sorry she'd gotten dragged into the conversation. Faced with way more information already than she wanted about Selma, Cissy didn't take the bait. Rachelle did, though.

"What kind of problems?" she asked, right on cue.

"The worst kind. The kind that involve men."

Diedre looked over, her expression skeptical. "You got man problems?" she called over the blast of the espresso machine.

Cissy tore off a small piece of her muffin. It was lunchtime, but she couldn't seem to get her appetite engaged no matter what she did.

"Sure do," Selma said.

It felt odd to hear that Selma was involved in some kind of relationship. She hadn't been with a guy at the funeral reception. Like Diedre, Cissy was kind of surprised. Selma had seemed single, unattached and maybe even not all that interested. With a small jolt, she realized she'd made assumptions about Selma like Sara and Larissa had made about her.

"How do you trust a guy?" Selma asked suddenly, as if she really wanted to know. "Really trust him."

Rachelle slid her a look. "The million-dollar question."

"We all have problems," Diedre said.

"Maybe you have to have a little faith," Cissy suggested.

"Do you trust your husband?" Selma gazed at her curiously.

Cissy dusted her hands, finished with her muffin, leaving about a third of it on the plate. "It's important in a marriage," she said, sliding from her stool.

"But do you?" Selma insisted.

Diedre and Rachelle were listening hard, as if waiting for Cissy's answer too. "Yes, I do. It's taken a while. I mean, marriage is . . . hard. But we have a son, and a home. Together."

Selma seemed to take that in. "I just want to have him with me more. A home . . . Wow . . . Wouldn't that be great?"

"You've got two homes," Rachelle pointed out to Cissy. "Unless your real-estate friend gets her way and you sell your grandmother's."

Cissy shook her head. "That house was never really my home. I mean, yes, I did live there when I was younger, but it wasn't a 'home,' if you know what I mean."

"But what a cool house," Diedre put in with surprising passion. "You got to live there. Lots of us never get that chance."

"It wasn't all that terrific," Cissy disabused them. "We Cahills seem to have trouble in the happiness department."

She left before the conversation could continue, always uncomfortable talking about her family. Stepping outside, she pulled on her shades, sliding them onto the bridge of her nose. The sun was bright, though it looked as if it were heading for a bank of clouds. It was a sheer delight after all the gray fog of the past few weeks. Cissy turned her face skyward and inhaled, some of her worry lifting with the change of weather.

She did trust Jack. She did. She loved him and felt safe with him, and that's all that mattered.

And then she saw the unmarked car, its two officers shadowy within the interior, engine running, double-parked on a side street, facing her. So, they'd followed her to Joltz and would undoubtedly follow her to the lawyers'.

She hardly knew how to feel. Sure, it was protection, but geez . . . It sure felt like more than just surveillance. . . . Almost as if she were under suspicion. . . .

Irritated, Cissy stalked to her car, threw open the door, climbed inside, and twisted the ignition. She pulled into traffic and watched as the car nosed into the street behind her, several cars back.

"Pain in the butt," she muttered and wondered if maybe Paterno's claim of protection was a cover for something else.

Jack wiped the remains of B.J.'s lunch from his face and got him out of his high chair and back on the ground, where he instantly started chasing Coco, who ran for the living room.

He cleaned up the kitchen, then collapsed the stroller and propped it against the wall. "Come on, Beej," he called to his son, who followed Coco from room to room. "Let's get to the park before the sun goes away."

Beej's running skills weren't exactly causing Coco concern. The dog's ears and tail were down, but she could easily keep ahead of his awkward chase.

Hearing Jack, Beej veered his way, grabbing his father's leg to keep from falling.

Jack lifted him into one arm and grabbed the stroller with his free hand.

They were heading for the door when the front bell rang. "Tanya," he said, remembering. He set Beej down and opened the door. But it wasn't the nanny. It was his father.

"Dad?"

Jonathan lifted his hands at the surprised tone of his son's voice. "Nothing's wrong. I knew you'd moved back in, and you weren't at the office, so I just stopped by."

"You called the office?"

Jonathan leaned down to B.J., but he tore away in pursuit of Coco again.

"I was going to ask you to lunch," Jonathan said casually.

"I already had tuna sandwiches with B.J. I'm babysitting while Cissy meets with the attorneys for Eugenia's estate."

"When's she going to be back?"

"Couple hours."

"What about Tanya?"

Jack gave his father a long look. "I can't get away right now, Dad. What's wrong?"

"Just wanted to see you. Is that a crime?"

Jack ignored his father's defensive tone. He knew his father, and it was just a matter of time before Jonathan got to the real point of his visit. There generally was an ulterior motive. Sometimes minor, sometimes not.

"Beej and I are on our way to the park. You can certainly join us."

"No, no. I'll only take a few minutes of your time. Just hold on about the park for a bit, and we'll be fine."

Jack threw a glance at B.J., whose attention was on the dog. "Want a beer?" he asked his dad, deciding he might as well give Jonathan his ear now rather than put off the discussion to some other time.

Jonathan accepted the long-necked bottle. "I've been

talking to investors in these oil-drilling sites in South and Central America. Getting the money men together with the operational teams. You know what I mean?"

"You're looking for investors in wildcat drilling?" Jack's father had tapped him for money more times than he could count, always with the promise of a fabulous return on his investment. Mostly Jack bobbed and weaved his way out of the deals, but Jonathan seemed to always come up with a new one.

"I'm brokering some deals. I was thinking maybe you might want to get in on the ground floor."

"I'd have to talk it over with Cissy, and now's not the best time for us. A lot of things need to be resolved, financially, with her family."

A cloud crossed Jonathan's face. "I'd hate you to miss out on this, Son."

Jack's smile was noncommittal. He let his father expound heartily for long minutes until B.J. grew tired of chasing Coco and came back their way, hanging on Jack's leg and looking up at him.

Jack picked up his son as Jonathan was saying, "I thought your magazine could do a small profile on me. Get some publicity going. It would be great if you were a part of this."

Jack had heard about a lot of get-rich-quick schemes from his father, some of them full of merit, most not. Unfortunately, even the ones that panned out never really worked, for Jonathan had yet to see any of them to their profitable end. Long before that happened, he was off chasing another idea, another dream. Sometimes his brother was in on the deal, at least peripherally. They both believed that "big killing" was just around the corner.

"It's a really great opportunity," Jonathan said for about the third time when B.J. started chanting.

"Park. Go park. Park. Park!"

"In a minute there," Jonathan cut him off a bit tensely, then launched into more particulars.

B.J. responded with, "Now, now, now!"

"Bryan Jack," Jonathan snapped.

Beneath Jonathan's bonhomie Jack heard nervous tension. This latest deal must be really important to him; but then, they all were.

"WE GO!" B.J. regarded Jack urgently.

"I promised him the park," Jack said to Jonathan. "We really have to go, if we're going."

"Put it off till tomorrow."

"Kind of important to follow through on promises," Jack pointed out.

Jonathan got his face close to B.J.'s. "Okay, little man. Why don't you go find some toys to play with? Your dad'll be ready to go in a minute."

"No, Poppa."

"Don't tell me no."

B.J. scowled.

"And remember, grumpy boys don't get to go at all."

"Dad," Jack warned, as Beej wound up for a siren wail.

"You can't just give in to him," Jonathan said, annoyed, over the escalating scream. "He'll never learn anything!"

"Except how to be disappointed over and over again?"

"When can we have a real discussion?" Jonathan demanded. "This is important to me, Jack."

"Dad . . ." Jack tried to comfort B.J., whose upset had turned to tears. Jonathan tossed his hands in the air as if everyone were conspiring against him just as the doorbell rang again.

This time Jack discovered Tanya on the porch. "I came to get my check," she said uncertainly.

B.J. held his arms out to her as if she were a savior, and Jack, a bit reluctantly, handed him to the nanny, who cooed at him.

"There you go," Jonathan said with relief as the little boy stopped crying.

"Go park!" he told Tanya. "Park!"

She turned her gaze to Jack. "You want me to take him to the park?"

"No, that's fine. We were just leaving. You don't have to."

"Don't look a gift horse in the mouth," Jonathan said, smiling at Tanya. To Jack, he added, "Didn't I tell you she was great?" He loved taking credit for discovering her.

"I don't mind," she said.

"She's the nanny," Jonathan declared, as if Jack were just about as dense as he could be.

Jack was about to explain that Tanya was no longer employed, when he caught her eye. "I'd be happy to," she said, hugging B.J. and smiling. "He's a great kid. And you're busy. It's no problem, really."

"You sure? He hasn't been Mr. Happy today," Jack warned.

"I think I can handle it."

"You're a fine young lady." Jonathan gave her a warm look.

Jack handed Tanya her check, then helped tote the stroller to her car. They strapped B.J. into the extra car seat she used. "I'll give this back to you, since you paid for it," she told him.

"I'm sorry things haven't worked out."

Tanya shrugged that off. B.J. waved at him from the backseat window, and, with a deep breath, Jack returned to his father, who immediately, and enthusiastically, launched into more discussion about his new venture. Jack silently wished he could have gone with Tanya and B.J., his attention drifting a bit as he wondered how many more times he would play this scene out with his father. It was always jab and parry. And inevitably Jonathan would leave feeling Jack wasn't a "team player" because he hadn't invested in the latest investment opportunity.

Jack did agree to some free advertising in his magazine, however, and Jonathan finally wound down. He seemed to want to try one more approach, but Jack walked him to his car, casting an eye to the sun, which was now fighting against encroaching dark clouds. Jack checked his watch, worrying a bit. How long had Tanya been gone?

"The boy's in good hands," his father assured him as he climbed into his car. "Don't you worry about Tanya, now."

Jack watched his father head down the street. He didn't have Tanya's cell number. He wondered if he should go to the neighborhood park and look for them himself. The dark clouds were winning, swallowing up the sun and darkening the sky as if night were approaching. It appeared the heavens might open up in a downpour at any minute.

His father was right about one thing, though, Jack reminded himself: Tanya was a capable nanny. Cissy's problem with her had been because of a personality clash. It had nothing to do with her love and care for B.J.

But he sure as hell wished she'd get back here.

When another fifteen minutes had elapsed and the first fat drops of rain hit the ground, Jack was through waiting. He grabbed his coat and headed determinedly for the door. Before he could fold himself into his Jeep, Cissy's car turned into the drive and pulled into the garage. Jack turned back her way, reaching her as she was climbing from the car.

"Is Beej in your car?" she asked.

"No."

"You left him in the house?"

The rain suddenly poured down in a torrent, pounding on the pavement, bouncing like silver pellets. Jack squeezed inside the garage beside Cissy, and they both watched the sudden flood as he explained, "Beej is at the park with Tanya."

"Tanya?"

"My father stopped by, and Tanya came for her check. Dad wanted to have a talk with me, and she offered to take him to the park, so I let her. I was just going to find them."

"How long have they been gone? Hopefully she got him back in her car before this rain started." Cissy grabbed her purse, then glanced at the rain some more. "I'll come with you."

"Maybe you should stay in case she comes back."

"The park's not that far. If we miss her, she'll wait."

They hurried to Jack's car, getting soaked as they ran. "So, what did your dad want to talk about? Swamp land in Florida?"

"Basically," Jack said.

Cissy heard the resignation in his voice as they climbed into his Jeep. He knew as well as she did that his father was a five-star flake.

The unmarked police car rounded the corner as they got in Jack's Jeep. Both Cissy and Jack glanced at it as they traveled the short distance to the park. There was no sign of Tanya's car.

They circled the park, peering through the silvery rain that blew in front of them in waving curtains. There was no one about. The parking lots were empty, the place deserted with the advent of the rain.

"Could they have gone to a different park?" Jack asked.

"That would be a first. Tanya takes the path of least resistance. This one's closest. Can I use your cell?" Jack handed it over, and Cissy dialed Tanya's cell phone number from memory. It rang several times, and then Tanya's voice said to leave a message. Cissy hung up and called her a second time, hoping Tanya might respond to the urgency of a second call on the heels of the first. But again, Cissy heard her message. At the end of the beep, she said, "Tanya, it's Cissy. I know B.J.'s with you, but it's raining cats and dogs. Can you bring him back? Jack and I are looking for you, but you're not at the park. Thanks for taking him, but we've got things to do. We really need him back. Soon."

She hung up, tamping down a growing panic.

Jack's expression was grim. "Want me to take you back to the house?"

"I can't imagine where they are." She pressed her knuckles to her lips. "She should have come back as soon as it started raining. Beej should be home."

"Isn't there a park about five blocks up? It has more swings."

"Yes . . ." Cissy's breath felt like it was trapped in her lungs.

"We'll go there," Jack said, shooting her a concerned glance. "Tanya's taking good care of him. Maybe they went for ice cream or something."

Cissy didn't say anything. She should never have allowed Tanya to be B.J.'s nanny, should never have listened to Jonathan. The man was no judge of character. Far from it! He was the worst. A flim-flam man. A womanizer. He probably *had* been involved with Tanya!

And now her son was missing!

She fought back a tide of paranoia. *Don't panic. Don't freak out.* Tanya wasn't perfect, but she loved Beej. That had never been in question.

"How'd it go with the lawyers?" Jack asked.

She understood his attempt to keep her from flipping into a full-blown panic, but it only deepened her anxiety. "It was fine. Uncle Nick's the executor, but we knew that already. There they are!"

Through the rain Cissy could see a woman carrying a toddler wrapped in a dark coat, hurrying down the sidewalk alongside the other park.

"That's not B.J.'s coat," Cissy realized, her spurt of relief fading quickly.

"And that's not Tanya."

Jack wheeled the Jeep around and back to the house. Before the vehicle was in park, Cissy sprang out and flew into their home.

No B.J. No Tanya.

"Where else would Tanya take him?" he asked her.

"Nowhere else. Well, wait . . . maybe her apartment?" Cissy ran out the door of the house.

"You have the address?"

She rattled it off, and Jack turned the Jeep around. Tanya lived past the airport. It wasn't all that far, but it felt like the traffic was purposely keeping them from their destination.

It was enough to send Cissy into overdrive. She wanted to scream at the delays.

"Come on . . . come on . . ."

They drove in silence for a few miles: Jack negotiating traffic, Cissy trying to keep herself calm. Finally, she admitted in a small voice, "It makes no sense. Tanya wouldn't take Beej to her place. Why would she? The only time they ever went there was because Tanya had to get extra clothes because she was going on a last-minute date."

"Where else do you want to look?"

"No, no. Keep going. We've got to get there. I don't know! I just want my son. I want him to be okay."

"He's gonna be fine."

"How do you know?" She was on the verge of hysteria.

"He's with Tanya. She's taking care of him." Jack said the words like a mantra.

They screeched to a halt near her apartment complex. Cissy scanned the parking lot. "There's Tanya's car!" There wasn't another space to be had in the lot, so Jack circled, looking for a parking place. Rain battered the windshield, pouring so hard it was like driving through a car wash. "Damn this weather," he muttered.

"Just let me out!" Cissy had her fingers wrapped around the door handle.

"Just a sec."

"Please, Jack . . ." Her teeth were chattering.

"Take it easy, Ciss. We'll find him."

Jack squeezed the Jeep into a lined No Parking zone. "Screw 'em," he said, yanking on the brake. Cissy threw open her door. "I'll go," he told her. "You stay—"

"No way!" She practically ran across the street to the dun-colored complex, a boxy monstrosity that had to have been built in the late sixties or early seventies, evading the newer, more stringent city planning restrictions.

Rain poured over her, dousing her in a flood. She ran toward the wrought-iron gate that led to the inner courtyard. The gate had originally been on an automatic lock requiring a visitor to ring to be buzzed in, but that lock was broken and looked to have been for quite some time.

Cissy shoved her way through, and Jack was right behind her. She hurried to Tanya's door and twisted the knob. Locked.

"Tanya!" Cissy beat on the door with all her strength. "Are you there? Tanya! Open up!"

She waited a moment, holding her breath. Then Jack pounded his fists on the door panels as well, yelling even louder, "Tanya! It's Jack and Cissy. Are you okay? We tried calling."

They heard the sound of a window scrape open to their left. "Hey," a disgruntled female voice called from one apartment over. "You trying to wake the dead? I work graveyard. Gimme a break."

"My nanny lives here. She's got my son," Cissy said rapidly. "We can't reach her. I'm scared to death something's happened."

"Keep your shirt on. I've got an extra key. Tanya and I swapped in case . . . something happened. I guess this is something."

Cissy was on one foot and the other. She wanted to scream for the other woman to hurry. Jack stood like a sentinel by the door, arms crossed, expression taut.

Finally, a woman in her thirties opened her door, running a hand through tousled hair and squinting at Cissy and Jack. "It must be raining like the devil."

"Please . . ." Cissy said.

"Okay, okay. You look harmless enough." She gave Jack the once-over and self-consciously smoothed her robe. Rather than give them the key, she twisted open Tanya's lock.

Cissy rushed inside, but Jack was even faster. Before she could react, he suddenly crushed her face to his chest. "Get out," he ordered the neighbor. "It's a crime scene."

"What?" Cissy gasped. She wrenched herself free and shoved Jack aside, fear surging through her veins. *Crime scene?* "B.J.?" she whispered brokenly.

But there was no sign of her son.

Instead, in the center of the room, lying faceup on the floor, was Tanya.

The dark, ominous circle of a bullet hole sat between her surprised eyes.

Chapter 18

"Where's B.J.?" Cissy cried, her heart racing, feeling as if she might faint. Oh God, oh God, oh God! He had to be here. Had to. She stared at Tanya's body, the blood oozing from the black hole in her forehead, the sightless eyes staring toward the ceiling of her bare apartment.

"Oh Lord . . ." the neighbor woman said, backing away as Cissy raced through the rooms, searching, her gaze scraping every nook and cranny of the tidy, one-bedroom apartment.

He had to be here. He *had* to!

"Call 9-1-1," Jack ordered the retreating neighbor.

"Beej," Cissy called, desperation creeping into her voice as an old cuckoo clock on the mantel ticked loudly. She hurried down the short hallway a second time, opening the bedroom closet door. Finding nothing, she dropped to her knees and peered beneath the bed skirt. Suitcases and a plastic tub of summer clothes were hidden there, but no baby.

She whispered, "Beej, where are you?"

What if he wasn't here?

There were only so many places he could hide.

What if . . . Oh God . . . She hated to think it, but what if the person who'd shot Tanya had B.J.? She couldn't think that way. Not yet. Pushing herself to her feet, she dashed into the minuscule bath. Heart thudding, half afraid that she might find his little lifeless body on the cold porcelain, she threw back the shower curtain, nearly ripping the plastic from its metal hooks.

"I'm looking outside," Jack's voice reached her.

Aside from a visible rust stain, the tub was empty. Cissy nearly sank to her knees. She didn't know whether to be relieved or worried. She just wanted her child.

Please, please, please keep him safe. Let me find him, she silently prayed, returning to the kitchen, keeping her eyes averted from Tanya's body. Through the open sliding-glass door, she spied Jack outside in the small court-yard, where a rusting barbecue and pots of last year's dead flowers had been stored. Rain poured down. But there was no child.

She swallowed back her fear. Whoever had killed Tanya wouldn't take Beej. Wouldn't hurt him. That made no sense.

Or did it?

A chill as dark as midnight touched her soul.

Jaw tight, skin stretched taut over his face, Jack walked back inside and shook his head. "I checked her car. Unlocked. Nothing."

"He has to be here," she said as if to convince herself. "He has to." Willing her child to appear, she threw open a pantry door. Brooms, cleaning supplies, towels, and a few canned goods filled the shelves.

Jack's hands grabbed hold of her shoulders as she stared into the empty pantry. "He's not here."

Her knees nearly gave way. "Oh no," she whispered, disbelieving.

Cissy's entire world spun. How had she let her son

get caught up in this horrendous nightmare? How could she have let him be in jeopardy? If anything happened to Beej . . . Oh God, she couldn't think that way. Wouldn't. "We have to find him!" Where? Oh Lord, where was he? She couldn't breathe, could barely hear over the panicked beat of her heart.

Jack pulled her against him and whispered into her ear, "We'll find him, Ciss. I promise."

Anger and frustration filled her. "How could you let B.J. go with Tanya?" Cissy demanded, rounding on Jack, ready to strike at anything, to accuse anyone.

He flinched. "Don't go there, Cissy. Not now."

"But I warned you. I told you she was . . . was . . ."

"You said you trusted her," he reminded, throwing her own words back at her, and she knew he was right.

"Oh," she whispered, her voice cracking. "I'm just so scared. So damned scared for Beej." Her insides turned to water, but she knew that Jack was right. B.J. was missing, most likely in the clutches of whoever had murdered Tanya. Horrible scenarios of her frightened child—in pain, in fear, lost and lonely—streaked through her brain. He would be looking for her, and she wouldn't be there. Tears rained from her eyes. Cold, certain fear crawled through her as Jack steered her into the living room.

"We'll find him. He'll be safe. You have to trust that, Cissy. Okay?"

She nodded, willing herself to be strong.

"Did you call the police?" Jack demanded, glaring at the neighbor, who'd returned.

"I . . ." She shook her head.

"Oh for Christ's sake!" Jack retrieved his cell, punching out numbers.

Cissy glanced down at Tanya's body sprawled across the rug, blood pooling beneath her. It was the second body she'd seen this past month. So much like Gran's. Cissy's stomach revolted, and she retched, barely able to keep the contents of her stomach down. Acid burned up her throat. What had happened here? Why had Tanya stolen their child and ended up dead? This didn't make any sense.

Marla . . . She's behind this. . . . You know it. She's a psycho.

A new fear crawled through her veins.

Marla wouldn't hurt B.J. Not her own grandson. . . .

But you think she killed Gran, don't you?

And Rory, her own brother?

What about Cherise?

Why would she stop there?

Why not murder Tanya and B.J. too?

"No!" she said, denying the evil thoughts.

Jack, cell phone to his ear, snapped back to attention. "What?" he said, but before she could answer, she heard a voice coming from his cell phone. The 9-1-1 operator.

Jack's blue eyes were as sober as she'd ever seen them. He stared at her but spoke into the receiver. "This is Jack Holt. I need to report a murder. A woman is dead, and a child is missing. The victim is Tanya Watson; she's our nanny. She's dead in her apartment. It looks like she's been shot and . . . and she had my, our, son, Bryan Jack Holt. He's missing. What? The address?" He looked at Cissy, who dully recited it, and Jack repeated it for the officer, then added, "Send an ambulance and help. We need help . . . Oh . . . wait . . ." He looked through the doorway to the parking lot, where a car was wheeling over the apron and into an empty slot.

Cissy recognized the unmarked police car and the men inside as the officers who had been watching her house and following her.

"They're here," Jack said and hung up as the two men flew out of the car, weapons drawn, their faces masks of determination.

The rain was finally diminishing as a tall Latino man with clipped hair and a weathered face yelled "Everyone out!" as he walked to the open door. "Now! Oh Jesus." He squatted next to the body and felt for a pulse, then looked up and shook his head as his partner approached. "Dead. Call it in, and we'll seal off the area. Start talking to the neighbors, see who heard what. Then phone Paterno."

"Already on the phone," the other, heavier-set detective said, clicking a cell to his ear.

"Our son is missing," Jack said. "He was here with Tanya, and we can't find him."

"You've searched?"

Jack nodded.

"You need to get out of the apartment. . . . Please wait on the porch."

"But he's not here," Cissy cut in. "We checked. We have to find him."

"I'll look again, but you have to leave. This is a crime scene." He was motioning with his hand to Cissy and Jack. "In just a minute we'll get your statements—yeah!" he said into the phone as he walked into the room. "O'Riley." He gave his badge number, then said, "Detective Perez and I are here at what looks like a homicide. Dead female. We're first on the scene. We were following Cissy and Jack Holt." He glanced up at Jack, who lingered near the doorway. "Victim's name?"

"Tanya Watson," Jack supplied again, his expression grim, lips blade thin, muscle working in his jaw. "Our nanny. I already called it in."

O'Riley nodded.

Propped against the exterior wall of the unit, Cissy tried to think clearly, to get a grip on herself though she wanted to fall into a billion pieces. She couldn't let herself. She didn't have time. She had to save her son. But from what? From whom?

The detective grunted. "Tanya Watson is dead. . . . What? I don't know all the details. We just arrived on the scene. The Holts say their kid is missing, that he was with the victim." O'Riley turned back to Cissy and Jack, peering at them over the top of wire-rimmed glasses, and Jack nodded. "Yeah, that's right," he said to Paterno. "Okay, we've got it covered, but we need more manpower, not just for the investigation but for the search. Okay."

He hit a button, said to Jack and Cissy, "More units are on their way. Just give me another minute." He punched out another number and had another conversation, similar to the first.

The scream of sirens split the air. For the first time, Cissy noticed that neighbors were peeking out windows or standing in doorways as more emergency vehicles screamed up the street.

Everything seemed surreal, just slightly out of focus.

A jet rumbled overhead, taking off from the airport not far away.

O'Riley said into the phone, "When the unit gets here, we'll start with the neighbors and scene . . . Will do." He clicked off his phone and said to Cissy, Jack, and Tanya's neighbor, "We're gonna want statements from all of you and all the neighbors. You live next door?" he asked the neighbor, who identified herself as Corinne Glenn.

"Yes."

"You heard the gunshot?"

"No . . . Well, maybe. I'm not sure."

"How's that?" O'Riley asked.

Cissy couldn't believe it. Everyone was standing here, under the overhang of the porch, asking questions while someone had stolen her child. "Aren't you going to look for my son? We have to start now! We have to find him! We . . . we can't stand here and discuss this. Whoever took him is getting away. Don't you see? Whoever killed Tanya—" Her voice cracked. "Whoever did that, who shot her, they . . . they took B.J. They took my baby!" Her voice rose steadily, and she was gasping, hyperventilating, barely noticing that a police cruiser had arrived and cops in uniform were setting up tape and barricades around the scene. More sirens. More cop cars. An ambulance, siren shrieking, screeched into the lot.

O'Riley nodded, eyes concerned behind his glasses. "That's what we're trying to do, Mrs. Holt. But we need some information. If you'll just be patient—"

"Be patient? Are you crazy? We don't have time for patience. Who knows where he is, what's happening to him!" She fought back tears, fought too against the urge to fall completely apart. Frantic, she looked from the cop to her husband. "Jack, tell them!"

"Minutes may count," Jack said grimly.

"We're aware, sir. As soon as we secure this scene, we'll start going door to door. Believe me, Mr. and Mrs. Holt, we want to find your child."

The crime-scene investigators trooped in, carrying kits into Tanya's apartment, the place she'd called home. Cissy's heart went out to the girl. But why had Tanya taken Beej away from the house? Why had she kidnapped her baby? More investigators arrived, more officers swarming the scene of the crime, uniformed men keeping the growing crowd of the curious at bay. Cissy felt the seconds of her life ticking away. To her horror, a news van arrived, parking at an odd angle on the street. To the media, this was news. This. Her worst nightmare. "Please," she whispered.

"Detective Paterno is on his way," Perez said.

O'Riley said, "Now, Ms. Glenn. Did you hear a gun-shot?"

"I heard something. A loud pop. I was sleeping. I work graveyard. Thought it was a car backfiring or something on TV. I didn't realize . . ." Her gaze slid into the open apartment door, where Tanya lay on the green carpet. ". . . I didn't know."

"You didn't see a baby?"

The woman swung her head side to side.

While O'Riley walked into the apartment again, Perez asked, "Did you notice anything or anyone else? A person? A car?"

"Nothing."

Cissy felt Jack's arm around her.

"Which vehicle belongs to the victim?"

"That one. The Subaru." Jack pointed to the car parked in its spot.

"Yes, that's it . . . but . . ." Cissy stared at the car. "Tanya always has B.J.'s car seat in the back. I've never seen the car without it. And I didn't see it in the apartment."

"It was in her car when she picked up B.J. this after-noon," Jack confirmed.

"You think the killer bothered with a car seat?" O'Riley questioned.

"Someone did. Someone who took my baby," she said.

He looked skeptical. It sounded insane. A person killing Tanya, then bothering with the car seat to kid-nap B.J.

Cissy thought she was going to die. She was shaking, trembling, tears running down her face. Where was he? Precious, precious baby? *Dear God, please, keep him safe!*

"We're gonna need a picture of your son."

"I've got one," Jack said, slipping his wallet out of his

back pocket. A smiling picture of B.J., taken at Christmas, filled the plastic compartment. He pulled it out and handed it to O'Riley.

Cissy's heart shredded all over again.

Who would do this to her child? And why, oh God, why?

Her knees buckled, and Jack caught her, held her tight, helping her stand upright. In a far, frightened corner of her mind, she wondered if she would ever see her son again. Fear crippled her. She was paralyzed with despair.

A killer had her son.

"Son of a bitch," Paterno said, snapping his cell phone shut and grabbing his shoulder holster off the back of his chair. "Son of a goddamned, friggin' bitch." He snagged his jacket from a hook and stormed to Quinn's desk.

"What are you swearing about?" she asked as she pulled her jacket off the back of her chair. "The Cahill case?"

"The nanny was killed, and the kid is missing."

"What kid?"

"Cissy's Holt's son." He was striding out of the squad room, heading for the street, Quinn on his heels.

"Wait a minute! What happened?"

"I don't know the whole story yet. O'Riley just called. He and Perez had the Holt duty, and somehow the nanny and kid slipped away. Man, I didn't see this coming," he said, kicking himself as he pushed open the door to what was left of the day. Sunlight was fading fast, dusk chasing through the city, clouds on the horizon.

"I'll drive," Quinn said, and he didn't argue. Her car was more agile in cutting through rush-hour traffic. She slammed the police light on the top of the car, then slid behind the wheel. He climbed into the passenger seat of the Jetta and had barely buckled his seat belt when she gunned the car out of the lot and onto the street. "We're heading south," he said. "It went down at the nanny's, Tanya Watson's, apartment, on the other side of the airport. Let's see, I wrote down the address." He looked at the piece of paper he'd torn from the tablet on his desk and told it to her. "Around Burlingame."

"Got it," she said. "I used to live down there."

"When?"

She slid him a glance. "In another lifetime. Don't ask."

He didn't. As private a person as she was, it wouldn't do any good anyway. And he wasn't really concerned about her personal history, at least not now. Reaching into his pocket, he found a piece of gum and offered it to Quinn. She shook her head and rocketed around a gas tanker as she hit 101. Unwrapping the gum, he tried to focus as the cars flew by in a blur. Why kill the nanny? That didn't fit into his theory about Marla Friggin' Cahill.

"Did you get through to any of the employees or volunteers who worked at Cahill House when Marla Amhurst had her baby?"

"I've talked to five or six people who won't say a word against anyone at Cahill House. They're hiding behind sealed records and patients' rights, but I still have those three names to work with, if they're still alive. One nurse moved out of the area, lives in Boise, I think. Another aide is in Oakland, and the third, a secretary, I'm still tracking down." She saw her exit and took a quick turn off the highway. "You know, just because Marla had another child, doesn't mean squat."

"Could be nothing. But it's a loose end that bothers me."

Quinn turned a corner around a gas station. "Only a few more blocks," she said. "So why would anyone kill the nanny? Does that make sense?"

Paterno frowned. "Maybe she was a means to an end."

"The end being the baby?"

"That little kid is Marla Cahill's grandson." Paterno didn't like the turn of his thoughts as a motorcycle blew past them, loud pipes roaring.

"Shit. You think the boy was the target." She shook her head, and the nostrils of her straight nose flared. "Then why not kill him too?"

"Don't know."

"I hope to God we don't find his body in a trash can somewhere."

"You and me both," Paterno agreed as she rounded a final corner and he saw the flashing lights of two patrol cars and an ambulance. A crowd had gathered, and one news van sat on the horizon. He caught a glimpse of Jack and Cissy Holt standing together on the front porch, each looking desperate.

"Crime unit's behind us," Quinn said.

"I'm gonna look around, then get the Holts out of here. Take their statements if Perez and O'Riley haven't. They don't need to hang out here."

"I'll stick around. Talk to Jefferson."

She parked the Jetta near the entrance to the lot of the apartment complex as Paterno unfolded himself from the seat. Before he'd even stepped on the curb, Cissy Holt was running toward him, across the parking lot. Tears streaked her cheeks, determination set her chin, and in an instant Paterno saw glimpses of her mother on her face. "Thank God you're here," she said before she reached him. "We can't just stand around here. We have to start looking for B.J.! He's missing! You know that, right? She took him!"

"She?"

"My mother."

"You think Marla's behind this too?"

"I don't know," she admitted. "But it's what you think, isn't it? So, if you're right, then she killed Tanya, and she has my baby, so let's move, Detective. Let's find that murdering psycho! We can't let her hurt B.J. We can't!"

The glare of headlights was blinding. The kid was crying in the backseat. He was probably wet or needed to eat or something. "You're going to be fine," Elyse said, squinting against the drizzle and fighting the pain ricocheting through her head. At least the damn down-pour had let up.

She had to be careful. The police would be every-where, and there were security cameras in places she'd never think of—on streets, in parking lots, in stores. She'd been prepared, of course. She had a stash of dis-posable diapers, baby food, a car seat, bottles and for-mula, even clothes that she'd bought over the past week. But she hadn't prepared herself for his crying.

God, would he never stop?

"Just a little farther," she said as she reached into her purse and pulled out a bottle of ibuprofen. The child-proof top gave her fits as she tried to drive and open it, but finally she managed to get the damned thing off and tossed several pills into her mouth. She swallowed them dry, then, on inspiration, pulled into a fast-food drive-through and quickly donned her dark glasses. The blond wig was already in place when she ordered some fries for the baby and a large diet soda for herself. Once they were through the series of windows, after she'd paid and collected the bag and cup, she twisted in the seat and handed the small container of fries to the boy, who quit crying long enough to be intrigued. He grabbed the bag, and though she knew that he'd spill more than half of the damned things, maybe it would keep him occupied for a while.

She jabbed her straw into the drink, then took a long swallow and felt better. Nosing into traffic, she headed still farther south, toward San Mateo. She'd take that bridge, hoping that if anyone had seen the car, they would remember it traveling in the opposite direction from her destination. She checked her mirror often as the night encroached but saw no one following her. It was a worry. She'd heard the newscasts, seen the picture of her car and herself in her Marla getup that had been taken by the damned medical school parking-lot cameras. She kicked herself for getting a ticket there; it had drawn the police closer. If she hadn't switched plates a few times, she would have been caught. As it was, she should probably get a new vehicle as well. But she wouldn't need one much longer.

She checked the rearview again, and the kid, finally, had calmed down enough to munch his fries, his eyes curiously studying the back of her head. Kidnapping Cissy's kid hadn't been part of the original plan, of course, but Elyse had seen a growing opportunity and taken it. Let Cissy twist in the wind a little, let her agonize over the whereabouts and safety of her darling boy.

Stealing the baby had been a bold act, but Elyse was happy with her decision. It complicated things, but the satisfaction of knowing that Cissy was worried sick, was sleepless and guilt-riddled, was worth it.

She drove through the middle of San Mateo and found the ramp for the bridge. She kept checking her mirrors, but it still appeared that no one was following her. All the commuters drove as if they were robots, some on cell phones, most listening to their favorite radio station, all anxious to get home.

She could have been invisible for all the notice they gave her.

Elyse was in no hurry. She drove carefully, turning north at the east end of the bridge.

She'd put another five miles behind her, heading toward Oakland, when she heard the first shriek of a siren.

Her heart jolted.

No! She couldn't have been found out.

She looked in her rearview mirror. Lights flashed as a police car roared up the freeway. Cars behind her were pulling over to the side of the road, and she prayed one of them had been speeding and was the cop's target. She thought of her switched license plates. Had they found out? She had a gun. In her purse. She could use it if she had to.

He was bearing down on her, his siren screaming, blue and white lights flashing wildly. She had no choice but to ease to the side of the road like everyone around her and pray that he would pass. Every nerve tight, she slowed into the far right lane.

The cop followed.

Oh shit!

What could she do? Blow him away? Risk someone seeing her kill a policeman? Every damned motorist had a cell phone with a camera. She slowed even further, onto the shoulder.

The cop blew past her, his siren deafening.

Elyse nearly fainted.

Her tense muscles relaxed.

"Loud!" the baby said, unconcerned.

"Oh yeah." Elyse took a few deep breaths and then slowly accelerated, easing into traffic, her heart still madly pumping, her headache sweeping back with gale force.

She kept the needle of her speedometer right under

the speed limit. Shaking inside, she was more than careful as she wound her way northward and finally reached
the alley behind the bungalow where Marla was hiding.

This ought to be good, she thought, hauling the baby
and a blanket out of the car.

"Down!" he said as she started carrying him to the
back door. "I get down."

"Not yet."

"Down."

"In a second." Elyse hauled him up the back porch,
and as she fumbled in her purse for her keys, she heard
a hiss. That damned cat again.

"Kitty!" Now the boy was a whirling dervish. Eyes on
the cat as it hissed again and slunk into the shadows, he
wrestled with Elyse to be free. "Kitty!"

"Yeah, that's what it is," she said as she found her key
and jammed it into the lock. "A cat."

"Want kitty."

"No, you don't. That's one nasty thing," Elyse said,
then realized she was making too much noise. That nosy
neighbor across the street was peering through her blinds
again, not that she could see anything. Nonetheless,
Elyse had to be careful.

She slipped inside the house, and the baby said, "Eew.
Stinks!"

"That it does," she agreed, reminding herself to get
more air-fresheners. If Marla would ever get off her
bony ass and clean the place, it would help, but it was
never going to happen. Well, she was in for a surprise
tonight. "Shh," Elyse said and fought the blasted headache
as she descended the stairs into the old, musty basement.

God, how could Marla stand it down here?

Her footsteps seemed to ring on the floorboards as
she passed the rusting washer and eased to the bookcase where she unlatched the hidden lock. With her
free hand, she pulled the door open.

God, the smell was worse in here.

The kid started whimpering.

"You're fine," she said tautly.

The door swung open, and Marla was inside, sitting in front of the television as always, her eyes glued to the news.

"Do you see that?" she said without looking up. "What kind of moron are you? Your picture's all over the place! They caught you on camera, there at the medical center. Jesus Christ, Elyse, how do you think we're ever going to escape?"

"Don't worry, I've got it handled."

"The village idiot would do a better job!"

Ungrateful bitch.

"Don't worry about that now," Elyse said. "Turn around, Marla. I think it's time you met your grandson."

Chapter 19

Marla gazed at her grandson as if he were from a different planet. "What have you done?"

"I brought him to see his grandmother. Go on," she urged, pressing a hand to B.J.'s back, but the boy was as reluctant to meet Marla as she apparently was to see him. "She's been dying to meet you."

"Mommy," he whimpered. "Mommm . . . meeee . . ."

"This is your Nana Marla," Elyse told him. This reunion was not going like she'd hoped.

"Why did you bring him here? Do you want us to get caught?" Marla was beside herself.

Elyse decided not to fill her in on the altered plans just yet. Kidnapping B.J. hadn't been part of their original scheme, but sometimes, when opportunity knocks, you've just got to go with it. Couldn't Marla see that?

"You've got to take him away. He can't be here."

"He doesn't know where we are. He's too little."

"Somebody will see him. Oh God, look! He's going to cry!"

B.J.'s face had crumpled and was turning red. Marla

was right. The kid looked ready to wail for all he was worth.

"We'll see your mommy soon," Elyse said hurriedly. "Don't worry."

For an answer, he threw back his head and howled. The noise was loud enough to wake the dead. Marla looked ready to throttle the kid, so Elyse dragged him upstairs. What the hell was she supposed to do now? The little house scarcely had any furnishings apart from what Elyse had found for Marla's secret room.

There was a beat-up chair in one of the two bedrooms, and Elyse carried the screaming child down the hallway, trying to shush him without scaring him. God, he could make noise! Were all children so *loud*?

"Shh . . . shh . . . ," she said, holding him awkwardly on her lap. What the hell was she going to do?

"Dad-*dee*," he cried. "Dad-*dee*."

"Make up your mind, kid. Mommy or Daddy."

She could hear Marla hammering with something downstairs. Now what? Muttering furiously, Elyse hauled the kid back down the stairs while he wailed "No-o-o-o!" and tried to grab onto the handrail. Her head felt like it was going to split in two.

"What are you doing?" Elyse demanded of Marla. "I could hear you! Someone else might hear that pounding too!"

There was a piece of pipe on the floor beside her. "I wasn't through," Marla said, glaring at her. "We've got to leave. I've got to leave."

"Not yet!"

"Look . . ." Her gaze centered on the television, where the news was just breaking on the murder of a young woman near Burlingame. Tanya.

Elyse stared in a kind of horrified fascination as Marla said, "You did that. You killed her."

"It's all part of the plan," Elyse said through her teeth. Why did Marla question her? When she *knew* what had to be done!

"Did they see you? Get your picture? Like when you killed Rory?"

"No."

"That picture of you in the newspaper? That artist's composite? They're saying it's *me*. They're blaming this on me."

"Well, of course they are." Elyse was fast losing patience, and the kid's continued crying was enough to split her head right open. It was all she could do not to shake him.

"You want *me* to take the fall for this," Marla said on a note of discovery. "*You* want to get away scot-free."

"That's not true. This is a partnership. Didn't I help you escape?"

"You never intended to share. That's why you've kept me down here. You want it all for yourself."

"I haven't kept you down here. You refuse to go upstairs! For God's sake, Marla, get a grip!"

But Marla was right. Elyse did plan to double-cross her. Did want the police to blame all the murders on her. Why not? It was Marla's relationship with her relatives that created the motive. Nobody knew Elyse was involved. They thought Mary Smith was Marla.

Elyse couldn't take it anymore, so when Marla ordered her to get the kid to stop crying, she hustled him upstairs again.

"Go home!" he sobbed. "Me go home!"

"We're going to my place."

"No-o-o!"

"Shhhh!"

It was dark now. The ground was wet, but the rain had ceased for the moment as Elyse hauled a whimpering B.J. back to her car. She strapped him into the damn car seat. Couldn't risk getting pulled over for not having him properly buckled in. Jesus, the rules they had these days.

Why did anyone ever have a child?

Across the way she saw someone peeking through the blinds of the old biddy's house, the lady with the cat. The bitch was watching her! Infuriated, Elyse jumped behind the wheel.

"Shut up," she warned B.J., who gazed at her with big eyes.

"Bad word," he said.

Yeah, well, he was just lucky she hadn't said the phrase that leapt to her tongue.

Damn! She could see the old bitch now as she'd pulled the blinds up and was watching Elyse like a hawk, her pointy face aimed in Elyse's direction.

Had she seen the kid?

Carefully, Elyse backed out of her driveway, resisting the urge to flip the old crone the bird. She had things to do. Family business to take care of.

And nobody was going to get in her way.

Cissy watched dully from the apartment parking lot as CSI techs did their work and the detectives canvassed the area, searching for witnesses, information. Jack was with her, his arms pulling her close. She squeezed her eyes shut and tried to block out her fear.

Everyone kept urging her to go home, get some food, get some sleep, take care of herself, but Cissy couldn't leave. Jack was one of the few people who understood. He stayed by her side as the afternoon wore into evening and evening into night.

It was only when a weary Detective Paterno made the effort to bring them up to date that both Cissy and Jack knew there was nothing left for them here.

"We've canvassed the area," Paterno told them. "Checked with the neighbors. People around the area."

"Did they see B.J.?" Cissy asked urgently.

"Several of them remember seeing a woman carrying a boy about B.J.'s age from her car. The description fits Miss Watson and your son."

"And?" Cissy gazed at him.

"She carried him into her apartment."

"Did they see anything else?" Jack asked.

"Not really. One of them reported seeing a silver car, but she wasn't specific about the make and model."

"A silver car," Jack repeated. "Like the one used by Mary Smith."

Paterno nodded. "A lot of silver cars out there," he reminded.

"The neighbor, Corinne Glenn, heard a 'pop.' Maybe the gunshot," Jack said. "Anybody else?"

Paterno shook his head. "We're still checking with people. But the crime scene's off-limits. There's no reason for you to stay."

"Where would she take him?" Cissy asked. "Oh God . . . She can't hurt him."

Jack said, "We don't know it was Marla. Maybe Tanya was into something we don't know about."

"We're checking into her history. How did you come to hire her?"

"Jack's father, Jonathan Holt, recommended her." Cissy's tone was sharp.

"Do you know how he knew her?" Paterno asked.

Jack's face was a mask. "I believe he learned of her through a woman he was dating. He meets a lot of people that way."

"I'll talk to him," Paterno promised.

The area had all but cleared out by the time the streetlights fully came on. The rain was a sputtering mist, as if being turned on and off by a spigot.

Cissy felt like her body wasn't her own. She wanted to pinch herself, make herself wake up from this nightmare. Reluctantly, she allowed Jack to take her home. Both of them looked through the pantry and refrigerator, but neither had an appetite.

"We have to eat something," Jack said, and he split a sandwich with her that he made from the leftover tuna salad used for B.J.'s lunch. Cissy took two bites and couldn't go on. She laid her head on the table and sobbed.

Jack wanted to die. If he hadn't trusted Tanya with B.J. she might still be alive and his son would be with them right now. Safe and sound. Cissy had given up blaming him, but he sure as hell was still blaming himself.

"Come on," he said, pulling her to him and guiding her upstairs. "We'll go to bed. Maybe by morning, Paterno will have found him."

"You think so?"

"We'll know more," he evaded.

"Jack, if anything's happened to B.J. . . . ."

"Shhh."

"I just can't bear it!"

"I know." He squeezed her hand, kissed the top of her head, prayed that his son was all right.

And inside, a deep, boiling rage took root. Whoever had taken his son would pay a price. Jack would make sure of it.

Paterno drove to the station before dawn broke. He hadn't slept. He'd tried to, but he'd watched the clock, his thoughts traveling various routes, all of them leading to Marla and her accomplice.

He'd left a message for Quinn. She was in charge of getting the background information on Tanya Watson.

Meanwhile Paterno was chafing for the hours to pass. He wanted the ME to get the bullet from Tanya's skull and give it to ballistics. And he wanted ballistics to compare it to the bullet that ended Cherise Favier's life.

He'd bet dollars to doughnuts they came from the same gun.

Now, he rubbed his face as he got himself a tall cup of black coffee, the terrible sludge offered at the station, the perfect stuff to keep him awake.

He would check with the feds later. It was really their case now, but Paterno wasn't about to back off one bit.

He sighed. He hadn't told Jack and Cissy Holt that he was worried for their son's life. He hadn't wanted to scare them. But Marla Amhurst Cahill had never shown the smallest bit of humanity, and if she'd taken the boy—or had hired someone to take him—it wasn't out of love and/or a crazy, obsessive need. Nope. The boy's abduction would be for other reasons. Monetary, most likely. Something to feed Marla's need for freedom and greed.

And he would be expendable.

Paterno popped a few antacids. Coffee and bicarbonates. Breakfast didn't get any better than this.

He wondered about Tanya. Why had she taken the kid? Was it simply that she went back to her apartment for some reason, and B.J. was with her? Or was she somehow involved in Marla's plot to systematically kill the members of her family? If that's what Marla was doing.

And if so, why hadn't she killed the boy and left his body with Tanya's? Maybe Tanya had her own agenda, something unrelated to Marla herself. Maybe she had wanted something from the Cahills and ended up working at cross-purposes to Marla. Maybe that put her in Marla's sights, and *blam!* She was permanently removed.

But why was Marla so careless? What was going on

with her? The crime-scene investigators—under Tallulah Jefferson's command—had scoured Tanya's apartment. They'd found hairs and bits of fingernails—clipped pieces—that didn't seem to match the victim's. So whose were they? Someone Tanya knew? DNA tests would take weeks to get results, sometimes longer, and Paterno knew he didn't have that much time.

He needed answers now. He needed to find Marla Cahill. Before she killed anyone else.

Before she killed her own grandson.

Cissy stood at the kitchen window. She'd watched the sun rise and glisten through the raindrops. She'd heard birds twittering and the groan and hum of their new furnace kicking into gear. She'd smelled the coffee Jack was brewing and felt the warm mug he pressed in her hand.

"Ciss?"

"What's he doing right now? He should be asleep in his bed. We should be waiting for him to wake up. What do you think he's doing?"

"Don't torture yourself."

"How can you stand there and not care!" she burst out.

Jack swallowed. "I care."

Cissy sank into one of the kitchen chairs. "I can't do anything. I can't think. I just want to go to sleep till they find him, safe and sound, but I can't sleep!"

"Paterno will call us as soon as he knows something. Or, the FBI."

"What if we never find him? What if we never know?"

"Don't think like that," Jack said sternly.

In truth, Jack was beside himself. His fury and fear were bone deep. If it turned out Marla was behind this, he planned to strangle her conniving neck himself!

The minutes crept by. He made toast for himself and Cissy. He practically had to browbeat her to get her to eat anything. In truth, he could scarcely choke down food himself, but he was determined to keep up his strength. There was a showdown ahead, and he planned to be ready for it.

It was barely nine when the feds arrived. They began to systematically set up for the expected kidnapping ransom call. Cissy and Jack hung back, watching and staying out of the way. Hearing another car screech to a halt in front of their house, Cissy rushed forward.

"Beej?" she whispered.

"Wait . . . ," Jack said, trying to stop her as she flew outside.

To Cissy's shattering disappointment, she saw Jack's father, Jonathan, and his brother, J.J., climb from Jonathan's car and hurry their way through the rain. Cissy sagged against Jack, who held her tightly as they came inside.

"Is he back?" Jonathan asked, white faced. "Have they found him?" Jack had called his father the night before to tell him about Tanya's murder and B.J.'s abduction.

Jack shook his head, and J.J., normally remote and completely self-involved, stared through wide, stretched eyes, as if looking at a harrowing vista only he could see. They both gave the feds a wide berth.

"Where's Jannelle?" Jack asked.

"I don't know, son. I just called J.J. and came over. God Almighty." He ran a shaking hand through his hair. "Have you had a ransom call yet?"

"No," Cissy repeated faintly.

"Why else would someone take him?" Jonathan said, as if he were puzzling it out himself. "Has to be ransom."

They all moved to the kitchen, and Jonathan sat

heavily onto the chair Cissy had just vacated. J.J. stood by the back door, gazing outside. Jack spooned more coffee grounds into the filter and watched the pot fill.

"You have to pay the ransom," J.J. said in a low voice. "Keep the police and FBI out of it. That never works."

"I think it's too late for that," Jack said.

"The kidnapper killed Tanya," J.J. reminded. "He'll kill again."

Tears of fear filled Cissy's eyes.

"Murdering bitch," Jonathan said angrily.

"We don't know it's Marla," J.J. said.

"We don't know anything," Jack reminded. "Let's not speculate. Let the feds take care of it."

"I'm surprised at you, Jack," Jonathan said. "You can't trust the police with your son's life!"

"What do you propose I do about them?" Jack responded repressively, gesturing toward the federal agents. His fists clenched. He didn't want this argument. He sure didn't want it in front of Cissy.

"Get rid of them!" Jonathan gazed at him as if he'd never seen him before.

At that precise moment, one of the agents separated from his partners and looked into the kitchen. "We're almost done here, Mr. Holt. Can I have a minute with you?"

Jack talked to the man, and Cissy waited in the kitchen with Jonathan and J.J. She appreciated their desire to help, but she would rather just be alone with Jack.

The agent explained the procedure if and when the kidnapper called. Jack nodded, listening but barely hearing. This was B.J.'s life they were discussing. Anything could go wrong. He wanted to kill whoever had stolen his son. He wasn't sure he wouldn't, given the chance. But there were rules of engagement. And he damn well wasn't going to break them. Not yet. Not while the risk was too great. Once B.J. was home. Once he was safe. Then the rules changed.

Returning to the kitchen, Jack said, "For now, we wait."

"For the ransom call." Cissy shivered.

Jack nodded, adding grimly, "And for our kidnapper to make a move, or a mistake, or something."

The downtown office of Treasure Homes Realty was a narrow building hosting a luxurious windowfront reception area with a lovely, wraparound rosewood desk. But that facade was for the client who needed convincing and dazzling. The real work took place behind a solid-core door that led to rabbit-warren work spaces, of which Sybil Tomini's was one of the largest. She, like the other agents, was part owner in the company, which didn't amount to diddly-squat when things downturned like they had just recently. Although the downturn hadn't affected everyone. Nuh-uh. Those sharks at Luxury Unlimited were selling multi-million-dollar palaces like they were tract homes.

Sybil looked at her desk and sighed. It was covered with stacks of papers: loan docs, inspection reports, earnest money agreements. She felt like sweeping it all into the trash. It was amazing how many deals fell through when the interest rate went up a half percent. There had to be an easier way to make a living.

And the rental real-estate business was no picnic, either. She was trying to ease out of that business entirely. There just wasn't enough money for all the problems rental units created. Whenever someone called in wanting Treasure Homes' rental department to lease their home, she did her damnedest to convince them to sell.

Her phone buzzed. Sybil waited for the receptionist to announce what she wanted, but no such luck.

"I'm here," Sybil reminded frostily. What was with these receptionists? This girl's IQ had to be in negative numbers. She always buzzed and then couldn't seem to verbalize what she wanted.

"Sybil?"

Oh for God's sake. "Yes?"

"There's someone here to see you. A Mrs. Owens?"

Sybil had to fight back a short bark of annoyance. She practically tugged her blunt-cut, straight black hair out of her head.

Mrs. Owens was a perfect example of why the rental market was such a losing racket. The woman was the nosiest old bag you would ever hope to meet. She lived across the street from one of Treasure Homes' rental tenants and complained and complained about them. Worse, she'd somehow gotten Sybil's name as the person to call.

"I'll be right there," Sybil said, at the same moment the receptionist said, "I'll send her back."

No! Sybil did *not* want that big mouth tottering into her work space.

She glanced down at her papers, made a sound of annoyance, then headed for the door just as Carrie, the stupidest receptionist on the planet, threw it open, nearly knocking Sybil in the teeth.

"Come on in, Mrs. Owens," she invited in a sweety-sweety voice she reserved for the infirm or mentally disabled.

Sybil made a mental note to fire Carrie's sorry ass immediately following Mrs. Owens's visit.

"Hello, there," Sybil said to the eighty-something woman. "Come right in." She gave Carrie the evil eye, and the girl just gazed at her blankly before heading back to her desk.

Sybil closed the door behind them and wondered if

she would make it through another day without a cigarette. She'd quit a month earlier. Thirty-one damn days.

With an effort, she dragged her mind back to the
problem at hand and, smoothing the skirt of her cream
designer suit, pasted on a friendly smile. Mrs. Owens
couldn't be more than five feet tall, probably weighed
less than a hundred pounds, but it was clear she was a
force to be reckoned with as she tapped her cane along
the carpet and worked her way toward Sybil's work
space.

"I'm glad to finally meet-choo," she stated primly.

Was there a note of censure in her voice? Sybil inwardly sighed. They'd spoken on the phone two, maybe
three times, but this was the first time the woman had
actually made her way to the office.

"You can use my chair," Sybil told her, as it was the
only one around. She rarely invited clients to her desk,
preferring to meet with them at a restaurant or at the
hotel lobby down the street with its niches and alcoves
and historical feel. Clients liked the smell of money,
and so did Sybil.

"I'll stand, if you don't mind. Don't really trust chairs
with wheels."

Suit yourself, you old harpy.

"How can I help you, Mrs. Owens?" Sybil asked po-
litely.

"It's Tilda. My friends call me Tildy. And you know
how you can help me. I've told you enough times."

All Sybil had heard was a long and loud rant about
Tildy's neighbor, the one who rented the little Berkeley
house through Sybil's company. For the measly com-
mission Sybil had scored from the deal, it was a total dis-
aster. Tildy was making her life a living hell.

"I told you she looked familiar, coming and going
like all get out." Tildy sniffed. "It's that woman. The one
on the news."

"Which one?"

"The one that escaped from prison, y'know? Marla whatever her name is. I saw her going in and out of the house you rent, I did!" She tapped her cane hard on the floor, pushing its tip into the carpet with disdain. "And she nearly killed my cat! Poor old Mr. Timms! That woman doesn't look where she's going!"

Sybil drifted, wondering if the Lundeens were really going to be able to find new financing. That house they wanted was close to a million, and the down payment was going to kill them if their current lender backed out, which it looked like they were. Shit. What did she have to do to make a sale go through?

"You're not listening!"

"I heard every word. Is your cat okay?"

"Traumatized, that's what he is."

"I'm not sure what you want me to do."

"Call it in! Tell the police we got 'er!"

"Mrs. Owens—"

"Tildy."

"Yes, Tildy . . . The woman who rented the house across the street is named Elyse . . . Hammonds, no, Elyse Hammersly. I checked her out. I've met her, and she is not Marla Cahill. She lived in Oregon, a suburb of Portland."

"Huh. Well, she comes and goes at all hours of the day and night . . . sometimes doesn't show up for days. And last night she was hauling somethin'. Looked like a kid to me, all bundled up in a big coat. The woman's a menace. Nearly killed Mr. Timms."

"Was the cat on Ms. Hammersly's property?"

"He wanders." The old woman shrugged her shoulders.

"But he's not dead?" Sybil tried to be patient. She straightened the papers on her desk.

Tildy nodded emphatically, her permed hair scarcely

moving, her chin stubborn. "Not yet! I'm telling you, that woman is a maniac!"

"She works odd hours, I think, but I'll talk to her about the cat. In the meantime, it might be a good idea to keep Mr. Tom in the house."

"It's Mr. Timms." Tildy squinted behind glasses that enlarged her eyes. "You just try to keep a cat in the house, miss. He's been able to go outside since he was a kitten, and he's not gonna stop now."

"Sounds like the street's dangerous."

"Only since you rented to that maniac! She's the reason Mr. Timms is short a few lives."

"I'll talk to Elyse," Sybil heard herself promising.

"Good. Do that! Somethin's not right over there."

Sybil thought she could use a cigarette . . . maybe a couple. Tildy was a nuisance, and probably unbalanced to boot. Sybil's aunt had started showing signs of dementia when she hit her eighties. It was bound to happen. "Do you watch the house all the time?" Sybil asked curiously.

"I keep up with the comings and goings in the neighborhood." Tildy nodded.

"I'm sure everything's all right."

"If it was all right, I wouldn't have gone to all the trouble to come down here."

"I appreciate your telling me."

"You're just fobbing me off, aren't you?" the old lady accused.

"No, of course not."

"Well, what're you gonna do? Anything? Maybe I *should* call the police."

"No, no, no. I'll go over there and check with Elyse myself."

"I'll be watchin' for ya."

I'll bet you will, Sybil thought. "I'll be by this afternoon. I've got a couple meetings, and then I'll swing over your way."

Sybil held the door while Tildy stubbed her way back out. She passed through reception and glanced back, seeming aware that Sybil might be humoring her. But Sybil knew she would never hear the end of this until she took care of things, and she was never going to get rid of Mrs. Owens unless she showed her she was acting on her information.

Like she had time to run out to Berkeley. Oh, sure.

"I'll be lookin'," she said again, then toddled through the door.

"What a sweetheart," Carrie said, meaning it.

"You're fired," Sybil responded, reaching inside her purse for her spare, unopened pack of cigarettes, fingering it like a good-luck talisman.

"What have you got?" Paterno asked as Janet Quinn ducked her head into his office.

"Not much. Tanya Watson worked mostly as a babysitter or nanny. She was taking care of a couple of kids who belonged to a woman named Geena Barrymore, a single mother who dated Jonathan Holt for a time."

"Nothing between Holt and Tanya?"

"Doesn't appear to be. Geena's moved on to a new guy too. Quite a while ago."

"You think there's any connection between any of 'em and Holt's grandson?"

She lifted her palms.

Paterno sighed. "I called Jonathan Holt this morning. He's with his other son, J.J., at Jack and Cissy's. The feds were there, setting up. Holt didn't have much to say about Tanya other than he barely knew her."

"What do you think?" Quinn asked.

"He sounded pretty shaken up about both Tanya's death and his grandson's kidnapping." Paterno inhaled and exhaled slowly. "I'm worried about what's going on in Marla's mind. I want to know what she wants."

"Maybe she'll keep the little boy safe," Quinn said.

Paterno didn't answer.

Because he didn't like the response he would make.

It was after three by the time Sybil was on her way to the bungalow that was causing Tildy such a problem. Why, why couldn't neighbors just mind their own business?

Sybil smoothed her hair over one ear and grabbed her cell phone. She was going to have to get Bluetooth. Something. Driving was such a bitch as it was.

She dialed Maureen Lundeen. How was that for a name? Using her own version of the sweety-sweety voice, she enthusiastically left a message, hoping everything was perking along toward closing. If Maureen needed anything—anything at all—just pick up the phone. Sybil would be happy to help with the lenders, if she could. She was at her beck and call.

As soon as she hung up, Sybil made retching noises. Good God. Sometimes she looked at the faces on the real-estate page, agents who'd hit the million-dollar mark in sales a thousand times over. They all smiled like they couldn't stop. How did they get their names out there? Why did people choose them to be their agent?

"I wish Marla Cahill had rented it!" she declared. "Then I'd be on the news. Then I'd get some publicity!"

She pushed her toe to the accelerator, frustrated. By the time she was finally pulling onto the residential street that led to the rental, she was hot, tired, and thirsty. The green salad she'd slammed down at lunch had been wilted and swimming in acidic fat-free dressing. She'd eaten it anyway, though she'd really wanted a bacon cheeseburger. But God. Real-estate agents around here were like pencils with boobs. She had to watch every calorie, and she was relentless about it. One of these days she was going to get a break. And she was going to seize that opportunity for all it was worth.

She pulled into the drive of the house and climbed from the car, searching through her keys. If she'd forgotten to bring them and had to drive all the way back . . . but no, her fingers closed over the bungalow's key ring.

She glanced over her shoulder to Tildy's house. The place looked deserted. Sybil waved anyway, just in case, and was rewarded with a twitch of the blinds. Well, okay, Tildy was on patrol.

Sybil almost felt sorry for Elyse.

She knocked on the door and waited. Long minutes passed, and Sybil looked anxiously toward the sky. The clouds were gray, their bottoms darker, as if they were just holding in the rain, waiting to let loose with a maelstrom. Peachy.

She knocked again, but when no one answered, she slid her key in the lock and twisted open the door.

She was hit by the smell. Rotten. Putrid. Like a wet, unpleasant slap to the face.

"Oh . . . God . . ."

Almost afraid to tiptoe inside, Sybil held the front door open for some fresher air and scanned the rooms. Not a lot of furniture.

What? Did something *die* in here?

Maybe Mr. Timms hadn't been so lucky after all.

Sybil pulled the lapel of her suit jacket over her mouth and coughed a couple of times. "Ms. Hammersly?" she called. "Are you here? Elyse?"

Moving carefully down the hallway, Sybil felt a shiver chase down her spine. Elyse may have been coming and going for a while, but she clearly hadn't been here lately. Last night, Tildy had said, but the old bat had to be wrong. No one could stand the smell without finding the rotted little corpse and tossing it out.

She checked through the upstairs rooms but found nothing to account for the odor. Stopping at the top of the stairs that led to the basement, Sybil called again, "Ms. Hammersly? It's Sybil Tomini from Treasure Homes."

No answer.

"Screw this," she muttered, grabbing her cell phone again and calling Rich, one of Treasure Homes' other partners, a real prick but at least the man possessed a brain.

Creeping down the stairs, Sybil kept one hand firm on the rail, the other pressing her phone to her ear. The basement was unfinished space, she recalled, with a wall that divided off one section that could be made into a bedroom or workspace. There was a narrow doorway to access it.

As she reached the bottom step, the smell reached out to her, nauseating. Horrible.

Sybil coughed some more, just as Rich's supercilious voice invited her to leave a message. "Rich, it's Sybil. I'm at one of our rental properties. The Berkeley cottage, and it's . . . weird."

Beep. Rich's phone suddenly cut her off. Didn't even ask if she was satisfied with her message.

"*Damn* it."

She clicked the phone closed but kept it in her hand as she stepped forward and spied a narrow, nearly secret, doorway to the closed-off area. Holding her breath, Sybil squeezed into the room.

She looked ahead, and all the hair on her body stood on end. In the bluish light of a television, she saw the back of a woman's head. The woman was watching the news. She sat still as a statue.

"Elyse . . . ?"

She eased around to get a better look at her, her fingers fumbling for the light switch. She snapped on the fluorescents. Illumination flickered uncertainly.

Sybil's mouth opened in a silent scream.

The woman seated calmly in the chair had been sitting there for some time. She gazed at Sybil serenely out of blank eyeholes. Her face—all her skin—was being systematically eaten by insects and larvae. The dead body was putrefying, melting into the chair.

But it looked as if someone had recently given her a manicure.

Sybil backed away as if burned, her fingers scrabbling on the phone, searching for 9-1-1. Screaming like a banshee, she stumbled up the stairs, through the house, out the front door, and, in full view of Tilda Owens's house, threw up that damned salad all over her cream designer suit.

Bayside Hospital
San Francisco, CA
Room 316
Friday, February 13
NOW

I can't believe that no one has come in to check on me. I only wish I had one more chance to tell Jack that I love him. . . . But it's too late. . . . I know it now. The doctor says it's time to take me off life support, that it's best to let me die and harvest my organs.

Oh God, no!

No, no, no!!! I'm alive.

I strain with everything I'm worth. Panic spurts through me. Certainly it registers on those damned monitors, right? Can't they see my heart rate soaring into the stratosphere? Don't they know I'm responding?

For the love of God, check me! Shine that bloody light into my eyes and watch me flinch, my pupils react.

Give me time. I'm waking up. You're giving up too quickly.

I struggle to move, to show them I'm alive, but nothing happens.

Stop this madness. Think of me.

Through all my fear, I hear the doctor say resignedly, "It's time. I'll call the family. . . ."

Chapter 20

Paterno had seen a lot in all of his years on the force.

He'd witnessed man's inhumanity to man, seen the effects of abuse, addiction, and rage. He'd never been surprised by how sick people could be to each other, but this . . . what he was viewing now, was something he couldn't imagine.

He'd gotten the call from a Detective Lee in Berkeley, who had responded to a 9-1-1 emergency call from a frantic landlord who had found a dead body in the basement of one of her rental units. The uniformed cop who had responded had quickly called his homicide department, and the cop there, Detective Lee, had put two and two together and rung up Paterno. Paterno had driven over the bridge at lightning speed, his guts twisting, acid roiling, as he walked through the cordoned-off bungalow. Already the place was swarming with cops and crime-scene investigators, and around the perimeter were news vans and neighbors, people who had been passing by but were now standing outside the roped-off area, hoping to get a glimpse of what was happening.

"Detective Paterno?" a female voice called, and he looked over his shoulder to see Lani Saito, the attractive Asian reporter from KTAM with the glossy black hair who'd confronted him earlier. Her cameraman was with her, training the lens of his shoulder cam at Paterno. It wasn't quite dark yet, but they'd already set a big lamp near the van to illuminate the area. "Could I have a word with you? Is it true that Marla Cahill is in this house? Is she alive?"

Paterno glared at the woman. How could she get information as fast as he could? "I just got here."

"This one's out of your jurisdiction, and since you're working on murders in which Marla Cahill is a suspect, I'm guessing that's why you're here. Is Marla Cahill in the house?"

"I don't have anything to say right now, Ms. Saito, but I'm sure the Public Information Officer will make a statement later, once we know what's going on." He forced a grim smile and managed not to snap the woman's head off. Jesus, what did the press want from him? Turning his back on her and her cameraman, Paterno walked to the perimeter of the crime scene and flashed his badge at a uniformed cop. "Paterno, SFPD, Homicide. Detective Lee called me."

"She said you'd be here. She's inside. Probably in the basement. Just put these on." The uniformed cop handed him a pair of shoe covers.

Paterno slipped the disposable covers over his shoes, then walked up the front steps to the little house that resembled all the other houses on the street. The yard was shaggy with winter, the shrubs needing a trim, the curtains drawn.

Inside, the living room was virtually empty. A couple of folding chairs and a small table sat on a scratched hardwood floor. No other furniture. No beds in the two bedrooms, no towels hanging in the bathroom, the bathtub home to spiders, and the stench permeating through the place was overwhelming. The minute he'd crossed the threshold, he'd been assailed with the scents of solvent, pine and air-fresheners, but beneath it all, overpowering in its intensity, was the unmistakable smell of death.

Carefully he picked his way around the techs who were dusting for prints, scanning for blood, picking up trace evidence and examining every nook and cranny of the little post–World War II cottage. Through a kitchen with a cracked linoleum floor from the fifties, Paterno made his way downstairs to a musty, dank basement that reeked—the scent of rotting flesh nearly choked him. He pressed on.

Evidence of flooding was visible in the cracked cement walls, and he noticed the washer was rusted. Cell phones rang and radios crackled as he made his way to an open doorway, a shelf pushed aside to expose a small room from which the horrible smell was emanating. He locked his jaw so he wouldn't gag and stepped inside.

He nearly retched anyway.

Sitting in a chair in front of a television with the volume turned low was the decomposing corpse of a woman. Her eyes were missing, and there were gaping holes in her face, exposing blackened muscle and bone. "Jesus," he whispered, his stomach ready to toss everything inside. The ME was examining her, and a small, fortyish woman was waving the beam of her flashlight over the twin bed pushed into a corner. "I'm looking for Detective Lee."

"That's me." She offered her gloved hand. "Susannah Lee. I go by Suze."

"Anthony Paterno."

"I figured." Seemingly unfazed by the grisly sight or the horrible smell, Lee said, "We think this is Marla

Cahill, though it's hard to tell in her current condition. But race, height, size are consistent. This place was rented a few weeks before Marla escaped, right after the holidays. Look at it. Is it weird or what? The bed's been made and used, there's evidence of the body being in the sheets, body fluids, insect larvae and eggs, that sort of thing. So someone moved her. And someone did her hair, check it out." Lee shined her flashlight over the dead strands of the corpse's hair. Combed and styled. "Look at her fingers." She shined the light on the rotting fingers, and, sure enough, the nails were polished. "Toes too." She focused the beam on the toes peeking out of sandals. "Someone's been here. Recently. Look in the wastebasket. Food from a local burger shop. What's left of the burger hasn't been here as long as the dead body."

Paterno glanced around the room. There were pictures on the wall, photos of Marla Cahill as a girl, and a comb and brush next to a silver baby cup . . . the cup that Cissy reported missing from her house.

Detective Lee was right. The person rotting in front of some game show was Marla Cahill, and, from the looks of her, she'd been dead for quite a while, probably killed soon after her escape.

"Cause of death?"

"Beneath the perfectly coifed hair . . ." she said, then shone the light on the back of Marla's head to reveal a bullet hole. "Looks like she was executed."

"Here?"

"We don't know that yet. Still looking for blood splatter. Whoever killed her went to a great deal of trouble to make her comfortable. A bed with sheets and an expensive coverlet, homey pictures, a television? What kind of nut job are you tracking, Detective?"

"Good question." He glanced at Lee. "Who found the body?"

"Sybil Tomini. She's with Treasure Homes. Her firm rented the bungalow to a woman by the name of Elyse Hammersly."

"Marla didn't rent it?"

"Don't think so. Ms. Tomini's in my squad car. I thought you might want to ask her a few questions. I've taken her statement, so once you've talked to her, she's free to go. She's been making noise about that for nearly an hour. And there's one other thing: we found this." She held up a scrap of blue material.

"What is it?"

"Looks like part of a piece of clothing, possibly ripped off when someone passed by." She held the flashlight's beam on the plastic bag. "But the weave's loose, and the material's fuzzy. Maybe part of a blanket. A baby blanket?"

"Jesus," Paterno whispered. He thought of the Holts, dealing with the FBI, who had set up shop in their living room, worrying themselves sick about their kid.

"I'll have the lab analyze it, and then you might want to take it to the Holts. See if they recognize it."

His jaw tightened at the prospect. "No one found a baby here," he said, though he was certain he would have been informed immediately if B.J. Holt or his body had been located.

She shook her head. "No baby. No body. Even this"— Detective Lee held up the scrap of material—"might prove not to belong to the kid." She met Paterno's gaze, and they had an understanding. They both felt B.J. Holt had been here with his decomposing grandmother.

Lee glanced at an officer near the door. "Would you show Detective Paterno to my car and Ms. Tomini?"

The young uniform nodded. "You got it."

"I'll send you my report," Detective Lee said, turning back to the bed as Paterno and the Berkeley cop walked through this tomb of a basement to climb the rickety stairs once more.

Outside, night had fallen. Paterno breathed deep of the rain-washed air, but the rank stench of death lingered in his nostrils, and he knew it would take days, and more than a few hot, steamy showers, before the odor would leave. It clung. For days. What the hell was going on?

It looked as if Marla's accomplice had murdered her. A friend? Deadly enemy?

Or both?

Did the killing make any sense?

Why risk springing her from prison if the intent was to kill her? What had been the motive? Had Marla's death been an accident?

A fight?

Premeditated?

A bullet to the back of the head screamed intent to kill.

But there was more to it than murder. Why not dump the body in the woods outside the city or the bay or *anywhere* and get the hell away? Why go to all the trouble of renting a house, hiding the corpse, and, for God's sake, dressing it and combing its damned hair? And what about bringing a baby here?

What kind of sicko would do that?

And why?

Sickos don't need reasons.

Marla had been dead for weeks from the looks of her. Why expose a child to the horror of a decaying body? The kid's own grandmother, for God's sake.

Maybe that's the point. Get the baby. But then why kill Eugenia, Rory, and Cherise? Why not Cissy?

Who *was* this person?

He shoved his hair from his eyes and noticed an old woman standing in the window of the house across the street. She was staring at the place while holding a big cat with a long tail.

Scratching his jaw, Paterno followed the cop across a patch of lawn and thought about the murder weapon. A gun. He figured the slug retrieved from Marla's rotting body would match the bullets found in Cherise Favier and Tanya Watson, all victims of the same demented killer. All from a .38, but not matching any other bullets found in any other crimes in the Bay Area.

Until now.

Paterno had little doubt what ballistics would turn up.

"This is Detective Lee's vehicle," the policeman said, but there was no one inside. Instead, a woman with blunt-cut, sleek dark hair, her cream suit stained orange and smelling like vomit, leaned against the hood, sucking vigorously on a cigarette as if the nicotine could obliterate the nightmare she'd so recently witnessed. The officer introduced them. "Ms. Tomini, this is Detective Paterno."

"About time!" Sybil took a long drag. "Did you see that . . . that thing inside the house?" Smoke streamed from her nostrils. "Awful . . . just awful. Can I go now?"

"In a few minutes. I just want to ask a few questions."

"I've answered dozens of them already. All I know is that the neighbor, Mrs. Owens, Tilda Owens, she's a widow and lives right across the street . . ." Sybil waved her cigarette toward the house with the older woman and the cat. "She complained to me about my tenant nearly running over her cat, so I decided to talk to Elyse."

"Elyse?" he repeated.

"Yes, Elyse Hammersly. She's my tenant, has been since the first of the year."

"You've met her? Talked with her?"

"Yes."

"And she's not the woman downstairs."

"That dead thing? No . . . oh, no, I'm sure not." But she didn't sound convinced. She took another drag of smoke and glanced down at her soiled suit, wincing a bit. "I mean, it's hard to tell." Shuddering, she shook her head, disbelieving that the moldering corpse could be anyone she'd actually seen or talked to.

"You've seen pictures of Marla Cahill, the escapee. Was she the woman who rented this place?"

"No. I rented it before she escaped, I'm sure. And I've met Elyse, and she's not Marla Cahill."

"I'd like to see the lease. You have a copy?"

"At the office, yes."

"Do you take any references or ID before you lease your property?"

"Of course." Sybil bristled.

"Can I see the records?"

"No problem. Again, they're at the office."

"I'll drive you there, and, when we're done, I'll bring you back here."

"I could just drive myself."

"Just in case Detective Lee or the FBI have any further questions."

"The FBI?" she repeated and sucked on her cigarette until the ash reached the filter tip. "Oh, dear God."

Paterno's thoughts exactly.

"I need to see you," Elyse said into the phone. On the other end, her lover was balking.

"I can't. People will get suspicious. I'm being watched, you know."

"We need to talk." She was desperate, her heart pounding as she drove across the Golden Gate Bridge. Traffic was thick, people pouring out of the city in rush hour, and she could barely think. Her head pounded, and she told herself she just needed to get home, to see him again, to . . . to . . .

The car in front of her slammed on his brakes, and she did the same, nearly plowing into the trunk of the red Pontiac. Her tires skidded on the wet pavement. "You cretin!" she yelled, though she could only see the back of his head as the wipers slapped away the rain. The driver was a teenager on a cell phone, and of course he couldn't hear her. The thrum of huge speakers and rap music pulsed through the night. And still he was on his cell.

"What?" her lover said breathlessly as if he'd been climbing stairs or running.

"Just meet me. Tonight."

"I'm telling you it's impossible."

"You show," she insisted as the stupid baby started crying again. The damned kid was driving her crazy. "I need some help, damn it, and we're in this together. It was your idea."

"Not all of it."

"You were the one who said we could do this, now for God's sake be a man." She was irritated, biting the inside of her cheek nervously, her fingers so tight around the steering wheel they felt fused to the plastic and metal.

"You're taking too many chances."

"I don't have a choice!"

"We need to cool it for a while."

"Cool it?" she said, her voice increasing in pitch, rising to a near screech. "Are you crazy? We can't cool it now."

"You're the one acting crazy!"

"Because I'm the one who's taking all the damned risks. If you knew what I put up with, dealing with that bitch! Just get your ass to the house," she insisted as her Taurus inched over the bridge.

"For Christ's sake, get a grip."

"I can't!" she yelled and heard the anger, the panic, in her own voice. She caught her reflection in the mirror and was surprised to see that her hair was frazzled and unkempt, her makeup running, her eyes staring as if she were freaked. Holy God, what was wrong with her? Nothing. Not a damned thing. It was everyone else. Yes, she was a little wired and nervous, but who wouldn't be? She was just under a tremendous amount of pressure, and he, the wimp, wasn't helping. Where was the strong, intelligent, sexy man she'd fallen for? "Listen, lover boy," she snarled sarcastically. "You damned well better meet me, or you'll never see the boy again. End of story." She clicked off, swore at the driver in front of her, and, when the phone rang and she saw it was Jack calling her back, she ignored it. Let him stew in his own juices.

Bastard!

So Cissy had changed her mind about the divorce.

So what?

That didn't change anything!

Paterno's cell phone jangled as he backed the Caddy into a tight parking space in front of the realty company. Sybil Tomini, sitting in the passenger seat, braced herself, as if she expected him to scrape the grill of a Range Rover with his back bumper. He jammed the big car into park and answered the phone. He hadn't been taking any calls for the past couple of hours, had half a dozen to return, but caller ID told him that Quinn was on the other end of the line.

"Paterno," he said as Sybil Tomini hugged herself on the other side of the wide seat. Into the receiver he said, "Just a sec, Janet." To the realtor, he held up a finger. "I'll be right in."

Sybil, already reaching into her purse for her pack of cigarettes and lighter, nodded. "I'll find the file." She climbed out of the car and lit up before she closed the door.

"I'm back," he said to Quinn as raindrops began to shiver from the dark sky.

"I got your message earlier," Quinn said. "You found Marla Cahill, and she's dead?"

"Has been for a while. Couldn't have been the doer in the murders. I'll tell you all about it when I get back to the station." He cut the engine and the lights. "We're looking for Mary Smith now."

"I've got something from that nurse in Idaho, the one who was working at Cahill House during the time Marla Amhurst had her baby."

Paterno grunted for her to continue.

"The nurse is a little foggy and really didn't want to talk to me. She's retired now, her husband fishes all day, and she doesn't want any trouble, but she said Marla had a baby girl who would be around twenty-six or twenty-seven now, which coincides with the dates in Eugenia's diary."

"Have you got a name?"

"Not for the child, but the adoptive parents were from Oakland—Ron and Christine Engles. I'm checking now to find out if they still live in the area."

"While you're at it, find out anything you can about Elyse Hammersly. Do a statewide search for priors. See if she was incarcerated with Marla Cahill, anything. She rented the house where we found Marla's body in Berkeley. I'll know more in a few minutes. I'm at the realty company now. I'll fill you in when I get back to the station."

Paterno dashed through the rain and headed into the front office. A door in the back wall was ajar, so he walked through. Sybil was at one of several utilitarian workstations, digging through a drawer. "I have keys to the file cabinets in the storeroom. I'll be right back." She headed toward a metal door past the other workstations.

Paterno waited, and Sybil returned with a folder. "I know I have this information on the computer too," she said, calmer now that they were away from the bungalow where she'd found the corpse. "But there's an agreement she signed . . . and I always take a copy of the renter's ID. Also, we require proof of employment and a credit history. Let's see . . ." Her fingers flipped through several folders before extracting one. "Here you go."

With a feeling of getting closer to his goal, Paterno began reviewing the documents.

"They might have found Marla," Jack said breathlessly as he rushed through the door. He'd been out jogging, working out some of his aggression while Cissy had been inside. His running gear was wet, his hair plastered to his head, his face tense, his expression dark.

Coco, from her little bed near the fire, lifted her head, letting out a disgruntled "woof" before returning to sleep.

Cissy's heart skipped a beat. Hope shot through her, but it was followed quickly by fear. "What about B.J.?"

"No. Don't think so. I just got a text message from a friend who'd seen it on the news. I've got a call in to Paterno." Jack was sweating profusely, his face red, his hair wet, his cell phone in one hand, his iPod in the pocket of his sweats. He walked to the television and flipped through the news channels.

Nothing about Marla. At least not yet.

"Wouldn't someone have told us? The FBI?" she asked as agents had been with them on and off since the kidnapping. Their phone lines tapped in case the kidnappers decided to call, all their mail searched for a note, the house under twenty-four-hour surveillance. So much for keeping them out of it.

"Not until they were certain, but you'd better brace yourself."

"Brace myself?" she said, images of B.J.'s tiny unmoving body filling her head. "Oh God, Beej—"

"I'm talking about Marla. It's possible that your mother might be dead."

A chill swept up her spine. "What do you mean?" Marla? Dead? A multitude of emotions rocketed through her. She loved her mother; hated her. The woman was loathsome, a horrible creature, and yet she had, in her distant way, raised Cissy, been there for her. Marla's was the face she remembered as a child, the person who had taught her to tie her shoes, who had enrolled her in private school, who had shown her how to French braid her hair, and so much more. Marla, in her own way, had consoled Cissy when she'd scraped her knee or had her heart broken, and yet, over the years, there had been a rift between them, one that had started with Cissy's teenage years and had never been bridged in the years since. But she'd always thought there would be time to make amends, if she ever wanted it. . . . Oh God . . . Dead? That seemed impossible. "Where's our baby?"

"I don't know." Jack's face was carved with worry, deep grooves around his eyes and mouth. Neither he nor Cissy had caught any sleep, and Cissy felt like the hours had dragged into a lifetime. She didn't know what she would have done without Jack, without him to lean on, confide in, cry with.

Outside, along with the FBI vehicles, was a news van, seemingly permanently camped out on the street. Most of Cissy's friends had called. Gwen and Tracy had stopped by; even Heather had phoned, clearly feeling sheepish about the way her affair with Donald had splashed across the news. Cissy was too worried about B.J. to even think about that issue. It was Heather's problem.

And Sara had brought over a pan of lasagna. "It's from Dino's," she'd admitted, fighting tears. "It was all I could think of to do." Jack's family had been in and out, and they'd received calls from the people she'd worked with at *City Wise* and also most of Gran's employees. Deborah had been devastated, wailing into the phone. Elsa and Lars had stopped by in person, Elsa delivering pies and a casserole while fighting tears. She said Rosa and Paloma were devastated as well, and Rosa was lighting candles at her church. Everyone was offering support, and yet most of the time Cissy wanted to be alone. She'd spent hours sitting in B.J.'s room, holding either his favorite stuffed animal or Coco and rocking in the chair they'd bought when he was born.

Now she was angry. Tired of waiting. Exhausted from the lack of sleep and frustrated by the lack of information. Where the hell was her little boy?

While Jack was in the shower, she called Paterno again and left a voice message. Damn it, where was the man? Where was her child? The house was getting to her; the doing nothing was driving her mad. She felt the need to pound her fist through a wall or scream or do any bloody thing to find B.J.

The phone rang, and she jumped.

She knew the drill. If it was a friend, get them off the phone quickly; if it was the kidnappers with a ransom call, keep them on the line. The FBI would be recording.

She picked up before the second ring.

"Hello?" Cissy said, her heart pounding.

"I've got him," an unrecognizable voice whispered in a tone that was absolutely chilling. Cissy gasped, her worst fears crystalized.

"But he's alive. Tell me he's alive."

"I did something you never did, you selfish bitch. I took him to visit his grandmother."

"What?" Cissy was stunned. "Who is this? Where's my child? I swear if you hurt him, I'll hunt you down and—"

Click.

"Wait!" she cried desperately, her heart in a thousand pieces. "Hello? Hello? Who are you? Oh God, please . . . Bring him back!" she screamed into the phone, but it was dead, the silence deafening, the rush of fear in her brain sounding like the hollow roar of the sea in a cavern. Thoughts of B.J. crowded through her mind, his laughing face, his impish grin and tiny teeth, his bright eyes. Tears streamed down her face, and she melted against the wall, the horrible words ringing through her brain.

I've got him.

"B.J.," she whispered brokenly, burying her face in her hands.

Chapter 21

Paterno examined the picture on the Oregon driver's license.

It wasn't anyone he recognized. But it was the picture of the woman who went by the name of Elyse Hammersly, the woman who'd rented the bungalow in Berkeley. The driver's license listed an address in Gresham, Oregon, as her last place of residence. With a little nudging, he'd had the information faxed to the office in San Francisco and called Quinn to start working on it. Sybil had also handed Paterno a second copy of the documents.

Now she asked, "How soon will . . . will the body be removed and I can have the place . . . ah . . . cleaned and aired out?" She was calmer and was apparently already calculating the weeks and months of lost rent.

"Not for a while. It's still a crime scene. But I'll let you know."

"The sooner the better."

"I assure you, Ms. Tomini, we want to solve this as soon as possible." He pointed to a blank line on the rental applications. "You didn't get any employment history."

"Oh. Sometimes it's not required. Elyse put down first and last month's rent, plus a security and cleaning deposit. We checked her credit history, and it was stellar. She was looking for work in San Francisco."

"She lived alone?"

Sybil shuddered delicately. "Apparently not."

"I mean, she wasn't married? No live-in boyfriend? Someone who came with her?"

"Not to our knowledge."

"How does she pay her rent?"

"We send all correspondence to the rental, though we haven't billed her yet because she paid in advance." Sybil walked around the desk to the spot where Paterno was standing and flipped over one of the pages he was holding. "See . . . Here's the receipt for cash. She hadn't opened a checking account yet, and since her credit history was so good, no red flags went up."

Paterno nodded. Hopefully Quinn was getting some information from Oregon. "She came into your office to rent the place. Did she drive?"

"I don't know how she got here, but she met me at the house, so I think she must've driven there. Yes, I remember . . ." Sybil frowned. "I thought it odd at the time. She parked in the back, near the alley."

"Do you remember the make of the car?"

Sybil shook her head. "Sorry, Detective, my mind doesn't work that way. I can remember houses in minute detail, the flooring, appliances, windows, cabinets, shades of woodwork, but when it comes to vehicles . . ." She shrugged. "I know it was a car, not a pickup or a van or an SUV, I do remember that much, oh, and it was light colored—white, silver, gray, maybe that champagne color? I don't know." She glanced out the window. "For example, all I know about your car is that it's at least fifteen years old and someone keyed it. . . . It's a Lincoln?"

"Cadillac," he said.

"Close."

Not really, but he didn't have time to argue the fine points of the Caddy, nor did he want to think about its marred finish. The vandalism still infuriated him. He asked a few more questions, got no more information, and left, heading straight to Jack and Cissy Holt's house.

A gust of wind ripped at his coat and rain pelted from the dark sky, promising a storm, but he felt a little better, as if he had a stronger handle on things. Finally, they were closing in on the murderer. He sensed it. Experienced that little zing in his blood whenever the net was closing around a criminal.

Now it was only a matter of time.

He slid behind the Caddy's steering wheel, swiped at the rain that dripped into his eyes, then fired the car's engine. Elyse Hammersly. At last he had a name to deal with.

And her picture.

Now all he had to do was find the bitch.

"What happened?" Jack asked, stepping into the hallway with only a towel wrapped around his hips. His hair was wet, his face a mask of concern.

"She called, oh, Jack, she called!" Cissy said. She was crumpled in the hallway, Coco whining and licking her face, the poor dog's tail wagging nervously.

"Who called?"

"The woman who has Beej."

"What did she say?" he asked tautly.

"She said she had B.J. and, oh God, I think, I mean I thought I heard him crying in the background." Cissy was losing it. She felt the tears roll down her cheeks, the fear congealing in her soul. "I don't know who it was. It was a restricted call. She was whispering, and, oh God, she sounded so . . . cruel, so angry, so . . . intense." She gazed up at her husband. "We have to get him back. Before she does something . . . something horrible. We're his parents; we're the ones responsible for his safety. We were supposed to protect him." She was falling apart, the hole inside her immense. "We *have* to."

"We will. I promise. Come on." He held out his hand. She clasped it, and he pulled her onto her feet and into his arms. Still wet from the shower, still smelling of soap and fresh water, he rocked her and whispered into her ear as she tried not to shatter into a million pieces.

"I'll find him, Ciss," Jack promised as she rested her head against his chest. He was so strong, not just in body, but spirit. How had she lost sight of that? Ever mistrusted him? "I mean it," he said into her hair. "If it's the last thing I do, I'll get him back."

She let out a broken sob and clung to him, all the while telling herself to pull it together. Whimpering and crying weren't going to help B.J. She had to be strong, to fight back the terror, to go out and find her child. Whoever had called her expected her to crumple, used her weakness where her baby was concerned, wanted her to feel this unending pain.

"What else did she say? Anything?"

"Just that she had him, that she'd taken him to see his grandmother, that I never had . . . Oh God, what was she talking about? I thought you said Marla was dead? She wouldn't . . . couldn't . . ."

"Shh. Let's find out." Jack pulled her into the bedroom, where he switched the towel for a pair of boxers, jeans, and a sweatshirt. He clicked on the TV as Cissy angrily brushed the tears from her eyes. "The local news should be on. . . ." He rotated through the channels until he found a station that looked promising. "Breaking News" swept across the screen, followed by the image of a small house, a cottage that looked as if it was fifty or sixty years old. A newswoman was standing in front of it, telling a chilling story.

". . . unconfirmed reports of the identity of the body inside, but just a few minutes ago we did see someone from the medical examiner's office wheeling out a body bag on a stretcher. Speculation is that the deceased person is escaped convict Marla Cahill." Marla's mug shot was flashed onto the screen, a black and white photo that showed little of the sexy, vibrant woman she'd once been.

Cissy pressed her hands to her cheeks.

Standing in the blowing rain, the reporter continued, "As yet the police have not confirmed or denied the identity of the victim, but neighbors of this tidy little bungalow report suspicious behavior." The camera flashed on the reporter interviewing an older woman leaning on a cane. The Asian newswoman wore a hooded parka emblazoned with the station call letters, KTAM.

Someone hovering just out of the camera's range held an umbrella over the older woman, who was wearing an overcoat and a plastic accordion-type rain bonnet.

With convictions as strong as her jutted chin, the neighbor, identified as Tilda Owens, insisted emphatically that she'd known for the past month that something was "fishy" at the house across the street from where she lived. ". . . all those late night comings and goings and the shades always drawn. I knew somethin' wasn't on the up and up. You can just tell. I thought it was probably drugs," she admitted, "but I guess I was wrong."

"Did you see Marla Cahill enter this house?" the reporter asked.

"I think so." Tilda Owens nodded.

"And you went to the police with that information?"

"I talked to the landlord."

The camera returned to the newswoman. "And that's what led to this search. One of Treasure Homes' employees apparently discovered a body and informed the authorities. . . ." Again the camera panned the average-looking house. "This is Lani Saito reporting for KTAM." The reporter signed off, and Jack used the remote to mute the television.

"So it's true." Cissy couldn't believe it. Her mother was dead. Shaking her head and biting her lower lip, she stared at the silent television, where an ad for a new sports drink flashed across the screen.

It was hard to imagine that her mother was actually gone and her son was in the hands of a murderess, a cruel, heartless killer. Why had the woman taken Beej? Why had her boy been with the nanny at her apartment? Who was the woman who had called? The voice on the phone had been hard to hear, but Cissy was sure it had been female.

"The feds recorded the call on tape," Jack said, glancing out the window to their van, parked on the street.

Cissy closed her eyes. Over and over again, she replayed the short, heart-stopping conversation in her head and came to the same pathetic, sick conclusion. She cleared her throat and stared at Jack. "We're not going to get a ransom call."

"Why do you think that?"

"Because this is personal, Jack. I don't know how, and I don't know why, but this woman hates me. I felt it, heard it, in her voice." She steeled herself against the awful, mind-numbing truth. "And I know for a fact that she'll stop at nothing to get what she wants. She'll hurt B.J. because it's the best way to get back at me."

* * *

The Cadillac's wheels were humming over the Bay Bridge when Quinn called Paterno on his cell. "Paterno," he answered, switching lanes as he reached the western edge of the bay, where the rain and wind seemed more intense.

"Okay, I've got information on Elyse Hammersly. She's sixty-four, nearly retired from a phone company in Portland, and has lived in Gresham, Oregon, for the last thirty-five years. She's never owned a home in California, and the last time she visited was in 1987, when a nephew got married, and that was San Diego. She and her husband drove through San Francisco, spent a night at the St. Francis, and continued to Southern California. On the way back, they stayed in Sonoma, did the wine country thing. Someone's obviously got hold of her ID, enough to access her credit rating."

Crap! He'd expected no better but had hoped the information he'd obtained at Treasure Homes Realty would lead them to the killer. "You check for any other Elyse Hammerslys in the area?" he asked, noting the swells of water just off the bridge, white caps rising furiously on the dark, choppy surface.

"Yep. Nada. Same with the DMV. If she's got a car, and we know she does, it's not registered under Hammersly. I checked all Hammerslys. Again, I'm drawing blanks."

"You tell the feds?"

"Oh, yeah. You'll be hearing from them."

He eased off the bridge and worked his way to Market Street. "Look, I'm going to inform Cissy Holt that we found Marla. I'll show her the copy of Elyse's fake Oregon driver's license. If we can't find anyone who recognizes her, then we'll have to put it out to the media. In the meantime, show it to Perez and O'Riley.

They staked out the Holt house. Maybe they saw her. She has to have been around."

"Will do."

Paterno clicked off and eased the Caddy through the dark night. The storm was picking up steam, blowing in from the Pacific, wind whipping through the streets, rain slanting from the black sky, the kind of night Paterno's grandmother had always said "Wasn't fit for man nor beast."

The wipers struggled to keep up with the rain's assault, and the glare of oncoming headlights made him squint as he turned onto the road near Alamo Square. Jack Holt's Jeep sat in the driveway of their house, the lights visible behind drawn blinds and curtains. An FBI van was parked up the street. Inconspicuous? Yeah, right.

Paterno eased into a parking spot along the curb, cut the engine, and tucked the copy of the lease agreement inside his overcoat. Turning his collar against the rain, he half-ran across the street and leaned on the bell when he reached the front door. Hell, what a night.

Before he'd straightened again, the door swung open, the damned yapping dog went off, and Jack Holt motioned for him to come inside, shushing the little beast as he said, "We heard about Marla. It's all over the news." Holt gave him a hard look. "You could have called."

"I wanted to come by in person."

"Took long enough."

Cissy was in the living room, seated on the hearth in front of the fire, looking as if she'd lost more weight, which was a shame. This ordeal was taking its toll on her.

"So it's true," she said, climbing to her feet and rubbing her arms as if she was cold from the inside out. "My mother's dead."

"We think so, yes. She had no ID on her, of course, and we didn't find any of her prison clothes, nothing to indicate that the body was hers."

"You couldn't tell?" Cissy asked uncomfortably.

"It had been a while since she died."

She went white as a sheet and swallowed hard, as if trying to keep whatever was in her stomach down.

"We'll need dental or DNA to be certain."

Cissy nodded tautly several times, processing. "She was murdered."

"We think so. Looks like a bullet wound to the back of her head."

"Who killed her?" Jack asked. "The person who has our *son?*"

Paterno sidestepped. "We'll know more after the autopsy."

"But she was holed up in that house." Cissy looked at him.

"Yes."

She picked up the damned little mutt and held her close. "You thought she had an accomplice."

"Could be a double-cross. Maybe your mother isn't the person responsible for the crimes."

Cissy said slowly, "I think whoever killed her called here."

Paterno's attention sharpened. "Called you?"

Jack nodded. "The FBI taped it from their van. They just came in and talked to us."

"I hadn't heard about the call."

"There's not much to tell. The woman basically taunted Cissy about having B.J. Said she'd taken him to 'see his grandmother.'"

Paterno glanced at Cissy, and she repeated the entire conversation. She finished with, "Then she hung up. I can't believe it. If Marla was dead . . . decomposing? What was she thinking? Beej was probably scared out of his mind." Her face tightened, and she blinked against tears.

"We found a scrap of cotton fabric there. Fuzzy. Blue. Could be part of a blanket. We're analyzing it."

"That damned bitch! What's she doing to my child?" Cissy was instantly livid. The dog whimpered, and she leaned over to let Coco down again.

Paterno asked, "Do you know anyone named Elyse?"

Cissy and Jack shook their heads.

"Elyse Hammersly?"

"No. Why?"

"That's the name of the woman who rented the house where we found Marla. We think she's also disguised herself as Mary Smith." He pulled the copies of the lease agreement and ID from his pocket and handed them to the Holts.

Cissy just stared at the grainy picture on the copy of the Oregon driver's license. Her pale skin turned ashen. "This woman is Elyse?" she whispered in disbelief.

"Wasn't she here after the funeral? Serving?" Jack stared at the license photo too.

"You know her." Paterno felt a jolt of adrenaline.

Cissy stared hard at the photo. Shock and fear registered in her eyes. "There has to be some mistake. This is a picture of Diedre Lawson, Detective. She works at Joltz. It's a coffee shop I go to. She's not really a friend of mine, but we know each other. No, you have to be wrong. I mean, I can't believe that . . . *Why?*" Cissy started to tremble all over. "Are you telling me that Diedre killed my mother . . . and has my son?"

Jack swore pungently through clenched teeth.

Paterno's brain was clicking. "Do you know that your mother had another child, a daughter, whom she gave up for adoption a few years before you were born?"

Cissy recoiled. "What are you saying? I have a sibling?

No . . . The only sibling I have is my brother . . . half-brother . . . in Oregon. James, who lives with my uncle."

"I know this is a shock, but we found out through your grandmother's diary, and records at Cahill House, that before your mother was married, she had a baby girl and gave her up for adoption. She was at Cahill House. That's how she met your father."

"No way!" Cissy held up her hands. "I mean, I would have known. Someone would have told me. Gran would have . . ." Her expression changed from denial to something darker, as if the muscles of her face were drawn by the fingers of fear.

"I don't know how to say this but straight out," Paterno said. "You have a half-sister, Cissy. She was adopted by a couple named Engles. Sounds like she's now Diedre Lawson."

"And Elyse Hammersly?" Jack spit out.

"And she killed my—our—mother and kidnapped my son?"

"It's speculation, but it fits. Do you know where Diedre lives?"

Cissy shook her head. "Rachelle would. She owns Joltz and works with Diedre." Cissy held up a hand as if to stop the tide of information. "Are you sure about this?"

"You're the one who came up with the name," he reminded them. "When I showed you the picture, I only knew the name Engles."

"This is unbelievable!" Jack was shaking his head, and he placed an arm around his wife.

Amen, Paterno thought as he called Quinn again and gave her the updated information. Then, after telling the Holts he would let them know the minute he tracked down Diedre Engles, walked out to have a discussion with the FBI.

* * *

Cissy stared at the door as Jack closed it soundly behind Paterno. Seconds ticked by. The wet spot on the wood floor where the detective's raincoat had dripped seemed to spread. Paterno expected her to just sit here and wait while her child was being held by a madwoman, a woman who could be her half-sister. But she couldn't. "Something about this doesn't make sense," she said.

"None of it makes sense." Jack was pacing in front of the fire, his gaze traveling to the pictures of Beej on the fireplace, then to the toy box where their son's stuffed animals, little cars, and Legos lay stacked and untouched.

That great gnawing pain started up again, ripping through her guts, slashing at her heart. In her mind's eye, she saw Beej standing over the toy box, and her throat burned.

"Do you trust the police to get our boy back?" Jack asked, his voice verbalizing the very question running through her mind.

She shook her head. "They haven't been able to protect anyone, not since Marla escaped. Look what happened to Gran and Rory . . ."

"And Cherise and Tanya." He plowed anxious fingers through his hair. Pain and despair darkened his eyes. "I can't stand it. I have to *do* something."

"What?"

"I don't know, but I can't sit around and wait one more minute. I'm going to find B.J."

"If you leave, the police will follow you."

A muscle worked in his jaw. "Do you think that we're going to get a ransom call?"

"No." She was certain of it.

"And even if we do, don't you think this person . . . Diedre has our cell numbers? If we didn't pick up here, she'd call one of our cell phones."

"She's got my number," Cissy agreed. The feds had made sure she got her cell phone operational, as she hadn't had the time. "It's on the new phone."

"Right. So if she's got Beej, and it seems like she does, then she would call your cell, right?"

"I suppose. But what is it you want to do?"

"I want to look for our boy. Right now we're doing everything *she* wants, everything *she* expects. She knows we won't go against the FBI or the police. That we'll stay here and wait. I agree with you. This isn't about ransom money."

"What do you want to do?" Cissy asked.

"Call Rachelle. She knows more about Diedre than anyone else, right?"

Cissy was nodding.

"She might tell you more than she would tell the cops."

"I don't want to screw up their investigation."

"I want my son back. I've got a friend who was in the special forces. He owes me a big favor. I think I'm going to call it in. You talk to Rachelle, I'll call Sam."

A part of her wanted to hold back, to let the police do their jobs. They had the manpower, they had the equipment, they had the knowledge. But Jack was right. They weren't related to Beej, and they hadn't been able to stop this horrible wave of killings. Too many people close to her had died already. No one had saved Gran or Rory or Cherise or Tanya. "How long will you be gone?" She hated the thought of being without him, of not being able to depend upon his strength.

"As long as it takes."

"You won't have a car. The Jeep's parked out front. If you take it, someone will see you."

"Sam will come get me, or I'll jog to Jannelle's. I still have a second set of keys for her Lexus, and her house is less than two miles from here."

"Uphill."

"Yeah, but I'm in great shape." He managed a thin, humorless smile.

"I don't know," she said, then looked into his eyes. Clear and determined, they held hers. She knew then she couldn't change his mind.

Reckless, bold, irreverent, and bullheaded—when Jack became passionate about something, he didn't back down, not even, it seemed, to the police or the damned FBI.

"I'm going, Cissy. Keep your cell on. One way or another, we'll find our son." He walked through the house, casually making certain all the shades were drawn, that no one could see inside.

"Maybe the police will find him first," she said hopefully.

"Good. Then I just look like an overzealous nutcase of a father. I don't care." He reached for his windbreaker hanging on the hall tree, then stopped as if a sudden thought had cut through his brain. "But you, Ciss. You stay here."

"After all your big talk about getting our kid back? You're telling me to 'stay,' just like you would a damned dog? I'm in this too."

"Someone's got to remain here, keep the police thinking that we're playing by their rules. There's a chance we're going to lose B.J., we both know that."

"*No!*"

"Okay, we're trying everything we know to keep that from happening, but if it does," he said, conviction running through his words, "it'll kill us both."

"Don't say it," she begged. "Don't even think it!"

"And I wouldn't be able to live with myself if anything happened to you. So you stay put. And safe." He slipped the windbreaker over his sweatshirt and found his running shoes.

"I'll be fine," Cissy insisted, stiffening her spine. "Do what you have to do, Jack. I will too." She felt a renewed sense of purpose as he laced the shoes. "You're right about one thing, though. This monster who's got him, Diedre or Elyse or whoever she wants to call herself, she's never going to bring him back to us, never going to let him go." She was keyed up, anxious, needing to do something. "Okay, go. Get our boy back."

"Jesus, I love you," he said, and she believed him. Strong arms surrounded her, dragged her tight as he kissed her hard, destroying the breath in her lungs with a passion that told her he thought he might truly never see her again.

That thought was crushing. She clung to him. What if she lost him? Lost their son.

He drew his head back. "I need a distraction, so that the police or feds won't see me leave."

"You act like you've done this before."

"Don't ask," he said, and looked around the connecting rooms of their house. "We'll turn off the lights in the back, just leave the one to the stairs and bedroom on, maybe a lamp here in the living room, but I want the kitchen dark. I'll slip through the garage and crawl out the window on the side of the house while you make a quick call from the landline, just to get the FBI's attention. Let the dog go outside to do her thing and take the receiver with you. If anyone asks about it, tell them you couldn't find your cell and were just dialing the cell number hoping it would ring so you could find the damned phone." He glanced around the house. "Tell them that the dog needed to go out, so you stepped onto the patio." He looked at her again, his features taut. "I only need a couple of minutes to cut through Sara's yard and get over her fence. Then I should be able to make my way to the street two blocks over. Two minutes. Got it?"

"Yeah."

"Okay," he said and started for the garage but stopped. "Wait!" Taking the steps two at a time, he flew upstairs and turned on the bathroom light and shower, so that the water was running through the pipes. He was downstairs again within a minute. "If anyone asks, I'm in the shower."

"And then what happens when the police wait around for you to come out as prune man?"

He flashed a smile. "Then, darling," he said, kissing her on the forehead, "we're screwed."

"You were right," Quinn said as she and Paterno climbed into her Jetta. "Diedre Engles was married briefly to Gene Lawson, her high-school sweetheart. And get this, now he's a cop with the state police." She rammed the keys into the ignition and flicked her wrist. The little car's engine roared to life, and she hit the gas. "I already talked to him, and he told me that yes, she was adopted, grew up in Sacramento with upper middle-class parents she hated. She always wanted to meet— and this is a direct quote—'the bitch who gave me up.' She spent years searching for her birth mother, but she and Gene split up before she found her."

"Why did she hate her adoptive parents?"

"Who knows? Gene didn't. They were decent enough people, if a little distant. Anyway," she said, rounding a corner fast enough that the wheels chirped, "Gene said the older she got, the more, as he put it, 'psycho' and 'obsessed' she became, to the point that when she refused counseling, they divorced. No kids."

"Does he think she's capable of plotting an escape and committing a string of murders?"

"He told me he didn't know what she was capable of, but that she was extremely smart: high IQ, but really messed up. His diagnosis: she's got some major wires crossed."

"So he wasn't surprised?"

Quinn stepped on it as a light turned amber, then switched lanes as if she thought she was a race-car driver. They were driving without sirens or lights, converging on the townhouse where Diedre Lawson lived. On this one, they were taking a backseat to the FBI, but Paterno would be damned rather than miss the snagging of the woman who had sprung Marla Cahill only to kill her.

"He didn't expect her to turn out to be a serial murderer, but surprised? No. He didn't have many good words to say about his ex-wife."

"They never do."

Quinn slowed to a stop two blocks from the townhouse. From here, they could watch the feds in action. Paterno stared through the rain-spattered windshield as the agents surrounded Diedre's residence.

Would there be a gun battle?

Or would she lay down her weapon and surrender?

He wasn't betting on it.

That would be just too damned easy. The truth of the matter was that he had a bad feeling about this showdown. It was true that the woman seemed to be slipping up, her actions in the last few murders not as carefully planned as Marla's escape or Eugenia's and Rory's murders. She was losing it. Definitely, he thought as he reached into his pocket for a pack of gum. But he still thought this was just too easy.

He felt in his gut that Marla's killer wouldn't go out unless it was in a damned blaze of glory.

Would that kid never shut up?

Jesus H. Christ, she'd fed him, given him a bottle, and changed his damned diaper. She'd even attempted to bathe him, but he had squirmed and struggled. She just wasn't cut out to be a mother, Diedre decided, just like that bitch who had borne her.

Marla!

Now there was a head case.

"Oh, shut up!" she yelled down the hallway to the room she'd set up for him, a room with a playpen and blankets and some of those dumb stuffed animals that always looked so insipid. She figured he'd wear himself out eventually, but man, oh, man, her head was thundering, pain throbbing through her skull. She popped another couple of ibuprofen, but she really needed something stronger, something prescribed by a doctor, a painkiller that would knock the throbbing ache out once and for all.

It was all because of Marla. Diedre didn't remember having headaches before she'd finally tracked down her real mother—in prison, no less! Talk about bad karma! Worse yet, she realized everything she'd wanted in life: a family with social standing; a beautiful young mother; a world of privilege . . . everything that should have been hers. Gone. Gone! Because her damned mother had given her up for adoption. Not that her adoptive parents were all that bad, but they were just boring, ordinary people who didn't really seem to care about her as she'd grown. She'd wondered about that, but it was all mixed in her mind. Then there was her father. All she'd learned about him, after digging for years, was that he and Marla had been involved in a very short, very hot affair, and guess what? Marla had ended up pregnant.

Marla's parents, Victoria and Conrad Amhurst, had been mortified at their daughter's promiscuity and condition. Talk about living in the dark ages! They'd talked her into going to Cahill House, where she'd met her husband, much to the horror of Eugenia. That old bat! She'd recognized Diedre before she'd died because she'd always kept track of her, through Cahill House. Hypocrite. She got what she deserved. Diedre still felt more than a little satisfaction when she remembered Eugenia's last frightened minutes as Diedre had forced her over the railing.

Served her right.

The baby's wailing had finally lessened a bit, and Diedre's headache abated a tad too. Thank God. She walked into the master suite of the Amhurst mansion and looked through the windows to the sea. It was weird to think that her grandparents had slept in here, even made love. Her skin crawled at the thought of it, but it suited her perfectly, and at least her own dead parents had left her a small inheritance that had allowed her to afford the rent on the townhouse, the place she considered her "cover," as well as the bungalow where Marla hid out.

Marla, who was going to go down for every murder Diedre committed. Diedre had her alibis all set, and Marla had none. It was perfect, though in the back of her mind, she felt a tiny little schism of fear cut through her brain, something that didn't seem to fit, though she couldn't quite sort it out. Whatever it was, it would have to wait.

Where the hell was Jack?

She checked her watch and frowned. She'd told him to come here, right? This is where they always met. This was the place she considered their "home." After all, she really did have Amhurst blood running through her veins, and once all of the other pretenders to the throne were dealt with, she truly would inherit it all.

That's not right. It's not what you planned . . . remember?

The headache behind her eye flared again, and she decided not to think too hard. She just needed Jack to show . . . and then . . .

The noise from the baby's room had disappeared altogether. Diedre tiptoed down the gallery hallway and peered through the door she'd left ajar. He was sleeping. Curled up with a lop-eared fuzzy bunny Diedre had bought for him. He almost looked angelic lying in the playpen, but she didn't step into the room, didn't want to risk waking him. She wasn't sure what she thought about him.

Walking back to the master bedroom, she let her fingers trail over the wrought-iron railing as she gazed down three floors to the foyer below. This incredible Queen Anne home was hers. This mansion that had been abandoned and left to go to seed because of Marla's incarceration would soon be brought back to life!

Marla would go back to prison . . . or . . . She frowned as she concentrated. Or she would be dead. Marla would be dead. That would be better. She'd decided that Marla had to die, right? So she couldn't drag Diedre down? She rubbed her forehead and shivered. She was just under so much stress that sometimes she got a little mixed up. Just a little. Despite what the ridiculous psychiatrist had said. What was it? Something about paranoia or schizophrenia or delusions. Didn't matter. He was a kook with his bald head and gray beard and tiny little glasses . . . always staring at her as if there were actually something wrong with her.

But she wouldn't think of Dr. Lazio Bennett III now. Not when she had time to spend alone with Jack. . . . Wait a minute. Was that right? Of course it was. Jack was one of the very few people who knew who she was. She didn't have to go by that damned alias around him, didn't have to pretend. He loved her as Diedre, and that was perfect.

She climbed the stairs to the turret and walked outside to view the sea. It was dark, a few lights mounted on the sea wall offering views of the raging, frothing whitecaps and angry surf. The sky was dark, the wind gusting and fierce, rain slashing from the black sky.

It was wild and savage, and she wondered what Jack would say if she suggested they make love here, on this balcony, with the storm raging around them.

If Jack would go for it. She turned her gaze inland, the wind blowing her hair over her eyes, and she saw the headlights on the road leading to the estate. Her heart skipped a beat, and she forced the door open and hurried down the circular stairs to the floor below. She was on the second floor when she heard the key in the lock, and a few seconds later, he walked through the front door and into the foyer.

He was wet too from his dash across the parking lot. He stood dripping on the floor, his gaze lifting upward to clash with hers. "Jesus Christ, Diedre," he said, no flash of a smile slashing across his face, no spark of intelligent humor in his blue eyes, "what the hell have you done?"

Chapter 22

Cissy looked at the clock for the fourth time in as many minutes. Jack had been gone over an hour, and she hadn't heard a word. Nor had the police called or stopped by. She chanced a peek through the blinds, and, miracle of miracles, the van that had been parked up the street for days was gone.

Had the FBI seen Jack leave and taken off after him? Had they considered him a risk to the investigation and arrested him? Where was he?

She paced in front of the fire, barely noticing the flames licking the porcelain logs or her own reflection in the mirror. What if she lost them both? Not only B.J., but Jack as well? She felt sick inside. Jangled. Her restlessness was making her crazy, her nerves wound tighter than a watch spring. She had to do something.

She'd tried to call Rachelle, but the number at Joltz rang on and on.

Again, she checked the street.

Once more, there was no van in sight.

Leave now! This is your chance! They might be back. Now, they won't know that you took the car out of the garage. You know there isn't going to be a phone call for ransom; Diedre or Elyse or whoever the hell she is plans on harming Beej, even killing him.

She grabbed her keys and threw on a jacket, and, as she walked to the garage, she twisted her hair away from her face and slipped a rubber band around the short ponytail. She didn't know where she was going, but she knew that sitting here in the house made no sense whatsoever. Sliding into the Acura, she spied Beej's car seat in the back. She almost lost it, her knees like water, pain cutting through her heart so deeply she swore it was physical.

She didn't dare call Jack for fear it might startle him. If he hadn't remembered to turn his cell to vibrate or silent mode, it might alert anyone he was stalking of his whereabouts. Even a text message might make some sound.

So where to? she asked herself as she hit the garage door opener and it ground open, the gears seeming so loud she cringed, the automatic light exposing the fact that she was in the car. Too bad. The FBI could just damned well follow her if they wanted. She was doing nothing illegal. In fact, *she* was somehow going to find her child. She just had to be careful to maneuver around Jack's Jeep, then close the garage. She didn't know how, but she intended to track Diedre Lawson to the ends of the earth.

Diedre is your half-sister.

Marla was her mother too.

God, how twisted was that?

She put the car into reverse and inched around Jack's Jeep, her tires sliding off the cement into the yard. As soon as she was clear, she hit the garage door opener and the door ground down. Backing into the street, she threw the Acura into drive and headed into the city.

She thought about Diedre or Elyse, a person whom she'd known for several years. How could she do this? Why?

It's because she's your half-sister. You heard her voice on the phone. She hates you, Cissy.

But why?

Because, in her distorted mind, you were the golden child, the chosen one. You lived with your mother. Marla didn't abandon you. You became a Cahill.

But Diedre had her own parents—two people who loved her.

But she's screwed up, and she wants what you have, including your baby.

"Not for long," she murmured, hands flexing on the wheel. She only had to figure out where, in all of the Bay Area, the monster was hiding her child.

Diedre stared down the curving steps to where her lover stood in the foyer below. Jack was angry? With her? Why?

"You blew it," he said, his blue eyes snapping fire as she descended the staircase.

"I did no such thing." The nerve of the man! He was just stressed. They both were.

"You didn't stick to the plan."

"Hey, I'm the one taking all the chances," she reminded him, irritated. "I'm the one who has to put up with Marla's whining! If you think that's fun, then you go ahead, babysit her for a while."

"It's a little too late for that, don't you think?" he said, looking around the darkened rooms. "Where's B.J.?"

"Here."

"*Where*, damn it?" He turned on her then, anger

seeming to pulse from him. She saw it in the throb at his neck, the twist of his lips.

"He's upstairs, sleeping like a, you know, baby."

"Show me."

"Oh, for the love of Christ—"

"Show me!" he insisted and grabbed her arm roughly, jerking it hard. His hair was wet, his face flushed, and he glared at her as if she were a demon straight from hell.

"Chill out!" she declared, yanking back her arm and cocking her head toward the stairs. "I said he's upstairs in the nursery sleeping." She started marching up the sweeping stairs in front of him, but he brushed past her, mounting the steps two at a time. At the curved landing, he looked down the unfamiliar hallways.

"Where?"

"The nursery."

"Which room is the damned nursery?"

"Oh, for the love of God. Relax." She reached the landing and led him along the hallway, which was really a gallery that cut in a semicircle above the foyer. Each of three doors opened to the gallery: the master suite, of course; a library on one side; a music room on the other. And farther down on each curved wing was another bedroom, one of which Diedre had designated the nursery. "Do not wake him up; he's been cranky all day."

He walked to the door that was ajar and pushed it open. It creaked a bit, and she hurried to catch up with him. "Damn it, Jack," she whispered, "do *not* wake him up."

But she needn't have worried. Her lover, it seemed, didn't have the heart to disturb the boy sleeping so soundly with his stuffed animal. Once he was satisfied that the kid was fine, he backed into the hallway and grabbed her wrist, pulling her toward the master bed-room. Now this was more like it! She felt a tiny rush in her bloodstream, sensed his warm fingertips on the inside of her wrist, as if he could feel her pulse.

Once inside, he closed the doors behind them, and she, smiling, said, "I thought we could have a private party up on the deck of the turret."

He stared at her as if he couldn't believe what he was hearing. "There's a storm raging out there!"

"All the more fun, don't you think?"

"What I think is that you've gone too far. It was *not* in the plan to kidnap the baby, and what the hell did you do to Tanya? You killed her!"

"I met her in the park and told her that I needed something she'd borrowed from me—an umbrella that I had at the coffee shop, for crying out loud. She got caught in a rainshower one day. So, I insisted that I needed it immediately. Tanya didn't want to bring B.J. back to her place, but I told her it would be just for a second, I really needed the damned umbrella, and then I followed her there."

"And shot her dead," he charged, his hand, stiff as a claw, shaking in the air beside him, as if he wanted to strangle her.

"How else was I going to keep her mouth shut? It's not as if she would just hand him over to me, now, is it?"

"But you weren't supposed to kidnap him! The point is that he's the one who inherits everything."

"Why bother with him? I'm Marla's daughter. If everyone else is dead, then I inherit."

Jack's face turned deadly. "You mean to tell me that you want to kill the baby?"

"I want to kill that bitch, Cissy," she retorted. When she saw his shocked expression, she rolled her eyes. "Don't tell me you care about her? She's in the way. I'll take care of it. And don't worry, I'll make it look like

Marla did it. I've left her DNA at all the crime scenes, and she didn't even realize it," Diedre said, proud of herself. "Fingernail clippings, hairs. And she has no alibi. I figure it'll be back in prison for her for the rest of her life."

"Diedre," he said softly, his eyes troubled. "Marla's dead. You know that, don't you?"

"What are you talking about? She's hiding out in Berkeley."

He gasped. Appeared thunderstruck. Shoved his hair from his eyes with both hands. "Haven't you seen the news?"

"Why? What are they reporting?"

"They found Marla! In the house in Berkeley."

"I don't believe it."

"When was the last time you went to see her?" he asked, and his shock seemed to give way to something else. Fear? Disgust?

"Earlier today . . . or maybe . . . yesterday?" She tried to shake the cobwebs from her mind.

"And she was alive?"

"Yes!" she said, but something in his words triggered a memory of a fight, of Marla's arguments, of her insistence that she couldn't live cooped up "like a damned convict" again. Isn't that what she'd said?

Diedre tried to think, but her head was pounding, the images distorted. She remembered parking the car and shuttling Marla inside.

"*This* is where I'm supposed to stay?" Marla had asked as she'd looked at the small bungalow. She'd shaken her head in dismay. "You're kidding, right?"

"No, really, it'll be perfect," Diedre had insisted, unlocking the door and glancing across the street to the house where an old lady was picking her mail out of the box and glancing toward the cottage. "Come inside, I'll show you." She'd finally unlatched the door and pushed it open and Marla, dressed in the jeans and sweater Diedre had picked up for her, had walked into the darkened interior. The house had been cold, of course, and dark with the gloom of winter twilight fading. All the blinds were dusty and closed. "You'll have to stay downstairs for a few days. I've got it set up, just until we know no one's seen you."

"Downstairs? As in a basement?" Marla grimaced. "Wonderful," she said sarcastically.

"No, it's all set for you . . . I'll get more furniture for up here, but it'll take some time."

"Jesus, this place is awful." Marla had snapped on a light and seen no beauty in the patina of the old hardwood floors, no charm in the built-in bookcases and fireplace. "Someone will see me here."

"No, no . . . we'll keep the blinds drawn."

"Great."

"Only for a little while, until we set the rest of the plan in motion," Diedre had pointed out. "We just have to get rid of anyone who stands to inherit the money that your father intended for you."

"My father," Marla muttered, walking to the fireplace where a mirror was still mounted over the mantel. Her gaze found Diedre's in the reflection. "My father was an A-number-one chauvinistic bastard. Always concerned about the boys. You know, he wouldn't have had a thing to do with you. Women were only good for screwing and breeding. Male heirs. That's why I had to come up with a son . . . oh, Christ, it's all ancient history now." She ran a finger over the mantel. "There's no furniture."

"I know, I know . . . I haven't had time."

Marla whirled to face her. "You've had all the time in the world. We've been planning this for years! The least you could have done was come up with a chair or two. And where the hell am I supposed to sleep?"

Diedre's hands fisted. This was not how the conversation was supposed to go. "Just give me a little time."

"For what? A sleeping bag?" Marla snarled.

"Look, Mom, I tried and—"

"Mom?" Marla repeated, facing her. *"MOM?"*

"You're my mother."

"I'm not your mother. I might have given birth to you, but that was it, okay? Remember that."

Diedre felt a rip in her heart. "I know you had to give me up way back when, but I thought, now that we finally found each other—"

"You found me," Marla reminded firmly. "I *never* came looking for you."

Diedre couldn't believe what she was hearing. "Wait a minute. Because I 'came looking' for you, and because I found you, and stuck my damned neck out for you—that's why you're here now, out of prison, free as a bird."

"Hardly."

"Without me, you'd still be in prison."

"Looks like I already am." She threw up her hands in exasperation. "Look at this place," she said, walking closer to Diedre. "I'm used to living in mansions with servants, not hidden away in some crappy little run-down bungalow! Jesus, Diedre, what were you thinking?"

"That you might be grateful," Diedre snapped. "And it's been a long time since you lived in a mansion, or have you already forgotten about the last, what? Nine or ten years when you were in a tiny cell?" She moved closer to this cold-hearted woman who had borne her. "You just have to wait a little longer, until we get our hands on the money. We have a plan, remember? First we have to get rid of a few people."

"I hope you include Eugenia on that list."

"She's not an Amhurst."

"But she knows about you." Marla walked to the short hallway leading to two small bedrooms. "We'll never be safe if she's around." Her mouth twisted in disgust. "You have to get rid of everyone who could blow it for us, and you have to make certain that the cops think I'm long gone, or better yet, dead. The prison clothes—they should be left somewhere, with some of my blood on them, so that when they're found the authorities will think I'm wounded . . . you know, maybe even dead." Her eyes narrowed thoughtfully. "That would be the best," she said, the wheels turning in her mind.

"So you'll stay here," Diedre said, resenting the fact that she'd done so much and her ungrateful mother didn't seem to give a damn.

"I don't see that I have much choice until you find something better."

"I can't do that until we get the money."

"Oh, for Christ's sake, can't you come up with something? My God, didn't your parents leave you anything?"

"It's expensive to—"

"Excuses!" Marla snapped, folding her arms across her chest. "It's so cold in here."

"If you could quit complaining for a second, I'll take care of it." Diedre marched to the thermostat, adjusting the temperature, trying to tamp down the anger that kept rising. "I thought we were in this together. A partnership. Whether you like it or not, I'm your daughter." The furnace rumbled to life, air blowing through the vents.

"Don't start with that."

"It's the truth."

"Is that what you think? Don't tell me that you sprang me from prison because you thought that you and I had some kind of bond . . . a mother-daughter thing going, because that's not how it is. I gave you up at birth because you were inconvenient in my life, get it?"

The headache Diedre had been fighting began to throb. Through her ears a great, rushing sound nearly drowned out the hated words. Still, she heard them, watched as Marla's red lips formed the syllables.

"Giving you up for adoption wasn't some great sacrifice because I loved you and thought you deserved a better life. I was just not ready for a baby, and I'm not really sure who your father is, okay? It was a time in my life I'd rather forget, but you came looking for me and offered me a way out of prison, so I took it. End of story."

Diedre couldn't believe it! How many years had she gone to the prison, pretending to be a person of faith, like Mary Smith, and met with another inmate, one who had passed the information on to Marla? How long had she worked in that joke of a job at the coffee shop, just to get close to Cissy? All this was part of Jack's plan . . . for the Amhurst money . . . that's what it was all about. "I–I'm your daughter."

"You're *not* my daughter. I wasn't there for you and I didn't want to be. I'm not about to sugar-coat this and claim that I pined away for you all my life. The truth of the matter is that I spent a few months thinking about you, and then I decided to pretend that you were dead, that I'd never see you again. I had a life to live; one without you. And I had another child, one I cared about, whose father I married. Cissy's my daughter, Diedre, the girl I raised. You're a stranger."

Diedre was shaking her head, disbelieving, fighting the fury that was burning through her. "I've done so much for you so we could be together."

"Oh, save me."

Pain boiled through Diedre. Despair darkened her

heart. Anger exploded in her brain. She was being rejected all over again. "You don't mean it," she said, but she knew. Marla was right. She'd used Diedre, played with her emotions, had never felt a pang of love for her firstborn.

"For the love of God, don't go through some freaky, maudlin routine with me. I've got no time for it. We've got things to do." She was walking from one end of the room to the other, pacing, thinking, her shoes tapping on the hardwood, echoing in sharp painful jabs in Diedre's brain. "Now, do I have a bed in this hellhole or what?"

The words rang through Diedre's head. The sharp click of Marla's heels cut through her brain. She winced, tried to keep her thoughts straight, but for the first time she realized Marla, her own flesh and blood, her damned MOTHER, had played her for a fool. She'd used Diedre's emotions against her. "Don't you love me?" she whispered. Her adoptive mother hadn't loved her, either.

"Enough! This is not about love."

"Of course it is!"

The rush in her head became louder. "You're my—"

"I used you to get out of prison," Marla cut her off. "You did it because this is the only way you'll get any chance at the Amhurst money. That's all there was to it."

"No!"

Marla let out a disgusted puff of air. "Sorry if I destroyed any of your fantasies."

Diedre didn't realize she was reaching into her purse, her fingers fumbling for the gun. She pulled it out and lifted it, pointing it straight at Marla.

The woman who was supposed to be her mother gazed at her with disgust. "Oh, for God's sake, don't go all overly dramatic on me."

"I risked everything for you," Diedre whispered, her

hand shaking as she held the gun. "Everything." Tears slid down her face. "And you didn't care about me at all."

"Put the gun down."

"Say you love me."

"What?"

"Tell me that you're my mother and that you love me," she said, the damned gun wobbling all over.

"Diedre . . . oh, for the love of God, you don't have the guts to pull the trigger," Marla said as a car backfired on the street. Marla turned, faced the window, and Diedre fired. One quick shot to the back of her mother's head. "I loved you," she whimpered. "I always loved you . . . so beautiful . . . why . . . Mama . . . Why . . . ?"

Now, at the Amhurst house, with the wind rising and screaming outside, Diedre stared at Jack. She blinked. Shook the image out of her head. It had been a dream, only a dream. A nightmare.

Right?

She'd visited Marla plenty of times since then . . . and . . . and . . . Her throat tightened. In her mind's eye, she remembered falling to her knees, holding the dead woman, crying and rocking. "You're not dead," she'd whispered over and over, "You are *not* dead. We have so much to do . . ." And she'd carried her mother downstairs to the room she'd prepared and Marla had slept and . . . and . . . she'd gotten better . . . that was the way it was. Diedre had visited her and spoken with her and fed her and . . . surely . . . oh . . . of course Marla was alive! She was just confused. And Jack, he was using it against her for a reason she didn't understand. She focused on him now, standing in front of her, half-crazed with anger. "Why are you lying to me?" she demanded, furious with him.

"Goddamn it, Diedre! She's dead, and I think she has been for a long time."

She was shaking her head, but the headache, the fog, returned. Through the rising mist she remembered the argument, the gun in her hand . . . a loud bang and Marla falling, spinning, turning, her face twisted in shock. Now she blinked rapidly, clearing her head. That was a dream. Surely. But Jack was reaching into his jacket, pulling out a videotape wrapped in a plastic bag.

"I thought you would try to deny it," he muttered, turning on the older model television and VCR, shoving the tape in the recorder. She stared at the snowy screen as he adjusted some of the knobs. "Here we go." He hit the play button, and a jerky image of a woman reporter standing in front of the bungalow showed on the screen.

The newswoman was holding a microphone in the rain, wincing a little with the blast of wind. ". . . prison escapee Marla Cahill was found dead this afternoon in the house you see behind me . . ."

"That's not right," Diedre murmured. She had dreamed of killing the bitch, but she'd never actually pulled the trigger . . . right? She hadn't killed Marla. . . .

". . . partially decomposed body from the house . . ."

A stretcher covered by a body bag appeared rolling from the back of the house, the rear porch Diedre recognized, to a waiting van from the coroner's office.

"No," she whispered, shaking her head.

"She wasn't supposed to die yet, not until we could frame her for the murders. You stupid, stupid bitch, what were you thinking? Are you out of your fucking mind?"

She glared at him. Instead of being proud of her for all the things she'd done for him, he was pissed as hell. Furious, he snapped off the television and the VCR. The house was suddenly silent. Still.

"You were not supposed to kidnap my grandson," Jack said, so angry he was shaking. "He's the link. I fought like hell for my son Jack to meet Cissy, and then when they were married, I thought I'd won the lottery. Then she started talking divorce, and you . . . you messed things up but good. I don't know why I ever bothered with you."

"Jack—"

"It's Jonathan," he said coldly, denying her the nickname she'd given him, the one like his son's. She'd thought it cute and playful, and he'd put up with it. Until now.

She leaned against the bed. Everything was changing, swirling in her mind. Did she actually kill the bitch then delude herself into believing that the corpse was actually alive? God, her head ached. She rubbed her temples, trying to think. She remembered several conversations with Marla. Her mother had sat in her chair or on the bed, not speaking, either smirking or pouting . . . or was it decomposing? But they'd had conversations, about the baby, about Rory, about her damned hair. Diedre remembered trimming her nails, listening to Marla whine in her low voice . . . that was it . . . always in the low voice. And only after she was in the room in the basement. That's when she'd started whispering. Was it possible she hadn't been complaining? How many times had Diedre wondered why Marla's voice had been so soft, why she'd spoken when Diedre's back was turned, why her lips had barely moved.

Oh, God!

WAS IT POSSIBLE?

Had she . . . Jesus, had she taken the kid into the house to visit a dead woman? When B.J. had complained of the smell, had it been the stench of decay and rotting flesh?

Images flashed behind her eyes. Horrible images of a decomposing body—maggots visible, flesh falling away—cut through her vision of her mother's beautiful face . . . oh . . . oh no . . . Her stomach revolted, bile rising, and she was trembling inside.

"You killed her too early!" he said again, snapping Diedre back to the present. Sweat broke out on her skin and the headache, that damned excruciating pain blasted through her. "What kind of idiot are you? Marla needed to be alive until *after* you took care of the people who needed to die . . . Eugenia and Rory and Cherise. That was the reason you threw suspicion on her. Remember? To prove that Marla was the killer? How the hell are you going to get out of it now?"

"You mean us," she said dully, fighting the pain. "How are we going to get out of it?"

"I should never have trusted you," he said, rage pounding in a tic under his eye. How could he talk to her this way, this lover who now wanted to be called Jonathan? This man she slept with, made love to, loved with all of her heart? "I knew it. This was a mistake from the get-go." He raked his hands impatiently through his hair. "What the hell were you thinking? After all the time we spent finding a way to spring her? To get our hands on the money? You go and kill her too soon!"

There it was again. The image of Marla lying dead on the floor, blood pooling from her brain. An accident . . . if it had actually happened. But now, Jack was saying they had planned to kill her. Her head was pounding so hard she could barely think. "This—you and me—wasn't just about money. You and I . . . we're going to get married. You're leaving your wife for me . . ."

"I'm not married. What did you think this was about?"

"It was about love."

"Oh, give me a fucking break, Diedre."

He, like Marla, sniggered at her thoughts of love. That's not how it had always been. He'd found her. While working as a donation solicitor at Cahill House, he had gone through old records and learned that Marla

Amhurst had come to the home to have her baby and give the child up for adoption. Using the information, Jonathan located her and ultimately seduced her. Or was it the other way around? She too had been searching for her birth mother, and then this handsome, sexy, intelligent, older man had shown up. Flirting with her. Making her feel so much better after her loser of a husband, Gene, had divorced her.

He'd spent years planning it, the ultimate score. He'd even set up his son to meet Cissy, to gain him the grandson and access to both the Cahill and Amhurst fortunes. B.J. Holt stood in line to inherit millions. But Diedre had believed Jack loved her. It had started out slow, their love affair, just a little flirting over coffee, then he offered to drive her home when her car hadn't started one night. Over time, he'd admitted that he'd known who she was, and when he came up with a way for her to meet the mother she'd never known, she leapt at the chance. Eventually, he'd suggested they help Marla escape, and together they'd hatched their plan, which now seemed hazy. All of her communication with Marla had been through her cell mate at the first prison. She and Diedre had never met until the day that the plan went into motion, and then, the first time they'd looked eye-to-eye, Marla had smiled.

They'd driven back to the city together. "You look like me," she'd said, tilting her head and studying Diedre. Diedre had been pleased until Marla added, "Much more like me than Cissy does." Her smile had been sincere. "Thank you."

Diedre had felt tears welling in her eyes, and then she'd outlined the plan to Marla . . . how to get their hands on the Amhurst money. Rory would have to die, of course, and James up in Oregon, eventually, and then there was Cissy. Marla had balked a little at that idea, at least at first. But prison had hardened her, and

Cissy had turned her back on her mother. Eventually, Marla had gone along with the idea of the killings, though, of course, she didn't know that Jonathan had ultimately intended to blame her and either kill her or send her back to prison. Diedre had thought that she could talk him out of it by staging Marla's death, having it look as if she were dead or on the run in Oregon, away from the Bay Area. She'd already talked to Sam, the man she'd hired to scare Cissy at the coffee shop, and he'd agreed to do whatever was necessary. Except nothing had turned out as she'd planned. Now Marla was dead.

How had she let herself believe Jonathan had ever loved her? How had she ever thought that Marla would love her as a daughter?

You're a fool, that's why. Just like that bitch of an adoptive mother had always said.

Now, Jonathan glared at her as if he actually hated her. "You screwed everything up. Everything. This had nothing to do with love. Ever. You and I, we were just using each other. And now, because you're such a stupid idiot, we're both going to go to jail for a long, long time."

"You bastard!" she hissed, snapping.

Smack!

She slapped him. Hard. Leaving a red mark on his face.

"What the hell?"

Rage, hot and wild, exploded deep inside her, and she saw Jonathan for what he was. How had she ever thought she loved him? He was a generation older than she, a man who had never forgotten his wife, never stopped loving Jill.

"I always suspected you were nuts," Jonathan sneered, clenching a fist.

Before she could answer, he struck, his fist crashing

into her chest. Pain exploded in her ribs, the wind rushed out of her lungs, and she doubled over.

Fury rose with the speed of a demon. She looked up at him and saw the hatred glinting in his eyes. "You are such a lowlife," she said.

"A little late for name calling," he spat. "Now what the hell are we going to do?"

She didn't think twice. Her purse was hanging from the bedpost. She lunged for the leather bag. In one quick movement, she reached inside and pulled out her .38.

Her heart thudded, reverberating through the pain in her skull. "I don't know what you're going to do, *Jonathan*," she snarled, aiming at his heart. "But I've got work to do."

"NO! Diedre—"

She fired. Point-blank.

With a startled cry, he stumbled backward. His handsome face was a mask of shock. "Diedre, no . . ." he whispered, disbelieving, starting to fall.

Blood ran from the wound in his chest, staining his jacket as he dropped first to one knee, then the other.

"You should have loved me," she said as he tried vainly to catch himself, smearing blood on the floor.

She blinked.

Realized what she'd done.

Dear God, no. This was all wrong. She loved him.

And yet he'd attacked her!

Her mouth went dry as she remembered how she'd met him, how he'd sought her out, how she'd envisioned a perfect life with him, even thinking she would become his wife. That, of course, had been a pipe dream, the kind of childish fantasy her adoptive mother had always teased her about.

Now she looked down at him, the man she'd loved with all her heart, watching as he bled out. Had he ever really cared about her? He'd said so, but words were cheap.

It had been his idea to not just shake down the Cahills, who were in control of the money, but the Amhursts as well. He'd offered it up and she'd thought it brilliant; he'd told her he loved her, and she, fool that she was, had believed him.

Liar! Prick! She sacrificed everything for him. For them. For his plan. She took all the risks, and now . . . now she realized that he loved his damned grandson more than he ever loved her!

"What have you done?" he said, staring up at her, trying to lever up on one arm and then falling back, his head cracking against the floor.

"What I should have done from the beginning."

Diedre fired again, and his body convulsed, blood showing at his nostrils and one corner of his mouth as well as spreading in a dark red stain across his chest. He was already dead. She knew it. But she shot him one more time.

The son of a bitch. He deserved it.

Cissy drove like a maniac through the streets, her gaze scanning the rain-washed sidewalks, her eyes searching for anything that might give her a clue. She tried to call Rachelle again, but still no one answered. *Think, Cissy, think,* she told herself as she pulled up to a light near a low-slung car with rap music blaring from its speakers, the throb of the bass a counterpoint to her own beating heart. Of course. The coffee shop was probably closed at this hour. The police were probably now at Diedre's apartment, but she wouldn't be that stupid, that obvious. The house in Berkeley was cordoned off, so that wouldn't be where she'd run with Beej.

"Come on, come on," she told herself. Where would

she go? Where? *She wanted to be you. She thought you lived a charmed, pampered life. So where would Diedre go.* Cissy thought hard. If Diedre had always wanted a life of privilege, like the Cahills, she would run to the estate on Mt. Sutro, though that was too risky. No. There must be someplace else . . . someplace she would feel safe . . . someplace connected to the life she wanted.

"Oh God," Cissy whispered, her pulse jumping as the wipers slapped at the rain and the light changed. The low-slung car beat her from the stop and roared around her, but Cissy barely noticed. Her mind was spinning wildly. Diedre didn't think of herself as a Cahill, but an Amhurst; therefore, she would take B.J. to—

Her cell phone rang, and she snatched it from her pocket, saw that it was Jack and flipped it open.

"Tell me you have Beej!" she cried.

"No."

Her heart dropped.

"Can you get away from the police and pick me up?"

"I'm already out," she admitted.

"Oh . . . good. Then pick me up at my father's place."

"What's going on?" she asked, desperate for answers.

"I'll tell you when you get here."

"I'm on my way." She did a quick U-turn at the next corner and stepped on it, making her way to Jack's father's condo in record time. Traffic was light, but the streets were wet, the wind gusting as she pulled into the short drive.

Jack was waiting and dripping wet.

"What are you doing here?" she asked as he opened the door and slid into the passenger seat.

"I came to borrow a car. It didn't work out. Dad isn't here." He said it bitterly, then added, "Let's go. Drive. North."

"To Sausalito?" she asked, glancing at him. She was

already backing out, heading toward the Golden Gate Bridge. "To the Amhurst mansion, right?"

He gave her a surprised look. "You figured it out?"

"I don't know why Diedre killed Gran, maybe because she knew the truth, but she killed Rory because he was an Amhurst. Marla too."

"And Cherise?"

"Oh . . . I don't know . . ." Cissy shook her head, but she wouldn't be deterred. "I just think she would go to the house."

"And, if Diedre's out to get all the Amhursts, you, your brother James, and B.J. aren't safe," he said solemnly as he pulled out his cell phone. "I'm calling Paterno."

"What if we're wrong?" she asked as she eased her car onto the bridge and felt the rolling gusts of wind buffet the Acura.

"Then we look like fools. Still—no harm—no foul." He left a message with the detective, then snapped his cell phone shut as Cissy drove through the stormy night, over the neck of water separating the Pacific from San Francisco Bay, seeing the winking lights of the city in her rearview mirror.

She felt Jack's worry and drove steadily onward. "How did you figure it out?" she asked, guiding her car up the hills of Sausalito. "I thought you were going to Jannelle's."

"I decided I didn't need the inquisition or the grief. I called Sam and couldn't get hold of him, so I jogged over to Dad's."

"It's another mile or so."

"Two and a half," he said, "but who's counting? Anyway, Dad wasn't in, but I went inside. I know a window that doesn't quite latch. I was drying off, trying to figure out what to do, whether to wait for him, call you, the police, or what. I was running out of ideas, but as I

was in his bathroom off the bedroom, using a towel, I
saw his computer monitor. It was on, and Beej's face was
smiling up at me. It's his wallpaper. So I touched the
keypad, and his computer opened to his e-mail. There
were hundreds of messages, all written by someone
named Elyse, love letters, every one addressed to 'Dear
Jack.'"

"Elyse . . . Who's Jack?" She blinked. "Your father?"

"Some people call him Jack, only a few, but apparently she did. Most of them were cryptic, but I figure
they were in a hot love affair and that Dad was in on
Marla's escape and the murders, too."

"Your father . . . and Diedre . . . ?"

"Sick, I know, but apparently Dad has stooped to a
new low. They headed up the long narrow road to the
old Victorian manor built high on the cliffs. It should
have been empty, but there were a few windows where
they could see slats of light cutting through the blinds.

Parked in the cracked, uneven lot was Jack's father's
SUV.

"Perfect," Jack said. "I'm going in."

"Me too."

"Either wait here for me or, better yet, drive back to
town and keep trying to get hold of someone at the police department."

She cut the engine. "My son is probably in there, and
I'm not waiting outside. You told Paterno what's up,
now let's go inside."

He hesitated, then reached into his pocket. "Then
take this." He handed her a small pistol.

Cissy violently shook her head. "I don't even know
how to shoot a gun. Where did you get that?"

His lips twisted. "Dad's closet."

"It's loaded?"

"Oh yeah."

"Then you use it. Really. I would never be able to pull

the trigger. I brought a knife. My Pomeroy 5000, all in one."

"All right, I'll take the gun," Jack said grimly. "Stick close to me."

They each slipped out of the car and closed the doors quietly. Here, on the cliffs over the sea, the storm raged, screaming inland, battering the house and rocks. A shutter banged loudly. Cissy followed close on Jack's heels. Fear pounded through her brain, but she didn't let it stop her. Inside this old, deteriorating home, her deranged half-sister, more murderous than their mother, held her child captive. Quietly, they walked up the rotting steps to find the front door unlocked.

Stealthily, nervous sweat drenching her body, Cissy followed Jack inside.

The feds and the crime unit techs had crawled all over Diedre Lawson's apartment. They'd discovered items connecting her to the crimes, shells for a .38, various disguises and wigs that had hairs that were certain to match those found at Cherise Favier's home. There were notes and a computer—a laptop—that had already been taken as evidence.

But no Diedre.

No baby.

Paterno walked outside and popped an antacid as the rain poured from the sky. The feds had been so certain they'd caught her that they'd pulled their van from the street in front of Jack and Cissy Holt's house.

But she wasn't here.

There was already a BOLF on Diedre's car and her picture was being circulated to the media, but he was disappointed that they hadn't nailed her.

Pulling out his cell, he listened impatiently to his messages, hearing a few he dismissed, then, lastly, a call from Jack Holt. "Holy crap," he said and rounded up Quinn.

"What's up?"

"We'd better get our asses up to Sausalito. Jack Holt's decided to be John Wayne." He quickly explained what he knew. "We'll call for backup if it turns out to be something more than a wild-goose chase."

She didn't argue, just got behind the wheel of her Jetta, and, as Paterno slid inside and pulled the door shut, she circled in a quick one-eighty and sped north.

The minute Cissy stepped into the foyer, she heard the muffled sound of a baby's cry. Over the rattle of rain on the windowpanes, the scream of the wind around the house, her own heartbeat thudding in her ears, she was certain she heard her child.

Her knees nearly gave way, and she motioned to Jack to climb the stairs that swept to the second floor above this wide foyer. The house was cold and dark inside, and though she had flitting little memories of playing here as a small child, they seemed in black and white, faded with the passage of time. There had been lush parties here once, and if she thought really hard she could imagine the ghosts of guests long gone, the tiny tinkle of glasses and laughter long forgotten.

But that was fleeting. A millisecond memory, for now Cissy was focused solely on finding B.J.

Behind Jack, she slowly mounted the stairs.

Near the second-floor landing, Jack stopped and tensed. He glanced at Cissy. The sound of a baby crying was closer. Nodding toward the big doors before him, he took the final steps. Biting her lip, Cissy opened the multi-bladed tool to its longest knife, wanting to force herself into the room. It was killing her to wait. She could hear the distinctive sounds of her baby crying, louder and louder, hiccupping and sobbing.

At least he's alive!

"Mom-mee!" he cried. "Mom-mee!"

Cissy tried to rush past Jack, but he held her back and she felt it too, that this was too easy. Where was Diedre? Motioning for Cissy to step aside, Jack tried the door, slowly edging it open.

Over his shoulder, she saw the silhouette of her son. Standing at the edge of a playpen in the darkened room and crying, his body thrown in relief by a dim fire. "Mom–mee!" he yelled unmoving. She couldn't see him clearly, but she knew he was upset.

"Oh baby," she cried, rushing past Jack into the darkness. "Baby, I'm here."

Jack tried to grab her, but it was too late. She flew into the room and tripped, landing on the floor and staring into the dead eyes of Jack's father, Jonathan!

Cissy screamed, scooting backward as Jack entered the room. He paused at the sight of Jonathan Holt's blood-soaked body, his pale skin, his lifeless eyes.

"Dear God," Cissy whispered, terrified, as she scrambled to her feet.

Diedre had killed Jonathan and left him in the same room with her baby!

Jack's stunned gaze lifted from his father as Diedre stepped from behind the open door on the landing, her gun trained on him. "Drop it!" she ordered. Jack didn't comply. "Drop it or I'll kill the kid! You, too. Let go of your knife," she said. Unlike Jack, Cissy dropped the Pomeroy utility weapon. Diedre trained her gun on Beej.

"No!" Cissy screamed, still far enough away from Beej not to be able to console him, not to see his little features, only to hear his sobs. It was so dark in here.

"Jack, don't let her do this!" she ordered but felt some-thing was wrong. Off. Jack tossed the gun onto the bed, then knelt at his father's side to feel for a pulse as the loose shutter banged loudly. *Bam! Bam! Bam!*

"He's dead." Diedre said it without inflection.

"This is what you do to people you love?"

"He didn't care about me," she said and slid a glance at the corpse. "He tried to tell me my mother was dead."

"She is. You killed her," Cissy said and through an open doorway heard the rush of the sea, smelled the salt in the air.

"No . . . that's a lie. She's not dead, not yet. . . . She's got to look like she did all the killings." Diedre said, but her face changed as if she weren't certain of what she was saying. In that moment, Cissy rushed toward the playpen to reach for her son, to hold him. She picked him up and let out an agonized scream. It wasn't her son at all! It was a lifesized doll propped against the side of the pen, hiding a baby monitor which was emitting her son's terrified cries.

"You bitch!" She whirled on Diedre. "Where's my B.J.? Where is he!"

"The only Amhurst heir, beside you and that half-brother of yours in Oregon? Don't worry about B.J."

"Tell me where he is!"

"Ciss . . ." Jack warned.

But Cissy was livid and didn't care that Diedre had aimed the gun straight at her heart. She wanted her kid, damn it.

"Step back!" Jack yelled, just as they heard the wail of sirens, faintly crying over the lash of the wind and the pound of the rain.

"You called the police?" Diedre demanded, stunned and furious, her voice rising over the wind and the cry-ing of the baby.

"Yes! Yes, we called them!" Cissy suddenly threw the doll at Diedre. Oh God where was he?

Diedre caught the rag doll handily.

Jack rushed her.

With a wicked smile, Diedre turned, aimed, and fired straight at Jack, the muzzle of the .38 spitting fire.

"No!" Cissy screamed. "Oh God, don't! No, nooo!"

Too late.

Jack stumbled backward. His face drained of color as he looked at her.

In a gasp of pain, he crumpled onto the floorboards.

"Jack!" Cissy dropped to the floor beside him and grabbed his head, forcing him to stare up at her. "Oh no, no, no . . ." She couldn't lose him! She couldn't! Quicksilver images of their life together flashed behind her eyes—their meeting at the boring party, his quick wit, the way he stared into her eyes when he made love to her, his joy at the birth of B.J., his pain when she'd insisted on divorcing him.

Now he was bleeding. Vainly, she tried to staunch the flow, to keep him alive, but it was impossible. Blood oozed upward between her fingers. There was just so much, so damned much. "I love you, Jack. Oh, God, how I love you. You can't die. You can't."

"Oh, how pathetic," Diedre said from her position in the doorway. Looming over them, gun in hand, she clucked her tongue. "I guess you've forgotten. A month ago you were going to divorce him."

Ignoring the taunt, Cissy felt for Jack's pulse, her sticky fingers touching his throat as she willed him to look at her, to hang on. The police were on their way. She'd heard the sirens. Fighting panic, her own choking fear, she willed her husband to focus on her. "Jack, don't you die on me, do you hear me? Don't you die! Look at me. Jack! Damn it, you look at me!"

"Don't die," Diedre mocked in a little-girl voice that irritated the hell out of Cissy. "Look at me, Jack! Jesus, Cissy, do you hear yourself?"

Blood was spreading over the floor, and still the baby was crying, calling for her. Her whole life was crumbling, all because of this hideous woman she'd thought was her friend. "Shut up!" Cissy turned to her husband. "Hang in there, you can do it."

"Too late," Diedre said.

Cissy ignored her, desperately trying to halt the flow as Jack lost consciousness.

"He's gone."

"I said, SHUT UP!" Cissy snapped. She had no time for this.

"I heard you, but you don't get it, do you? He's dying and you're next. All of you are going to die. You're going to join Gran, isn't that the stupid name you gave Eugenia? You're going to die as easily as she did, or that moron Rory, or Cherise—that one was a surprise to both of us. She saw me, you know, right after I scared you at the mansion. Couldn't let her get away with that."

"Go to hell."

"Funny, that's where I think you're going, sister."

Cissy worked desperately to save Jack. "Sister?" she repeated, praying for the sound of the police breaking into the house. "You're not my sister."

"Same blood."

"You're a monster. You killed everyone related to you including your own mother. Why was that? Spring her from prison just to kill her? Because she gave you up? Is that it? Because she couldn't love you?" *Don't antagonize her,* a part of her brain warned, but Cissy couldn't stop herself. Her nerves were frayed, her heart dying already at the thought of losing Jack, adrenaline pumping furiously through her system while B.J. wailed.

"I—didn't . . ."

"What?" Cissy demanded, looking up to see a bit of confusion on Diedre's face, a moment of hesitation. Diedre's eyes clouded for a second. "Marla . . . No, I didn't . . ." She raised the gun and aimed at Cissy.

This was it, Cissy realized. They were all going to die and poor B.J. . . . Oh, God, if that bitch harmed one hair on his head, she'd . . . She saw the knife. The one she'd dropped on the floor. Only inches from Jack's body.

"You did, Diedre, you killed your own mother," Cissy stated harshly.

"No!" Diedre was shaking her head, as if to clear her mind . . .

What was Cissy saying? That she'd killed Marla? Oh God, was that possible? Diedre couldn't remember, couldn't think, the roar in her head was deafening, the pain so tortuous that she gritted her teeth, had trouble holding onto the gun. Jonathan had said the same thing, and then there was the video, and she remembered, oh, God, she remembered pulling the trigger on that bitch who had given her up and borne another daughter. A daughter she'd kept. A daughter she'd loved and nurtured in . . . in this very house . . . this mansion. . . . No . . . that wasn't right . . . it was the Cahill mansion where Cissy had grown up, the privileged daughter . . . wasn't it?

"She loved me," she said now and felt what? . . . Tears? Oh God, tears were running from her eyes.

Cissy didn't wait. Without thinking she picked up the knife and rolled to the balls of her feet. Spinning low, gathering force, she slung the knife underhand straight at Diedre.

Diedre shrieked.

The slim blade slammed into her gut, sending her backward through the door. Shocked, her eyes suddenly clear, the gun in her hand wobbling slightly, Diedre fired.

White-hot pain exploded in Cissy's side. She spun to the floor, could barely breathe. Blood flowed from the hole in her torso, hot and wet, but she didn't care. She had to stop this madwoman before the bitch killed B.J., who was still sobbing.

Diedre stumbled onto the balcony. The fingers of both her hands grabbed at the knife in her abdomen. With a horrid sucking sound, she pulled the weapon free. Blood oozed from the blade as she stared dully at her wound.

Cissy struggled to her feet. Before Diedre knew what hit her, Cissy hurled herself toward her maniac of a half-sister. Together they fell against the fancy railing. Diedre's back pressed into the heavy metal. The knife fell from her hand, slipping through the wrought iron, and falling two floors to clatter uselessly in the foyer.

Where the hell were the police?

Despite the blood running from her abdomen, Diedre fought wildly. She grabbed hold of Cissy's wrist, twisted her arm so that she heard tendons popping. Blinding pain ripped through her. "You're going to die, Cissy," she hissed. "And you're going to die tonight, and that little boy of yours, he's going to be with me."

"Leave B.J. out of this!"

"He's what it was all about. Jonathan planned his conception long before you even thought of it." She pushed harder, and pain screamed through Cissy's shoulder.

"The police are on their way."

"Too late for you and they won't hurt me as long as I have him . . ."

"It's over, Diedre. Give it up! Your plan failed. You can't get the money now."

"But I can get rid of you, and that's worth it." She gave Cissy's arm another hard wrench. "You didn't even know how lucky you were. Neither will your kid."

Charged with injustice and fury, Cissy wouldn't let her win. Couldn't.

But Diedre was strong and determined.

With a violent twist, Diedre flipped them both around, and Cissy, bleeding, was bent over the wrought-iron railing. She sensed the century-old bolts give a little. She was weakening, and Diedre was stronger. Diedre, eyes glowing with victory, pushed hard and bowed Cissy over the railing so far that Cissy thought her back would break. The pain in her side burned hot, and she grabbed at anything she could, the top of the rail, Diedre's hair, her neck.

"Die, you pampered little freak," Diedre snarled. Cissy felt her body giving up, her strength failing. Twenty feet below was the hard floor. With an effort, she wound one hand on the rail and held, knowing that if she was pushed any harder she'd do a back flip and fall, to land with a bone-breaking thud. Like Gran.

Pain screamed up her spine, and she was certain it would snap.

Agony tore through her muscles. She felt ligaments pop, tendons tear, and all the while her baby was crying. *Oh God, please help me, please . . . Jack . . . I love you . . . B.J., darling baby . . .* The room spun, her brain swam. She flailed with one arm while holding on for dear life with the other.

Her shoulder shrieked with the pressure, and blackness played at the edge of her consciousness. *Don't let go. Whatever you do, don't let go!*

But she couldn't think, couldn't fight any longer. The sweet bliss of unconsciousness threatened to pull her under. All she could hear were her frightened baby's cries and the pounding of her own heart.

It's over, she thought. The railing shifted beneath her, and the hellish pain in her spine forced her to let go. As her grip loosened and she started to give up, she saw something big and dark and looming behind Diedre. His face was twisted into a mask of hate. Blood smeared his skin.

In those last moments of awareness, Cissy saw Jack blast the gun. Diedre's body jerked. She shrieked and fell hard against Cissy, grappling with her, both of them careening for the stairs.

Cissy tried to scream, but it was too late. Diedre's weight pushed her down. They spun down the stairs, screaming, Diedre's body hitting the railing, Cissy's tumbling after her.

Cissy tried to call Jack's name, but then she was lost to darkness.

Bayside Hospital
San Francisco, California
Room 316
Friday, February 13
NOW

What's this? A priest? Murmuring prayers over me, pleading for my soul? Oh, no . . . Please, Father, listen to me. . . . I'm not dead, I'm not even sure I'm dying. . . . There are other voices, whispers. . . . I've heard their voices before, and they're saying their good-byes. . . . Who are they? People who care about me? People who love me? They think I'm dying. Oh, no, no, no . . . They come in and they sob, they cry and touch me, whoever they are. Familiar voices offering prayers for my soul.

Then there is silence, only the sound of the machines monitoring my responses . . . the damned machines that don't show the fear that makes my heart pound or the ventilator that doesn't register when I draw in a horrified breath. . . . I hear someone moving through the room, and a series of clicks. . . . Oh God, they're turning off a machine. The ventilator? No . . . Oh no . . . I feel a weight . . . it's hard to breathe . . . impossible, oh, please do not do this . . . stop! . . . Help me! Please! Dear Jesus, help me! I can't hear anything anymore, nor smell. For the love of Christ, I can't breathe . . . I . . . can't . . .

Epilogue

San Francisco
May 14

Cissy opened her eyes and fought the headache that had been with her since the night at the Amhurst mansion, the night she nearly died. Had it not been for Paterno and the EMTs, she probably wouldn't have made it. Nor would her husband or child.

As it was, they were safe.

She rolled slowly out of bed and stretched, feeling pain in her back. It might be with her the rest of her life; then again, she was making a "remarkable" recovery.

Slipping out of the covers, she hobbled into the baby's room. No longer on crutches or a cane, she fought the pain and was able to walk on her own.

"Hey there, big guy," she said as she found her son standing in his crib.

"Big guy!" B.J. said, raising his little arms to be picked up.

With difficulty she lifted B.J. into her arms and kissed

his head. Oh God, she loved this child, and to think that she'd almost lost him. In the aftermath of the battle with Diedre, the police had found B.J. safe, if frightened out of his little mind. Between Jannelle, Deborah, and Rosa, the baby had been cared for and brought to the hospital daily while Cissy recovered.

"Let's go wake up Dad," she said.

"Dad-dee wake!"

"Not yet, but he will be." She let B.J. down to do the honors and watched as he ran into the other room. Coco, who had been curled in her bed in the corner, stretched and followed after him.

Life was nearly normal.

Nearly.

There were still reminders—issues to be discussed, decisions to be made. Jonathan had been laid to rest and Diedre allowed to die when they'd finally pulled the plug.

Cissy shuddered when she remembered the horror of meeting her half-sister. If it hadn't been for Jack, she would have been pushed over the railing and surely dead. As it was, he'd caught her on the third step, just as the police arrived. The police had swarmed through the building, but she remembered little of it, only pieces of the ambulance ride to the hospital as she was in and out of consciousness, all the while wondering about her baby, her husband. Later, in the hospital, she'd learned that Jack would survive, no serious complications from a clean wound that had just nicked his spleen.

Anthony Paterno had found the baby locked in the basement, terrified but unharmed. Time would tell if there would be emotional scarring for Beej as well as the rest of them, but apart from a little extra neediness, he seemed pretty resilient. Cissy refused to worry about that now. What good would it do? She just wanted to hold tight to her husband and her baby boy. Nor would she allow herself to dwell on Jack's father's part in the horrible scheme to kill them all. Or how, when it came time to pull the plug on Diedre, the only family she had, Diedre's adoptive, widowed aunt had agreed to take her off life support.

For now, she would push all those dark thoughts aside. It was over. She, Jack, Beej, and even Coco were happy. Gran's miserable little dog had won them all over and burrowed into their hearts.

Cissy peeked into the master bedroom where Jack was playing peek-a-boo with Beej, much to the boy's delight. Each time Jack ducked his head under the blankets, Beej squealed with delight and said, "No, Dad-dee! Don't hide!"

"Good morning," he said, smiling up at her from the rumpled bed. "Is it my imagination, or were you a wild woman last night?"

Cissy smiled. "You mean apart from the 'Ouch, my back' fifty times?"

"Love talk."

She laughed. "I have a surprise for you. Happy Valentine's Day," she said, throwing open the blinds and letting the spring sunshine stream into the room.

"What? Am I in a time warp? Isn't it May?"

"But we didn't get to celebrate, so I bought you a very special and sexy gift."

"And you're giving it to me in front of our son."

She walked to the closet and pulled out a paper shredder. On its top she'd pasted a red bow with a purple heart tied to it.

Jack frowned. "Okay, I give. Have you gone out of your mind? I hear it runs in the family."

"Not funny, Jack," she said, but smiled as she plugged in the machine, turned it on, and first shredded the heart, then the ribbon.

He looked totally confused.

Then she pulled the unsigned divorce papers from the nightstand and slowly, page by page, shredded the entire document.

"Like I said before, Happy Valentine's Day!" Laughing, she grabbed the basket of diamond-cut paper and tossed the shreds into the air like confetti.

Jack took her hand. "How about I give you a Valentine's present too?" One of his eyebrows arched devilishly, and she shook her head.

"I have a feeling your present might not be appropriate in front of our child."

He grinned and glanced at his watch. "Point taken. Just when is nap time for the little guy?"

And they both laughed.

You've turned the last page.

But it doesn't have to end there . . .

If you're looking for more first-class, action-packed, nail-biting suspense, join us at **Facebook.com/ MulhollandUncovered** for news, competitions, and behind-the-scenes access to Mulholland Books.

For regular updates about our books and authors as well as what's going on in the world of crime and thrillers, follow us on **Twitter@MulhollandUK**.

There are many more twists to come.

MULHOLLAND:
You never know what's
coming around the curve.